W9-CAM-232

A Pale Distorted Shape Was Creeping About the Room . . .

slithering over the shabby furniture. It was the stray light of a car, which must be turning outside in the road, for the light managed to reach the door in front of her. Her shadow leapt up, small and wavering. It was alone.

Was that reassuring or more terrifying? Before she knew, something cold and flabby, a body which felt not quite formed, fastened on her from behind.

If she could have screamed she would have done so. Perhaps it would have brought her no help, but at least it would have convinced her that she was still herself—for the thing which had fastened on her was seeping into her body.

She couldn't move or cry out, only writhe inside herself as she felt the parasite within her body. Before long her mind was unnaturally calm, peaceful as the surface of water into which something dreadful had plunged. Its depths were invisible to her. . . .

THE PARASITE

RAMSEY CAMPBELL

PUBLISHED BY POCKET BOOKS NEW YORK

POCKET BOOKS, a Simon & Schuster division of
GULF & WESTERN CORPORATION
1230 Avenue of the Americas, New York, N.Y. 10020

Copyright © 1980 by Ramsey Campbell

Published by arrangement with Macmillan Publishing Company, Inc.
Library of Congress Catalog Card Number: 80-13179

All rights reserved, including the right to reproduce
this book or portions thereof in any form whatsoever.
For information address Macmillan Publishing Company, Inc.
866 Third Avenue, New York, N.Y. 10022

ISBN: 0-671-41905-6

First Pocket Books printing September, 1981

10 9 8 7 6 5 4 3 2 1

POCKET and colophon are trademarks of Simon & Schuster.

Printed in the U.S.A.

to all my friends in Chapel Hill
particularly
Manly and Frances
Dave and Jo
Karl and Barbara

Acknowledgments

Among the many who helped this book, I especially want to thank

Chris Clarke, for one of the images which brought the story alive; and Matt, for various other stimuli

for help and hospitality in some of the locations, Gary and Uschi in Munich; Tony and Marge in Manchester; Jack Sullivan, T.E.D. Klein, Kathy Murray, Kirby McCauley, Jay Gregory in New York

John and Ann Thompson and Tony Beck, for details of the university setting—not the personalities, who are my inventions

Peter Valentine Timlett, for expert advice on out-of-the-body experiences (though he should not be held responsible for my imagination, and would, I know, want me to make it clear that amateur experiments with these techniques can be dangerous)

three of my favorite film critics, whose accounts of teaching film were helpful: Philip Strick, David Thomson, Robin Wood

Carol Smith, Thom Tessier, Tim Shackleton, George Walsh, Kirby again, for suggestions that improved the book

my wife Jenny for many things, not least for advice and criticism while the book was being written and for the Tarot readings.

Finally, I had better say that the shop which is the setting for the finale of this book does not exist, nor did "Peter Grace" live in the location described.

Contents

PROLOGUE

"Did you hear me?" her mother called. "I said Wendy's here"—and all at once it was too late: the night had crept up on her, and she didn't want to go.

There was nothing in her room to help her. Sandwiched in its case, her tennis racket leaned against one wall. Posters froze wild birds in flight. Elvis Presley sneered above her bed, his hair shining like oil. Spines of encyclopedias offered her fragments of words, none of which inspired an excuse.

She retrieved her coat from the wardrobe, where she'd hidden it after laying it out, in the hope that might wish Wendy away. Buttoning the coat, her fingers felt hot and swollen, prickly with nerves.

From the top of the stairs she heard her mother saying, "Look after her, Wendy, won't you. Don't let her get too excited."

The Magic Flute was playing. Her father hung back in the living-room doorway, afraid to lose the opera. "What is this film, did you say? *Rock Around the Clock?*" He knew perfectly well, but meant to imply that it wasn't worth knowing. "I'm surprised that it interests you. Well, you must find out for yourself."

Couldn't he tell that it was a lie? Just because the girl thought Elvis was sexy didn't mean that she wanted to watch fat Bill Haley sing three notes. Her moist hands

1

squirmed, suffocated by her pockets. Resentment gagged her more than nervousness. How dare her mother suggest she was less mature than Wendy! Couldn't she both prove her maturity and save herself by admitting the lie? But her parents were waving, the door was closing, and she was outside in the icy night.

Beneath the streetlamps Wendy's eyes looked bruised with makeup. Scent crept from beneath her pink coat. By comparison, the younger girl was dressed childishly, which made her feel irritable and vulnerable. Already her knees were burning with the cold.

At least she wasn't going up the hill, where the water tower no longer resembled the maze of tall arches among which she'd used to play hide-and-seek with her friends. Now it was a looming crowd of legs, its body hovering above a scrawny glimpse of daylight as a spider stands over a wrapped fly. The night changed everything.

Even the main road was changed. Beneath the lamps the terraces glared as though trapped in the stasis before a storm. Two nurses marched like nuns toward the hospital, once a workhouse. Suppose they asked where the girls were going? But they vanished laughing into the hospital, leaving her alone with Wendy's footsteps and her own, with the repetitive brushing of Wendy's knees against her calf-length skirt, with her fears.

A young couple hurried by, their breath and their parcels of fish and chips steaming. Queues of cars passed each other on the narrow road; their scoops of light caught dust, petrol fumes, a moth. Soon they were gone, and the tarmac gleamed bleakly. "What do you think we're going to do?" she said uneasily.

"Oh, just sit around a table, I expect, like they did in that story." Wendy sounded glad to talk. "Or maybe Richard will sit there with a pencil and see if it writes anything. I expect it'll write something stupid, if he has anything to do with it. You know what Richard's like."

They were approaching the town. Houses and gardens were dwindling, sometimes into terraces of cottages. Glimpses of bright rooms—warm, impregnable, aloof from her—reminded the girl of home. One last secret charm reassured her a little: as long as she stayed on this pavement, on the far side of the road from the house, she might be saved.

Saved from what? She had seen death, her grandmother more soundly asleep than whispers could penetrate, fretted lips gaping in a silent snore. Richard liked to scare people, but she was too old to be scared. Why, only last year he'd told everyone that the girl who had been dug up outside town had just been murdered, when in fact she was fifty years dead.

They passed the pale squat unlit hall, the Kingdom Hall of Jehovah's Witnesses. Next to it, behind the Windmill pub, hens clucked sleepily. It was a comfortable sound, but by no means encouraging, for it meant that they had reached the terrace which contained the house.

But it was only a house where someone had died, months ago. Nobody but Richard insisted that he had been crying for help; nobody but Richard said that the house had an unpleasant reputation—at least, nobody else had said so to the girls. Or were there rumors which had given Richard the idea for his latest horror fib?

Beyond the terrace, people sat morosely on a bench outside the bus station. Disraeli stood on a pedestal, ignoring the traffic lights beneath him, which were stepping down to green. There was safety: far too distant. Wendy had already crossed to the opposite pavement, had braved the short path beside the lit bay window and was ringing the bell.

Seated figures glided by in slabs of light like amber. Glowing splashes trailed over the pavement, over the shiny blunt toecaps of the girl's shoes. Then the bus was past, and Richard was frowning at her. "Well, what's she waiting for? Does she want crossing over?"

She drew a breath so fierce it bruised her chest. She

wasn't a baby, she was ten years old. Wendy might be older, but she was more mature than Wendy. She strode across the deserted roadway, past the dark uncurtained bay, into the bright house.

The living room seemed crowded with people, sitting on a plump, though somewhat faded, suite. In fact there were only five people, but all of them were staring at her as though she had no right to be there. A boy whose chin sprouted a few unequal hairs complained, "She's rather young for this, isn't she?"

"Oh, she's all right. Leave her alone." Wendy sounded both annoyed by the reflection on her judgment and a little embarrassed; perhaps, deep down, she agreed.

Richard stood between chairs in the bay, peering out through a crack in the curtains. A boy with hair like Elvis and a reasonably even moustache said, "Is that everyone?"

"No, there's Ken. He has to come from near the Comrades of the Great War Club."

Glancing at the moustached boy, Wendy brightened. "I didn't know you were coming."

"Who, me? I wouldn't have missed it for anything." He patted the arm of his chair, as though to make a dog jump. "Besides, you might need looking after."

The younger girl thought him pompous and conceited, and a very bad substitute for Elvis. After a token protest at the way he had summoned her, Wendy sat beside him. She had withdrawn into the adolescent world, where people seemed to do things which they didn't want to do and which, when they did them, they didn't enjoy. The girl felt excluded, barely tolerated by the group. She sat on the couch, beside two girls who ignored her. She wished she hadn't come.

Did Richard want to scare her? He was looking at her as he said, "I heard something else today."

"What?" one of the girls demanded nervously.

"I don't know. It sounded like—" Was he pausing for effect, or choosing his words? "It sounded like someone ill trying to get hold of things, groping about next door, trying to pick something up."

He leaned against the chipped mantelpiece and gazed at his listeners. He was obviously enjoying himself, but was he lying? He must have heard mice, the young girl told herself. But she was struggling to gain sufficient courage to say that she'd decided not to go into the house.

The doorbell rang. Everyone started, then pretended that they hadn't, or giggled uneasily. "Stupid," one girl snarled—it wasn't clear to whom. Had Richard's parents returned unexpectedly? Oh, please let it be— But he returned from the front door to announce, "All right, it's time. Ken's here."

He led them out of the house. Between it and its neighbor was an arched tunnel, narrower than the stretch of the young girl's arms. The edge of headlights on the road withdrew from the passage, which was at once very dark. The girl's footsteps rang shrilly between the walls, mocking her nervousness.

At the end of the passage were the doors to two backyards. Richard pushed one, which tottered open, scraping over stone. Beyond it the kitchen of the deserted house protruded into the yard, toward a large coal shed. There was room for little else except darkness thick as mud and, in one corner of the yard, an anonymous shrub, starved and restless.

As they crept into the yard eyes gleamed at them from the coal, which scattered rattling as the awakened sleeper leapt on the wall and fled, mewing. "Shut up," Richard hissed at giggles. He was fiddling with the back door of the house. He must be copying a film, he couldn't know how to do it properly. There came a snap of metal; he must have broken his knife. The girl relaxed, only just suppressing an audible sigh—then saw that the door was open.

Richard's flashlight reached into the darkness. It spread over the flags of the kitchen floor, dimming. Wooden legs with knobbly ankles stood in the shadows;

deep in the darkness, something gurgled moistly.
"Well, keep up," he said irritably to the others as he
stepped within.

The young girl tried to keep up with Wendy, who was
clinging to the moustached boy. As the flashlight swung
to make sure everyone had followed, a nervous drip
glinted on the lip of a tap. The drip was trembling,
ready to fall. It must have been the tap which had
gurgled. "Shut the door," Richard ordered.

Beyond the kitchen was a larger room. The patch of
light crawled over the floor, picking at the pattern of
the carpet, leaving it incomplete. Why couldn't Richard
raise the torch beam? Nobody could see so far into the
house from the road. In the unlit room draped chairs
loomed, squatting fatly beneath their shrouds. The air
smelled of hovering dust.

As they ventured into the hall, a thin silhouette
sprang up to meet them. A sharp hook of panic snagged
the girl's heart. Everyone halted, gasping or swearing,
except Richard. In a moment they were scoffing and
jostling, for it had only been the cross that separated
the front-door panes, outlined by headlights. But the
girl had felt caged by their panic. As they'd surrounded
her, instinctively huddling together, they had seemed
capable of crushing her among them. They and their
indifference dwarfed her. Her fear was bigger than she
was.

"Keep it quiet," Richard muttered, and padded
upstairs. His light doled out a couple of stairs at a time.
Shadows tugged at the banisters, which shifted creaking beneath her hand. Nervousness and dusty breaths
parched her throat; underfoot, the unseen carpet felt
like a thick wad of dust. She was trapped in the midst of
the uneasy procession. She could only stumble upstairs.

All the doors on the landing were ajar. As the light
wavered into the rooms, they looked impossibly large
with darkness, which seemed less still than it ought to
be. Carpet muffled the creaks of the landing. How
could the answering creaks—surely they must be

echoes—sound clearer in the rooms? This seemed not to trouble Richard, who strode stealthily into the front bedroom.

He switched off the flashlight. A streetlamp lit the room, though only through two cramped windows. An indeterminate pattern swarmed on the wallpaper. As the others pushed her through the doorway she saw a large table which seemed not to belong to the room, surrounded by a dim bed, a dressing table, a couple of chairs; rough squares of paper laid around the table's edge spelled out the alphabet—"Don't shut that door!" Richard hissed urgently.

He tugged a drawer out of the dressing table and propped the door open. "No handle on the inside," he explained, amused by their muffled dismay or suspicion. "Come on then, before my parents get back."

The girl advanced, because there was nothing else to do. "Go on," said the boy with the wispy chin, shoving her. Was he annoyed with his own nervousness? Before she knew it she was sitting on the bed, hemmed in by the wispy boy and, nearest the door, by Wendy.

"Right," Richard said triumphantly. "Now." From beside the dressing table he produced an object like a homemade wooden roller skate, whose wheels were capable of veering. His gesture expected a reaction, and received one: strangled laughter, nudging, giggling. "He's going to write with his feet," someone sniggered. The girl joined in the almost hysterical mirth, though she felt the shrillness of her laughter excluded her from the group.

"Shut up!" Richard said savagely. "Do you want someone to hear us and call the police?"

They subsided gradually into silence. There was an interlude of subdued jostling as they each placed one hand on the skate in the center of the table. "Now what?" demanded the wispy boy.

"We wait," Richard said.

They did so, more or less silently. "My arm's going to sleep," one girl muttered. "So am I," complained her friend. Minutes after they had spoken, their words remained, hovering as though the air had grown stagnant. The room seemed to be darkening, as if with the approach of a storm—the young girl's eyes must be tired, that was all. Headlights trailed over the ceiling and dragged at the pattern of the wallpaper, which shifted slyly. No light reached the ajar door, beyond which stood blackness. She imagined how much of the dark house she would have to brave to escape.

Boredom or unease was growing. "How long are we going to have to sit?" protested the wispy boy. Free hands were exploring. "Oh, *get* off," one girl cried furiously.

"I don't think this is going to work," said the boy with the moustache. "The planchette's too heavy. You need something lighter."

At once, accompanied by an odd sound which seemed to come from deep in the house, the wooden skate began to quest toward the edge of the table, advancing and recoiling like a trapped rat.

"Of course if you're going to *make* it move—"

"I'm not doing it," Richard said resentfully.

"Well, somebody must be." He gazed at each of them in turn. She noticed that his moustache was glistening: with sweat? Nothing he saw in their eyes seemed to please him. "Well, it's certainly not me," he said as though denying a bad smell.

The skate faltered and was still. Richard was glaring—because of the interruption, or because he had ceased to be the leader? "Are we just going to sit here and argue?" he demanded.

"We're supposed to ask questions. What was the name of the fellow who died here?"

"Allen. Mr. Allen."

"All right." The moustached boy sat forward like an executive at a conference; perhaps he was imitating a film. "We'll see if it's him." Slowly and loudly, as though addressing a retarded child, he asked the skate, "Are you Mr. Allen?"

He was answered at once, by stifled giggles. He permitted himself a faint smile: the joke was really too childish for him. Only Richard held himself solemn, furiously so. The girl restrained herself from giggling more loudly than the others. Why was she afraid to draw attention to herself? Because the room was so dim?

Again she heard the faint sound, which was perhaps not so deep in the house, after all: a feeble restlessness. A mouse? No, it must be the noise of the skate, made to sound distant by the oppressive atmosphere—for the skate was moving. It turned purposefully and went straight to a square of paper, where it halted.

That seemed comfortingly meaningless. One letter could tell them nothing. Then the girl saw that two additional squares interrupted the alphabet, on opposite sides of the table: YES and NO. NO, the skate had said.

No, it was not Mr. Allen who was advancing through the house, making doors squeak in the downstairs hall and now on the landing. It must be only a draft. But it was not Mr. Allen who had come into the room, whose feeble restlessness was clearly audible now, though its position was obscure. Richard's head turned, searching. Reluctantly he said, "That's what I heard."

Now the sound was more definable. Yes, it was like someone very old or very ill fumbling about in the dark—except that just as she was close to locating it in one part of the room, it seemed to reappear elsewhere. Her fingers on the skate were paralyzed, they felt glued together by sweat, but they were trembling. Neither her hand nor the rest of her body could do anything about her panic.

Perhaps everyone was waiting for somebody else to be the first to flee. Before anyone could move, the skate began turning. Though their arms were heavy with exhaustion and nerves, it was quicker now, more efficient. I AM, it spelled rapidly.

The moustached boy sat forward, awaiting the rest of

the message. His free hand wiped his glistening moustache. The others watched unwillingly as the skate dragged their hands about the table. When it had finished they sat stiffly, not daring to remark on the message in case that lent it power. Only the moustached boy mouthed it silently, frowning: I AM EVERY-WHERE IN HERE.

"I think we'd better go," stammered the wispy boy. His last word sprang into falsetto, but nobody laughed. Nor did anyone move, for the formless sounds were groping about the room, hemming them in. Headlamps slipped rectangles of light into the room; the rectangles turned into gliding parallelograms and vanished. The girl kept her gaze away from the light, for it might make the source of the groping visible.

The skate darted into the center again, and dodged about the table. Its swiftness seemed almost gleeful. One of the girls was sobbing dryly and incessantly; it sounded as though she was choking. The skate picked out its message deftly, then rested beneath the crowd of their fingertips. DO AS YOURE TOLD, it had said.

A wave of resentment, violent as electricity, flashed through the group. "Fuck that," said Ken, whom the young girl had yet to hear speak. His voice proved to be high and thin, unsuited to the protest; it breathed out beer, the smell of bravado. His chair creaked as he made to stand up. The sobbing girl managed to gulp herself space between sobs for words, to cry, "Don't let go!"

Perhaps she believed that while the presence was occupied in spelling messages it would be unable to do worse. And indeed, the sound of unlocated fumbling had ceased—but the young girl felt it had only come to rest. She thought she could hear the faintest of shiftings, like the movements which betray the serenity of a cat as it prepares to leap on its prey. She dared not look.

In any case, she had to watch the skate, for it was darting urgently about the table. Their fingertips clung to it as though it was their sole protection from the dark. Before the message had ended, the girl was seized by a fit of trembling. Everyone stared at the table, unwilling to meet anyone else's eyes. She felt as though her hand was trying to shake her body to pieces. The message was expanding in her mind, like an afterimage in sudden and absolute darkness.

ALL EXCEPT ONE GO OUT.

"Oh, that's too fucking much," Ken protested. "That's just fucking stupid." He was speaking at the top of his voice—to impress them, or himself, or someone else entirely? His piping voice was scrawny in the dark. Nevertheless Richard, at whom he was glaring, turned defensive. "I didn't make it say that," he retorted. "I'd have said who the one had to be, wouldn't I?"

At once, as though it had been waiting for his cue, the skate pounced. It rushed toward the bed, sweeping letters to the floor, jerking their arms with such force that Wendy fell against the young girl. Wendy began shuddering as though with fever—for the skate was pointing straight at her.

"No," Wendy cried. "I won't. I won't." She sounded hardly able to form the words. She managed to stumble to her feet, and fled toward the landing. The young girl struggled away from the wispy boy, who shook himself impatiently free of her.

As she sat up, regaining the place from which Wendy had elbowed her, she realized that the skate was pointing directly at her.

Wendy's flight had released the others. They retreated from the table as though it was diseased. None of them glanced at the young girl; indeed, they seemed to have forgotten her—for in their haste they shoved the table against her, knocking her backward on the bed.

The bed was not empty. As she fell back, she glimpsed a face upturned on the pillow. A convulsion seized her whole body; she arched upward, straining her spine—anything rather than touch what lay in the bed. Was the face only an accident of shadows on the lumpy pillow? Perhaps, for as she wrenched her neck in peering wildly, she saw that the face was incomplete. But as her hand tried to lever her away from the bed it touched, through the bedclothes, a thin yet flabby limb.

She heard someone stumble over the drawer in the doorway and kick it aside. The door slammed. "Hey, Richard," said the muffled voice of the wispy boy, "did you realize we've left that kid in there? Was she supposed to be the one?" Several of them giggled, relieved; perhaps they had known they were shutting her in.

She kicked the table away and ran blindly to the door. Her gasp of terror had hurt her chest, leaving her no breath with which to cry out. She heard Wendy from what seemed a great distance. "You haven't really left her in there, have you? You silly fool, she's only a kid! I'm supposed to be looking after her!"

"All right. Calm down." It was the voice of the moustache. "The door isn't locked, is it? She's braver than half you people, anyway. I didn't hear *her* whining." The handle of the door rattled. There was a thud, and a silence.

When he spoke again his voice was low with anger. "What sort of games are you playing, Richard? The handle's come out and the door won't budge."

The dark closed around the young girl, like the embrace of fever. The door shook as shoulders thumped it, but it held. Now the babble of angry voices was retreating from her. Was Richard calling, "It's all right, don't fret, I'll get something"? The voices faded down the stairs, leaving her alone with silence.

It was not quite silence. Behind her, something dropped softly to the floor. She could neither turn nor cry out, but she knew without turning what the sound was: the fall of bedclothes. Had something else got down from the bed?

She could move her hand now. She hooked her finger .

in the hole where the door handle ought to be. She dragged at the door, though her hand was trembling so violently that it threatened to jerk out of the hole, but it was no use; the door refused to budge. Now she was trapped there, unable to let go of the door, held fast by the dark as though it was a marsh.

When she was seized from behind she was not even able to scream. They must be hands, for they had fingers, though they felt soft as putty—far softer than putty, indeed, to be able to do to her what they began to do then.

PART ONE

THE FOLLOWER

I

"Discerning a director's personality in his films can be rather like doing a jigsaw puzzle," Rose said, "except that sometimes the pieces are blurred."

Trevor gazed up at her, smiling ambiguously. As he sat back, crossing one leg over the other, his sharp nose poked forward like Punch's, the curtains of his long black hair parted farther. "Why can't it be your method that's blurred?" he said.

Rose smiled, glad of a pointed question to enliven the last day of term. "Well, because it seems to have worked for me over the years, I suppose. I hope I haven't given you the impression that I decide in advance that a director's films are going to express his personality. On the contrary, it's a question of looking to see if they do. But I remember when I saw a group of Hitchcock films and all at once I realized that despite the different scriptwriters and studios, not to mention actors cast against his wishes, the films had an absolutely consistent personality, a way of looking at things that could only be Hitchcock's. As soon as I saw that, his films became enormously more interesting."

"But if you can't find a personality you say it's a weak director. That's like dismissing all the filmmakers who don't fit into your theory. Suppose they're in the majority? Maybe when you think you've found a personality it's just a series of coincidences."

17

"I don't think so, Trevor," She wished some of her other students would join in, but they were gazing at her as if she were a rather dull film. "In fact you're right, the faceless directors are in the majority, but doesn't that make the consistency of people like Hitchcock all the more remarkable? To me what makes film so fascinating is the way that self-expression is often so much of a struggle. That, and the ways a good director solves the problems of unpromising material. You remember how our feeling that Paul Newman has gone to bed with Mary Poppins actually works in favor of Hitchcock's film."

That made them laugh, and begin to talk about miscasting. "Once I saw Terence Stamp playing a Mexican with a Cockney accent," someone said.

"The worst of the lot was John Wayne saying, 'Truly this was the son of Gawd.'"

Before long they flagged. They must be as eager for the end of term as she was for New York. Only Trevor wanted to continue the discussion. "I still think you can't call a director the author of a film. It isn't like writing a book, where the author is in complete control."

"Heavens, I wish that were true!" she said. "It isn't for me, I'm afraid. But I don't think it is for any writer, you know. Any writer has to be influenced by things he's read or experienced but doesn't consciously remember, not to mention how he's learned to tell a story or whatever form he uses to express himself. A writer must be partly at the mercy of his subconscious, just like everyone else."

Trevor seemed to feel she'd tricked him, performed some sleight of mind. She couldn't tell if the others were even listening. "I think we'll call it a day," she said. "Have a good Easter, since I don't suppose I'll see you before."

She packed her briefcase and emerged from her office, into the low corridor. Lighting, more or less concealed, flared down the walls. Beyond the Henry Moore drawings, Gainsborough's portrait of Mr. and Mrs. Andrews gazed haughtily at her. Quivering afterimages of light exploded before her, and she had to shut her eyes. She hoped she wasn't due for a migraine. Certainly she felt on edge for something to happen—presumably New York. As she made for the Center for Communication Studies, beneath the lid of the overcast sky, a jumpy nerve tried to pluck at her lips.

She walked through a glade of saplings taped to poles, the thin tips of branches sprinkled with green, and she felt happier at once, for there was Bill. He stood straight and tall and smiling quietly to himself outside the Center, a converted chapel bristling with aerials like garden rakes. Beneath his graying hair his face with its dark bushy eyebrows and strong clear lines looked young, by no means six years older than Rose. The first time he'd waited for her on a date, when they were students at Sussex University, he'd looked exactly like that, strong and patient and dependable. A tingle of sexual electricity shivered upward through her, as keenly as ever.

When she reached him he hugged her quickly, affectionately. "Had a good day?" she said.

"Apart from the fact that a plague of the zombies seems to have infected my class, I suppose I had quite a good day."

"Oh dear, end-of-term lethergy."

"Fifteen different varieties of gaping incomprehension, more like. Like being confronted with one of those sideshows where you have to throw pennies in the holes. Thank God for Hilary—thank God for mature students."

"Yes, I know how you feel . . ." They were strolling downtown, past the Children's Hospital whose windows were a zoo of teddy bears, past the gilded masks on the gates of the Philharmonic Hotel. Beyond the

Mersey, the green afterglow sank through the deep lake of the sky; above the Pier Head, clock faces were misted suns.

"Still," she said, "I can't entirely blame the students, not when they know that when they leave here their degrees won't ensure them a job. Some of them are going to be overqualified for what's available. Can we expect them to drug themselves with knowledge for its own sake?"

"Why not? It's certainly preferable to the shit they do use. I'm sorry, I'm just not receptive to special pleading today. If I'd sat around moping when I left school I wouldn't be where I am now. I don't like having got there only to waste my energy."

She had the impression that something else had made him irritable. "We'll both feel better for New York," she said, squeezing his arm, and all at once was eager to be there, among the Jacob's ladders of bright windows, the parks watched over by skyscrapers, the street smells of pretzels and kebabs and lunchtime marijuana, the sleepless shops and restaurants, the nervous energy, the constant high of New York. That much she'd learned from their American agent, Jack Adams, and his letters; but for her Gene Kelly was dancing along Broadway, King Kong was perched on the Empire State Building, Brando was mumbling through broken teeth on the waterfront. No doubt New York was nothing like the films. She was sure it would be full of surprises.

Downtown at Lewis's she still felt excited. She had always liked big stores, where the profusion of new clean things reminded her of childhood birthdays. Scents drifted from pastel displays of cosmetics, toddlers rode in plastic cars with fat wheels bright as finger paints. She bought blouses trimmed with lace, and a dress which glowed like a butterfly's wing when she held it up against the light. She would look pretty for Bill and New York.

Bill wandered away to the book department while

she paid. Eventually the salesman returned, having vanished behind the scenes to check her Diners Club card. Rose hurried to the descending escalator, and the top stair caught her heel; for a moment she was afraid of falling headlong. A spark of migraine pricked her vision, a group of toddlers watched her, their eyes painted into the sockets. Really, she had no cause to feel nervous, now that she had Bill and her work.

But where was Bill? Blind mauve faces craned toward her on necks as long as arms; wigs roosted on their heads. There he was, at the far side of the book department. She made her way through the crowded aisles, past a bookcase five shelves high full of MYS-TERIES OF THE UNIVERSE. *Did Spacemen Colo-nize the Earth? Was God an Astronaut?* One book was called *Astral Rape*—the pleasure without the pain, she thought, and couldn't help giggling, though a bald man stared at her.

Without warning she felt on edge. Again she looked for Bill. He was only three aisles distant now, glowering at the cardboard labels on top of the bookcases. Presumably he was looking for their books, but there had never been a section for books about the arts. She was halfway to him when her stomach tightened, her fingers began to shake.

Before she turned she knew what was wrong. The bald man was still staring at her. His head, which looked perched on top of a bookcase, shone like plastic beneath the fluorescent lights. His eyes were bright, flat, expressionless as glass; she thought of a display head stripped of its wig. When a fat pink tongue squeezed out between his lips, it was as if a plastic head had come to life.

Was he a store detective? Did he suspect her of theft? But she could see him with unnatural clarity, even the spider-legs of hair protruding from his nos-trils. His forehead was beaded like a boiling egg. No, he was no detective.

Unable to think for dismay and rage, she forced her

way through the crowd to Bill. Cash registers purred and sang. "Ready to go?" he said. She glanced back, but there was no sign of the bald man. He wasn't worth mentioning, not when she had to find out what had upset Bill.

On the train home Bill produced from his briefcase the source of his mood—a *Times Literary Supplement* review of *The Same Old Movie Scenes,* by W. & R. Tierney. "'. . . difficult to know how seriously the writers take their subject . . . they strain to make a case for clichés as formal conventions supplying the artist with a context for experiment and personal expression . . . book lacks the disciplines of semiology and structuralism . . . jarring attempts at humour . . . sense of academics slumming . . .'"

"Never mind," Rose said, "it's only one woman's opinion," but she knew that a hostile review could embarrass and depress him for days.

"*Films and Filming* quite like us." He tilted his glasses to peer at the magazine. "'The Tierneys' new book is especially good in showing how supposedly clichéd scenes have developed . . . brilliant and specific analysis of conventions in the urban thriller . . . combines insight and humour with common sense . . .'"

"I wonder which of us is which?" Bill said of that comment, giggling, as they climbed the steps to the tall cottage of St. Michael's station. The train dwindled, a kite's tail of lit windows.

They headed for the Mersey, along a path which was just visible, glimmering like whitewash, between ivied banks. The muffled glow of the moon was caught in lattices of trees. "Sometimes I wonder if I'm losing touch with my students," she said.

They ducked beneath a pipe thick as Bill's midriff. A car hid among brambles. "You're not still blaming yourself for that John Wayne business?" Bill said.

"I wouldn't say blaming, exactly." She had taken her

students through *Rio Bravo,* the most enjoyable Western she knew and one of the most fruitful to analyze, but her students could see only John Wayne's politics: his presence wiped out the rest of the film for them, destroyed its personality. "But one has to take their feelings into account," she said.

"Take them into account, yes, but don't indulge them. You're trying to get them to open their minds, not cling to their prejudices."

"I know." It was just that sometimes she felt frustrated—felt that she contained untapped resources, though she had no idea what they might be. "But there used to be times when students would give me insights I hadn't had before."

"Well, we still get that in our collaborations, don't we? Don't look so glum. 'You could be a wonderful dancer instead of letting people set fire to you.'"

"*The Story of Vernon and Irene Castle.* 'It's no use knocking there, everybody's dead,'" she responded, laughing.

"*The Diabolical Doctor Z.* 'With luck your boyfriend may have a rich and fulfilling life as a paraplegic.'"

"*Beyond the Valley of the Dolls.* 'Soldier who fell for your country, you did not fall upon deaf ears.'"

"Oh, that was the Roger Vadim film—what was its name? *Hellé.*" They were quoting from their book of unforgettably bad lines and plots from films, *Watch Out for Sodomite Patrols!* A television showing of *Sodom and Gomorrah* had given Bill the title and the idea for the book, which had sold spectacularly: many of their students had bought it, which had pleased her most of all. "Anyway," Bill said, reminded of that, "our books aren't out of touch."

As the path led them onto higher ground, alongside a field where cows were large pale standing stones, the clouds rolled back above the Irish Sea. Gulls sailed down like flakes of the lonely full moon, the river was a torrent of milk through which a luminous liner was

gliding. Where the river widened to the sea, beneath
the intense sharp-edged disc of the moon, the darkness
looked vast and mysterious as outer space.

Fulwood Park shone through the gap in the hedge at
the end of the path. The Italianate villas stood in
gardens like small parks, screened by trees. One villa,
lit for a party, was bright as a ship. Beside Rose,
beneath a railway bridge which had been boarded off
from pedestrians, the wind from the Mersey hooted, an
enormous insubstantial owl.

Infrequent streetlamps lit the private road of Fulwood Park, conical drops of milky light frozen as they
were about to fall. Everything looked theatrical: the
red bole of the postbox, the chained bollards which
fenced off a garden for residents only, the mass of
clover which covered the pavement, each pale leaf
separate and distinct, embalmed by the icy light.

Among the villas, the Tierneys' pebble-dashed house
and its Siamese twin looked cozily out of place. The
twin's windows were lit, but it had felt unfamiliar ever
since old Mrs. Winter had died of a fall near the
riverside path one subzero night a couple of months
ago. No doubt Rose would meet the new owners when
she came back from New York.

She had emerged through the hedge, and was making
for their gateless drive, when she started and glanced
sharply along Fulwood Park. Patches of light and inky
darkness led toward the main road, beneath the trees.
Someone had just stepped into a patch of darkness.

A minute later she was in their house, which was
warm as a bed, and as welcoming. Bill headed for the
kitchen while she took the mail into the living room.
When she turned the dimmer switch the Victorian suite
brightened quietly; on the cushioned seats, embroidered lovers smiled through leaves. On the sideboard—
dark rich wood, glossy as a black cat—the Chinamen
which Uncle Wilfred and Aunti Vi had left her reached
toward each other with tiny perfect porcelain hands.
She sank gratefully onto the sofa and read the mail.

"Here's a letter from Gerhard," she called. "He's traced our German rediscovery."

"Fine. The book is shaping up." *Rediscoveries in Film* was to consist of interviews with neglected innovators. "And we couldn't ask for a better reason to go to Munich."

"Oh dear, there's a set of proofs for correction."

"Perhaps you could make a start on them while I cook dinner. I'll finish them before we leave."

He sounded happier; routine always calmed him. Why wasn't she as calm? Abruptly she stood up and turned the switch. The wall lamps dimmed like candles in a mine. She went to the velvet curtains, which were heavy as quilts, and peered through the window. Above the conical streetlamps branches glared, frozen explosions of wood. The road was deserted, and all at once she stepped back, shaking her head wryly at herself. Of course, the man she'd glimpsed five minutes ago had been wearing a crash helmet; that was why his skull had looked smooth and gleaming.

II

When the airport bus reached the bridge into Manhattan, Rose was struggling to wake. She felt as if she were still flying over the Atlantic. But there was the New York skyline, cut out of a dark blue evening sky which had soaked up the last of the light. Rank on irregular rank of lit windows, brilliant perforations in computer cards, mounted toward brazen wisps of cloud. Already she sensed how the city was teeming; she thought it must never sleep. Yet even when the foothills of the skyscrapers towered over her she felt she hadn't quite arrived.

She tried to concentrate on Jack Adams, her American agent and Bill's, who occupied the seat in front of them. He was a tall swarthy man with a dimpled chin, whose limbs moved restlessly, propping one another. "David Tracy had gone underground," he was saying. "That's why we had the trouble finding him. A seventy-eight-year-old underground filmmaker, isn't that something? We should be able to arrange today for you to interview him."

"I'm glad we're doing this book," Rose said to wake herself up, "adding to the literature of cinema."

"Well, sure. So long as it makes you good money as well." He folded his arms, disentangled them. "Listen, when you do your interview in Munich, maybe you can introduce me to your German agent. I need to get together with someone over there."

At Grand Central Station he snatched their luggage from the belly of the bus. "Listen, why don't we take a cab from here. I invited some people over to welcome you to New York."

Pavements breathed out steam. Knots of pastry fumed on a stand. A man and a poodle trotted by, both wearing crimson nail varnish. Sirens howled along the angular stone valleys, bicycles dodged across intersections against the lights.

Jack despaired of the taxis and hurried the Tierneys into the subway, where trains were tapestries of painstaking graffiti. During the ride he showed her a subway map which looked like a tangled skein of colored wools, but her sense of direction was bad enough as it was. She was a burden her sleepwalking body was carrying.

Jack lived on West 89th Street, on the tenth floor. Though the main room was a maze of bookshelves, it was obsessively tidy. The books were interrupted by Mexican figurines, a tarantula beneath a glass dome, a clock whose hands and face changed colors incessantly.

Breughel prints humanized patches of whitewashed wall.

Rose hadn't much time to explore, for already guests were arriving: the editor of a science-fiction magazine, lecturers on cinema, a girl escorted by a publisher's editor who said to Jack, "This is Diana who you wanted to meet."

"Oh, sure, okay." Visibly embarrassed, Jack said, "These are two of my authors," as though the Tierneys were a pair of ornaments. "Help yourself to drinks," he said to everyone.

Rose introduced herself to Jack Daniels, a bourbon. Soon she was happy to drift from group to group, sampling conversations, as the party grew. " . . . The last anyone heard of him was he got so stoned at Frankfurt he forgot what books he was selling . . ." " . . . and Asimov says to her, 'Don't say that, that's what my wife keeps saying' . . ." Bill was in a corner, playing author. "There's no point in criticism that isn't honest," he was declaring, "no point in being too sensitive on behalf of other people."

Rose chatted about films and watched Diana, the small slim young woman with the large dark eyes, who had been introduced to Jack. Diana was wandering aimlessly, disoriented perhaps by Jack's rebuff. When Rose went to the bar to pour herself another bourbon, Diana ventured over, and Rose took pity on her. "Do you know many people here?" she said.

"No, not many. I guess it shows."

"Well, neither do I, so we can get to know each other."

"I'd love to if you don't think I'm being too selfish. I mean, everyone here must want to meet you."

"That's all right. You aren't going to scare them away."

"Hey, that's strange. I knew you were going to say that. I'll tell you something—I feel like I already know you. Do you ever have that feeling?"

Her eyes were even wider now, her gaze was more

intense, and all at once Rose seemed to feel it too: a rapport with Diana which she couldn't quite define. Behind her a writer was saying, "One night I brought her to fifteen orgasms on the studio floor." The two women looked at each other, then they burst out laughing. They were certainly in rapport now.

"That man is his own bad publicity," Rose said. "The trouble is, I know people who think all writers are like that."

"Every job has its big mouths. Not like your husband, I can tell he's a sweet person. Listen, if Jack's too busy to show you New York I can do it if you like."

"That would be nice," Rose said, and would have said so even if Diana hadn't looked steeled for another rebuff.

Before Diana could go on—she looked eager to speak now—her escort came over. "You brought your cards, didn't you? The guy from Doubleday has to leave in just a few minutes, but I said you'd give him a reading."

"I'll see you later," Diana said apologetically to Rose, and made her way to a corner table, where she took out a pack of Tarot cards. Jack joined Rose at once; perhaps he had been waiting for Diana to leave. Alcohol had calmed his limbs.

"It's really good to meet you," he said. "I mean, I knew Bill through his letters, but you were kind of a mysterious figure. I want to tell you, you're no disappointment."

"Yes, yes, dear," the loudmouthed writer was rebuking his girl friend as she tried to interrupt his erotic saga, "but we're talking about *me*."

"Jesus, that guy." Jack looked ready to blush. "His editor brought him."

"Don't worry, Jack, I didn't think he was a friend of yours."

"I just thought, well, you might be, uh, embarrassed. See, you kind of remind me of someone."

"I hope I'd like her."

"Sure, I think you would. Would have, I meant to say. I knew her back home. I mean, New York girls are okay, they're lively, interesting, you know. But they come on too strong."

Did he mean too brash, too competitive, too sexually willing? Perhaps all three. "She isn't—?" she said, and trailed off, like a hundred moments in films.

"What? Oh, you mean is she dead? No, I guess she's still alive back there. We were going together for a while—matter of fact, we were engaged. But her parents broke it up—you know, I had no prospects, that kind of bullshit. And—Jesus!" he said, struck by a memory. "Yeah, they said I talked too dirty for her. I'd forgotten that. They ought to hear the girls down here. I don't use those words, except when I have to do that or punch someone out. I mean, she didn't mind, it was her parents who minded. We understood each other, Kathy and I." A gulp of bourbon made him cough, but he seemed to welcome the harshness. "Still, I needed to get away from there. I had to do that before I could do what I really wanted. And that's what you see me doing here, right?"

Rose sensed that he wanted a woman as much as she had wanted a child until she'd grown used to her sterility. She patted his arm. "You'll find someone."

"Yeah, maybe. That Diana seems kind of interesting. Say, look, she's cornered Bill."

So she had. She was leading him to her cards. He looked bemused, too polite or too drunk to resist. Rose made her way toward them: this promised to be entertaining.

"Blue eyes, gray hair, fair skin," Diana was saying. "You're King of Wands." She handed him the rest of the pack. "Shuffle them how you like, then cut them three times to your left."

When he'd chosen a heap she began to deal from it, face up. "This covers you, this crosses you, this crowns you, this is beneath you. . . . This is strange. Are you into the occult?"

"No, not at all."

"Maybe someone very close to you?"

"No, I can't believe that."

"Are you sure? All the cards have several meanings, but that interpretation feels right. If it feel right it nearly always is."

"I'm sure there's nothing of the kind."

Diana brushed a coil of her reddish hair back from one slightly pointed ear, and continued dealing. "Well, I don't know. I'd really like to tell you how they feel to me."

"By all means do so."

Perhaps Diana couldn't hear that his tone was consciously patient. "The atmosphere you're in is conflict—Eight of Wands reversed," she began. "Working against you is the Moon—occult forces. Your aim in the matter is love, friendship, union—the Two of Cups. Yet your motivation, or the motivation of the matter, is imposture, falsehood—the Two of Swords."

An audience was gathering, as though around a poker school: would Steve McQueen have the ace in the hole? "Now this *is* interesting. The influence just past is the Hierophant reversed, the influence you're moving into is the Hanged Man reversed—both refer to something whose effects are far-reaching."

Bill clearly found this less interesting than she did. She pointed at the rank of cards: Five of Cups, Knight of Wands, Three of Cups, Nine of Swords. "There's a marriage, but with frustration and bitterness. A time away from home in strange surroundings. Your hopes in the matter are victory, fulfillment. But what will come is death—of something," she added, the impersonality leaving her voice, "it needn't mean a person. You have to remember that the cards show possibilities, not certainties. But can you relate what I've told you to anything in your life?"

"No." After a pause he decided to go on. "Since you ask, I think it's utter nonsense."

"I guess the cards can be read another way," she said

reluctantly. "They might mean that you and your wife are going to disagree over something—a book, maybe. The Moon could be something, say an insight, that has to be brought out. You may need to destroy some barrier to understanding. Maybe that's going to happen here in New York."

"I'm sure they can be made to mean anything you like."

Visibly hurt, she began to gather in the cards. The audience wandered off, disappointed or embarrassed. "I do apologize," Bill murmured. "It's my fault. I shouldn't have agreed to it in the first place. I don't believe in that kind of thing, but I didn't realize you did—not at a party. Look, can I get you a drink?"

He hurried away on that errand, relieved. "Oh, this is awful," Diana wailed to herself. "I didn't mean to upset him. He must think I can't relate to people at all."

"For heaven's sake don't worry, Diana." Rose felt protective; she could almost see Diana as the younger sister she had never had. "He shouldn't have been rude to you." She herself had been taken aback by the strength of his reaction.

"You don't agree with him?"

"No, not entirely."

"Then could I read your cards to see if they relate to his?"

Rose was both intrigued and uneasy. "All right," she said.

Her card was the Page of Swords. When Rose had prepared the deck, Diana began to deal: Three of Swords reversed, Five of Swords reversed, Queen of Swords, the Moon, the Tower, Queen of Pentacles reversed— Abruptly she shuffled them into the deck. "Listen, I must be too tired. I'll read your cards another time, okay?"

Bill returned, looking mischievous. "Let me introduce you to an English party game where the winner is whoever thinks of the worst line from a film . . ." He'd saved the situation and retrieved the party, which continued until the Tierneys showed signs of tiring. Everyone agreed they'd won the game with their favorite routine from *The Greatest Story Every Told* ("What's your name?" "James. What's yours?" "Jesus Christ." "That's a good name.") Departing, people invited them for drinks and meals. "I'm sorry we didn't get much chance to talk," Jack said awkwardly to Diana. "Maybe the four of us can have dinner one night. I'll give you a call."

In the bathroom Rose washed quickly, wary of a lurking cockroach. She and Bill had been so popular that it seemed perverse to harbor doubts, yet in a way it was their success that troubled her. When she'd read the proofs of their latest book the text seemed unadventurous, lacking in new insights, written with an eye to popularity. Were she and Bill suffering from success?

She heard Bill on the phone. When she returned to the bedroom he was boyishly excited. "I've just spoken to David Tracy and he sounds very enthusiastic about being interviewed. Says he has enough stories about the early years of Hollywood to fill a book—it's just that nobody ever asked him before. I hope I'm as lively as that when I reach his age."

His excitement was infectious. They hugged each other from sheer delight, and she forgot her momentary depression at once. Before long they were making love, which always seemed to make unfamiliar rooms warmer, more welcoming. They were hypersensitive with traveling and wakefulness, and their caresses felt electric. Bill came urgently almost as soon as he entered her, while she pressed him close to her with all her limbs; then he hugged her tight and stayed firm within her while she reached her own orgasm, slow and warm and profoundly relaxing.

Nevertheless, afterward she found she couldn't sleep. The room was stifling. She opened the window and padded to the edge of the balcony. Streetlamps pinned discs of light to the pavement, which glittered as though alloyed with frost. The street was deserted except for a glimpse of a figure vanishing into Amsterdam Avenue. She hurried back to bed, shivering. In her sleep she ran back and forth along the street. Every door was locked. She was scared to turn any of the corners, for she'd forgotten which corner the bald-headed figure had turned.

III

New York was doors in the wall of Grand Central Station which opened not into rooms but, like a childhood surprise, onto platforms. Seen from the Empire State, it was a grid of valleys, it was a launching pad miles wide. It was a man who gave the rebel yell at the end of a Pierre Boulez concert, a Japanese waiter performing a meal like a juggler, masochists prowling nighttime streets with keys at their belts, a French pavement café in the basement of Carnegie Hall, the tortured explosion of Picasso's *Guernica* filling a room. It was 42nd Street, which sounded like a song and looked like dozens of childhood cinemas lined up for offers: men muttering a litany of drugs for sale, a pretty black girl asking Bill, "Going out, honey?" New York was a million different impressions, one of which was David Tracy, the most insufferable man Rose had ever met.

He was staying in one room of a Brooklyn flat. Though the rest of the flat was deserted—his friend was out at work, presumably—Tracy had insisted on staying in the cramped room, amid the heaps of ragged magazines and fractured books, the stench of his cigars.

At first she had thought he was being gallant. "I can't say much more about that," he'd said abruptly, glancing at her, in the middle of a sordid anecdote about a former star. Obviously he'd felt that wasn't clear enough, for he had ignored her questions and had cut short his answers to Bill. "Well, I'm getting tired. I could talk to you again Thursday night, Bill. You'd need to stay overnight. There's only room for you."

Before Bill could show he was as furious as she was, she'd responded, "That would be fine, wouldn't it, Bill?" Their book was more important than their feelings. To have answered for Bill was a kind of triumph over Tracy.

Still, the more she thought about the incident, the angrier she grew. No wonder she felt irritably nervous. She was glad to be staying tonight with Diana: she could do with some female company. Besides, Diana could read her Tarot while Bill was out of the way.

Juggling packages of food, she let herself into the building with the key Diana had given her. Above the hunting howls of police cars, horses whinied nearby, in the Claremont Stables. Holding the door ajar with one foot, she stumbled backward into the foyer. The door slammed, and she sat down in a yielding lap.

She'd recoiled before she saw what it was. Furniture lurked everywhere, as though a room had taken over the building: a small bare table stood in the foyer, looking robbed of a telephone; a wardrobe stood beside the lift, comparing doors. The girl who lived below Diana was leaving. Nothing sat in the chair into which Rose had fallen except cushions.

When she'd waited minutes for the lift, she toiled upstairs. The few windows resembled slices of smoke, beyond which dark walls loomed. Wallpaper the color of old newsprint soaked up much of the brownish light, which seemed thick as gravy.

The second floor was almost indistinguishable from the first: a long bare stone-floored corridor in which her footsteps sounded flat and harsh, as though in an empty street. A sofa sat like a public bench. A loitering chair held open the doors of the lift.

As she made for the last flight of stairs she glanced into the vacated flat. A few rolled scraps of carpet huddled against the baseboard. Ghosts of furniture lingered on the walls, looking paler for having been exposed to light.

She'd turned away, toward the stairs, when she heard movement just beyond the door. She might have glanced back, but she had no time before the fist punched the back of her neck.

It felt more like a club, spiked with knuckles. The packages of food hit the stone floor before she did. Her knees tore. Would she be able to turn before the next blow? But the corridor imploded like a television image, a distant point of light which contained her body, and she was wrenched away into the greedy darkness.

IV

Rose woke with a headache of the kind that violent awakening can cause. She lay trying to quiet its rhythm. Bill's movements sounded distant; perhaps he was proofreading in the workroom. But why did the bed feel so narrow? Why was the light tinged with red?

As soon as she forced her eyes open she was frightened, for the ceiling was too close and entirely unfamiliar. It glowed dull crimson, except for the blurred whitish disc which hovered above the lampshade. She made herself turn her head, for someone was approaching.

He was padding toward her across floorboards which looked patched with dusty rugs. His face was more than black: its blackness boiled out of his cheeks, engulfed his mouth. The congealed light helped obscure his face. She could see only his eyes, moist marbles of yellowish gelatin.

She didn't cry out, but her hands clenched within the blanket that covered her. She felt the blanket pucker in her hands, and gape like ragged mouths. Behind the man, a woman emerged from an inner room. It was Diana.

Her appearance was not reassuring. With her small pinched face, her legs wasp-striped by socks, her hair that was neither short nor long, she looked trendy, anonymous. Outlined against a fluorescent glare, her face was by no means clear enough.

But she hurried forward anxiously. "You'll be okay now, Rose. This is John who lives next door. He's a nurse."

A friendly smile gleamed amid John's beard. Rose tried to sit up for him, until pain seized her by the forehead and by the scruff of the neck. "Now just relax. Just let me take a look here." He sounded like any of her childhood doctors. "This is where he hit you, right? Now how about here—can you feel this?" His hands were gentle and firm as Uncle Wilfred's had been.

"*O*-kay," he said. "You'll have a headache for a while, but you haven't got concussion. I have to go to Bellevue now, but I'll be back early in the morning if you need anything."

She needed Bill. His presence would reassure her that everything was stable, that the everyday world wasn't full of lairs, of lurkers waiting for her to turn her back—but if she phoned him, he would only come running. Not only would that spoil their book, but she could imagine the contempt of the insufferable Tracy. That above all was a reason not to phone.

Instead she grabbed her handbag. Nothing had been stolen; her passport was still there. Her name, her cramped photograph, the Englishness of it were profoundly reassuring. Still, why should she have been afraid of not being able to prove who she was?

"The cops want you to go and make a statement when you're better," Diana said.

Apart from her headache, Rose already felt better. The attack seemed less shocking than inevitable, one of the chances you took in New York. It seemed to have happened to someone else, not to have touched her at all.

"Maybe you could use some soup?" Diana said. She and Rose had planned to cook an elaborate dinner, but now Rose found the prospect of lying in state almost appealing. She glanced around the large narrow room. A Scriabin score perched above the keyboard of a battered piano. Above her couch, shelves heavy with leaning books clung precariously to the wall. Another couch was a battle of lumps; beside it a sweater salaamed on the floor. The apartment looked more lived in than Jack's—though Rose had yet to catch him dusting: he must work like a phantom charwoman, rumored but never glimpsed.

Over sounds of stirring, Diana called, "What do you think of Jack?"

"I like him now that I know him."

"That's how I feel. I mean, he puts up so many barriers until you get through to him. Like at the party, he felt he had to tell me the names of all his clients. He's scared to let go of his role in case you don't like him as he is. But I can tell there's more to him."

Rose was glancing at the ragged spines above her: *Catch-22*, Brautigan, Hesse, *Astral Rape,* Kafka, *The Psychedelic Experience, The Tarot Revealed, The Tarot Explained, A Primer of the Tarot* . . . "I like Bill," Diana was saying. "He sounds just like one of the Beatles, right? You know, I didn't come to the party to meet Jack. I wanted to meet you."

"Why, because you'd read something of ours?"

"No, never."

Rose had pulled out *Astral Rape*. IF SOMEONE COULD REACH THROUGH THE WALLS OF YOUR HOME AND KIDNAP YOU, red letters blared on the glossy black cover, WOULDN'T YOU BE SCARED? PERHAPS SOMEONE CAN.

"Have you read that? That's a scary book. Just imagine that guy Peter Grace reaching inside your body. I'm glad the Nazis couldn't find his secret, aren't you?" Diana placed a small table beside Rose. "Oh, you haven't read it—but you're interested in the occult, right?"

"No, not really." Rose stuffed the book into its gap, adding to its dog-ears, and felt abashed: after all, she'd pestered Diana to read her Tarot. "Sorry, Diana. You'll understand that I'm rather on edge. I used to be afraid of all that kind of thing, but I grew out of that. I'm interested really."

"Sure, I knew you were. It's like I was saying—I felt I ought to meet you. You have psychic glimpses too, don't you?"

"What do you mean?"

"Like premonitions."

"No." Watching Diana's disappointment, she grew impatient with herself. But Diana's missionary fervor had made her dizzy headache worse.

"I have them." Diana looked and sounded rather like a defiant child. "That's why I came downstairs to look for you. Excuse me, you don't want to talk about that."

"Yes, I do. I don't want to bottle it up."

"Well, there isn't much to say. Barbara, you know she was moving, she came up to use my phone because her van broke down. Well, we were having coffee when I got this feeling. We ran down in time to scare him off—we heard him running away. He must have tried to drag you into Barbara's flat. Wait, let me just get the soup."

When Rose sat up, the room tilted with her. She managed to prop herself precariously. "Want me to help you?" Diana said.

For a moment Rose was ten years old again, and desperate to be looked after. Then Auntie Vi had sat by the bed and held the spoon, but Rose didn't need that now; that was past, hardly even a memory now, more a feeling. "Good heavens no," she said.

Diana's face ducked quickly amid the cover of her hair, toward her soup. "Thanks anyway," Rose said.

It was vegetable soup, thick with chunks. Rose was wary of drinking it in case it returned in a similar form. Just in case she had concussion, oughtn't she to avoid solids? But the first mouthful seemed to strengthen her like liquor, stabilizing her head.

Diana was rolling a fat cigarette and gulping soup from a mug. Behind her a window too small for the room overlooked a fire escape. "Do you do drugs?" Diana said.

"Only alcohol. You go ahead if you want to."

Diana looked away, and seemed to feel rebuked. "I've been offered it a few times," Rose said, "but I'm always afraid it would bring on a migraine."

"It might." Diana glanced up sharply. "You have migraines?"

"Less now than I used to. None since a year ago." Why had Diana's question been so eager? She breathed out a cloud of sweetish smoke; the red light dimmed as though a fire was sinking. "What sort of thing did you use to see?" Diana said.

"Oh, a kind of tiny diamond that would break into fragments and spread across my whole field of vision. The first time was awful, because I didn't know what was happening—it was like reality exploding. I still see a spark now and then."

"I know people who have that." Diana's voice was slower, reflective. "And some people see intricate oriental patterns. I remember that because it sounds like an acid trip."

"I wouldn't know about that, Diana." The smell of cannabis made Rose's head swim. Was it affecting her? She heard a tap abruptly relieving itself, a blurred voice muffled by what seemed all at once an infinity of intervening walls. She felt restless, but when she tried to stand up her legs were water, pouring over the edge of the couch.

"I used to do acid," Diana said. "My Tarot says I may not go far in a job but develop inwardly instead. It kind of brings us back to what I was saying about your perceptions."

"Really."

"Yes, I believe so. See, certain things can heighten your perceptions. Drugs can, of course, and I'll tell you what someone once told me—being at a séance can sometimes give you special talents."

Rose felt obscurely threatened, perhaps by the looming cannabis. "But migraines heighten your perceptions naturally," Diana said.

"Not mine, I'm afraid."

"Maybe you don't let it get to you. John says most cases experience the heightening just before a migraine. I figure there's a connection between the flickering you get with migraine and the strobing you see on a trip. You know ergotamine—that's the only migraine cure that works—derives from LSD."

Rose was growing drowsy. "If you'll excuse me, Diana, I think I'll try to sleep."

"Sure, I'll turn off the big light." When she did so she said, as though the dark would help her to persuade Rose, "But if you ever have glimpses, you oughtn't to suppress them. I believe you're never given more to bear than you're capable of bearing."

Rose tugged the blankets over herself. Why couldn't Diana leave her alone? Shrunken voices resounded in the corridor; a vague oval hovered beyond the bars of the fire escape—the back of Diana's head. Rose closed her eyes determinedly. She hoped that her floating sensation, the heaviness in her skull, were the beginnings of sleep.

Her own warmth lulled her. Within her eyelids was a soothing glow. She drifted. Faint sounds of New York touched memories: streets, faces. Close by, Diana's footsteps reassured her that she was not alone, though they were receding beyond her sleep.

They weren't Diana's footsteps. They were darting out of the vacated flat. The dim corridor was a tunnel, beyond whose distant mouth the staircase rushed away like the lit end of a train. She fled toward it, in terror of the touch on the back of her neck. Dimness thick as mud hindered her limbs. The blow seemed to buckle her spine. She fell.

Suddenly she realized she still had a chance. If she could just let go of her body, she could escape. He would have caught only the shell of her. No sooner had she realized this than she was sailing out of her body, out of the corridor. She had barely time to glimpse him, a shadowy figure tearing out his hair in frustration at her ruse. She soared gleefully, delighted to have beaten him. She was safe, and more free than she had ever been in her life.

And she was no longer dreaming—for she could see herself lying on the couch, asleep.

She would have screamed if she had been able to scream; but she had left her mouth down there on the couch. There below her, yards below her, lay her body, and she was something else. Her body looked doll-sized; the dimness had turned her face into wax. It looked alien; she seemed never to have seen it before; but even that was less terrifying than the sight of her left fist, which was poking its knuckles uncomfortably into her left cheek—for she could feel nothing.

Unless she regained her body at once, she was dead. Darkness surrounded her, eating away her sense of herself. She was unable to move in any direction. It seemed that everything she could have used to fight the darkness lay slumped on the couch. Only her thoughts were struggling, and they were being crushed by darkness and by her panic into a last intense point of consciousness, rapidly dwindling.

Then her clenched terror seemed to explode, and she

way lying on the couch. But she was paralyzed, robbed of all sense of how to work her body. The smell of cannabis hovered over her. Nearby in the dimness, her fixed eyes could just distinguish a figure with a bloated head. Was it watching her, waiting to see what she would do?

In a moment she felt herself mesh with her body. Her gasp was inadvertent, far too loud. The dark figure leaned toward her; light flared before it; the shadow of Diana's head bloomed momentarily on the wall, as she lit another cigarette. Headphones tethered her to a stereo turntable. "You okay, Rose?" she called.

"Yes." She was too grateful to be awake and in her body to do more than lie there limply. But oh, she wished that Bill were here!

"You sound, uh— Anything wrong?"

"Nothing." But keeping it to herself wouldn't help her nerves. "I had a nightmare," she said reluctantly. "It was like a dream I had once, not long after I'd had my first period. I came down with a fever and had to stay in bed for a week."

Her words were steadying. "I dreamed that someone was looking for me—I don't know who, someone frightening. So I just drifted out of my body so that they wouldn't be able to find me. I remember floating downstairs and listening to my parents talking. The strangest part was, I seemed to leave all the sensations of fever behind."

Diana sat forward like a reporter. "Did you ever ask your folks whether they'd said what you heard them saying?"

"No, of course not. It was only fever. Besides, I could have overheard them from my room." The memory was blurred and oppressive; she wished she hadn't mentioned it. "I've had all kinds of strange incidents, Diana. There's no point in making too much of them. Why, when I was studying for my finals I used to stand back from the curb for buses—I really used to see them, even though buses never came along our road."

The tip of the cigarette reddened Diana's face, which looked dissatisfied. "You know what your dream sounds like?"

"Yes, of course." The phrase hovered above her, on a shelf. "Astral projection."

"Right, only we usually call it an out-of-the-body experience."

"Yes, well, I'd rather not talk about it just now, Diana. I'll try and get back to sleep." Still, their talk had helped her realize why she'd had the nightmare just now: Diana's attempts to persuade her that she had psychic powers, perhaps together with a sly effect of the cannabis.

But she couldn't sleep. She managed to relax a little, and lay hoping for Bill's return. She needed more reassurance than Diana could give. She had never before had a nightmare which stayed so vivid in her mind, refusing to blur or grow confused—as though it was not a dream but a memory.

PART TWO

INITIATION

V

Halfway down Fulwood Park, Rose halted, gazing at the beech tree. It was more like a handful of trees, sprouting from the immense bole. All winter it had stood dormant, a great arrested explosion of wood, silver against the chill sky. Winter had held the explosion in check. Now its tips flamed green; countless wooden filaments were multiplied by leaves, unfurled by the spring.

Spring had overwhelmed the pavement, which was a palette of grasses and ferns. In gardens, gorse shone yellow, illuminating its prickles. Opposite the postbox, the blond grass of the field regained its green; wild flowers expressed the yellow tinges of their stalks. Even the postbox looked to have sprouted roots of grass. In the residents' garden beyond the bollards, birds flew up like resurrected leaves. Everything made her eager to hurry home and write.

Before she reached the postbox, Miss Prince emerged from a drive. Tight waves of hair, frostily white, capped her head like a wig. She was tearing small flowers out of her driveway with her stick. Her right leg was lame, and appeared to snag that side of her face with a perpetual grimace of pain. "Good morning," she said icily, as though Rose were a stray tradeswoman.

She had been the Tierneys' first visitor in Fulwood

Park—canvassing for the election. "You do realize," she'd said in a tone which had dared Rose to try her patience further, "that this is a Conservative area?"

"Well," Rose had said, amused rather than offended but anxious to be rid of her, "we're rather in the middle."

"But that's worse than nothing." Since then she had hardly spoken to Rose, even when Rose had had to leave her the house key before going to New York. "Good morning," Rose said now, glancing at the woman as if she might be the new gardener, and walked on.

But how stupid, how petty! She tried to shrug off the incident, to think of her book. All of a sudden the road resembled a graveyard of stucco; the villas were elaborate boxes carved out of bone, so delicately carved that they were too fragile to be disturbed in any way. She had very seldom seen anyone emerge from them. Packs of watchdog cars sat in the drives.

Still, she was home. Dew or rain glittered, pinpoint rainbows, on the lawn within the curving drive. Because she had yet to see the new people, her home felt incomplete, a twin whose counterpart was ailing. She knew nothing at all about them, except that they owned a crimson Fiat, which stood gleaming like a commercial in the drive.

She filed the meat in the refrigerator, then she searched for the notebook. In the living room an advance copy of *Shared Nightmares* lounged on a chair; Victorian idylls, orientally delicate, were embroidered on the suite. In the dining room, wine bottles lazed in racks.

Oh, surely Bill hadn't taken the notebook absentmindedly with him to the university! She trudged upstairs, growing oppressively hot. When Mrs. Winter had lived next door, the Tierneys had often wandered around the house naked; trees screened them from the road.

Her blurred face skimmed over the black tiles of the

bathroom. She found the notebook in the bedroom, on the floor at Bill's side of the bed. Damn—he'd written one of the passages she had looked forward to writing, for it was crossed out in the notebook: "Directing films, Clint Eastwood seems frozen by the mirror of his lens . . ."

She sat in their workroom and strained at a paragraph. Her words seemed stiff and cumbersome, obstacles that hindered her thoughts. Of course this was only a rough draft, to help her and Bill write *The Meanings of Stardom* quickly once term was over, so that they could move on to *Rediscoveries in Film.*

What would she rather be doing, for heaven's sake? Following Diana's lead, developing her so-called psychic powers? Yes, she ought to be sailing around beneath the ceiling while her body took it easy on the bed; that would make her name—Rose the Astral Moth. She wished that memory—nightmare, hallucination, whatever it had been—would hurry up and fade.

Nor had Diana's dictionaries of the Tarot been encouraging. The Three of Swords reversed was mental alienation; Five of Swords reversed was connected with burial; Queens of Swords meant sterility, the Moon was darkness, terror, the occult. There were other meanings, but these seized her attention: the Tower meant catastrophe, the Queen of Pentacles reversed was evil, suspicion, fear. "Those cards didn't mean anything. I was tired," Diana had reassured her, though how could that affect how Rose had shuffled the cards?

Her ideas were chafing against one another without sparking. She saw no point in forcing herself to write. She typed a postscript on Bill's letter to Jack. "See you in Munich—where we'll drink you under the table!" Writing letters often made her banal.

The aerogram slipped, silent as Valentino, into the postbox. Above the white fire of the river, clouds like mountains softened by snow rode the sky. When Rose strolled back she found two people standing in her driveway. "Can I help you?" she called.

The small woman in the shabby coat turned first. Her face looked aged by resignation. A Band-Aid held her glasses together, hair the color of dust sprouted from beneath her headscarf. "We're all right," she said gripping her husband's hand. His shoulders towered above her, expensively padded by a brand-new overcoat. He turned.

He must be her son, not her husband. Perhaps he was twenty, but his smooth flesh looked babyish. His cheeks glowed as though rouged; his blank eyes looked overwhelmed by chubbiness. The whole of his chin glistened with saliva.

"Sorry," Rose said, apologizing as much for her instinctive shock as anything, and retreated inside her house.

She couldn't help it: she hoped the woman wasn't her new neighbor. Perhaps she was only visiting, like the other strangers Rose had seen recently in Fulwood Park: a fat man who dodged quivering from side to side of the road; a youth with hair twice the span of his head; a thin girl who stood gazing at her cupped hand as though it held a treasure. How many residents must be peering from the shelter of their curtains? Well, Rose wasn't going to. She climbed the stairs, feeling vaguely expectant. Perhaps an idea was about to declare itself.

Before she reached the landing, the doorbell rang.

She started, and felt guilty. The woman's son had looked not merely harmless but helpless. Besides, while Rose could see a woman's face in the lowest of the front-door panes, obscured by the frosted glass and surrounded by an aura of fragments of flesh, the woman seemed to be alone. When Rose opened the door she came face to face with someone entirely new.

Was she a gypsy? She carried a capacious tartan handbag, the sort which might hide items for sale, or pamphlets. But she wore a mauve sweater set, and looked like the keeper of a stall at a parish rummage sale, hardly a door-to-door saleswoman; her timid smile was ready to retreat. Beneath the pale crust of makeup she was middle-aged.

"I'm sorry if I'm bothering you," she said, and had to clear her throat. "I'm Gladys Hay. We have the house next door."

VI

Gladys seemed afraid to enter. As soon as she'd braved the hall she halted, her small plump hands burrowing mouselike through a mass of papers in her bag. "You shouldn't let me in your house just because of who I say I am," she said reproachfully, and produced a crumpled smudged envelope bearing a South African stamp. Colin and Gladys Hay, it said, where old Mrs. Winter had used to live.

"I do hope I'm not bothering you. I heard you typing before."

"Don't worry about that, I've finished now."

"Are you a typist?"

"No," Rose said with a hint of pique, "I'm a writer."

"A writer? A writer of books?" Her small square face looked trapped in embarrassment, her cheeks burned as if slapped.

"Yes, Bill and I have written a few. There's one." Rose had meant to put Gladys at her ease, but her gesture seemed too casual, affected.

Gladys ventured timidly to gaze at the book. *"Shared Nightmares*. Ooooh," she said with an extravagant shudder. "And you write with your husband. You must be very close. We are too, Colin and I. We look after each other."

She'd sat down and had opened the book. "Would you like some coffee?" Rose said.

"Oh, yes, please." She glanced up anxiously. "Only if it isn't any trouble."

Rose was quite glad to retreat to the kitchen; Gladys was rather overwhelming. Shortly Gladys followed her, accompanied by the muffled rustling of her handbag. She sat, slipping a little, on Bill's homemade pine bench. Her face reddened at the slip, and doled out a short self-conscious laugh. "Is that your greenhouse?" she blurted as though anxious for distraction.

"It belongs to both the houses. The lady who lived next door before you used to grow vegetables. Bill and I used to pay for half. We aren't much good at gardening, unfortunately."

"I'll see if I can do something—that is, if you don't mind. I'd like to share. I'm used to people who are neighborly." After a pause she said, "You left the country before we had a chance to meet you," but she'd seemed about to say something else.

"That's right." Rose poured the coffee. "I felt strange for days after we came back, as though I was dreaming. The Englishness of everything seemed so unfamiliar. You aren't from England originally, are you?"

"No." Gladys was delving into her bag; papers rustled, objects clinked. "I carry all my things about with me—I'm afraid they might be stolen. It's a compulsion, Colin said." She produced a tube of green-and-brown capsules. "Excuse me if I take these for my nerves."

Was she avoiding Rose's question? Her accent went with the stamp on the envelope. "You're from South Africa," Rose said.

"Yes, we are." She sounded ready to defend herself, though Rose wasn't about to attack: her books sold in

South Africa, her bank invested there; life was compromises. "I wish we were still there," Gladys said.

She mustn't have meant to sound so defiant, for she hurried on: "Don't think I'm ungrateful for England. We came here through America and Canada, but I couldn't have stayed. If there's any security left in the world, it's here. People are starting to realize that now. But I can't help it—I feel I was driven out of my home, that my parents made for me."

The tranquillizers seemed to have made her confiding. "I wasn't always as nervous as this, you know. Not until my parents died. I was so close to them, I couldn't believe they were gone. I can't believe that people of their character can be lost to the world. But I've learned to be patient. That's the right way to feel, don't you think so?"

Her appeal was so heartfelt that Rose said, "I'm sure you're right to feel that way, Gladys."

"I hoped you'd say so." Glady's smile wavered. "But at the time I felt my life was meaningless, except for Colin. If I ever lost him I don't know what I'd do. He made me see that I shouldn't waste my life. We built a new life together, and then the blacks began to turn on us, on our way of life. The things they do now to their victims in Africa—no grievance can justify that." Her face was red with anger now. "I would never have believed I could say this, but I'm glad we left while we were still able to."

Rose felt it safest to change the subject. "What is Colin?"

"A psychiatrist. Just for the moment he's working at home. He'll have an office in Rodney Street—someone told us that's where doctors go." Reluctantly she added, "You may have seen some of his patients."

"Why, he doesn't treat mental deficiency, does he?"

"Oh, you mean Mrs. Kimber and her son. Colin isn't treating the son, he's treating the mother."

"I have a friend in psychiatry. She works in a sort of

psychiatric commune down South. Their ideas are based on Laing, R. D. Laing." Gladys looked baffled and unimpressed, and Rose went on, "They're opposed to orthodox methods—no drugs, no electric shock treatment, no forcible treatment."

"I couldn't trust that kind of thing, communes and the rest of it. It's all part of the way everything is sliding toward chaos." She seemed to be nerving herself to change the subject. Was she daunted by all strangers, or only by writers? "Really, the reason why I called," she blurted, "was that I wanted to invite you to our party next week. Next Friday."

"I believe we're free then," Rose said, a little warily. "I'll mention it to Bill when he comes home."

"Oh, I'm so pleased. Who else should we invite?"

"I really wouldn't know, Gladys. We know hardly anyone round here by name."

"We'll have to be friends, then." Perhaps the tranquillizers were wearing off; all at once she seemed more nervous. "I mustn't keep you any longer," she said.

Nevertheless she dodged into the living room for a last murmur of awe at *Shared Nightmares*. As she scurried out she said, "That looks as though it ought to be one of a pair."

A porcelain Chinaman squatted on the sideboard. His right hand, delicate as a squirrel's, ought to be introducing his companion, a mirror image of himself; but he was alone.

"There should be another one. Where is it?" Dismay made Rose sound accusing.

"Is it on the floor?" Gladys scuttled about like a mime of panic. "I'm sorry," she wailed. "I didn't mean to upset you."

"Don't be silly, Gladys. You aren't to blame." Still, Rose found her nerve-racking. As quickly as she could without hurting her feelings she ushered Gladys out.

Miss Prince must have broken the figurine while she was supposed to be looking after the house. The old bitch probably thought it was too cheap to be worth mentioning. But the figurines had belonged to Uncle Wilfred and Auntie Vi, and evoked memories of staying with her relatives in their Southport flat, her final visit most of all—the soothing murmur of the waves, the sense of complete safety, far from whatever had made her so ill. She had been ten years old, afraid of being left alone even for a moment. She'd washed herself obsessively as though she could scrub away the fever or whatever had touched her. Her aunt and uncle had helped her recover, they'd made her feel that nothing could harm her now. She'd been happy to go home and look forward to next year's visit, but before then they were gone, her uncle first and Auntie Vi only months later, pining away.

And now she'd lost half of the little she had of theirs. For a moment gazing at the space where the Chinaman should be, she felt dizzy. It looked like a dark blotch in the air, a gap into which she was falling. If that was a threat of migraine, she had never felt like it before. She closed her eyes for a while, then she headed for the kitchen. For some reason she felt that it would be not at all a good idea to lie down.

VII

Everyone wanted to meet Rose, especially Colin. His bronzed head, topped with sun-bleached hair like plush, was set firmly on a strong neck. His shirt was white as marble. His amazingly blue eyes—yes, he looked like a travel agent's poster, Rose mocked herself

impatiently. Still, he was clearly delighted to meet her
and Bill, and to introduce them to everyone there.

The Hays' house resembled an enormous radio, a
battle of overlapping wavebands: stock-market reports,
discussions of mental research, what was wrong with
the country, how to rationalize the political system, a
song or two, amateur comedians who laughed while
telling jokes, a trait which Bill couldn't bear. Tables
were crowded with bottles, mounds of sausage rolls like
dormant caterpillars, plates of stuffed eggs which Rose
had provided to save Gladys from panicking.

Gladys was clutching a soft drink and had cornered
Bill. Hilary, his mature student, had been trapped by
Frank Sherratt, owner of the Vision group of cinemas,
who wore his Lancashire accent as the badge of a
self-made man. "Can you tell me why I have to go all
the way to London to see so many films?" she had
made the mistake of asking. Her boyfriend Des was
arguing with Colin, and Rose was afraid that the scene
might turn ugly.

Des had looked aggressively out of place at once.
He'd sauntered in, thumbs in his blue denim pockets,
surveying the party like a barroom brawler choosing a
victim. "I'll tell you what apartheid is," he was snarling
now. "A jackboot stamping on a black face, that's
apartheid."

If secondhand Orwell was all he could muster,
perhaps Rose needn't worry. Besides, people were
being introduced to her: a bank manager, cigar protruding from his mouth like a gargoyle's rusty spout; a
weary headmaster; a magistrate chained with neck-
laces, manacled with bracelets; a newspaper editor,
whose face looked too young for his piercing dispas-
sionate eyes.

"Interesting that you should use that image." Colin
touched his eyebrow, a tiny ironic salute. All his
movements were elegantly terse. "I've often felt that
South Africa has become the scapegoat of the world, a

convenient distraction from one's own shortcomings—
just as the Jews were the scapegoats of National
Socialism. In particular your unions use South Africa to
gain themselves power under the guise of taking a
moral stand."

"I'm in a union," Des said ominously. "At Ford's car
plant."

"Why, yes, your plants are quite famous. You and
your cronies care for the English system of government
as little as South Africa's."

"What fucking system? The one that robs the
workers who earn the money so that it can subsidize
fascist governments?" He was brandishing a bottle of
Scotch, which he had almost emptied by himself. "I'll
tell you what I want to see, mister. The blacks will blow
the lid off your country any day—I want to see the
workers seize power here. Then maybe we can start to
work for a world that's run by the people."

"And you would dance in the ruins. But would you
rejoice in the bloodshed? Yes, I suspect you might."
Colin's sudden anger faded quickly. "Have you any
idea of the aims of apartheid? Evolution must be given
time to work—it must be engineered, if necessary.
Some people are capable of evolutionary leaps, but not
the blacks. Many of them refuse even to be educated to
white standards."

"That's the same fucking system as here. Breed a
working class and make sure they don't get too
ambitious. Build them shithouses to live in, split up the
families and the communities, keep their wages down,
tell them they aren't worth educating—"

Gladys had come in and was listening nervously.
Rose felt responsible, even though she and Bill hadn't
known that their invitation to Hilary would include
Des. She moved away from a group of young people in
expensive casual clothes who wanted to tell her their
experiences in India, Africa, Tibet. Looking straight at
Des, she said, "Colin, could I speak to you alone?"

Des scowled at her and staggered back, sucking his bottle. "Yes, certainly," Colin said as she led him through the group of young explorers, toward the drinks. "What about?"

"Oh, I just wanted to shut him up. I do apologize for him."

"Now, really, that's not good enough." His smile was wide but brief. "I was quite enjoying him. Now that you've swept me away, you must find a topic to compensate."

"You were talking about evolutionary leaps." It was all she could think of except South Africa. "Of course they aren't the same thing, but a friend of mine has some ideas about heightened perceptions. I don't know what you'd think of them."

"Even if they aren't the same thing, you can't have one without the other."

He seemed so interested that she told him all Diana's ideas: LSD, migraine, even séances as a trigger for new perceptions. "I should think you disapprove of LSD," she said.

"As a tool it has its uses. But what you say about séances is extremely interesting. I should like to meet your friend."

"You'd have to go to New York."

"Ah, well." His smile grew wider. "Never mind."

All at once, as though it was a musical theme making its way through an orchestra, everyone seemed to be talking about séances. The young explorers had overheard Rose and were spreading the word like an infection—though why should she think of it in those terms? Now it had reached Hilary, who was muttering at Des. "A séance?" she said loudly, eager for a diversion. "That would be fun."

"It would, wouldn't it?" Bill said, smiling at Rose. Everyone seemed enthusiastic but Gladys, who demanded nervously, "Why do you want to do that?"

Des staggered at her. He was the reason Rose was

nervous; what other reason could there be? "Not so fucking rational after all, eh?" he said with exaggerated care.

"I don't mind at all if you attack me," Colin said. "But now that you insult my mother I must ask you to leave."

"Must you? Who's making you?" Eventually Des stumbled to the car, his walk wandering independent of him. Rose helped support him and watched Hilary drive away.

She stood in the driveway, gulping night air. Gravel bit dully into her feet through her shoes. On the bay beyond New Brighton, foghorns lowed. The air tasted acrid; the few street lamps looked enfeebled. She hoped they had called off the séance.

Colin had seemed anxious to avoid another scene. He'd smiled reassuringly at his mother, promising her that he wouldn't let things get out of hand again. Mightn't he have given in to her unease? But someone had switched off the hall light. As Rose went reluctantly into the house, there was only a glow seeping out of the living room.

The living room table was bare. A lamp craned its jointed neck out of the darkness; its metal cone laid down a blurred disc of light. At the edge of the disc, pairs of dissimilar hands clung together, chopped off at the wrists by the dark. They were immobile as meat on a slab. They looked too precise, too pink, their hairs wiry and glinting, their nails like embedded shells.

Above them faces hovered, stained and bruised by shadows. Bill's face looked amused but a little self-conscious, an adult at a children's tea party. The sight of him helped Rose step forward, though her guts felt liquid, burning. "Thank you for the party," she said to the Hays.

"Aren't you staying?" Bill frowned; shadows flooded his eyes. "What's wrong?"

"I'm just tired and headachy." A nerve tried to tug

her smile crooked. "You stay if you want to. Excuse me if I go to bed," she said to Colin's hovering face.

"Of course." But he looked puzzled, almost disturbed. Did he suspect that more was wrong than she was admitting? Everyone was staring at her. Obviously they would be, since she was leaving.

"You're sure you don't mind if I stay?" Bill said.

"No, I've already said so." The room in which she'd often sat with old Mrs. Winter was invisible, expanded ominously by the dark, which felt somehow larger than the night outside. "Good night all," she stammered, and hurried out.

She was glad to be able to switch on the lights in her own living room. The Chinaman squatted on the sideboard, reaching out vainly for his twin. "I'm sorry if you would have preferred things left dusty," Miss Prince had said haughtily. Though she hadn't admitted to the breakage, Rose was sure it had been her doing.

In the bathroom Rose's face dodged from tile to black tile. Her face looked rudimentary, as though an embryo were imitating her. She finished in the bathroom as quickly as she could, then she lay in bed, trying to make sense of her feelings.

Perhaps she knew what she had feared: that the séance, however playful, might catch old Mrs. Winter in its net. So Rose believed she was still alive somewhere, in some form? She wasn't sure, which meant it was best not to play. She could accept her own eventual nonexistence simply because the concept was impossible to grasp—but she refused to believe that one day Bill would cease to exist, because she could imagine that. To believe would be almost like wishing him dead.

In a way her fears were comforting. After all, there was no reason to suppose that Mrs. Winter was still bound to her house. She hoped the séance would be wholly unsuccessful. Feeling reasonably calm, she switched off the bedside lamp.

The séance was waiting for her. The hands crouched

close together around the rim of the circular table, a meeting of blind pink creatures with five legs. Some of the fingertips were pressing against the table, for crescents of white had invaded the mauve beneath the nails. The bare bright table was a stage with darkness for an audience. She was floating above the stage, gazing down.

Oh God, no—please, not that again! Her hands clenched on the blankets. Her fingernails were bending, an acid thread of panic burned from her throat to her stomach. The sensations helped her hold onto her body, reassured her that she hadn't drifted helplessly into the dark.

She wasn't at the mercy of the dark, only of her own imagination. That was how she could see the table so vividly. But she seemed to be able to feel the power of the séance, fumbling blindly and mindlessly in the dark for something to play with, however dangerous. For a moment it seemed that it might drag her out of her body.

Then it seemed to pass her by, though her skull felt thin and irritable. She bit back a gasp of relief: she felt in danger of gasping herself out of her mouth. In any case the gasp would have been premature, for she wasn't alone in the dark. The search had touched something.

Perhaps it was only one of those stray nightmarish thoughts that come in the depths of the night and insomnia, and are so difficult to deal with. There was a face on a pillow in a dim room. She would stumble in the dimness, fall on the bed, into its arms. The cold flabby face would open its dead eyes, grinning.

Had she dreamed that as a child? Was it only a dream that had waited in the dark to be touched? If she let go of the blankets, she could switch on the lamp—but she could only lie there, praying that the face in the dark would go away before she saw it clearly.

At last it seemed to fade into the dark. She could

reach out for the lamp now, and in a moment she would—just another moment. Before she could move, she heard a scratching at the front-door lock.

Of course it was Bill. His progress was hesitant and fumbling because he was drunk. She could hear that he was reduced to all fours on the stairs. Now he was in the room, padding about in the dark so as not to waken her. But she wasn't sure of any of this until he whispered, "Are you asleep?"

"No. Come into bed, quickly."

When he did so, she held tight to him. "What happened at the séance?" she demanded at last.

"Nothing at all. Why, what on earth did you expect?"

He sounded surprised by the intensity of her question. She clung to his waist, trying to think of acceptable terms for what she wanted to say. But he was snoring.

Had she had what Diana would call a psychic glimpse? She never wanted such a glimpse again. Bill's warmth was like a fire, holding back the darkness. She breathed in his warmth, his smell, to soothe her, help her float away on bourbon into sleep. Still, her thoughts were restless. If what she had sensed had somehow been real, how could it be safer for her to be less aware?

VIII

Emerging from the bathroom, where the cover of the jade-green toilet seat said Après Moi Le Déluge, Rose passed her parents' room. On the chest of drawers her childhood self was beaming. She'd had to sit in the shop in the Southport arcade while the glaring lights made her eyes smart and her armpits prickle. She'd kept still, since the photograph had been for Uncle Wilfred and Auntie Vi. In the frame she looked unreal, glowing in her best dress, like a ghost of the childhood she had already been leaving behind.

They had died within months of each other, just as she reached puberty. Everything had changed: her body seemed no longer hers, and Southport had become a tomb—no more evening promenades along Lord Street, where music drifted from the bandstand beneath trees budded with lights; no more swoops of the Big Dipper while her aunt stood gnawing nervously on a toffee apple. She hadn't been able to speak to anyone for days.

She had forgotten that until today. The memory was almost uncomfortably vivid, the sense of being trapped in her unfamiliar body. She hurried down to the front garden, where Bill and her parents were waiting.

The four of them walked down arm in arm to the Wigan Road. A lorry-load of glass went by, carrying a reflection of the linked quartet descending the hill, like a shot from a musical film. Two girls rode ponies along the opposite pavement.

On the Wigan Road the pavement made the party walk in twos. Shoppers of all ages were pedaling back from the market. "Oh, I know what I meant to say to you," her father said to Bill. "We were wondering if you'd like our old tandem."

"Well, ah, hmm. What do you think, Rose?"

She remembered breezes sweeping through her hair, hedgerows merging into a green flood, fields sailing leisurely, her feet pumping in time with her father's. "We could give it a try while we're here."

"It just needs a little first aid," her father said. "The, ah—what do you call it, the—oh, good God, what the devil is the thing the lever operates, Margaret?"

"The gear-change."

"Yes, of course. I just couldn't think of it for a second."

"I'm not very good mechanically," Bill said, like a bionic man admitting a fault.

"I'll show you what to do."

The concrete tip of the hospital chimney was stained like a cigarette. Houses drew in their gardens, pressed closer to the road. Some houses had turned into shops; through doorways behind counters, Rose glimpsed sofas warming themselves before hearths. Hens clucked in back gardens.

"Now let me tell you all the news," her mother was saying. "Pat next door finally went into show jumping and won herself a sprained wrist and a broken ankle. Old Mrs. Lewis died and left nothing but debts. You should have seen the relatives after the funeral—they looked as if they could have killed her. Oh, I read a story to the writers' circle, which everybody liked, except the fat poet. Did I tell you how he embarrassed us all when he read out his poems? Every couple of verses he burst into tears. Are you all right, Rose?"

"I'm fine." Only the abruptness of the question had startled her.

"You don't look fine. She doesn't look well, does she, George?"

He stooped to Rose as though examining a stamp collection for his shop. "A bit fashionably thin, perhaps. We'll feed you up, Rose."

"I'm perfectly all right." The night of the séance was safely past. In the morning she had been unable to recapture any sense of the presence she'd glimpsed; it had returned to the dark in which it had awakened— the depths of her own mind, of course. Why, she had never needed to be afraid. If the séance had attracted anything, it would have gone to the Hays' house.

She felt even better for coming to Ormskirk. Some part of her would always regard it as home. There was the bus station, its bench loaded with bored children. There was Disraeli, green as cabbage, ignoring the upstart traffic lights. There was Abblett's shop, behind which she could never find traces of the theater where Shakespeare had appeared. And there was the market.

It spilled into the roadways, turned the pavements into narrow crowded aisles, hid the shops, deafened the streets. As far as the clock tower at the crossroads, and turning the corner to the left, the pavements were a mass of stalls. Vegetables were lined up next to trinkets, a dog examined a dangling corner of fabric, a pair of breasts lay in the road. Clothes, naked without a wardrobe, shivered on wire hangers. Rose glimpsed herself trapped dimly in a mirror among crowds of empty coats. In the aisles, shoppers moved like a slow-motion dream.

The smells of meat were memories brought to life. The paperbacks on the bookstall seemed to have been there since her childhood. As she glanced at wartime covers—forties clothes, bland idealistic faces— someone touched her arm. "Isn't this a coincidence! I was asking your mum about you just the other day. Are you Bill? Lovely to meet you at last."

It took Rose a few moments to recognize Wendy. She'd grown hearty, eager to talk to anyone, now that she was a nurse. She joined them for lunch in the bar of the Snig's Foot Hotel, which had always sounded to

Rose like a Lewis Carroll monster. Soon Rose felt
mellow, drinking deceptively bland ale and listening to
Wendy, who was arguing with Bill.

"The only thing I don't like about my job is people
dying. I like coming home feeling I've worked hard.
This country is making it too easy for people to live off
other people." Each time she made a point she turned a
beermat over, like an attempt at a card trick. "I've no
patience with strikers. But as long as we give social
security to every nigger who comes here and can't find
a job, we can't withhold it from our own."

"You're content to be paid far less than me for a job
which must be at least as taxing as mine?"

"I've heard that sort of thing before, from people I
don't like." The beermat snapped like an ace in the
hole, displaying an advertising slogan. "You see, Bill,"
she said more gently, "I chose to stay here and look
after my mother. Nobody forced me to take up nursing,
so what right have I to complain? But I'll get married
one day, Rose. There's a young doctor who sometimes
takes me out to lunch."

Perhaps Rose looked dubious, for Wendy said, "It
isn't such a bad life. I still go to parties when I can. That
reminds me, someone at a party was asking after you."

"Who was that?"

"I don't think I caught his name. I was chatting about
things we used to do when we were children. He knew
you, or he'd heard of you."

"You were revealing my childhood indiscretions,
were you?"

Why had her father's tankard stopped halfway to his
mouth? Her mother had closed her eyes tight in her
nervous way. Wendy said, "Oh, just things in general.
Childhood things."

"But what were you saying about me?"

"Oh, just how you—how you always wanted to write
and then grew up and did it. Is that the time? I must be
going." Though she wasn't in uniform she said, "I'm
not supposed to take so long for lunch."

Rose's parents relaxed visibly. They'd taken a dislike to Wendy just about the time Rose had entered grammar school, aged eleven. Had they thought her not intelligent enough for Rose, or too flighty? It was rather presumptuous of them to be protective still.

When she'd downed another pint of ale and Bill had won on the fruit machine beneath the stairs, only to bang his head on the ceiling, they ambled home past denuded market stalls. Rose felt pleased with everything: the parish church with its tower and separate steeple; the double image of hands and shadow on the clock tower at the crossroads, as though the clock was dreaming of being a sundial; the little allotments like gardens in front of the cottages above the railway.

"Do you enjoy interviewing?" her father was saying to Bill.

"No, not especially." He shrugged apologetically when Rose glanced surprised at him. "I went off it when I had to interview a director in New York. Rose was promised elsewhere that night," he said, remembering not to upset her mother with the truth. "I got what I wanted, but it was like pulling teeth. Besides, the man was a pain in the arse, as Rose can tell you."

Beyond the bus station, the first terrace of the Wigan Road had changed. Two bay windows housed grocery shops which Rose remembered, Morris's and Smith's; but beyond them, separated from them by empty houses like teeth which needed filling, there was a new butcher's.

"Damn," her mother said. "Mince. I knew there was something."

"I'll buy it, mummy." Hurrying before her mother could argue, she stepped over the butcher's sill.

But there was no shop. There was only darkness, far larger than the room she'd glimpsed. As it sucked her in, its stenches choked her: blood, rawness, corruption, and something worse—something old and dead yet in some sense alive, which was advancing to meet her. She could almost see its eyes, if anything was left of them.

She threw herself backward, into daylight. The shop reappeared as though a light had been switched on, but the stench remained. Rose clung to a squat brick wall at the mouth of an arched passage between the houses. Would she be sick, or collapse entirely?

"Good heavens, Rose, what's the matter?" At last her mother, who was chatting, noticed. She gazed at Rose's face, then wrinkled her nose. "Yes, it is a bit smelly in there, isn't it? You wait here." To Rose's horror, she went into the shop.

Bill and her father came to support Rose. "Sit on the wall for a bit. Do you want to put your head between your knees?" But Rose had to stare at the shop, at her mother leaning unconcernedly on the counter, at the facade which shone innocently, at the curtained window above the bay. She was sitting outside one house of a shabby terrace, surrounded by her family, in broad daylight; yet nothing could have made her cross the sill again, even to drag her mother to safety. She could only sit clenched within herself, willing her mother to hurry up, hurry up, please—At last her mother emerged, and Rose hurried them away.

Perhaps she'd had too much to drink. That might explain the irritable heaviness which filled her skull and made her want to brush the oppression from the back of her head. Perhaps she had suffered momentary dizziness as she'd entered the shop; but that could not be the whole truth. She had had a glimpse of malevolence which nobody else could perceive. Even when they reached the hill and climbed leisurely toward home, arm in arm, she felt vulnerable. If the glimpse had been real—and if it hadn't, what did that tell her of herself?—then such things could happen to her anywhere, at any time.

IX

They were pedaling easily downhill. A breeze streamed past Bill's shoulders and over her face. He was holding the handlebars casually, proud to have found his balance so quickly. As her legs moved in unison with his, she enjoyed the hint of a double entendre. Their ride transformed the houses into a fleet of ships, sailing leisurely by. She had forgotten how intensely she enjoyed cycling.

They had almost reached the side turning, just before the hill plunged toward the Wigan Road. Her parents had gone inside the house, having admired Bill's performance. Now there were no spectators, only the long fertile gardens and the trees which swarmed greenly in the sunlight.

"Let's go a bit farther this time," Bill said. He adjusted his glasses as though they were goggles, and cycled past the turning.

She felt the hill grow abruptly steeper. It forced her to pedal more quickly, so as not to lose the rhythm. The main road sounded full of lorries, an elephantine race of them, frustrated by single file; she imagined the cottages shaking. All at once she knew—"No, Bill, turn," she said urgently. "The brakes won't work."

"Of course they will." He sounded almost patronizing, now that he was in the driver's seat. "They've been working perfectly."

She knew that as well as he did; her father had overhauled the tandem conscientiously; but that wasn't the point—she *knew* the brakes would fail. The cycle was hurtling downhill. Already it was too fast. She heard the lorries thundering closer, unrestrained. "Just try the brakes," she pleaded. "For my peace of mind, will you try them!"

He reached impatiently for the levers on the handlebars. His fists closed around them, closed tight—and the tandem gathered speed. She could see the lorries now, wreathed in their fumes, great stained blocks of metal pounding by, like the hammers of a machine for crushing. Bill was tugging at the levers. "But good God," he cried, "how do I stop it, how do we stop?"

"Turn it, turn it across the road, we'll fall off, doesn't matter, drag your feet on the road—"

Her heels were screeching over the roadway, but seemed to have no braking power at all. Ahead on the main road, only yards away, she heard the gasp and wheeze of air brakes. Nobody had seen their plight; it had only been a driver slowing so as not to collide with the lorry in front, before accelerating onward.

Bill was wrenching the handlebars round, too fast; he was losing control. As his feet reached wildly for the road, the whirling pedals cracked against his ankles. "Oh, *Christ,*" he snarled in pain. The bicycle was falling, but how close to the main road would they fall? The front wheel rammed the curb; the seat punched Rose in the groin; the machine mounted the pavement and careered into a driveway, thumping Bill against a gatepost. There it halted, pedals subsiding.

She stood clutching the frame. Her bruises began throbbing. For a while she was frozen by shock and relief, and the threat of further pain. Bill leaned panting on the gatepost and gazed into space. At last he said, "If you knew the damn brakes were faulty, why the hell didn't you say so before?"

"Because I didn't know then. I only knew just now."

As soon as he noticed she was trembling he came to her and held her. "I'm sorry," he said. "I shouldn't be blaming you, God knows. It's a good thing you thought of the brakes when you did." He held her, though he was shaking as well, and she could only wonder if he realized that the woman he was holding had changed— changed beyond anything she recognized herself.

There was no doubt of that now. Something was developing within her: a seed was growing. What had planted it? The attack on her in New York, the séance at the Hays' party? She knew only that she was aware of things she had never sensed before, things nobody else seemed able to sense—

Such as the danger of the brakes. If she hadn't had that premonition, she and Bill would have been under a lorry. She ought not to think of these glimpses as somehow separate from her; they were part of her, an extra dimension of herself, and perhaps she could learn to use them. However unpleasant her glimpses had been in the Ormskirk shop and after the Hays' séance, they hadn't been able to touch her: they were perceptions, that was all. If they were an occasional but necessary side effect of her developing instinct for danger, couldn't she bear them? She *must* develop that instinct, she told herself, and yet she felt that the choice had been forced on her. Deep down she was simply grateful to be safe with Bill, two weeks later now, lying in bed at home.

She turned her head on the pillow, which was cool against her cheek. Between the digits of the clock, a colon pulsed away the seconds. Beyond the window, birds gossiped shrilly. She lay trying to grasp her sense that something was about to happen.

Nothing further had happened in Ormskirk. She'd avoided the shop in the Wigan Road, and had suffered no more premonitions. Perhaps her life was calming down. But today she had been wakened by a twinge of anticipation, so muffled that she couldn't tell whether it was promising or threatening.

She felt restless. She slid out from beside Bill, who was still asleep, and gazed from the window. The

Mersey broke the sunlight into smithereens which never quite recombined; above the water, seagulls gleamed like fragments of shell. This was the river the Fulwood Park merchants had watched from their villas in the 1830s, awaiting the sight of their ships returning from the Orient. The Fulwood had been a sailing ship. The stroboscopic glittering of water drew her away from her sense of the house.

The snap of the letter box recalled her. On the mat the envelope displayed the red-and-blue stripes of an air letter, which seemed encouraging. New York, 81st Street. It was from Diana. For a moment her expectancy was urgent, piercing, then it blurred again. When she'd hurried into the kitchen and switched on the percolator, she ripped open the envelope.

Dear Rose,

It was so good to hear from you. I so enjoyed meeting you, and kept hoping you might write. It looks as though we may meet again quite soon, but I shall speak of that farther on.

But first I should answer your question on behalf of your friend as to whether being in close proximity to a séance could increase a person's psychic powers. I doubt whether I can add much to what I said in person to you. But I have read of someone's having attended a séance and discovering that he was a medium. The big problem must be to adjust to the new perceptions. If your friend is having this experience, maybe she ought to consult a professional occultist for advice.

I wonder if you are growing interested in the occult yourself? Did you ever read about out-of-the-body experiences after your experience in my apartment? Some of the books which I think have been published in England are one called *Techniques of Astral Projection* by Crookall, another called *The Projection of the Astral Body* by Muldoon, and that weird but fascinating one called

Astral Rape—which, now I remember one particular chapter, you maybe ought to read before we hit Munich.

That is my main piece of news, which perhaps you have guessed. I shall be coming to Munich with Jack. We are good friends now and understand each other much better.

As for me, I have grown interested in the Christos experiments, a kind of astral projection where you can go into the past, supposedly. It needs a group of people to handle it. I have been discussing it with my occultist, who lives near where I work in the Village. You could meet him next time you visited New York if you wanted to.

I look forward to seeing you in Munich! Love to Bill also,

Diana

It sounded oddly unlike Diana; both the language and the handwriting were stiff as a school essay. Perhaps that was how Diana felt one should address a writer. As the percolator boiled, Rose slipped the envelope into the pocket of her dressing gown.

She could hear Bill sneezing himself awake, as usual. No need for him to read the letter. Whether it helped her she wasn't yet sure. Diana did seem knowledgeable and gifted, but how reliably so? Enough so to have come to Rose's aid in the empty flat.

Expectancy paced Rose all day. It sat invisibly behind her on the bus, and seemed to hold the back of her skull gently but oppressively. Its meaning remained muffled, and was intensely frustrating. Her surroundings glittered with threats of migraine.

At least the day's lectures went well. The students were eager to argue, prepared to follow through their arguments. Afterward, dark crawling blotches followed her home across the gray sky, lay like mud in the river. The villas were soaked in dimness. They looked as blurred as her expectancy felt.

Bill had cooked moussaka. Smells of meat and cheese drifted through the house. "There's a letter from Jack," he called. "He and Diana seem to be getting on well together."

Feeling rather guilty, she read the letter. A paperback reprint; an offer from *Film Comment* for magazine rights to their interviews; see you both in Munich. She wished she felt more elated, less oppressed.

"My student Hilary left Desmond the Red," Bill called. "He'd started knocking her about."

"Best thing she could have done."

"Yes, she's far too intelligent for him. Her trouble is, she's too sympathetic to people."

Rose poured Beaujolais while he served dinner. "I'm glad for Jack," she said.

"Yes, he deserves someone. Actually, I'm glad for Diana too. Maybe he can cure her of some of her weirder tendencies."

"Possibly," she said, not looking at him.

After dinner he played a new recording of Mahler's Eighth. Ouside a wind was rising. It rushed across the field and soared over the house, tugging at trees until leaves ripped loose and it seemed that branches would take flight, as the choirs sang, "Come, Creator Spirit, fill our souls . . ." She loved the symphony for its romanticism, yet tonight it seemed bombastic, a convert's missionary rant. Several shots of bourbon allowed her at least to enjoy the melodies.

She needed the bourbon to dull her expectancy, to help her sleep. In its vagueness her anticipation seemed false, merely irritating, a self-indulgence. By the time she squirmed into bed it was blurred enough to ignore.

She lay on her side, one arm draped around Bill's waist, and listened to the rustle of the trees. As she began to drift, she thought that it was the lapping of the river, creeping closer to the house, close enough to be heard. Between her thoughts was darkness; each time she drifted deeper. The wind was soft now, or was it

Bill's breathing? The low rhythmic sounds lulled her, and ushered her into a house.

She began to struggle. Though she could see only the dark doorway, she would rather die than go through. She could hear whispering. They couldn't make her go in, whoever they were. But her captor was the dark; it was enormous and impalpable; her struggles were pointless, ineffectual. The house closed about her like a mouth.

And perhaps it was a mouth—for it was certainly alive. The walls were not of brick but of teeming corrupt flesh. It had come alive just as soon as she had entered. She had awakened what lay dormant there, the presence which had seeped into the fabric of the house. Underfoot the floor felt soft, moldering. As if the foundations were gelatin, the house was sinking into darkness as though it were a marsh.

There was a worse fear. Might her growing panic loose her from her body? It didn't matter that she was dreaming; indeed, that might make her more vulnerable. She dug her nails into her palms until she felt the skin parting. She woke, and was lying beside Bill, surrounded by whispers.

Perhaps the whispers were more distant, less encircling. Were they in the room, behind the curtains, or just outside the window? She was fully awake now. They were the rustling of foliage, that was all. She mustn't panic, not while her sense of her body was so tenuous.

She lay and tried to hear the sounds clearly. They ought to guide her back to reality. Were they leaves, or the lapping of water? Perhaps both, for they sounded distant, yet somehow close. Their rhythm was jagged, insidiously fascinating. They sounded unpleasantly like a chorus of low voices, whose words she was in danger of hearing. Her heart seemed to shake her entire body.

They were voices. They were searching for her in the night. Sibilants hissed clear of the vague murmur, as though reptiles were hunting. She was sure that they were saying, "Rose. Rose."

Perhaps the voices were in her head, for their rhythm had insinuated itself into her body. Her limbs were shaking in time with the rhythm. She couldn't feel her pulse, only her entire body at the mercy of the vibration. She had no control over her body, no hold on it. Surely her shivering must awaken Bill—oh, please let him wake before she was shaken loose!

She must wake him. She struggled to reach out, to grab him, but her body refused to move. The whispers deafened her mind; her jerky trembling shattered her attempts at thoughts. Only instinct remained to her. She made one violent effort, like a silent scream for help, and managed to reach out for his hand.

She felt her hand pass through the blankets.

X

The shock was too great. Her heart must be pounding uncontrollably, her body must be blazing with panic, her mouth parched as dust; but she could feel none of this. In fact she could not feel her body at all. In that case, she must be dreaming.

Yet how could a dream be so vivid? She could feel the texture of the blanket—warm, fibrous, slightly prickly—as she had never felt it before. The sensations were too awesome to be simply frightening. For a moment, since this could only be a dream, she let herself be overwhelmed by awe. In that moment she was dragged out of the shell of her body into the dark.

Bill lay below her, his lips fluttering with a snore. He was distant, unreachable, and so was the thing that lay beside him: her body. She could see her face, a dimly luminous mask of slack flesh; she could see her body breathing with a parody of life. It was a fake, a dummy placed in the bed to reassure Bill. She could feel her true body, hovering in midair, faintly palpable as a breeze.

At once her thoughts appalled her. It wasn't true, her real body was down there beside Bill, all she had to do was struggle back to it—In a sense her panic was reassuring, for surely it must wake her. But she was in the grip of a kind of vertigo, in which she was aware of nothing but her helplessness, the floating insubstantial victim that she had become. She glimpsed her body dwindling, whirling away as though the dark room had become a vortex, and she was rushing toward the wall. Surely the wall would halt her—oh, please—

She felt the bricks: rough, porous, cold as metal yet containing a kind of inner warmth. There was no pain, but that was hardly reassuring. Nothing was, for she had reeled out into the night.

She was nothing. That was why no barrier could hold her. Even her panic seemed lost to her; since it couldn't wake her, it had turned into a kind of harsh agonized incredulity, monotonous and inescapable. Sensations overwhelmed her: the immense overpowering chill of the night; a sourceless light which showed her that she had no form, nothing visible at all. How could she see if she had no eyes?

She was alone. The whispering had stopped, she couldn't tell when. There was no moon, and the sky was sealed with clouds; yet everything was visible, glowing from within, as far as the horizon. Trees were intricately lurid, smoldering with colors. The unbroken sky glowed like dull brass, the river burned like ice.

Shock seemed to have paralyzed her in midair. Now, as though drawn by a force against which she had no notion how to struggle, she began to rush helplessly toward the river. This is a dream, she thought, a dream, a dream. The monotonousness of the repetition helped dull her sensations, a little. But everything was more solid than she was, and relentlessly visible: the dusty road like a swathe of mist below the chained Fulwood Park garden, a demolished television set whose screen displayed a patch of wild flowers, a couple walking hand in hand over the grassy plateau above the river promenade. Everything was real except her.

The plateau fled beneath her, each blade of grass a separate filament of muted light. She swooped uncontrollably toward the strolling couple, so close that she could see the glimmer of their eyebrows. Without warning the woman glanced up. Her glowing lips parted; awe or fear seemed to kindle her eyes. Had she seen Rose—and if so, what exactly had she seen? Before she could do more than think of the woman as a potential ally, whose awareness of her might act as some kind of anchor, Rose was plunged deep into the river.

Oh God, she would drown! She could swim, except that she had no limbs to propel her to the surface. The water was dark as mud, and felt as thick; it filled her, choking her. Yet though she felt stifled, she apparently had no need to breathe. She could only endure the pressure of the depths, the pollution that blinded her, the currents that seemed to drag at her tenuous substance, threatening to tear her apart. She felt in danger of dissolving, of merging with the sluggish water that glowed like poisonous fog. Misshapen litter groped toward her, unfurling sodden tendrils clogged with filth. They invaded her substance, and there was nothing she could do.

At last her floating seemed to grow less aimless. She was going somewhere, though she had no idea what had given her purpose, nor what that purpose was. The river oozed through her, dragging its deformed burdens. Please let her be almost free of its torments, please let it be over now—

When she emerged from the river, she was beneath the earth.

Despite the total darkness, she knew where she was. Perhaps they were only memories of smell and taste that she was experiencing, but they were suffocating her. It was worse than being buried alive, for as she was drawn onward, she felt things squirming in the earth. They were squirming within her. She felt composed of rotten flesh.

Anything would have been a relief from this—even the sensation of rising uncontrollably through stone, which felt cold and massive, threatening to trap her like amber. It was the foundation of a house, for she emerged inside a wall—like a rat, except that she could not scrabble.

She was desperate to be free of the wall, to be able at least to see, and in a moment she was. There was a floor, which felt treelike, though less vital. Rising above it, she found that she was hovering in a darkened room.

Such relief as she was able to feel, she felt now. At least she was in someone's home. Perhaps she could rest here and grow calmer, before she tried to think her way back to her own home, Bill, her body. Even when she glimpsed the figures in the dark, she did not immediately panic.

There were more than a dozen of them. They sat in a circle, on chairs. Masks were tied over their faces, as though they were surgeons ready for an operation. At the center of the circle, on the otherwise bare carpet, lay a small object made indistinguishable by the dark.

She dreaded knowing what they planned to do. Their masks were black, and she could see nothing of their faces except their eyes, which glimmered white as grubs, with glistening bruises for pupils. Did the still object in their midst have small delicate hands? Was it a baby? She would soon know, for the faces leaned forward into the circle—and she was being drawn downward, into their midst.

When they looked up, their whitish eyes glowing, she felt a surge of panic worse than any she'd experienced. They knew she was there. They were reaching up to drag her down. The circle of their hands closed like the mouth of a carnivorous plant, the thick tendrils of their fingers eager to grasp her. She was falling helplessly into their midst, and the thought which saved her from utter panic was part of the nightmare too: they couldn't catch her, for there was nothing of her to hold.

But they could.

As soon as she was inside the circle, they closed on her. They felt more like a spider's web than fingers, thick as the cords of a web must feel to a fly. They clung stickily to her, and at last she was aware of her substance, could feel how fragile it was. At last she knew instinctively how to struggle, desperately as a fly in the clutch of a spider, but the hands were clinging to her or within her, and she was dreadfully afraid that any struggle would tear her substance. The masked faces loomed above her. Their eyes looked swollen with triumph.

Then she seemed to hear a voice, cold as a reptile's, hissing, "No. Not yet. He's saying no."

The circle of hands moved apart at once. Oh God, they would tear her to pieces! But they must have relinquished whatever power they'd used to hold her, for she was rushing backward the way she had come, through the chill foundation of the house, the swarming earth, the discolored river. Somewhere a hand was tugging at her shoulder. The sensation was less convincing than a remembered dream, yet she was certain that if someone tried to awaken her body without her, she would die. Distantly she felt her eyelids flutter open.

She flooded back into her open eyes. The sensation was almost unbearable. She could feel her eyeballs, thin-skinned gloves of liquid, about to burst with the onslaught of her return. The shock ripped through her chest like a saw. Above her, out of focus, hovered an object with eyes. She screamed.

Even the touch of the hand on her forehead, trying to soothe her into awareness, was hardly reassuring, for she had almost forgotten the sensations of her own flesh. "It's all right, love," Bill was murmuring. "It's all right. You were having a nightmare. I couldn't wake you."

At last his face came into focus. The bedside lamp illuminated his halo of rumpled hair. She managed not to flinch, though the sensation of flesh stroking flesh was alien, too intense. "It wasn't a nightmare," she babbled. "I wasn't here. I didn't know where I was."

"It's all right. You were here. I was trying to wake you for about a minute."

A minute! How long had he lain snoring, unaware of her plight? "I was outside my body," she said through twitching lips. "I couldn't get back. I could feel everything I touched."

"No reason why not," he said reassuringly.

"I don't mean that." Her body felt more stable now, far more so than her mind; the hectic feverishness was fading. "I could feel everything more vividly than when I'm in my body."

"I've never dreamed that."

Of course he meant to be reassuring, but all she could hear was that she wasn't reaching him. "I wasn't dreaming!" she cried, almost hysterical now, for she could still feel the clinging touch of fingers within her. "I was somewhere else, somewhere real, can't you understanding that? It was a séance, of course that's what it must have been. They called me and I couldn't stop myself. It *wasn't* a dream! Can't you see what it's done to me?" She was holding onto him now that he'd begun to feel familiar, but she was by no means sure that he could anchor her. "Oh God," she cried, "what's happening to me?"

"You'll be all right. I'm here." He was stroking her

hair, slow, almost hypnotic caresses, but she couldn't risk feeling lulled. She couldn't think what else to say to him, and that made her even more tense. After a while he murmured, "Do you think perhaps you ought to mention it to Colin?"

Perhaps that was the truth of it: everything had been hallucination, a lingering aftereffect of the attack on her in New York. She clutched at the explanation more desperately than she was clinging to Bill. Hallucinations were curable. "Yes," she said, and thought she sounded hopeful.

"Will you be able to sleep now?"

When she grew rigid, aware of how little of her terror she had been able to communicate, he said, "All right, I'll stay awake until you're ready to sleep again."

As she felt now, that might be never. He sat up, arms around her, and did his best to stay awake, but in an hour he was snoring. No doubt he had settled into comfortable dreams. She turned nervously, seeking a position in which she would feel locked within her body. There was none. The bedside lamp shone steadily, but was far less reassuring than her childhood night-light had used to be. The walls and ceiling looked frail, worthless as protection. Eventually dawn tinged the curtains. The soft light made her think of a searcher, reaching stealthily into her room.

XI

"I'm not quite sure how I can help you," Colin said.

Rose was sitting in the dining room. Framed diplomas decorated one wall. The table had been banished to the living room; a desk had taken its place. The couch which the table had ousted stood diagonally opposite the desk. The rest of the room was Mrs. Winter's, but there was no sense of her presence, nor of any presence but the Hays'.

Rose sat on the couch. Beyond the closed kitchen door, Gladys was muttering over her preparations for dinner, rebuking ingredients peevishly. Beyond the window, the lawn looked moistly new. Unkempt leaves pressed their veins against the greenhouse windows. Trees, intricate masses of green fans, swayed above the wall. Momentarily, until she controlled herself, Rose experienced their woodenness, their inner life.

She felt disappointed, almost betrayed, and worse. She had hoped Colin would explain everything, would help her believe that she had simply dreamed she wasn't dreaming, that her sensations were extraordinarily vivid. She had tried to persuade herself of that, but however much she yearned to believe her explanation it wouldn't help her sleep, for she was afraid to repeat the nightmare.

At least her insomnia was something Bill could understand, a reason for her to seek Colin's advice. Nevertheless, when Colin had opened the front door she'd felt timid, ashamed of herself; after all, no doubt he didn't expect to work on Saturdays. She had sounded like Gladys. "Are you very busy?"

"No, not at all. Just dealing with some correspondence." He wore a roll of Scotch tape on one finger. "In fact I'm glad to see you. We were rather wondering if our party had put you off."

"No, of course not. What made you think that?"

"Well, perhaps I was unduly harsh with your friend. A case for treatment rather than for retorts, wouldn't you say? But I did feel he'd outstayed his welcome."

"Oh, good heavens, he wasn't our friend. We didn't know what we were inviting. You may have done some good indirectly. Hilary—you remember Hilary—finally plucked up the courage to leave him."

He frowned slightly. "Relationships aren't as stable as they used to be—like everything else, I fear. Still, there's no point in suffering a partner who is out of sympathy with one."

"I don't know about that. One shouldn't admit defeat too easily."

"You're absolutely right. I'm talking only about extreme cases." He'd ushered her into his office, and was tidying his desk, stacking envelopes, clearing small plastic containers into a drawer. "Excuse my bringing you in here," he said. "We'll go through in a moment, where it's more comfortable."

Wasn't that her cue to tell him why she was here? Before she could make herself speak, he said, "I must tell you that you were the star of our party. All our friends were most impressed by you."

Her smile, and its wideness, took her unawares. "Thank you," she said, blushing.

"I hope that makes it seem worthwhile in retrospect. Perhaps I'm being overanalytical, but I thought you seemed upset by the party game."

"Which party game?"

"The table-turning, or whatever they meant it to be."

She forced herself to take the cue. "That was partly what I wanted to talk to you about."

"I promise that the next time we invite you there'll be nothing of the kind."

"No, I didn't mean that." His smile waited for her to go on. "It's very difficult for me to talk about," she said at last.

"Would you like to try?" To her surprise, he came and sat beside her on the couch. "I'll sit over there if you prefer," he said.

"No, I'd rather you sat here. I don't want to feel like a patient." Did that sound as though she expected him to treat her without payment? Surely she didn't need treatment, only advice. "I can't sleep. I keep having nightmares. Only," she managed to say, "they're more vivid than that—more like hallucinations."

He might be able to glimpse her secret fear in her eyes—but would he be able to reassure her? "The idea of hallucinations particularly bothers you?" he suggested.

"Yes. It terrifies me."

"Why?"

She could tell that he knew. "Because it might mean that I'm losing my mind."

"Which frightens you. Yes, I can see that it does, understandably enough. Well, let me try to set your mind at rest a little. In my experience, a fear of insanity is a pretty reliable indication that you aren't going mad. It's neurotic, which is quite a different thing. Nobody thinks himself saner than a madman. As for hallucinations, all sorts of things can cause them, by no means usually madness. Would you like some tea?"

His voice was so soothing that the appearance of a question startled her. "Well, yes," she stammered.

He glanced into the kitchen. "Gladys, we'd appreciate some tea if you would be so kind. Rose is here."

"Oh, I thought it was one of—"

"Rose is just asking my advice." Rejoining Rose on the couch, he said, "Now, try to tell me in as much detail as you can what's troubling you. Take your time."

"I think it began in New York." She told him about the attack in Diana's building, about her subsequent dream and its aftermath at Diana's. "It could have been just an aftereffect of the mugging," she said, and went on to relate her panic on the night of the séance. She dreaded having to talk about her sense of an awakened presence, and her glimpse in Ormskirk.

She was describing her sense of the power of the séance when Gladys bumped open the door and shuffled in, laden with a trayful of chattering china. "Let me relieve you of that," Colin said, taking the tray. Gladys insisted on pouring the tea, only to grow flustered once she realized that Rose had fallen silent. "Sorry. I won't be a moment," she wailed, as the stream wavered dangerously toward the edge of a cup. "I'll just do this. Do you mind if I just pour myself one? Sorry."

"She does tend to allow things to overwhelm her," Colin confided to Rose when they were alone. "But she's been a help to me. When I'm tempted to despair, she gives me back my sense of purpose. You might be surprised how firm she can be about some things. I appreciate your thoughtfulness with her." He patted her hand, as though to wake them both from musing. "However, we were talking about you, weren't we? What you say about the séance is quite fascinating, I think."

She preferred not to dwell on that subject, she wasn't sure why. Even to describe her last experience seemed a relief. She told him as much as she could, including the dark room and the voice that said "No," but she couldn't bring herself to describe the touch of fingers within her.

"That's all?" He looked engrossed, almost boyishly eager for more. "There was nothing earlier, I suppose?"

"There may have been." She described her adolescent fever, the premonition of pursuit, her vision of disembodied flight.

"Yes. Interesting." His fingertips met, and caged his mouth; his index fingers tapped gently at the corners of his lips, as though to unlock them. His fingers sprang away. "I wonder," he mused, "if there may not have been something even earlier? These things often seem to start in childhood."

Rose cried out. A hot stain was spreading over her breasts. Pain made her think it was blood until she realized that her hand had twitched the teacup. Whatever thought had jerked into her mind had vanished, driven out by pain.

"Gladys, have you a towel?" In a moment Colin brought Rose one with which to dab herself. "I'm sorry," he said. "I timed my question badly."

Did he think that had dismayed her? Perhaps he was right; her skin was prickling wildly; there seemed to be a darkness in her mind, and she was too close to the edge. "What things start in childhood?" she said, and told him the answer she wanted to hear: "Bad dreams?"

"Bad dreams—perhaps." He frowned, closing his brows over his eyes. "I'm not quite sure how I can help you," he said.

The darkness was very close. "Can't you help me sleep?" she pleaded.

"Oh yes, quite easily. Librium will do that. But I'm not fond of tranquillizers—they're a negative drug, I think. They treat the symptom, not the cause."

"But what is the cause?"

"I'm not sure. I hope that doesn't disturb you. Frankly, I think that anyone in my profession who claims always to be sure is a charlatan. Suppose this: suppose your experiences are neither dreams nor hallucinations?"

"I don't follow."

"Suppose they are actual perceptions of some kind?"

Why couldn't he play the role she expected of him? "Surely you don't believe that," she said accusingly.

"Psychiatry is in its infancy. Not only can't it cure everything, but there are times when it is too eager to do so. We have very little idea what the mind is really capable of." He was lecturing. "Put it this way," he said, more conversationally. "If someone told you that they could project themselves astrally I think you would be skeptical. But since, after all you've told me, you insist that you can't, I'm inclined to wonder whether you can."

She could only stare at him. "Understand, we're hypothesizing," he said, not reassuringly enough. "But I'm struck by the number of points your descriptions have in common with other such accounts. I take it you haven't read any of the literature? No, I thought not. In the same way, descriptions of LSD experiences often tally in suggestive ways. Much of the mind is uncharted, you realize. We know too little about these visionary states."

She'd begun to feel like an unwilling experimental subject. "But what am I supposed to do?"

"If the experience is real, you mean? I would suggest that you try to go through with it. Undoubtedly you will be nervous to begin with, but suppose you learn to control what is happening? That may be easier than you think. My thought is this, you see—that if you genuinely have these powers, it will be more harmful to repress them than to develop them."

"But what if I don't want them?" she said desperately.

"Perhaps you haven't got them at all. I'm sorry, I should have more regard for your feelings. Perhaps once you have the tranquillizers you'll never experience anything out of the ordinary again. Tell me just one thing: the voice that you say released you from your nightmare—could it have said, 'She's saying no'?"

"It's possible. Why?"

"It may have been the voice of your own mind, saying that you weren't sufficiently prepared. I take it that you can't say what kind of a voice it was." He gazed at her as though that ought to be completely reassuring. "Well," he said after a while, "I'll get you your capsules. They should help you over the worst of it."

He took his time over finding them in his desk. As he dropped the box into her hand she thought he grimaced faintly, disappointed. "Please let me know at once if anything further happens. Or if you need reassurance," he added, with a hint of self-mockery that seemed infuriatingly mischievous. "Of course, if you decide that there's any truth to my hypothesis, do remember that I'll help you in every way I can."

Once home, she opened the box of Librium. The green-and-brown capsules made her think of insect eggs. Bill glanced at them and smiled encouragement, perhaps too widely. "Was he a help?" he asked.

She couldn't begin to tell him what had happened, not until she gained some control over the turmoil of her feelings. "Yes, I think so," was all she could say.

A few minutes after swallowing two capsules she would have been happy to sound more definite. Relief welled up from her solar plexus; it felt like ointment that was bathing her, calm, cool, all-embracing. She was no longer afraid to sleep. In a few moments she was dozing. Yet she felt a twinge of guilt: wasn't this relief too easy, a coward's solution? How soon might she resemble Gladys, apologizing nervously for taking drugs?

XII

"Oh God," Bill cried in half-amused disgust. For a moment she thought it was meant for the book she was reading. "Listen to this, will you. They've printed 'Geiss' for 'Geist.'"

"Which means . . . ?"

"Well, it certainly doesn't mean what we wrote. Instead of Vincent Price being possessed by the ghost of his ancestor, he's possessed by the goat of his ancestor."

It was July. Tomorrow they would fly to Munich. Bill sat on a relocated chair, bemoaning the German translation of *Shared Nightmares*. The furniture had been moved around the room for the summer, to avoid the floods of sunlight. The deep pile of the carpet was clogged with shadow. Rose sat on the sofa, on the embroidered silvery vines. It stood close to the open hearth now. One day perhaps they'd replace the open fire, which she loved, and the gas fires in the other rooms, with central heating—if they stayed here long enough, and if they could bear the domestic upheaval. She was reading a book called *Out of the Body*.

At least the Librium had allowed her to do that. It had achieved more: each night she'd felt less vulnerable before sleeping, and it had seen her through the frustrations of examining, or marking papers, of arguing the low marks with the tutors from the training colleges. At least a dozen students from one college had submitted virtually identical papers, like a problem in structuralism: "Decode the Ur-text from its imitations."

Rose wasn't using Librium now. The drug had let her think calmly about Colin's advice, and Diana's. She'd begun to feel that her clinging to rationality might itself be irrational. Wasn't it absurd to explain away all that had happened to her by one blow on the back of the neck?

On impulse she'd gone to the library. It would be fun to leaf through *Astral Rape,* to see if it was as diverting as its title. But the copy had been stolen, as had most of the copies in Liverpool libraries. Oh no, she didn't want to order it, she'd said hastily. All the books about astral projection were on loan—it was a popular subject—but one of the staff had been reading *Out of the Body,* and had yielded it to Rose.

Reading the book was a series of shocks, as though she were encountering in print a text she'd planned to write. Each account had something in common with hers. The voyagers, as the book called them, always felt awake; their senses were never blurred, as in dreams. The continuity of the experience was always linear, without the dislocations of dreams. Some people felt their bodies vibrating invisibly; some thought that the vibrations became the astral form. Outside their bodies they felt weightless, or light as mist. Some felt they had died or were going mad—but most found the memory reassuring afterwards, for it proved they could live outside the body; life after death was possible. Though in many cases it was a once-in-a-lifetime experience, some voyagers learned to control their trips. It was mostly a question of growing used to the ease of it, they said. "To think of moving is to have moved," one voyager reported.

"Did you leave the key next door?" Bill said.

"Oh no, not yet. I'll do it shortly."

How much of the text was nonsense, delusion? Some of the accounts seemed preachy as descriptions she'd read of LSD trips, with which they had something in common: the heightened vividness of colors, for example. Though the sheer number of astral reports was impressive, surely there were dreams which most people experienced at some time—of flying, of falling, of running without being able to move. Too many of the accounts seemed credulous or willfully eccentric. She didn't want to be associated with cranks.

She leafed through a chapter of theories and cosmologies. Life after death was determined by one's expectations at the moment of death, some said. There were dozens of exclusive heavens, each populated by members of a different religion, who believed only they could be saved. That would make Bill laugh, but she decided to keep the book to herself. Here was another vision—it could hardly be more than that—which maintained that there were planes of astral evolution after death; the one nearest the living was crowded with the newly dead, enclosed by fragments of their past lives, obsessed with their lost sexuality and with achieving some kind of sexual release, until they forgot their mundane preoccupations and moved on—if they ever did. It couldn't be more than a theory, but she found it oppressive. She leafed onward, through references to an English group of the 1900s, founded by someone called Peter Grace, which had tried to push astral research too far. It had led to infanticide, madness, and (the book said vaguely) worse, but at least it was comfortingly distant, although some of the Nazis, Himmler in particular, had apparently tried to rediscover its secrets.

"Would you like to go for a walk on the prom?" Bill said. "It's a pity to waste a day like this."

"Yes, I'd like to, in a few minutes." Was he trying to distract her from the book? He wasn't helping her resolve her feelings. She felt that she was making it too easy for herself to dismiss the book as trash, to avoid pondering her own experiences. At least she was in good company, supposing that she wished to join them. On Holy Thursday, 1226, St. Anthony of Padua was said to have appeared in two places simultaneously. In 1774, Alphonse de Liguori appeared before witnesses at the deathbed of Pope Clement XIV, although de Liguori was imprisoned in a cell at Arezzo, where he had slept for five days after fasting. Goethe met a friend on the road in dressing gown and slippers, while the friend was dreaming of meeting Goethe. As a child, Thor Heyerdahl had been terrified under anesthetic that he couldn't return to his body. While ill in Paris, Strindberg imagined himself at home, so vividly that he felt he was there, standing by the piano—and was seen there by his mother-in-law, who wrote to ask whether he was ill. At the end of a visit to his friend Theodore Dreiser, John Cowper Powys promised impulsively to reappear later; two hours later Powys appeared, shining, in the locked apartment, though he was thirty miles away. Toward the end of his life, Hitler was observed to enter brief trances from which he could not be roused—and at these times his aides, who were often miles distant, were convinced that he was close to them and watching them. At the moment of his death, D. H. Lawrence told Aldous Huxley that he could see himself outside his body. Here was one of his cries from his deathbed: "Hold me, hold me, I don't know where I am, I don't know where my hands are . . ."

"Don't you want to go out?" Bill said.

His impatience was clearly directed at the book. In fact she was glad to leave behind Lawrence's struggle to cling to his sense of himself. She thought Lawrence had been too passionate for his own good—in terror as in everything, presumably. Still, she was glad to emerge into the sunlight for a while.

The postbox was a tube of crimson neon. The sky was parched of clouds. The villas baked like pastry. Everything radiated heat; scents of gorse and roses drifted as though in search of shade. The intensified colors—the overwhelming blue of the sky, the outpouring of green—seemed to converge in the focus, unbearably white, of the sun.

The couple who lived opposite the Tierneys were tramping through the residents' garden in hiking boots. The man's moustache was a thin black line in a bluish shaved penumbra; fragile bluish curls decorated the woman's head, as though it was a cake. "Good afternoon," she said coolly. "Was that your party some weeks ago?"

"No, it was next door to us."

"Oh, I see. The psychiatrist's house. There was so much noise that we thought one of his patients must have got out of control. Does he intend to continue bringing his patients here?"

"I think he's found somewhere in Rodney Street now." Rose had glimpsed nocturnal visitors, but hadn't seen their faces—friends of the Hays, presumably.

"I hope you aren't mistaken." She sounded as though she would hold Rose personally responsible for errors. "Well, we mustn't keep you," the woman said, and stalked onward.

At the end of the garden, a fallen square of concrete fence gave access to Otterspool promenade. The Tierneys climbed down to the road which led to the rubbish tip. Dust swarmed above the road in the wake of a lorry, like solidified heat haze. Beside the road, the shell of a television set was turned to a selection of grasses and wild flowers.

Rose halted, staring. "I haven't seen that before. At least—"

"It's been there for a while."

They ducked through a gap in wire netting and followed the path onto the grassy plateau. From the top they could see the sweep of the Mersey as it rushed down from the distant Pennines and out to the Irish Sea. The glittering ripples made her think of code, too rapid to decipher.

Just now she had been ready to tell him everything, but the chance seemed to have passed. She had been leaving *Out of the Body* where he could see it in the hope that he would broach the subject. If only he would give her that much help—

His gaze jarred her out of her reverie. "What's the matter, Ro?" he said wistfully. "You were with Colin a long time that day—you must have told him something. Don't you want to tell me?"

"You know I do. It's just so difficult to put it into words." She felt nervous and clumsy; this would be harder than telling Colin. Gulls passed overhead, an explosion of white, whose shadows touched her too quickly even to hint of coolness. "I'll try," she said at last. "But don't interrupt until I've finished. Please."

"All right." He seemed slightly offended that she felt the need to ask.

Smooth brick-red paths sloped to the promenade. Boys on skateboards rushed toward the Mersey. Children were everywhere, catching Frisbees, throwing a chewed ball for a terrier to chase; there was even a hopeful group running about the plateau with a grounded kite. A little girl whose legs were patched like old clothes with Band-Aids stood on her head against the promenade railings. Adults sat on benches or in brick shelters with portholes, or wheeled prams beside the river.

"I've been peculiar," Rose said with an effort, "since the night I stayed with Diana." Was there a glint of wry agreement in his eyes? "The night after I was attacked," she said, "I felt as though I was going to float out of my body. That could just have been dizziness, an aftereffect, I know. As a matter of fact, I dreamed that it actually happened. Well, when we came home I felt that it was going to happen again. This was weeks later, during the séance."

"Oh, that stupidity. I wish I hadn't joined in."

"Oh, Bill, you did promise not to interrupt. Don't make it more difficult for me." The river lapped quietly, gently rocking its burden of light, offering a sense of calm—but it reminded her of her plunge into the muddy depths, and she stayed well back from the edge. "Then—" she said, and her words seemed to clutter her mouth, to be impossible to dislodge. "Then one night it really happened. The night you couldn't wake me."

"What really happened?"

"I seemed to leave my body—to go outside the house. I couldn't stop myself."

"You dreamed you left your body," he said mildly, as though correcting a freshman.

"I knew you'd say that. I'm not getting at you—I felt the same way when Diana tried to persuade me it was real the first time. But this last time *was* real. I'm sure of it now. I saw that television set by the road. I'd never seen that before."

"I told you, that's been there for months."

"Yes, but *I* hadn't seen it."

"You must have." His voice was firm and reasonable, and seemed intolerably patronizing. "What other explanation can there be? Really, Ro, it isn't like you to want to believe that sort of thing. Was that why you couldn't sleep?"

"Yes, I was afraid it might happen again."

"But then what on earth is the point of reading that book? 'Some voyagers report that their astral bodies can be stretched like chewing gum,'" he quoted, and looked dismayed when she didn't laugh. "Why invite another of these nightmares? Seriously, Ro, you must know that's all they are."

"I've told you that I thought so until very recently." She felt alone, isolated by her plight. Lampposts held up brackets for lifebelts along the promenade; many brackets were empty, their belts stolen or flung away. "Just suppose these things were real," she said. "Would you look after me?"

"Of course I would. I'll always look after you. But they aren't real, they can't be. Look here," he said, invoking rationality, "what did Colin say?"

"He wasn't sure. He thought they might be real. He felt I shouldn't repress them if they were."

"Colin said that? *Colin* did?" For a moment she thought that his dogmatism was shaken. "The stupid twat," he said. Strolling couples began to glance at him. "Why did he want to tell you that kind of shit? How is that supposed to help you? The stupid bloody turd! Jesus Christ Almighty!" If Colin had been present, Bill would certainly have knocked him down. "And whose idea was it," he said dangerously, "that you should read that book?"

"My own."

Her quietness calmed him. He looked embarrassed, anxious to leave behind the strollers who had over-heard him. He hurried down the promenade. Beyond the far end, cranes bunched like skeletons of plants at Garston docks. A wind had begun to sweep the river, and ruffled his hair. As she caught up with him and took his hand, an airliner from Speke Airport rose leisurely over the cranes.

"Don't read any more of it, Ro. It can't be doing you any good."

"I'm not sure. It doesn't disturb me to read about the subject now. Don't you see that's reassuring? I want to be sure that I haven't been harmed." Beside the promenade, gorse blazed amid sullen green; she could almost feel the prickles. The intensified sense was more awesome than disturbing. "There's one thing that appeals to me," she said. "To feel that you may be able to survive outside your body."

"Appeals?" he repeated sadly.

"Yes, because it means you can survive the death of the body. Wouldn't you like to think we would still be together?"

"Obviously I would." He sounded as though they were discussing a dream—pleasant but unreal. "But if there is life after death, then it exists whether or not you mess around with this other thing."

They leaned on the railing. An oil tanker glided massively by, leading its brood of tugboats. Above the plateau, the kite's tail described the wind. On the far bank of the Mersey, fumes streamed from tall chimneys, concrete pens with black felt tips. Chimneys like fat stumpy mountains were manufacturing their own clouds. The smoke vanished in the enormous empty sky.

"I wasn't being honest before," Bill said abruptly. "I said I would help you, but that isn't true, because I wouldn't know how. I feel inadequate."

"Oh, Bill, there's no need—"

"No, let me speak now. No interruptions." He gazed across the river; the glare of the sky seemed not to touch his eyes. "I just don't want us to grow like my parents," he said. "I never told you, but it used to be like bloody Northern Ireland at home. My father was a Catholic, my mother was a Proddy—she took Catholic lessons so as to get married. Religious battles every night at teatime."

"Never mind, Bill, you've left that behind."

"You're right. And I had to do it on my own." His nails plucked at his moustache, like tweezers; hairs drifted away on the wind. "They wanted me to follow them in the shop, you know. They used to say I could always write between customers. They never actually tried to discourage me from studying, but I could always tell they thought I wouldn't make it, not having been to grammar school. Well," he said defiantly, "I did make it, and I'm where I wanted to be."

Why did she feel obscurely accused? "I know you are," she said, and after a pause, "So am I."

"Are you? I hoped you were. I couldn't have made it without you." His smile was tentative, almost pleading. "I can't help it," he said, "I feel threatened."

"Threatened by what?"

"By what you've been saying. I know you think I should be more amenable to change. Maybe I planned ahead too rigidly, but I thought that was what you wanted. But this is more than change. Suddenly I feel I don't know you."

"Really?"

"No, not really. Just over this one thing. But Ro—please don't encourage it. Please, I'm asking you. You don't want to have to go back on drugs."

"It hasn't happened since that night. For many people it happens once in a lifetime."

"Just don't encourage it, that's all I'm saying. Let me return that book to the library for you."

"There's no need for that," Rose said sharply. "In any case, I'll have no time to read it before we leave. Don't worry, Bill, I'm all right now. Truly I am, now that I've told you." Certainly she felt relieved, though perhaps only that she'd discharged the task.

As they turned toward home she saw the kite. Its long tail sketched great restless loops, wild yet graceful. The kite soared, plunged toward the ground, soared as though drawn by the intensity and vastness of the sky. Bill took her hand. His fingers felt as though they were caging hers.

XIII

Bavaria calmed her.

Life had the lingering pace and taste of beer. During the day they explored Munich; Rose had never seen so many churches—cool forests of pillars, blossomings of stucco. At twilight they took Gerhard's cat hunting field mice while they strolled among the Aschheim cornfields, startling pheasants which startled them. Gerhard was in Frankfurt, sorting out problems for one of his authors.

Soon Jack and Diana had arrived. Before long the women had found an excuse to talk alone. Diana had guessed that Rose's psychically gifted friend was Rose herself. She'd listened enthralled, and had accepted everything—even the masked group which had seemed to call Rose out of her body, and which Diana felt had been a magical rite of some kind, invoking anyone or anything that might be near, not necessarily Rose. "You mustn't waste your gifts," she'd said, her tone canonizing Rose. "Suppose you can use them to help other people? Just think how much you'll grow as you develop them."

Rose wasn't so sure, but it seemed not to matter; she had left her problems behind. And now it was twilight, and Munich was turning into a dream.

Lions crouched half-buried in the facades of buildings. Gilded clocks shone high in the air, holding the last rays of the sun. Slate decorations on the capitals of pillars flapped away into the sky, for they were pigeons. Massive swordsmen the color of mist stood on guard above the streets. Cherubs with faces smooth as eggs supported balconies. They looked peaceful as the first hour of sleep, before dreaming. Everything was peaceful, except for Bill.

Diana had invited herself and Jack to meet Josef Dietrich, the director. "No, I'm not Mrs. Tierney," Rose had heard her saying. "I'm, uh—I'm their agent's secretary. Oh, you didn't know we were here too? Sure, we'd love to come along." Rose could tell that Bill was wishing he had resisted Diana's pleas.

When the tram squealed leisurely around a curve Rose reached forward to massage Bill's shoulders, but he shrugged her off, muttering, "It's all right." The tram had left behind the Hauptbahnhof, the nightclubs where bouncers enforced absurd prices; now the route

led through residential streets. Balconies were giant
window boxes, glowing with flowers.

"Maybe you two could figure an angle on some new
stars," Jack was saying. "Go out to Hollywood or
wherever and interview them. Something that the mass
audience is going to want to read. What do you say?"

"Well, we'll put our heads together." He glanced
back for Rose's agreement. "But just now I'd like to
keep my mind clear for Dietrich."

Diana was reading from Rose's Berlitz phrasebook:
"'Go away, keep your hands to yourself, leave me
alone, stop or I'll scream'—Jesus, what kind of holidays
do these guys have?" Bill's shoulders clenched, but she
wasn't annoying him; he was standing up—here was
their stop.

The tram moved off toward the Nymphenburg
Palace, reeling in its gleam along the tramlines. Bill led
his party into a side street, between two birch trees like
sentries. The few houses were set in spacious gardens;
poplars swayed gently, almost imperceptibly; bushes
were formed into glossy shapes of gnomes. Giants,
mysterious luminous incarnations of the sunset, hovered on the walls of houses: Lüftlmalerei, Rose had
learned they were called—paintings on the air.

No figure adorned the house before which Bill
halted. Wide balconies stood out from the bone-white
walls; the balconies were crimson with flowers, slashes
of blood against the bone. Like its neighbors, the house
was caged by sharp railings. Low bushes squatted about
the lawns.

A grille in the gatepost considered the names of the
party. Its bars glimmered, a paralyzed snarl. Eventually a man in uniform appeared, leading a spiky
Doberman. "Come," he said with the voice of the
grille.

All the way along the drive the dog kept nosing at
Diana, who flinched away. A smile glinted in the man's
bland face. Around them the lawns were wide and dim;

nobody could creep up on this house. The bushes looked to be dissolving into shadow.

As the man knocked on the pine door, the dog squatted alertly beside him on the steps, baring teeth like the spikes of its collar. The knocking was complicated, obviously a code. A buzzer sprang the door open, revealing a bright pale hall.

At the foot of a gracefully curving staircase, a man leaned on a stick. Gray hair barred his balding skull. Piercing eyes gazed from beneath eyebrows wiry as strips of steel wool. For a moment he stooped over the stick, as though pinning down his surroundings, making himself their center.

Then he strode forward, limping slightly. "Mr. and Mrs. Tierney," he said. "You are exactly like the picture on your book. You must introduce me to your colleagues. Thank you, Günter," he said, closing the door.

"Jesus, I don't like that dog," Diana said.

"I am so sorry. Has he bothered you? He belongs to my son. All this is my son's property. He is in chemicals. I told him, don't go into films, it will break your heart." He smiled apologetically, as though he'd let them overhear that by mistake. "Now here is my room."

The room was very large and very white. Rose was reminded of a film set, for its contents looked isolated, cut off from one another: a modern suite surrounding a Persian rug in the middle of the room; shelves of books on cinema; swords crossed on the wall, above a shield; a desk with a typewriter, telephone, a framed photograph of Dietrich as a young man standing with a young woman, both dressed in thirties clothes, amid mountains.

Dietrich lowered himself on the lever of his stick into a chair. "Does everyone like brandy? I can have something else brought without trouble." As he filled a trayful of glasses he said, "Shall I start at once? Perhaps it is better if I start talking rather than we waste time on—*wie sagt man?*—small talk, yes?"

Bill switched on the cassette recorder. "As soon as you're ready."

"I was born in 1897. Do you want that kind of thing?"

"What? You're eighty years old? Why, that's incredible. I'd have said sixty." Diana subsided as Bill frowned, but Dietrich said, "Yes, I try to keep myself well. One needs something to occupy the mind, even if it is only the body."

"We did research your biography," Bill said. "I thought we sent you a copy."

"Yes, I remember now. Well then, you know all that. We shall speak of my career. It was my father who brought me into films. He was a famous stage director in Berlin, but the cinema excited him—he could see its possibilities. Reinhardt angered him. You know of Max Reinhardt, who wanted films to be nothing but recordings of plays? And there was the Kinoreformbewegung, the ones who would make it a crime to interpret Schiller in a film. Puritans and philistines, they are two heads of the same animal. They would stifle the imagination, and today they are succeeding. Oh, I forget," he said with apparent irrelevance, "does either of you speak German?"

For a moment Rose failed to realize that the question included her, for she was listening for something in his monologue, hiding there or waiting to be said. "Bill does," she said.

"Good. You may know that they allow me to speak about films at the University. I spoke to the tutor about you, and he would like you to address the students. Here is his number for you to call."

He sipped his brandy and favored it with a smile. "Now, you must know that the First World War was the midwife of our film industry, since we could import no films. So Universum Film Aktiengesellschaft—Ufa, you know—hired my father and me too, as his assistant. My leg was broken in a fall from a horse on my father's estate, and saved me from the war." He sounded obscurely bitter, as though over a lost opportunity.

"So I assisted him for some years. I worked with Asta Nielsen, our greatest film actress. Even more than my father, she taught me what film could do. Well, in a while you could tell which scenes I had directed. So one day Carl Mayer called me in and asked me if I would like to direct his script."

"That would be *Oktoberfest*," Rose suggested.

"Why, yes! You have seen it?" His delight faded. "No, I thought not. I read in *Sight and Sound* that a copy was located, but I think they spoke too soon. Well, it was not my best. Mayer, you know, had just made *Hintertreppe*. A girl who throws herself from a roof because a crippled mentally defective postman falls in love with her and kills her lover with an ax—today they would make that a comedy, yes? I think Mayer got nervous and thought he needed popularity, and so he thought of a detective story. He grew unhappy writing it, and yet he would not be satisfied until it was finished—that was how he was.

"Well, I had grown up with the films about Stuart Webbs. He was a detective with a peaked cap and a pipe. You have," he said satirically, "someone similar in England, I believe? So I helped Mayer complete his script, and took the credit for directing. It had some scenes I liked."

"Kracauer says it was years ahead of its time."

"Yes, he says so, but the other books ignore it. Film history, like any other kind, is rewritten by the victors. Still, let me tell you my favorite films. Erich Pommer, who produced *Caligari*, became chief of production at Ufa. He wanted visions. He would not be welcome today," Diettrich said wistfully. "Now they want politics, they want ideas small enough to grasp without opening their minds. Except perhaps Herzog—he at least tries to make films which express something larger than himself. Well, Pommer encouraged me to make my best film, *Die Wiederkehr*—that is, The Return."

"That's another we weren't able to see," Rose said.

"Would you like to see it now? Come, then." He led them down rough whitewashed steps beneath the graceful staircase and switched on the cellar light. "Here is what is left of me."

The rooms seemed full of screens. Even the whitewashed walls resembled them. One screen stood in the middle of the floor, faced by several folding chairs over whose shoulders a projector craned. In a corner, beside piles of cans of film, a movieola screen bulged, trapping a glimpse of Rose in its gray bubble.

"I have an extra copy of *Die Wiederkehr*." Dietrich gestured at the movieola. "I reedit it sometimes. I feel there is a better way to organize it, an insight to be found."

He closed the door and dimmed the lights while they sat in the folding chairs. "It will not be too distracting if I talk." He seemed to feel they might dislike the film.

A young couple was climbing in the Alps. Rose knew their faces from other films: Gustav Froehlich, Asta Nielsen. Though Nielsen was twenty years older than Froehlich, she looked magically young. Faults in the copy infected them with nervous jerkiness.

They had found a deserted village. As they ventured beyond it, their shadows grew wide as the night. From those shadows, glimmering figures emerged: the villagers, returning. They were bearing the corpse of one of their number down from the heights. Strangely, they were smiling.

"Not only the lighting is ahead of its time," Bill murmured, "but the performances."

"Well, the lighting was what Mayer wanted. I will take the credit for Froehlich. You saw him in *Metropolis?* Here, you see, he doesn't act as though he's sending semaphore. I should have gone to Hollywood instead of Murnau, except Germany was better without him and his boy friends."

"Why didn't you?" Diana demanded.

"Because I wanted to make German films. I never imitated Hollywood, as Pabst did. Next I made a ghost story, *Die Tanzes*, which I cannot show you, because the film people let it become lost after the war. They wanted most to lose *Die Wiederkehr*, I think. You see, Hitler was interested in it for a time, because it is about reincarnation."

"Yes?" Diana said eagerly.

"He must have thought I knew things he wanted to know, but my film was all imagination. Thank God, other things distracted him, and I was not summoned."

The room was flickering like migraine. Rose felt irritably oppressed. Before she could change the subject, Dietrich had done so himself. "Well, *Die Wiederkehr* wasn't too much of a success, so they asked me to make operettas. One critic said I had more wit than Lubitsch, anyway. Then the thirties came, and I made a war film, like everybody."

Rose had seen it: *The Standard-bearer,* who was a young soldier in World War I and who, after the commanding officers of his battalion had been wiped out, led his companions to victorious death in the Austrian Tirol. It looked like the work of an artist overcome by propaganda.

"Then the Nazis came. Should I have fled to Hollywood like Sirk and Lang? But there were still German films to be made. So they want me to make a film about the British in the Boer War. Very well, I film caricatures everyone will know are caricatures. I make comedy with a straight face. But what happens? The audience believes this is how the British are, because this is what they want to believe."

"Just give me a minute to change the cassette," Bill said.

The climbers had spent the night in the village.

Nielsen was determined to find out what lay above, in the mists. Since Froehlich refused to go with her she climbed alone, leaving a note. At last he and a party of villagers found her, frozen to death—but she was smiling.

"Can you go on with what you were saying about Hitler?" Diana said.

"About the secrets he wanted to learn? I can tell you what I have been told. I thought you would not be interested."

When Rose held up one hand, an unconscious gesture while she tried to interrupt, she saw that it was trembling. It felt perfectly still. Panic seized her as she remembered the vibrations which had shaken her out of her body—then she realized that it was the light which made her hand flicker. Diana had already replied, "I sure am."

"Well then, I wonder what you know. Perhaps you know that Nazi leaders were interested in such things. Himmler thought he was King Heinrich I reincarnated. Some say he created a magical order of himself and twelve generals of the Schutzstaffel, the SS. Some called him the Black Jesuit, and Hitler called him his Ignatius Loyola. You have heard of the Ahnenerbe? Himmler founded it to do research into German racial origins. Well, within it he created a section to do research into the supernatural. Why was that, do you think?

"Maybe all this was only Himmler, but there are other things. Do you know who was first to be persecuted by the Nazis? Not the Jews, no, but the occultists. Some say the Nazis were destroying those who might oppose them—that Hitler was. You see, some say he had occult powers."

Bill had fitted the new cassette and was staring at it, more or less patiently. "You should say if I am boring you," Dietrich said. "I am happy to talk all night, but it is long since I had the chance."

Was the film nearly over? Its glare kept snatching at

Rose's hands; the walls stepped forward and dodged back, as if playing a game in which their movements mustn't be glimpsed; tattoos of light and shadow crawled on Dietrich's face. Perhaps Bill would steer him away from his theme—but Bill seemed resigned. "It's all right," he said. "I'm in no hurry."

"Well, so they say Hitler had occult powers. Who says so? Not only madmen. Important men have said things. Albert Speer says that he felt psychically— yes?—psychically drained whenever he left the Führer. Hermann Rauschning, President of the Danzig Senate—he was present when Hitler saw an apparition that terrified him. He says that Hitler screamed, "It's he, he's come for me!" Can you imagine something that would terrify Hitler? Some say it was something he had called to him, to give him powers.

"What powers? That is the question, is it not? Some say he could see the future. How else could he be sure that your Allies would do nothing when he strengthened his army, and occupied the Rhineland, and annexed Austria, and occupied Bohemia and Moravia? Still, many of us can see the future sometimes, though perhaps we would not have such faith in ourselves.

"There is more. I have a friend who has researched these things. He is anxious still. Such things do not vanish without leaving a mark on the world, he says. Do you know that Hess once saw Hitler where he could not be, in the shadows of a room where Hess had called a confidential meeting? They all saw him, yet when Hess put on the light there was nobody there. Do you know also that Hess found Hitler in a trance from which he could not be awakened, until—these are the words of Hess, you understand—'he flew back into his eyes'? To see Hitler standing in a trance, staring as though he were dead—that frightened Hess most of all. Perhaps these were reasons why Hess fled to England. He felt what Speer felt, you know, but he said Hitler drew vitality from those around him. Of course Hitler said Hess was mad. Who knows? Most of the men who were close to Hitler felt he could overhear them at distances which would be impossible for an ordinary man.

"Well, we know he was not ordinary. These are tales to tell at the fireside, perhaps. But my friend says one thing that is not so pleasant. It is something one would rather not believe—but I think of Hitler's interest in my film. My friend says Hitler wanted above all the power to be reborn."

"But he didn't get it," Diana said anxiously. "I mean, he didn't have the power."

"I do not know."

There was silence except for the hectic chattering of the projector. On the screen, figures with chalky blobs for faces advanced jerkily as crippled puppets. The cans of film were slimed by the light; the piles appeared to squirm, their segments shifting. Apprehension clenched Rose's skull.

"One hopes not, of course," Dietrich said. "They say that toward the end Hitler became senile. He lost his memories, he couldn't concentrate. But my friend says people didn't read these symptoms right, that they were only signs that he was preparing to take his leave of that body. He still had his will, you know. He slept only three hours, and they were after dawn. My friend would tell you that those are the ways of a magician whose power is strongest at night.

"Well, maybe he did not achieve what he sought, but there are things that prove he sought it. Have you heard of the man with the green gloves? He was a Tibetan monk who lived in Berlin. He made predictions in the newspapers. Hitler would often go to him—why, do you think? When the Russians entered Berlin they found a thousand corpses of Tibetans dressed as German soldiers. Perhaps you know about the Dalai Lama of Tibet—at the moment when he dies, they say he is reincarnated. That would have interested Hitler, do you think?

"My friend says Hitler searched more widely. Himmler had the Ahnenerbe find out all they could about an occult order that was formed in England by a man called Grace. You would know of this, perhaps."

"Certainly not," Bill said. "Why on earth should we?"

"I thought that, being English—well, no matter. Perhaps it is not well known. No doubt that is best, if its purpose was the same as Hitler's. Well, we must believe he failed. Nothing in England could have helped him, could it? Perhaps he foresaw his doom and was trying anything, however desperate. Yes, I think we must believe he failed. But my friend thinks that is too simple, he thinks we are too eager to believe we are safe. You see, even the Dalai Lama must be reborn as a child and be trained as a monk once again. But Hitler wanted to be reborn with his personality intact."

Again the only sound was the insect whirring of the projector. Trapped light fluttered on the bare walls. Flickering nagged at the edge of Rose's vision, like migraine. Her head was in the movieola screen, shrunken and distorted and blanched. She turned away from that, and glimpsed Jack. His fists were wedged beneath his chin. He looked fascinated.

"Could we meet him?" Diana said. "Your friend, I mean."

"For what purpose?"

"To find out what else he knows. I mean, you said he thinks people are too eager to forget. Maybe we could publish what he tells us—that way people would have to know. It could make a neat article, don't you think, Jack?"

"Sure, it's a possibility." He sounded professionally wary but intrigued.

"Perhaps he won't want to talk to you," Rose said. "He may not want the publicity."

"We wouldn't have to name him."

"Oh no, he is prepared to talk. He wants to be known. But yes, maybe he would prefer not to be named. Well, I have your number. I will see what he says."

Froehlich was old now, and dying. He managed to struggle once more to the Alpine village, though he had no idea why he was doing so. A young woman was waiting for him. She had been born on the day Nielsen died. She reminded him of memories that only Nielsen had shared. He began weeping, crying that she was young now, while he was dying—but that didn't matter here; she was leading him gently up the mountain, into the mist.

All at once they halted, twitching feebly and repetitively. Their faces grew white as bone, as though their skulls were melting their way through the flesh. The light jerked Rose's limbs, which seemed about to drag her to her feet, toward the sudden blinding glare which had consumed the climbers.

Dietrich switched off the projector, in which the film had stuck. The last frames had been burned to a crisp. "Well, it doesn't matter any longer. Now we shall go upstairs."

Light welled up, steadying the shadows. The cellar was merely a workroom, which looked as though Dietrich had tried to fill it, only to find that his life's work was too meager. To Rose the light and the transformation seemed too glibly reassuring.

She followed Dietrich and the others into the hall, which was bright as an open sky. "Before we move on to your later career I'd like to check a few of the dates with you," Bill was saying, audibly relieved that the interlude was over. "When did you work with Asta Nielsen? I wonder if you might have any anecdotes . . ."

XIV

As they emerged into the Odeonsplatz, the sunlight seized them. Beneath the blazing sky, the steps from the underground station looked translucent as shell. Across the square, the Theatinerkirche shone like yellow sand; its onion domes gleamed green as leaves. A lion taller than a man lay in the shade of the Feldherrnhalle arches. At the far end of the Ludwigstrasse, lions were elevated on a triumphal arch.

As they turned toward the Hofgarten, Jack drew alongside Rose. "You've taken some weight off since New York," he said. "You look better for it."

"Oh, thank you." It seemed a wry compliment, to praise the effects of her anxiety.

In the arcade which walled in the Hofgarten, large paintings glowed beneath the arches. "We'd better hurry," Bill was saying, "If we want to be on time. He doesn't sound like the kind who'd wait for us."

"I really hope you won't be bored," Diana said. "Except for you we wouldn't have anyone to translate."

"Oh, it may be quite amusing in its way."

Jack dawdled, to be out of earshot. "Listen," he said to Rose, "I wanted to ask your advice." His arms were trying to fold themselves; his hands grasped each other's elbows and recoiled, like birds seeking to perch. "You know Diana pretty well. In some ways you're kind of alike. What I wanted to ask you—do you think this stuff she's getting into can do her any harm?"

Why, Diana seemed able to breeze through the whole business; it was Rose whom it was troubling. "Did you read *Astral Rape* yet? Some of the stuff Dietrich mentioned is in there." Diana might have been talking about the latest best seller. When Dietrich had called to say that he'd arranged for them to meet his friend, she'd reassured Rose: "It's okay. It's all in the past. It needn't worry us—it's just fascinating."

"I think she's just eager to learn about things, Jack. I don't think she takes it very seriously." And what about you? her mind was demanding of herself.

"Well, that's what I figured. I just wanted to be sure. See, I've met people who are so bad at handling the world that they'll believe anything that seems to explain things. But sure, Diana's too intelligent to take all that stuff seriously. Still, we could get good money for this story if the guy is weird enough."

"Come on, gang," Diana called, "or we'll be late."

In the subway beyond the formal garden, their shrill echoes dodged about beneath the white-tiled ceiling, like blind birds. The tiled wall at the far end appeared transformed into dazzling light. Little else was visible: the subway walls were a vague gray presence framing the dazzle; pedestrians were faceless silhouettes, their outlines unstable with light. The looming crowd of silhouettes parted to let Rose through—but one silhouette blocked her way. It was overpoweringly large, as were its hands that reached toward her, gloved raggedly in light.

For a moment it seemed not to matter that she was with friends. She was alone, half-blinded, with the faceless bulk and the babble of echoes. Then a voice said, "Tierney."

It sounded too weak for the bulk, almost piping. "Yes, that's us," Bill said. The silhouette turned blankly to him, until he spoke German. Rose heard him naming Diana and Jack.

Abruptly the figure hurried toward the light. *"Gehen wir,"* he urged them. It occurred to Rose that he'd met them here, rather than at the Chinese Tower as they'd agreed, in order to observe them without being seen. Now the obscurity, the crowding blacked-out faces, seemed to disturb him.

When he emerged into the light, Rose almost laughed, for his appearance was absurdly reassuring. He looked like a beer-hall waiter, fiftyish and fatherly and red-faced, his belly a shelf which would help him carry an armful of tankards. All he needed was an apron.

Then she noticed that his eyes were glancing everywhere, ready to send him back into the burrow of the subway. His face was bland as a balloon, but his eyes looked trapped, constantly darting to compensate for the slowness of his body. His nervousness made her own body feel clenched.

The English Garden disoriented her. Avenues of gravel led between tall trees; shadows of foliage lay stranded on the gravel, or attempted feebly to swim. Sunbathers were displayed on a wide green. Women shook rattles at prams. For a moment Rose was in England, then her intuition located her; though the garden was meant to resemble an English park, it felt German—she couldn't have said why.

"Well," Bill said with a hint of impatience, "what am I supposed to ask him?"

"Ask him about Peter Grace's occult research," Diana said, and when Bill grimaced wryly: "Ask him if he knows what Hitler found out about it."

As they talked the man watched them warily, sidelong. He seemed particularly daunted by Jack's tallness. As soon as Bill put the question he began to mutter rapidly. A weak ingratiating smile kept flinching from his lips, unable to grasp them. His voice was indistinct, as though he was afraid of being overheard, although the nearest stroller was thirty yards away. Twice Bill asked him to repeat phrases.

Rose found his high-pitched mutter nerve-racking, all the more so since she understood not a word. They were approaching a bridge beside a small waterfall. Across the green, she could see the Ionic columns of the Monopteros temple, standing above an explosion of flowers. The shining columns, the wide brilliant sky, the liquid chords of the waterfall, seemed lethargically peaceful. They would be peaceful, except for the muttering.

He had stopped, and Bill was translating, unable to restrain a faint superior grin. "He says that Himmler was known to be a medium. He used to boast about it, said he was able to call up the dead for advice—on a hot line, one assumes." He turned his back on the man, to allow his grin to widen. "Our friend here says Himmler tried to raise Peter Grace, the famous Englishman, so famous that I've never heard of him. But he failed, because he was only able to raise spirits from the distant past. What nonsense! Do you want some more?"

"Yes, please," Diana said. Rose could tell she was keeping her temper by an effort. Perhaps she was wishing they'd brought the cassette recorder, but the man had forbidden that. "Ask him what Hitler's powers were," Diana said.

Beyond the bridge stood a green metal post taller than Rose. An orange bulb protruded from its top, like a cartoonist's bump on the head. Beneath a grille was a handle which you turned to call the police. POLIZEI, a sign above it said, HILFE! Rose was obscurely grateful for its presence, for the man's nervousness was growing.

His eyes shifted more rapidly. Around him several avenues converged, but that seemed not to be the problem. Cyclists rode by; some carried children before them, like mascots. Prams nosed into the avenue; couples strolled, bound to each other by their arms. It wasn't the gathering of people that troubled him. He was glancing, more and more nervously, at the expanse of grass and sky. He made the open brightness of the park seem treacherous.

She stared at him. Had she misheard? Perhaps not, for Diana was gazing at him too, and Bill was frowning. Trees closed in; shade groped stealthily over the gravel.

"Oh, it's all very vague," Bill said irritably at last. "He says Hitler could see into the future—well, we've heard that one before. Then there's some other non-sense—ingenious, I'll give him that. He thinks Hitler's scorched-earth policy at the end of the war wasn't meant just to destroy Germany so that the Allies would gain nothing. It was supposed to be a sacrifice, to call up something that would carry him away. Mind you, Hitler could just have been mad enough to believe it."

"He said more than that, didn't he?" Diana demanded. "He said something about 'astral.' What did he say?"

"Sure, I thought I heard that. What is this, Bill? Are you censoring the guy?"

Not to know would be less bearable than knowing. "Come on, Bill," Rose said. "You mustn't hold things back."

"It's incredible to me that we're wasting a perfectly good day on this nonsense. You in particular, Jack."

"If we can break into a market with it, it won't be wasted."

"Well, as you wish. Still, I think this will be too grotesque for any kind of publication. He wants us to believe that Hitler could project his astral body—that's what *Astralleib* means, presumably, or something equally foolish. Apparently when Hitler became absentminded at the end, we ought to take that literally. That's why he didn't mind staying in the bunker. Do you know why he had himself shot? Have a guess. Because if he were taken prisoner, the forces he'd invoked might call at the wrong address to pick him up. It seems he wasn't in his body when they shot him. He'd stepped out to meet his friends."

He was laughing openly, and seemed determined that they should join in, especially Rose. She tried to smile nonchalantly, to show that none of this bothered her; there seemed no reason why it should. Jack and Diana were visibly puzzled by his behavior, perhaps embarrassed.

The man had noticed it too. His fingers, which resembled raw mottled sausages, clutched Bill's arm. A smile, presumably intended to be winning, managed to cling to his lips, though they trembled with the effort and looked ready to collapse. Snatching an envelope from his pocket, he thrust it into Bill's hand.

"What's this, the booby prize? I feel as though I deserve it, I'll tell you that." Bill inserted a finger to tear the envelope. The man dragged at his arm; his face crumpled inward, a rubbery mask of panic giving way at the mouth; he began to jabber. He was glaring at the sky, which a gap in the trees above them had left clear. His eyes looked near to rolling back.

"Do you know what he says he's just given me?" Bill stuffed the envelope into his pocket, as though it was a fanatic's pamphlet, to be giggled over at home. "It's supposed to be a letter from Hitler to Himmler, just before Heinrich tried to surrender to the Allies—that's one thing Adolf didn't foresee, it seems. Our friend refuses to tell me what it says, and I mustn't read it while he's here. Since the war, copies have been circulated to Nazi sympathizers. Well, I suppose that could be true."

He seemed happier now, having enjoyed the dramatic interlude. The man had begun muttering again, more rapidly as they came in sight of the crowded open space around the Chinese Tower. "There is very little time left," Bill translated satirically. "Too many people want to resurrect the secrets Hitler sought. Not only Germans want this—people are plotting all over the world. They want to achieve what he nearly achieved. What is that, I wonder? Ah, here it comes," he said as the man mumbled something, "the paranoid payoff. Nobody is safe until these people are destroyed. There will be nowhere we can hide."

They had reached the beer garden. Beside the

five-storied pagoda numerous wooden tables stood on a bed of gravel, their round tops painted green. The smell of hot garlic butter drifted from the self-service counters of a lodge. Most of the tables were occupied, some by nuns drinking beer, but a table on the far edge of the glade was empty save for birds squabbling over the remains of a pretzel.

The man strode nervously toward the table. Again he seemed less wary of the crowd than of the open space. Dogs kept wandering from between tables, almost tripping Rose; liter steins of heavy dimpled glass gleamed everywhere, piercing the edges of her vision. The clinging heat and the abrupt gleams felt like migraine. She was almost as glad as he was to reach the table.

Diana caught up with Bill. "Ask him if Hitler had been reborn," she said at once.

"You must be joking."

"No, really, you must ask him that." Her impatience was near to panic. "Really, you've got to. Please ask him, Bill, please!"

"I don't believe it. You really, seriously, want me to turn to this poor addled creature and say—?"

"Yes, you must. Otherwise," Diana added, with a cunning change of key, "We won't have a payoff to our story."

"Oh, all right. I expect a good stiff drink as compensation, though." When he turned to the man he looked in danger of a fit of giggling. At last he spoke. It occurred to Rose that none of them could be sure what he was asking—but the man's glare of horror and his gasp of "Nein!" told them.

"Okay, so he hasn't been reborn." Diana relaxed visibly. "Now you have to ask if he knows when it's going to happen."

"Oh, Diana, really. Enough is enough. I refuse to make myself look any more of a fool."

Rose had begun to sympathize with him. At the same time she felt edgy, frustrated. Was Diana infecting her?

"Go on, Bill," she said gently. "Just that one question."

"Really, this is too much. Bill Tierney, author and part-time weirdo." Nevertheless he turned wearily to the man and prepared to speak.

But the man was staring at the sky. Around his glaring eyes the skin was twitching. A hint of his panic seized Rose by her guts, until she saw that he was only staring at a cloud. Its shadow touched her with a sudden violent chill, and Diana shivered.

It was only a cloud, for all that it vaguely resembled a face. Blue sky shone through gaps in it, which closed and parted again. In a moment she would be able to look directly at it, to see that it was nothing but a cloud, to see how the sunlight was reflected from two points in it, glaring down.

The man leapt away from the table and ran stumbling toward the trees. He gabbled something which made Bill frown, uncomprehending. The man fled between the trees, his face quivering likc gelatin. A minute later, distant trees had caged him.

"It seems to me," Bill said, "that we all deserve a drink." His voice broke the tension, and made it possible for Rose to look at the cloud—but she'd realized suddenly that though she was shivering, no shadow had darkened the table. She looked up quickly, nervously. In every direction, as far as she could see, the sky was absolutely clear.

XV

Rose leaned on the edge of the balcony and gazed over Aschheim. The moon was a bright disc sliced from the empty sky. The asphalt was a path of frozen milk which the headlights of lorries could not melt. Moonlight lay on the balconied tiers of concrete like a promise of snow; across the cornfields, moonlight and shadow performed magical passes in trees. The unquenchable fireworks of planes sailed up from Munich Airport, slow and gentle.

When the moon began to swim through clouds, and Rose felt she was beginning to drift while the moon stood still, she went inside, away from the sky. Although nothing had happened since yesterday, she preferred not to dwell on the glimpse she'd had above the Chinese Tower, though she'd deduced what it might have been—a small flight of birds.

Afterward, Bill had grown tense. Perhaps he felt he'd lost them information by scoffing at the man. This morning he had thrust the letter at Diana: "It's all yours. Just count me out in future."

The letter was blotchily typed, and looked inexpertly photocopied. Its date was 21 April 1945. Rose had seen the signature in history books: the initial like a stroke of lightning, an inverse Z, half a swastika; then the name, the H just recognizable, followed by a cramped descending scribble like a black larva. The gray paper felt slimy. Though Diana could have asked Gerhard to translate the letter when he returned, she'd seemed to dislike its presence, and had mailed it to herself in New York, for later translation.

Rose locked the window and padded across the floor, which was softened by sheepskin rugs. Books shared the guest room; some were hers and Bill's, rendered incomprehensible to her.

As she climbed into bed next to Bill, he woke. "Don't switch the light off," he grumbled indistinctly, and fumbled out from beneath the bedclothes. "I'm bursting."

He didn't bother to put on his glasses. She heard him stumbling downstairs, his bare feet slapping the open treads of the staircase. He was tugging at the bathroom door, but the bathroom must be occupied. His footsteps flopped downward, toward the ground-floor toilet.

She lay listening for his return. Gerhard's cat wandered in and rubbed against her cheek. She was too sleepy to reach out and stroke the cat; the warmth that Bill had left behind felt comfortable; the cocoon of the quilt made her feel light and delicate, a figurine protected by soft packing, drifting weightlessly toward sleep. The touch of the cat's fur was lulling. The silence of the cat's retreat enticed her toward the silence of sleep.

Dread seized her without warning. It was far worse than being wakened by a cramp. Panic wrenched at her entire body, like an electric shock. Its message was all too clear: Bill was in danger. He was lying, or would lie, at the foot of the stairs, surrounded by blood. He was crippled, perhaps dying.

She must reach him. Please let there still be time! At least she could cry out from the top of the stairs, to warn him. But she could do neither of these things. The wrench of panic had been more than physical. She no longer had limbs that could walk, nor a mouth.

For a moment she struggled to regain her limbs. Her

body felt like an unknown intruder, pressed close against her back. If she could only grasp it, it would no longer be alien, it would be her own familiar body that could rush to Bill, to save him—

But wasn't there a quicker way to reach him?

No sooner had she thought it than she was at the door. It felt cold and glassy, and hindered her not at all. At once she was beyond it, as though it had given way like a shell, throwing her vertiginously out above the stairs.

She hadn't been prepared for this. Seen from above, the stairwell was more daunting than the open night had been. She felt disoriented, giddied, vulnerable. The house was threatening to turn over, to spin her into a vortex of panic from which she would never escape. This time she could not pretend that she was dreaming.

In that case she must not panic, for Bill was in danger. She must go down, see what the danger was. "To think of moving is to have moved"—she remembered that now, for she had already proved it to herself. The danger must be on the stairs. She had only to think herself down.

At first it was horribly unpleasant, far worse than being drunk, for she couldn't catch hold of anything to steady herself. Walls toppled toward her, ready to engulf her; the stairs swayed and whirled and seemed anchored to nothing. Whenever she thought of what she was doing, rather than how quickly she could save Bill, her instincts faltered, stranding her in midair.

Then she saw the cat. It lay just below the landing, and was rolling an oval cake of soap back and forth on the stair, pretending to let it escape, recapturing it just as it reached the edge. When Bill came stumbling blindly upstairs, he had only to tread on the soap—

The cat looked up and saw her. Its fur stiffened. A moment later it had fled, emitting a strangled mew which, under other circumstances, she would have found funny. What exactly had it seen? No time for speculation—the soap was still there. She couldn't move it or warn Bill until she regained her body.

She turned, and came face to face with the mirror.

It was not quite deserted. Though the reflected landing looked empty, a shape hovered there. It was pale as mist, and as blurred. Its outline looked unstable. Perhaps it had a face, which seemed incapable of holding still. Like the outline, the face appeared to transform uncontrollably. It looked vulnerable, unsure of itself.

For a moment she was caught, unable to think. The appearance in the mirror was all she was. It looked unstable enough to turn into anything, to become terribly deformed. It was drawing her in, engulfing her sense of herself.

Beside it in the mirror were the staircase wall, the stairs, the cake of soap. Bill! She glimpsed him, prone on his spreading blood. She must look away from the mirror, she must drag herself away. It didn't matter how she seemed to look—she knew how she felt, who she was. She had only to think of her body. "To think of moving—" She had only to think. Think, oh God, think! The word was cluttering her mind, a crowd of inane repetitions which grew more meaningless, leaving no room for thoughts: think, think, think, think—

The bolt clicked back on the toilet door, and she heard Bill's bare footsteps.

At once she was calm—the calm of despair. She was too late now, there was nothing she could do. No time to grasp her body. If Bill saw her as she was now, he would refuse to believe in her—in fact, his mind would refuse to see her. She would have been in time if only she had been able to feel her body a moment ago, the limbs awaiting her return, the chest breathing patiently, taking charge for her while she was away—

With hardly a transition she was back. The stairs whirred through her, the door was a hint of chill. She had only to match her body, to feel its position exactly, the position of each limb, each finger, each toe. It was easy, she need only let it happen, remember how easy it was, avoid panic, relax. But how could she, when Bill's footsteps on the stairs were counting the seconds to his injury or worse? How could she fit into this cumbersome unhelpful glove of a body, which pressed against her like a sack of flesh, refusing to move, thrusting her out, remaining stubbornly separate from her? Bill's footsteps were quickening: four, five, six—

She felt a whoop of air rush into her mouth. It tore at her throat and set her coughing. It seemed to pump her head thin as a balloon. When she staggered to her feet, the room tilted drunkenly. At least she could grab the wall to steady herself, and was able to rush to the top of the stairs and cry "Watch out, Bill! On the stairs!"

Her words might be too late, or too imprecise, or made indistinct by her coughing. She ran down, almost falling. Edges of treads cut into her bare feet.

Bill had halted, and was peering at the stairs. "What's this—soap?" He sounded almost as though he was accusing her of its incongruity. "It wasn't here when I came down. How did you know it was here?"

Rose leaned against the wall, trying to reclaim her breath from her coughing. Suddenly she realized that the bathroom door was open. Diana stood there, staring at her. Her expression told Rose that she knew what had happened.

Bill blinked at them. Though he was half-blind, could he tell that some message had passed between them? Snatching the soap, he said both apologetically and in a bid to close the subject: "Oh, of course it must have been the cat." But as he hurried upstairs, his shoulders clenched nervously.

Rose followed him. She avoided looking at Diana, for she could sense Diana's urging: tell him now, take the chance! In one way Diana was right—but she didn't know Bill.

By the time Rose reached the bedroom, he was

either asleep or determined to appear so. His face seemed locked into itself. At once she felt ashamed of her resentment: why shouldn't he sleep? He was safe, that was the main thing. Why should she insist on giving him more worries? She was beginning to wonder if she might grow to handle these experiences by herself.

When her breathing had eased and her throat was less raw, she slipped beneath the quilt. She felt neither exhausted nor especially insomniac. She lay gingerly exploring her thoughts, and was suprised not to be more disturbed. Her own resilience heartened her. It was comforting how quickly one grew used to things, however daunting they seemed at first.

Was she gaining strength? Even the glimpse in the mirror seemed less disturbing now. What had she expected to see, for heaven's sake, other than something that was hard to distinguish? In any case, she had conquered its lure. If she ever had the experience again, she must avoid mirrors.

Though her thoughts were rushing too swiftly for her, they were on the whole reassuring, and led toward sleep. She was almost asleep when something landed softly on the balcony. By the time she managed to focus her eyes it was rising, pale and vague, into the sky. A bird, only a bird! She subsided, and trusted herself to her thoughts, which were drifting wider, making way for sleep.

XVI

A cushion of wind pressed into Rose's face as she passed the corner of the Viktualienmarkt, which was loud as an aviary with the flapping of market stalls. Wind tried to snatch her breath, to tug her head back by the hair. It groped into her sleeves, it grabbed the ankles of her denims. Her hair lashed her face.

In the Odeonsplatz, the fur of the stone lion was unruffled. Sparks spilled over the backs of trams and danced away on the wind. In the Hofgarten, the jet of a fountain was a flailing leaf whose edges frayed into spray.

The walls of the pedestrian subway glowed like fog. They felt chill, and weighted down by earth. She glanced back as wind muttered close behind her, but the boxy dimness was deserted.

Once she reached the gravel path into the English Garden, the wind blew away her momentary nervousness. Soon she was at the bridge. A few distant figures trudged, heads down, over the grass, but the park was swept almost bare of people. She turned aside from the green, toward the waterfall beside the bridge.

The waterfall was small but deafening. It plunged over low rocks bearded with moss, a smooth slope of water that looked combed, then exploded into foam and rushed onward. Trees leaned over it, shouting. A few benches sat by a gravel path, at the mercy of the wind. She ventured to the water's edge, to be sheltered as much as possible by trees.

She sat on a rock which trailed grass in the current. Before reaching the waterfall, the river forked; the farther branch ran deeper into the park, bearing reflections of leaves and glimpses of sky amid its glittering. Like the Isar River which it fed, the Eisbach had a greenish chalky pallor, a muted color which helped coax her thoughts from hiding.

Yet now that she had contrived herself this chance to ponder, there seemed little that was painful to resolve. Perhaps simply being alone had given her thoughts room to fit together. After all, she trusted herself now; she was no longer desperate to deny what was happening to her. She wasn't going mad, nor was she secretly afraid that she might become so. She was growing, along with her gifts. Saving Bill had given her that strength, or had increased it. She felt less frustrated than expectant now.

Wasn't there still a risk of going too far? She thought not. At least, that was not the immediate risk. The real danger was that in developing, she might drift away from Bill. Why, he'd seemed to want her to admit that she wouldn't be able to find her way to the University—but she had a keen sense of direction now. He couldn't even adjust to this, the least of her new gifts.

In the city she could hear, piercing the uproar of the trees, the sound of chimes falling over one another, juggled unevenly by the wind. Was she approaching her problem in the wrong way? She ought not to let him restrict her development. But that seemed unfair. She was underrating him. Of course it would take him longer to adjust to what was happening, but she could help him if she really tried. Surely she knew him well enough for that.

Shadows reached over her, fishing in the river. Sunlight kept seizing the back of her head, which felt shaken by the wind, an ominous persistent feeling. She must remember that some kinds of weather confused her new perceptions. Still, she was growing calm; she had only to think of ways to guide Bill gently toward her revelations; in time she might find a proof which he would be unable to deny. One of the shadows that were reaching for her was a man's.

She turned hastily, almost slithering into the river. A dislodged rock fell, splashing her legs. He stood just behind and to the side of her, on the grass between the rocks and the gravel. The hood of his black duffel coat tried feebly to peer over his shoulder. Beneath his carefully trimmed and layered hair, his face resembled one of those she'd seen hovering all over Munich: smooth, symmetrical, difficult to read. Had he been looking at the river, or at her?

He was looking at her now. From his widening smile, she might have been a long-lost friend. She couldn't help feeling expectant, however uneasily. If only her senses weren't so muffled by the buffeting and clamor of the wind!

He moved closer before he spoke. "You're looking well. I am glad."

His accent sounded so English as to be almost a parody—as though he was straining to fit in with the garden. Never mind his accent: what about his words? Did she know him, as he obviously thought he knew her?

Amid a clutter of stray thoughts and stifled feelings, a memory was stirring. She *had* met him recently, briefly, but he looked somehow different—that was why she couldn't place him. Had he been at the party next door? No, she was instinctively sure he had nothing to do with Colin or Gladys.

"I'm sorry," she said, struggling to find her balance on the slippery rock. He was crowding her; why didn't he move back? "I believe we've met, but I can't recall—"

He was reaching for her, to help her up; that was why he hadn't stepped back. She felt on the edge of a slapstick disaster: what if she fell into the river and took him with her? Certainly he seemed to be stooping dangerously far. But his hand was strong, and now the other hand had closed around hers. She rose toward his smile.

Something was wrong. His smile had slipped awry, and so had the top of his head. There came a minute tearing sound as the wind scalped him. In a moment his hair was bobbing on the river, sailing away like a pelt of a small brown animal. So the slapstick had materialized—but she felt no urge at all to laugh.

"Please don't run away from me again," the bald man said.

XVII

When he let go of her hand she thought he was going to push her, but there was no need. She was on the edge of the rock; there was nowhere to go except backwards. She could hear the river trying to outshout the trees.

His smile was changing, with a dreadful slowness: his face looked like a recalcitrant mask. At last the grimace was firm. It looked intended to mock pity.

"I don't want to harm you." He showed no sign of moving back. "I just want you to listen to me."

"All right." Her voice felt as unwieldy as his face had seemed; she struggled to make it sound convincing. "I'll listen to you. I won't run away, but I'd like to sit down. Shall we sit on the bench over there?"

"You promise to listen? You won't—" His head began to turn—to judge how close the bench was, perhaps—then his gaze pounced back at her. "No, I can't take that chance. You've got away from me too often."

Her hands were shaking, as much with frustrated

rage as with fear. If she could just persuade him to take one step backward she could knee him in the groin, claw his face. If she tried that where she stood now, she would endanger herself as much as him.

He'd found a new expression, a lopsided grin which, on someone else, might have looked apologetic. "It's a good omen that we should meet here, don't you think?" he said. "Appropriate, I mean, to find a Rose in an English Garden."

Grotesquely, he was willing her to smile. She managed to force the corners of her lips to rise. If she could make him trust her, take him off his guard—

But he seemed to dislike what he saw in her face. With a visible effort he said, "I'm sorry. You're wondering how I know your name. Well, you see, I know all about you. I spent years finding out. I've been looking for you for years."

The worst of it was that he clearly felt he sounded reasonable. It was like having to guess both sides of a conversation when you could hear only one—except that the penalty for failure might be the river, or worse.

"I've read some of your work," he said. "The book of lines from films—I enjoyed that." His voice turned shrill, to show that he was quoting. "'Watch out for Sodomite patrols!'" he squealed.

He began to laugh, a dry clicking that seemed unable to escape from his throat. He was trying to ingratiate himself with her. Perhaps this was her chance. Prickling swarmed over the palms of her hands as she said, "I'm too near the edge. Could you step back a little?"

"Don't worry. Just tell me if you think you're falling. I'll catch you."

Her hands clenched, clawing at her palms. Her face must have betrayed her dismay, for he said sharply, "I don't know who's trying to trick me, but don't try. I don't want to do what I had to do to you in New York."

Surely she'd misheard him. Her mind felt ponderous, a swollen object in her head which his words couldn't quite touch. But he said, "I'm glad I didn't hurt you. I didn't want to do it, but you never gave me a chance to reach you. You were always with people. I had to make sure you wouldn't run away again."

His hands groped toward her, palms up. Should she leap before he pushed her? It might not be so easy; he might run faster than she swam, and drown her. In any case, his hands apparently meant to reassure her, to calm her down. That alone would have convinced her he was mad. Beyond that, she seemed unable to think.

"You understand I didn't set out to harm you." His voice crept through the uproar of the trees. "I couldn't take the chance of someone turning you against what I had to say, that's all. That's why I had to get you alone. You listen to too many people. You ought to be more careful. You're too trusting."

A gust of wind grappled with him, and sweat glistened in his eyebrows. He was near to panic himself, which made him far more dangerous. That was all the more reason why she mustn't panic, why she must smile at him, pretend she was willing to listen—for suddenly, from the corner of her eye, she had glimpsed a chance.

She managed to smile encouragement. It felt like a smile, surely that was how it looked. She mustn't look away from him, mustn't let his attention stray from her, for the glimpse was still there, at the edge of her vision: bright blue, bright yellow, moving between distant trees. Surely they were colors worn by people, who were approaching. She dared not look to be sure.

The bald man stared at her, as though they were challenging each other to blink. Her eyes felt smoldering, rough with ash; she could see each raw crack in his eyeballs. Sweat stung her palms. On the slippery rock, her legs had begun to tremble.

"I don't like your husband. We're going to have to think carefully about him."

It didn't matter what he said: the more he rambled, the better. She must smile as though he was being entirely reasonable. If he suspected that she thought otherwise, there was no telling what he might do. Her feet were cold from the soaking; she could no longer feel how near the edge she was. But the colors were approaching, and she was sure by now that they were glimpses of clothes. So long as he didn't notice until they were close enough—

"Well, we're alone now." She managed to speak without faltering, though her teeth felt desperate to chatter. "But you still haven't told me anything."

"I know that." He sounded dangerously resentful. Was there nothing that was safe to say to him? The two figures strolled closer, across the grass. Just let him talk another minute, just long enough for Rose to be sure she would be heard through the uproar—

"I hope you don't think it's easy for me." He was being reasonable again, but there was an edge to his voice. "Do you know how many times I've worked out what to say to you? And every time you were with someone, or someone got in the way before I could tell you. It's difficult enough to get clear in my mind so that you'll understand, without all that."

Her gaze was struggling to glance beyond his shoulder; a nerve dragged her mouth awry. "I'll do my best to understand," she pleaded.

"That's what you say now. Let me tell you, it won't be easy for you. I wish I could make it easier. You must brace yourself, that's all. There's no point in my beating around the bush, that will only make things worse for both of us. The simple truth is that when you were young, you were—"

Did he say "infested" or "infected"? As he turned, distracted by the crunch of gravel, the wind snatched the word. It didn't matter, for the two girls had reached the path.

They were teenagers. To Rose they looked dismayingly young; physically and emotionally they would be no match for him. That was why she didn't cry for help, but only called unevenly, "Excuse me, can you direct me to the University?"

The two girls stared at her. For a moment they

seemed content to smile; then one said, while her companion's smile grew apologetic, "Ich spreche nicht Englisch."

They didn't speak English, and were strolling onward, unconcerned. Rose tried to struggle past the bald man, and to remember the phrases on the emergency page of her phrasebook. She could think of none. "No, wait!" she cried. "Please wait—this man won't leave me alone!"

Her heel skidded on the rock. The river spat over her ankle, chill and soaking. Before she could regain her balance, he was holding her by the shoulder, not even exerting his strength. Only his hand prevented her from falling. He turned to the girls almost casually and addressed them in German.

He was talking about Rose, for both of them were gazing at her. Their expressions grew pitying and fearful. They spoke nervously to each other, and hurried away.

Rose began to fight. Never mind if she fell in the river; if the girls saw that, surely they would help her, no matter what he'd told them about her. She couldn't reach his face, for he was holding her at arm's length. As she raked at his hand, she felt his skin gather like dirt beneath her nails. She tried to kick, but the leg nearest him was her only support. "Help!" she cried, and remembering at last, "Hilfe! Hilfe!"

The teenagers glanced back as though afraid she might be chasing them. They ran over the bridge, and were gone. Beyond the bridge stood the post with the grille for calls for help. "Please, call the police!" Rose screamed. "Please! Polizei, Polizei!" But their retreating footfalls were lost amid the clamor of the trees.

Dry sobs interrupted her breath. She darted her hands at his eyes, not caring how much damage she did so long as she escaped. He grabbed her wrists deftly and dragged them down to her waist, pinioning her on the brink. Now she couldn't even overbalance him, a ruse which had occurred to her too late.

"Now you're going to listen to me." His voice resembled a terrier's: snarling, high-pitched, vicious. He was panting hot stale beer into her face. His eyes were glancing everywhere, and looked almost too swollen for their sockets. He was as afraid as she was.

"I'm sorry if you're frightened." He didn't sound sorry, and looked secretly gratified by her trembling. Perhaps he was a sadist as well as deranged. "But that can't be helped. You'd better get used to the idea of being frightened. You're going to be far more so."

Yes, he was excited by her fear; it seemed to make him feel strong. He pressed against her on the rock as though in a grotesque dance or a double suicide. Yet despite his closeness he seemed less oppressively vivid—for she was growing aware of something new.

"It will be a pity if you're harmed," he was saying with the daunting single-mindedness of a fanatic, but his words seemed distant, beyond the boundary of what was happening to her mind. Something was trying to break through her fear. She was afraid to let it come, for it was quite alien. Was it madness? Was that her only chance to escape him?

He seemed not to notice. "There are more important things than you," he was muttering. "The world must be purified before it's too late"—and all at once his words were only sounds, irrelevant to what had happened within her.

It was energy: that was what it must be, for it made her entire body tremble. It left her no room to be afraid of him, yet she couldn't welcome it, for it was too sudden, too unfamiliar. She was not at all sure that her body or her mind would be able to contain it—but even less could she control it. Would it overwhelm her, this torrent of power that was rising from the depths of her?

The bald man felt her trembling, and grinned into her face. He seemed about to speak. Without warning, as he stared into her eyes, his mouth began to jerk uncontrollably, wrenching his lips awry. She felt his hands grow clumsy with fear. They seemed not so much to let go of her wrists as to struggle free of any contact with her.

As she lunged at him, to escape the river's edge, he recoiled as though she were diseased. Had he known, part of her was as frightened as he was, for the power that flooded through her, sweeping her mind free of thoughts, seemed to have nothing to do with her. It was as though the power had borrowed her face for a mask, to glare out through her eyes.

He was backing away. A corner of a bench bit unnoticed into his thigh. "It doesn't matter what you do to me," he babbled. "There will always be others. I'm not alone."

Her eyes glared at him. Rose hid in a corner of her mind, observing. "You are wasting your time," her voice said.

Disinterestedly she watched him flee, slithering on the grass, stumbling to his feet. His dwindling figure seemed beneath her notice, as did his ravings, which she had already begun to forget. Nor did his identity matter. She felt that she knew, deep down, who and what he was, but it wasn't worth straining to reach the information. She failed to observe when he vanished into the distance. She was aware only of her power, which faded into the depths of her as a sunset is absorbed into the sky.

As it faded, and she realized she was whole, her gratitude welled up. The power had saved her, as nothing else could. Her trembling slowed, merged with the rhythms of her body. Her pulse grew calm. She was intensely aware of herself. She felt not at all exhausted, not even physically shaken. She began to feel a sense of enormous well-being. At last she had glimpsed the extent of her power. The newness had frightened her, but it was part of herself. Her mind and body felt transformed, aglow.

Eventually she recalled that she ought to meet Bill. Yes, she was late; he must have finished lecturing, no doubt he was waiting for her—but wait until he heard what she had to tell him! She strode into the shadow play beneath the trees.

But ought she to tell him? She needed nobody's help now. What would telling him achieve, except unnecessary trouble? Nevertheless she felt it was important, perhaps crucial, to tell him, though she couldn't quite understand why. Yes, it *was* worth the strain of persuading him. No, certainly he shouldn't be left alone to find out by himself how she was developing, nor—perhaps this was the true reason why she was anxious to tell him—should she be left alone with her powers. She began to hurry through the shadows of the trees which stooped over her, shutting out the light, leaving her half-blind. She must share her new self with him. It felt oddly vulnerable, overshadowed by looming. The sooner she found Bill, the better. She must find a way to coax him into believing, before it was too late—

Something reached for her mind and swallowed her thoughts.

Once, as a child, she had been given anesthetic. She'd struggled against the formlessness that had seeped into her mind, wiping out her thoughts. She had been afraid that when she woke she would no longer be Rosalind. But this new invader was far worse than anesthetic, for it was not formless. Only because it had settled over her mind, like preying wings, was she unable to glimpse its form.

She cried out and clutched her forehead, as though to cage her thoughts. Trees shook and roared in the deserted park. Her cries were lost in the flood of sound. Now even the uproar was receding, or her mind was completely engulfed. The last of her thoughts was lulled, hushed. She could not even cling to her panic.

She was walking. Paths met paths, trees spread carpets of shadow for her. Before she reached the University, she met Bill. He was strolling along the edge of the park, and looked pleased with himself.

"See, you couldn't find your way after all," he said, grinning. So that was why he was pleased. "Were did you get to?"

She couldn't think. She was struggling in darkness, about to panic. Then a memory lit up: the endless pouring of the waterfall, the chorus of the trees. She must have lost track of time there. "I was walking by the Eisbach," she said.

"Did anything happen? You look a bit pale."

"No," she said at once, surprised by the question. "Nothing at all."

XVIII

As the plane left the ground the last raindrops streamed away from the windows, barring the glass with translucent lines. Soon the glass was clear. The dwindling landscape brightened and grew precise, an abstract composition of a multitude of varied rectangles. Microscopic villages drifted through veils of cloud; roofs sparkled minutely, pinpoint windows glinted and vanished. Lakes filled slowly with light, scored with tiny ripples, then dimmed. As the plane climbed, Rose saw buildings scattered over the land like pale dust; some of the grains were arranged in lines. The landscape fell away, and the plane emerged above the clouds, a bright still field of almost insubstantial curls.

Before long she felt cramped. The man in front of her insisted on reclining his seat as far as it would go. She was trapped in a wedge-shaped cell. The seat belt seemed restricting as an infant's harness; her feet shared space with a carrier bag full of books and liquor. The slipstream was a constant roaring in her ears. She tugged at the plastic tube above her, to gain herself a fraction more of air.

When the meal was served, the man sat up—but as soon as he'd finished, his seat slumped back again. Bill had fallen asleep; his forearms levered at the folding shelf, edging his plastic tray of debris closer to a fall. Rose passed the tray to the stewardess and was dragged back into her seat by the belt.

She was bored. Her discomfort made the window seem too small, a dwarfed fragment of a boundless glare of blue and white, like an epic film reduced to television. The journey was too short for an in-flight movie. The books at her feet were all in German. She leafed desultorily through the glossy *Lufthansa Logbook*. At last she was driven to gazing at the safety instructions. Red arrows poked at cartoon passengers, who leaned forward in attitudes of despair, clutching their heads. Passengers slid down a yellow chute and hurried away; in their haste they'd left their mouths on the plane. A woman helped a child don a life jacket. Panic had frozen the child's face into a blank mask, identical in three pictures. However the woman turned her head, its outline remained exactly the shape of a strawberry.

Rose sank back and, closing her eyes, retreated to memories. Gerhard had liked Jack, and they'd agreed to work together. Gerhard had placed the Josef Dietrich interview in *Der Stern*. Diana was still coaxing Jack toward making her his secretary. The Aschheim house had felt full of success and the promise of success.

Occasionally Rose had caught Diana glancing at her when she thought Rose wasn't looking. She'd seemed anxious, puzzled, almost wary. Was she daunted by Rose's growing sense of inner strength? Well, she was very young in many ways; that was why Rose was fond of her, perhaps too indulgently. Touring Bavaria with Diana had been like showing the world to a child, and she remembered Diana's cries of delight as vividly as the places and events themselves: the Wieskirche, whose interior shone with gilding and golden frescoes, like a shrine to sunset; Neuschwanstein Palace, Ludwig II's castle high in the pines, the walls of its rooms and halls like a feverish dream of an art gallery; men sailing high as mountains, beneath great triangular gliders, soaring from Alpine peaks where flowers grew that could be found nowhere else in the world.

Still, she was glad to be going home. She glimpsed the swarming of Ormskirk market. Why had she thought of that? Ormskirk wasn't her home now. Her thoughts were beginning to drift. As she blinked herself awake, she almost had another glimpse: a nightmare in Munich—she must have dreamed something there, and forgotten. She tried to grasp it, but it was lost. She'd better stay awake until the flight was over. She didn't want to risk losing her sense of her body, not here.

Why not?

The thought made her mind leap. That was the way to escape her cramping. At once, not only her seat belt but her entire body felt constricting. Ouside, just beyond the shell of the plane, the clouds were loftier than mountains, more untrodden than the highest snowfield, and beyond them was the freedom of the sky; yet she was trapped in the cabin. She need only let go in order to break free of the shell.

With an effort she controlled her thoughts. She mustn't allow herself to be tempted. She might get lost, blinded by clouds or by her awe. The sky was too large, too high. She mustn't risk it. But her mind was possessed by a yearning for freedom. Was she being too careful, perhaps?

Sooner or later she would have to discover whether she could leave her body at will. That must be a necessary step toward controlling her experiences. Could anywhere be safer than here? The sky was clear of danger; it looked pure, unblemished. Her intuition told her it was right to try—and it had been her intuition that had saved Bill. She should try. She was confident of being able to return at will.

How could she coax herself to leave? Now that she examined it, the idea seemed ridiculous. The cabin was too solidly present: the patrolling stewardesses, the oppressively muffled roar of air, the feeble breaths from the dwarfish throat of the air conditioning, the lolling heads of dozing passengers, all dragged her back into the everyday. But that was irrelevant. She need only trust herself, let her instincts guide her out of the trap of the cabin.

She let her eyes close. Once she relaxed, her instincts would do the rest. "To think of moving—" The muffled roaring sounded to her as though the sky was trapped. Imagine the fields of the sky, wider than the world—At once a stranger was lurking behind her, pressing close: her body.

Too fast! The cabin snapped into violent focus as she retreated into her body: stale tobacco smoke sneaking down the cabin from the smokers' territory, a child whining tunelessly and constantly as the jets, another child intoning a toneless plea: "Have my sweets now. Have my sweets now"—the trap of boredom.

She lay back, to give her body time to relax. She hadn't realized her control would be so effortless; that was all that had shocked her. Now that she knew how easy it was, now that she knew how it would feel, she could prepare to try again.

She coaxed her mind to widen. It flowered gradually. She let it reach out without straining, let it venture to consider the breadth of the sky, the promise of greater freedom than her mind could grasp. She felt the thoughts possess her, but the sense of dislocation from her body was more subtle, hardly perceptible. She knew only that the cabin felt suddenly more claustrophobic—because she was closer to the ceiling.

She was gazing down at the lolling heads. If she looked, she would see that one of them was hers. That was unimportant. She could bear the cell no longer. The ceiling felt oppressive as fog, but it was ridiculously thin, no barrier at all. Certainly it could not restrain her.

At once she was free, and transformed into light.

It seemed to overwhelm all her senses. It annihilated time. She was buoyed up by the light, possessed by it. Though the sky and the clouds were blinding, the sensation was in no way painful. The winds that tugged at the edges of clouds passed straight through her. The sensation was intensely exhilarating. She felt full of a shout of joy that would resound through the whole of the sky—except that she had no voice.

Either the first shock of freedom was less prolonged than it felt, or her instincts were guiding her, for she found she was still hovering beside the plane. Passengers were lined up like peas in a metal pod which lumbered across the sky. Their heads in the windows resembled dolls' heads, arranged in ranks too symmetrical to be real. Beyond a window, one head was her own.

For the first time that sight was less disorienting than reassuring. The plane was keeping her body safe for her. She felt detached from the momentary pang of apprehension. She was superior to it and to the contents of the plane, including her body. If anything, she ought to be less vulnerable out here than in the plane. Here she was in absolute control.

Ecstasy seized her. She soared above the plane, plummeted toward it, swooped away. Not even a hawk could have been so effortlessly skillful. The shining clouds swayed enormously, the sky danced with her. She was tempted to fly in the face of the plane, an ecstatic challenge. Suppose the pilot saw her? To risk

distracting him was irresponsible. Her power demanded self-discipline. She turned and plunged into
the clouds.

They felt like snow blindness. Pure white engulfed
her. They felt less solid than Rose, a dream of
snowdrifts. Their piercing chill was no dream; it was
exhilaratingly real.

When she emerged, the plane was half a mile away.
She sped to catch it, not in panic but for the joy of
flight. The plane seemed likeably absurd as it plodded
bulkily onward over the clouds. It kept her company on
the awesome luminous plateaus above the world. For a
while she played with it, swooping around it, making it
turn nose over tail, a gigantic toy. She felt no vertigo at
all.

At last she ascended as high as she dared go. The
clouds became small islands on a misty sea. The 747
was a glinting pin with minute wings, far below. On the
horizon, where she could see the curve of the world, a
microscopic jet plane threaded clouds with molten
wire.

Now she could see whole countries. The world
looked too small to reclaim her; its hold on her was
weakening. Her awe was close to terror, and it was
lifting her free of the pull of the world.

She sensed the infinite darkness beyond the thinning
sky. It was colder than she could bear to contemplate.
Either it was infinitely lifeless, or alive in ways her mind
could not encompass. Was part of the darkness leggy
and alert? She was possessed by a vertigo far worse
than physical giddiness. The world was only a speck in
the darkness. In a moment she would lose it, she would
be alone in the dark—or perhaps not alone.

All at once her terror seized her. It was bearing her
away; she was falling into the darkness. The world had
no hold on her, nor had her body, that submicroscopic
speck contained in a pinpoint of metal which hovered
above the dot of the world. It was the ultimate

childhood nightmare of being lost in the dark—and the dark was reaching out for her with its infinite limbs.

Without warning its power faltered, seemed to flinch back like a spider whose web had been torn. She was no longer alone with the dark. She hardly dared grasp what she felt, not because it might prove to be untrue but because it might grow clearer. Somewhere, so distant that her mind recoiled from imagining, a presence was aware of her.

That was scarcely comforting. Even in the midst of her panic, she could only be grateful that her sense of it was so numbed and blurred. Was it a single entity, or many? Perhaps it was both, and more. It seemed vaster than a country, and she feared to glimpse even a hint of what it was.

Yet the sense that her plight was being disinterestedly observed gave her back some sense of herself. She was both the soaring victim of the edge of space and the germ which was her body, though both were invisible to her; the two of her were linked. Minute though it was, she had grasped the concept of her body now. It was a thread that would lead her back—it was stronger than gravity.

With a plunge that would have torn any breath from her, she swooped toward the world, the bright cross of the plane. Roaming winds shrilled through her, then she felt the arms of the seat beneath her arms, the cushion behind her head, the buckle resting on her waist. It seemed almost too easy a victory, but it appeared she was quite safe.

She kept her eyes closed while she settled into her body. Its solidness was profoundly reassuring. She lay experiencing each muscle, the whole of her flesh and skin, until her body felt like armor which nothing could penetrate.

At last she opened her eyes. A dream fluttered within Bill's eyelids. Heads slumped, dozing. She checked her feeling of superiority; she mustn't allow it to tempt her.

She must learn her capabilities but, above all, avoid unnecessary risks. She was venturing into a transformed world where anywhere might be inhabited and nowhere was entirely safe. Bill was muttering in an incomprehensible language of dream. She smiled at him, glad of the reminder. No power was too costly or too dangerous while it helped her keep him safe.

PART THREE

EARTHBOUND

XIX

Something made Rose look out of the window.

Had it been movement? At first that seemed un-likely. The garden lay torpid beneath the August sun. The parched grass was straw yellow, almost white. The clear blue sky looked solid as a backdrop. The bricks of the garden wall were a battle of blazing reds. The trees above the wall appeared to shimmer, green fire poised on the instant of gushing upward, into the sky.

She glanced toward the greenhouse. Its panes were almost opaque with light, and resembled metal. Through the glare she could just distinguish vines, which climbed frames in the center of the greenhouse. Their leaves crowded some of the panes that faced her. Gladys had been watering the vines, but mustn't know how to prune them, if that was what one did with vines. It looked like a jungle in there. Perhaps Rose ought to read up on greenhouses—she shouldn't leave Gladys to do all the work.

Of course, Gladys must be in there now; that was what had attracted Rose's attention. Yes, there was movement beyond the panes. The glare, and the patches of condensation on the panes, made it look unhealthily pale. Rose was squinting irritably, trying to disentangle her vision from the net of vines and be sure it was Gladys, when the percolator boiled.

She carried a mug upstairs to Bill. He was sitting in their workroom, head on one side, staring into the trees. One hand was splayed on his scalp, fingertips digging in; it looked as though he was trying painfully to trap thoughts. Before him on the desk lay their workbook.

"Are you stuck?"

"What?" His fingers leapt away from his skull; tousled hair tumbled over his forehead. "No, not really." But he was gazing at his unfinished sentence on the page as if there were no chance of remission.

"There's no need to rush it, is there? It's not as if there's a deadline. We still have the rest of the summer."

"Yes, I'm aware of that."

Of course she shouldn't interrupt him, but usually they helped each other past temporary blocks. She set down the mug in front of him and glanced into the garden. From up here the greenhouse was easy to observe, and it was empty.

"Was Gladys in the greenhouse before?"

"I really wouldn't know. I've been trying to do something with this." He was glaring at the book as though it was a student's deplorably inadequate essay. "Oh, get away," he muttered, and it took her a moment to realize that he was snarling at a dangling lock of hair.

She went downstairs slowly, growing depressed. It wasn't Bill's irritability, though that had been increasing, nor the unwieldiness of their new book. In fact the book seemed unimportant, and perhaps that was the problem.

Though her skill as a writer had suddenly grown, though she was all at once able effortlessly to marshal thoughts and ideas, the task seemed minor, little more than a hobby. It no longer involved her enough to be satisfying. She felt there were more important tasks for her to perform—but she had no idea what they were.

Nothing spectacular had happened since the flight

from Munich. At first she'd felt afraid to be tempted into another ecstasy, but gradually she'd realized she had control. Now and then, prompted by instinct, she made herself aware of her entire body, strengthening her control. That was all that was necessary; she didn't need Bill as an anchor—but she loved him, however frustrating his stolidity was sometimes. She loved him, and that was something she must never lose.

Surely there was no danger of that. If she must keep her new gifts to herself, hadn't she the strength to do so? They weren't so overwhelming: they'd sharpened her memory, improved her control of her mind; her intuitions were keener, she experienced places more vividly. None of that was difficult to handle.

But she felt there was more to come. The sense of imminence frustrated her, muffled her intuitions. If there were to be further developments, couldn't she glimpse at least a hint? Still, she ought not to force her growth, in case she overreached herself. If she couldn't trust her instincts now, she could trust nothing.

She slid open the patio doors of the dining room and sat outside on Bill's homemade rustic bench, leafing through the new *Film Comment*. Sunlight rebounded from the glossy pages; the print appeared to char. The David Tracy interview read well. She couldn't detect the strain of Bill's questioning.

A gout of dark blood squeezed out of a harebell and flew away humming. Grasshoppers made the lawn buzz like wire. Behind her the house gaped dimly as a cave, as though transformed by an ominous mystery. When she could hear the nagging of the mystery no longer, she fetched the letter from the sideboard. As she unfolded it, the photocopy paper squeaked beneath her nails. It felt unnatural, a parody of paper, and looked like the ghost of a page.

My dear Heinrich, Ignatius Loyola,
    Do not take as my last word the testament which I plan to issue, as-those cowards who are eager to

betray me will do. Do not be disheartened if some of those whom I appoint to rule Germany betray me. You and Goebbels know that time does not matter, for now we have allies who are not ruled by time. I look forward to the death of my body, for then I shall shed that suspicion which has been my companion for so long, that this flesh is poisoned.

You know that time, above all, was the enemy I fought to overcome. Now I am victorious, and it is my ally. It will destroy my enemies and multiply those men and women of character who will destroy the poisoners of all nations.

Those men and women must not mistake the death of my body for my death. These words are meant for them. They will take my words as a promise of the dawn of that day of which we spoke. You and Goebbels must instruct disciples, who will spread my word that the day will be soon when I, and others of my kind, will lead mankind in purging itself of international Jewry and its henchmen, and those others whose poison hinders mankind from reaching its goal.

Do not lost courage. Those whose purposes are true will soon rediscover the secrets of which we have spoken. Those secrets were lost in order that they might not be misused by creatures without character, who are not fit to learn them. The day of the true leaders of mankind is soon. They will deal ruthlessly with all imperfection in order to achieve mankind's goal. When I speak again, and call myself by name, you will know that the new day has dawned.

(A. Hitler)

Rose folded the letter quickly. When she'd stuffed it back into the envelope, she wiped her fingers on her skirt. Of course he had been mad. If Himmler had received the letter, would he have betrayed his leader?

Rose thought so—surely he couldn't have been so deluded. The letter seemed too blatantly deranged to be a forgery. One thought disturbed Rose: assuming that Hitler had been psychically gifted, had his gifts destroyed his mind?

She picked out Diana's covering letter. The envelope bulged as though the Hitler page was trying to force its way out, protruding a slick gray tongue. "That is one weird letter," was all that Diana said. "Jack isn't sure if it's worth showing around. Maybe you could research Hitler's involvement with the occult and build an article around the enclosed? I can give you one strange detail to research: the occult meaning of April 30, when Hitler had himself killed . . ."

Bill emerged into the garden and stood blinking. He looked taken aback by the brightness, almost tearful; his face seemed to shrink into itself. "The thirtieth of April," Rose said. "Does that mean anything to you?"

"Why should it mean anything to me?"

"It doesn't matter. If it isn't in the diary I can ring the library."

"Oh, don't bother. It's Walpurgisnacht, the German equivalent of Halloween, when all things evil are supposed to—oh, you know the sort of nonsense."

Neither his mockery nor the sunlight entirely reassured her. The lips of the swollen envelope were being forced wider. "That's strange," she muttered, almost to herself. "Why would he plan to have himself killed just on that date?"

"Because he was mad." She was about to nod dubious agreement when he said, "I wish you wouldn't swallow everything she says."

"What on earth do you mean?"

"Diana. You're letting her influence you far too much. Really, Ro, I'm surprised at you." He sounded almost jealous. "Falling for a young girl like that."

"If you dislike her so much you shouldn't have invited them here."

"It isn't a question of disliking her. Besides, if Jack's employing her then we have to put up with her, I suppose. But when you two get together—"

"Yes?" she said ominously. "Go on."

"I don't know what you talk about, that's all, and it worries me. The way you sloped off for hours together in Munich, for example."

"Oh, Bill, don't be ridiculous. You say *you're* surprised at *me,* but really—"

"Never mind saying I'm ridiculous." Apparently she'd scraped a hidden wound, but before she could touch it more gently he demanded, "What about New York? Are you going to deny that? You smoked pot with her the night I met Tracy, didn't you?"

The nerve jerked into life beside her mouth. "No, as a matter of fact, I did not. But I wouldn't need your permission to do so."

"You don't need me for anything. You certainly don't care about my feelings." He was plucking at his moustache, flicking away hairs. "Don't do that," she said irritably, but he was bullying onward: "After all we talked about, you're still getting rubbish from the library. What's this latest item—*Astral* bloody *Rape?* What kind of garbage is that?"

When the library informed her that they were holding the book, she'd left the card on the sideboard; she certainly didn't intend to hide it from him. "I don't know what kind of book it is," she said in an attempt to calm him down, "since I haven't read it. But after what we heard in Munich it interests me."

"That's another thing. That bloody fool and his forged letter—how in God's name could you take them seriously? I'd expect it of Diana, but never of you."

His skepticism seemed unbearably ponderous. Worse, she was beginning to feel the same about him. His childhood had made him skeptical of all faiths, but couldn't he ever grow? Not only was he locked into his mind—he seemed determined to possess hers too.

Her resentment chose her words. "Listen, Bill, I think it's about time you tried to understand. There are things I haven't told you. You know I've been having premonitions—yes, you do, don't let yourself deny it! There was the time the brakes failed, and the time I saved you on the stairs at Gerhard's. I saw that was going to happen, and I saved you. You know perfectly well that I couldn't have seen it ordinarily. Diana has premonitions too—she knew something was wrong that day in her building. Bill, don't you see that if we hadn't trusted these feelings neither you nor I might even be alive now?"

"You're right about one thing—I *don't* understand." Sunlight on his glasses shuttered his eyes. "I can't understand how this can have gained such a hold over you. Suppose you have had a couple of premonitions? Nearly everyone has them. If you have them often you're bound to be right some of the time."

"There's more to it than that. I don't only think so, I *know*. Don't you trust my judgment any more?"

"Let me finish." He held up one hand, like a traffic policeman—but a secret doubt tweaked the skin around his eyes. "Just suppose your premonitions were genuine? How can you allow them to delude you into believing the rest of this nonsense? I don't understand you any more. Half the time I don't know what you're thinking or feeling. You aren't what I married."

Through her anger she felt a momentary but violent fear of being left alone. At once she grew angry with her fear. "I'm beginning to feel you aren't quite what I bargained for either. You can't own me or my thoughts, Bill."

"It isn't a question of owning. It's a question of sharing, and we aren't doing much of that. My God!" he said, close to rage, "you talk as if it's all my fault—as if I won't come halfway to meet you! What about you, for Christ's sake? You're so deep in yourself I can't reach you. You don't even know what's happening to you." He strode into the house, his glasses glaring blindly. "You just wait here. By God, I'll show you something."

Though the sunlight seemed to be intensifying, Rose felt cut off from the heat. She was furious that he'd trapped her into this squabble, which seemed not worth her time—but that feeling was also a trap. She mustn't let herself think that their marriage was no longer worth the effort. Her new gifts weren't worth that hidden price. Besides, some of his accusations were true. To dismiss him as lacking in perceptiveness and sensitivity was both unfair to him and dangerous to their marriage.

When he reappeared he was carrying their workbook. He looked abashed and reluctant, but he began at once: "I wish I didn't need to say this, but we've got to talk about it. You aren't writing as you used to."

He sounded as though he was criticizing a student, not a collaborator. "Listen, this is the sort of thing I mean: 'Laughton's paroxysms of disgust with his hunchbacked body draw on the actor's own disgust with what he regarded as his own deformed sexuality'—well, I suppose that can pass, though I don't think very many people are interested in Laughton any more. But look here, what about this: 'In *David Copperfield* (1935), the first closeup of Basil Rathbone's Mr. Murdstone smoking a pipe looks exactly like a preliminary sketch for Rathbone's Sherlock Holmes of four years later, so that Murdstone's unrelenting repression casts a disturbing light on Holmes's emotionless insights . . .' How many people will get anything out of that?"

"But I won't suppress my insights. That won't improve our books."

He glanced at her; a glare of sunlight exploded in front of his eyes. "I didn't realize you thought they needed improving. You used to be quite proud of them. Look," he said more gently, "I've read through all this, and I've tried to be objective. I can see you're trying to

do something new, but it hasn't helped the book.
You've lost touch with our readers."

"Which readers?"

"The ones who've helped us to succeed. Listen, Ro,
some of this reads like an encyclopedia. It's just facts
and insights, no personality there at all. That's not why
people buy our books. They aren't students who are
being paid to learn. They want humor, they want to be
entertained, and I thought we were quite proud to be
able to do so. You don't want to throw that away, do
you?"

Beside her mouth the nerve felt like a splinter.
"Well, I expect you can do the popularizing."

"Yes, I suppose that's about my level."

How many of these hidden wounds were there? How
long had he been brooding, hiding his thoughts from
her? "Oh, Bill, we don't need to argue like this. Don't
you think we should try sometimes to reach a different
audience—people who know about films? Don't you
think we should be striving constantly to develop?"

"No, I don't. We know what we're good at, and
frankly I think that's writing, more than lecturing. How
can you just dismiss our popularity?"

"By that standard Harold Robbins is the greatest
living writer. Oh, for heaven's sake, Bill, aren't you
ever dissatisfied?"

"Yes, ever since you started turning into someone
else." The discs of light which hid his eyes made her
think of pennies on a dead man's. "I know you're
dissatisfied," he said sadly. "I've known ever since you
told Jack that at last we would be adding to the
literature of cinema. At last was what you meant,
wasn't it? I think you saw that didn't please Jack too
greatly, either."

She mustn't be drawn deeper into the squabble.
They'd never had this kind of argument, the kind that
reduced to ammunition everything they'd shared, to be
hurled at each other as viciously as possible. She

wouldn't be reduced to such banality. But wasn't that resolve simply another way of feeling superior to him?

"Listen, I'll tell you how I feel," he said. "I feel like Joel McCrea in that Preston Sturges movie—I'm happy to entertain the people. To reach the people—that's some achievement, you know. Now you seem to want to wander off into elitism. Well, there's no use trying to involve me in that. It doesn't tempt me at all."

She couldn't believe he was serious; his speech sounded bombastic enough for the worst of Hollywood. "Oh, Bill," she said half-laughing, "this working-class heroism isn't like you."

His face grew bland with suppressed rage. "It's obviously more like me than you've bothered to realize." When he spoke again, his sadness seemed almost disinterested. "I don't think you're aware how much you've changed."

He turned violently. Colin was standing in his office, smiling at them. "Come inside," Bill muttered. "I don't want that damned twat involved."

She'd had enough. "I'm going for a walk."

"In that case I'll try and make sense of this book."

"No doubt you'll do better without me to hinder you."

By the time she reached the field beyond the Fulwood Park hedge, she felt caged. He meant to lock her up in dullness, in his refusal to look beyond the known. He had everything he'd aimed and worked for, and he wasn't prepared to risk a fraction of it—but how long had he numbered her among his possessions? He must adjust to her growth or lose her: just now she didn't care which.

The worst of it was that she felt he didn't trust her. He thought she was incapable of coping with her growth. Or was it possible that he still didn't believe in her gifts? Surely not even he could be so stolid.

She felt oppressed by his lack of faith in her. It was a barrier which cut her off from the wide bleached field,

the bottomless blue sky, the swarming of light on the
Mersey. A liner, which looked weightless, glided
leisurely by. Gulls wheeled, bright as fragments of the
highest cloud. She was tempted to lie in the grass and
drift wherever she might.

That wouldn't help. She mustn't use her gift as a drug
to escape the problems of her marriage; all too soon it
might become addictive. To choose not to abuse her
gift—that was a kind of strength, certainly. She
strolled, and at last the August day touched her, melted
the barrier. Darkness was somewhere near—in the
future, perhaps? A train plunged roaring beneath
Fulwood Park, and she thought uneasily of the crawling
infested earth.

XX

When Rose set aside the book she felt pleased with
herself. At least she'd learned enough to make a start.
Her mind had grown quicker, greedy for information,
able to retain more. Surely that was a gift for which she
could be wholly grateful.

The sky was closing. Darkness rolled lethargically
toward the horizon. The bleached grass seemed to give
out light which it had stored. The house felt stuffed
with dull heat.

Gladys was still in the greenhouse, as far as Rose
could tell. She had glimpsed movement in there while
reading. Well, she'd learned enough from the book to
be able to help—she'd collaborate with Gladys for a
change.

That was unfair: she must stop using Bill as a scapegoat. She couldn't expect him to make an effort without expecting as much of herself. Yesterday evening they'd hardly spoken to each other; they had treated each other like invalids, wary of touching in case that reopened a wound. Their marriage had been so rational, so settled in its peace, that the confrontation had been all the more painful. Now that it was over, they'd tried to outdo each other in forbearance: "I'll make dinner." "No, that's all right, I'll do it." "That's perfectly all right. I will." If only they had been able to laugh at all this—but they were shrunken into themselves. In bed they had lain apart. Bill had slept first, loudly.

Late this morning he'd woken her gently. "I have to go down to the library. Shall we meet at the Grapes about six and eat at Zorba's? Then we can relax a bit and talk." It seemed he intended to forget their argument, until he said, so reluctantly but apologetically that she couldn't help loving him, "If you like I'll get your astral book for you while I'm at the library."

She took him too much for granted. She must take the trouble to understand him. Of course he had to research the last of their interviewees, whom he would meet at the National Film Theater—but had he chosen to do so today in order to let her read over her work by herself, or did he simply mean to leave their book alone until they'd talked? She'd told him not to borrow *Astral Rape;* she wasn't sure now that she wanted to bother with it—and besides, he might have taken the chance to read it first and prepare his objections.

Perhaps he was right: perhaps her writing was becoming too introverted. She would read it over when they'd talked. To free it from introversion would be a kind of growth, after all. She must get closer to Bill to compensate for her development. It had been difficult enough for her to accept: how much more so, then, for him!

That was enough sitting and thinking. She was being introverted about trying not to be introverted, for heaven's sake. It was time she helped Gladys. Reflections obscured the panes of the greenhouse, but she hadn't seen Gladys emerge.

The dark sky was thick and sluggish. Reflected clouds oozed through the greenhouse. The lawn was a network of livid scratches. Dimness nested in the trees, shifting restlessly. The threat of a storm seemed to cling to her skull like a cap, sizes too small. As she hurried down the garden, parched claws of grass scraped her ankles.

She pulled open the door to the greenhouse and halted, dismayed.

At first sight the interior seemed fertile as a jungle, and as overgrown. Melons and cucumbers swelled from beds of soil; above them on shelves, tomatoes dangled beneath leaves; vine leaves fountained over the ceiling and cascaded down. Humidity swarmed prickling over her skin. None of this had halted her. It was the stench of rottenness.

For a moment she had to hold dizzily onto the doorframe. Could Gladys really be in there? Yes, she could hear movement within. Gladys must be hidden by the tangle of vines which climbed down the center of the greenhouse, from the tubs of earth two feet high and almost as wide. The vines looked neglected now.

A breeze hissed through the dry grass and tugged at the back of her T-shirt, peeling it away from her skin. At least the breeze might clear the stench a little. The thickening sky made her feel irritable, apprehensive. Get it over with, for heaven's sake. Taking a deep breath, she strode in.

She had to slow down, for the closer she came, the more she could see that was rotten. The skins of the melons had split, exuding green froth. Most of the tomatoes were black; several lay burst on the concrete path. Traces of puddles remained in dips in the concrete. The place looked as though it had been half-drowned and then abandoned.

No use blaming Gladys. Could she have done any better herself, before she'd read the book? She could imagine Gladys's clumsy efforts: well-meaning, agonized, trapped in self-doubt. She shouldn't have left Gladys alone with the task.

Her held breath was nearly exhausted. She made herself hurry to the far end of the greenhouse. For a moment she thought that the shrivelled cucumbers had broken out in boils, then she saw that the excrescences were whitish and writhing. Did she glimpse movement in one of the tubs? Never mind. She rushed herself past the vines, before her breath gave out. But Gladys was not there.

There was nowhere she could hide. Beyond the vines were only beds of strawberries. All of the fruit was blackened; some resembled clusters of glistening eggs, which had hatched grubs. On the windows above them, more vines were paralyzed in the act of groping for a way out. Rose felt caged by green, which glowed sullenly; as the daylight failed, the presence of green intensified—the presence of rottenness, which was overwhelming her.

Nonsense. In a moment she'd go out, before it was too dark to find her way over the splattered path. First she wanted to see what she'd heard moving. Had an animal strayed in? Straining her breath through her fingers, she peered into the corners. The vine leaves were a lair of shadows; where leaves sagged against the panes, condensation gathered like gray scum. There was no sign of movement, except outside, beyond the panes.

It was not beyond the panes. It was behind her, reflected: a vague incomplete bulk, swaying toward her.

She whirled. "Oh, you damn fool," she gasped at herself. It was only the mass of vines above the tubs;

they were swaying in a breeze which had managed at last to penetrate the greenhouse. The same breeze swung the door with a slight creak, swung it closed. No need to worry: the door didn't lock. Six quick steps and she would be out of the greenhouse—except that between her and the door, something was moving.

She stood absolutely still. The breeze was blundering about outside the panes, which vibrated faintly. Yes, there was another sound. Though it was less indeterminate than when she'd mistaken it for Gladys, it was still difficult to distinguish. It was large, and sounded sluggish or crippled. It might be wakening slowly or doing its best, with its deformed body, to make no noise.

That was ridiculous: how could she know such details when she could see nothing? Perhaps a tramp had crept in here to sleep and was trying to crawl out without being seen—but would even a tramp take refuge in a place like this? She thought of things that grow in rottenness. It occurred to her that the growth of rot in the greenhouse seemed too quick, too total.

Never mind thinking. Just get out. She was strong enough now not to panic. She need only stride out of the greenhouse before panic could reach her, before it robbed her of control. Her imagination was treacherous, and might conspire with whatever was lurking, put her at its mercy.

She began to tiptoe forward. The panes looked coated with dimness; green rot crowded her, glowing luridly. Everything was intensely present, uncomfortably close. Cucumbers protruded from beneath their leaves, like stumps of shrivelled limbs; tomatoes hung like bags of rot; the cracked lips of melons foamed. On the concrete, spilled seeds gleamed on burst tomato skins.

Before she reached the wooden tubs, she saw movement between her and the door.

She had to clench her teeth in the flesh of her wrist to

stop her gasp. Then her teeth began to part in a weak
smile. Again the movement had been nothing but the
vines, which were swaying feebly, irregularly. Perhaps
that was what she'd heard before; perhaps that had
conspired with her overheated imagination, the dimness, the humidity oppressive as fever, to scare her—

How could the vines stir in a breeze when the door
was shut?

She gazed at them with a kind of fascinated despair.
Their movement was not entirely irregular. They were
being thrust apart with painful slowness by whatever
stood behind them, if it was standing.

Now the sounds were far too clear. They sounded
moist and tentative, but determined. She thought their
source was clumsy, lopsided as an infant, but she could
tell it was considerably larger than an infant—perhaps
incomplete, then. A muffled creaking told her that it
was clambering out of one of the tubs of earth.

Something glimmered through the tangle of vines.
She didn't dare turn away, but she tried not to see, to
be aware only of her hand groping behind her, along
the shelf. Surely there must be a weapon, surely—

Her fingers sank into a fruit which felt like a balloon
bloated with slime. She mustn't recoil, mustn't take
time to shudder, only to reach out, sure there was a
weapon that she'd glimpsed before. Her fingertips
touched metal: a point, not very sharp, in fact quite
blunt; a bunch of tines which entangled her fingers,
threatening to make her jerk nervously and hurl the
weapon to the floor. Then she had grasped them, and
began to draw the gardening fork stealthily toward
her.

There was a gap in the vines now. She couldn't see
what had pushed them apart, but something gleamed
beyond the gap. Though it seemed to have the texture
of flesh, it was moist, and the color of lard. If it was
peering at her, why could she see no features at all?

She gripped the handle of the fork so hard that it

bruised her palm, and tried to force herself to step forward. Now—now, before it grew stronger, before she saw its face! Her feet might as well have merged with the concrete; she could hardly feel them. Now— before it sensed her fear! All at once she remembered that she'd felt this fear of drawing attention to herself before, on the night when the séance next door had awakened the presence.

The thing was only waiting for her to reach the vines. Even if it couldn't move fast, no doubt it could topple toward her like a spilling of entrails. Once she saw it clearly, that would hold her paralyzed until it could totter high enough to embrace her.

Why couldn't she smash her way out of the green-house? It was only glass. But how badly might she injure herself? How long would it take her to escape? Long enough for the whitish thing to clamber out of hiding, to flop closer, closer, as she struggled amid broken glass?

Without warning her control gave way. What flooded her was not so much panic as rage—rage with herself for having ventured in here, with the gathering storm for having muffled her instincts, with the lurker for reducing her to the state of a terrified child. She lurched forward, the fork poised to stab and gouge. "Don't you dare touch me," she cried, "you—"

God, she'd called attention to herself! Drawing back her arm so far that it blocked her vision, she stabbed viciously at the gap in the vines—so viciously that she missed. The vines entangled the fork, dragging it down. The force of her blow overbalanced her. As the net of vines fell toward her, her free hand plunged into the gap and touched something.

Perhaps it was leaves, a slippery mass of leaves grown together so close that they felt like an unbroken surface, but how could they feel so cold? How could leaves writhe, snuggle slimily against her palm? She wanted desperately to believe they were only leaves,

that her hand had simply thrust between them, that
her fingers hadn't really sunk deep into a soft mass.
She threw herself backward, and managed to keep
hold of the fork. But the concealment of the vines
was collapsing, and she couldn't help closing her
eyes.

Panic made them open at once. There was nothing to
see: the vines had revealed only the tubs of earth, the
wide mouths gaping darkly beneath the fallen tangle.
Or was there movement deep in the nearest tub, like a
blurred glimpse of a nest of maggots? Was it retreating,
or preparing to emerge?

She pressed against the shelf and edged past, keeping as far from the tubs as she could. The nearest
mouth looked enormous and dark; it could contain
far too much. Wood scraped her spine. The pain made
her grip the fork harder, terrified to drop it. Then
she was past and grappling with the door, listening
for sounds amid the bluster of the breeze, deformed
sounds behind her. In a moment she had wrenched
the door wide and was stumbling over the grass,
scrubbing her free hand against the seat of her
jeans.

She ran and locked herself in—but by the time she
had scalded her hand clean beneath the tap and finished
convincing herself that the house was secure, she felt
she had caged herself. The greenhouse was too near. It
possessed her thoughts and infected her home. Perhaps
what she'd glimpsed was unable to emerge, perhaps it
was less physically present than she'd feared, but even
the hint of its nearness was frightful. She roamed the
house, hands at her throbbing temples; her thoughts
felt like hammerblows. Were her gifts only making her
more perceptive—or could they attract the things she
perceived?

The clouds had lumbered onward, bearing their
burden of unshed rain. Sunlight flooded the garden,
and gave her the courage to glance from the window.
For a moment she stared, then she grabbed her

handbag and fled toward town, Bill, normality. Through the vines which obscured the panes she had glimpsed, pressed close to the glass and facing her, something like a face and hands.

XXI

Bill wasn't in the library. None of the faces which stared at her over the tables, like animals disturbed while feeding, was his. A crowd of her footsteps scuttled after her beneath the dome of the Picton reference library. He wasn't in the Art Library, from whose gallery she had a warder's-eye view of readers at tables; he wasn't in the tiered arena of the International. In the latter, Hitler stared from a book, *The Psychopathic God*. His face looked half-formed, and close to a secret panic; it hovered in the glossy darkness of the cover. His painted eyes resembled boils.

She wandered the city center in search of Bill. On Manchester Street, King George V and Queen Mary stood like survivors of a giant chess game; in the Bluecoat courtyard, Captain Pottle was conducting the Merseyside Police brass band in Beatles numbers. But Bill wasn't in the Bluecoat art gallery, nor in any of the bookshops, the restaurants, the snack bars.

Dark clouds oozed across the sky. A last gasp of sunlight reached the towers of the Liver Building. Against a sky like muddy depths they looked too bright, and skeletally brittle. Around Rose, Church Street had grown intensely clear; department stores shone violently, everything was close and vivid—the textures of bricks and plate glass and flagstones, the discords of neon and window displays, clusters of flowers vibrating in concrete tubs, the restless random patterns of the crowds. The ponderous sky boxed her in. Was her mind clinging to appearances in order not to glimpse a truth?

Stores were casting out their customers. Staff locked grilles over windows. Men stood with their hands on locks, forbidding her to enter. Waves of the crowd flooded toward bus stops and car parks. Before long the street was swept almost bare. At least the downtown streets were open and well lit, and she was not entirely alone.

But her companions were not heartening. A newspaper seller's leg protruded from his tin lair, like a spider's. An old woman sat on a bench, her head nodding rapidly and constantly with the automatic restlessness of a caged bird. As Rose climbed Bold Street she passed a man with frayed sleeves, sitting on the pavement against a shop wall, reading yesterday's *Liverpool Echo* in the light from the window. Behind him, hats were raised on poles, like skulls. Each time the paper stirred in a breeze he snarled, "You bastard." He sounded unnervingly gentle as a sadist.

The breezes seemed hardly to move the air. The sky was low as the roofs. Rose felt soaked in rusty oil; muddy dimness filled her eyes. The cab of a lorry ran up Leece Street, and made her think of a severed insect head, still moving. Outside the Children's Hospital, a glove was trapped in a drain. The fingers fluttered, struggling feebly to drag it clear of the grid.

By the time she reached Egerton Street, the light was almost doused. She hurried into the pub, less wary of the rain than of the darkness. The interior was less bright than she'd hoped—but bright enough to show her that Bill was not there.

Black wood surrounded her, soaking up the meager light. Lanterns stifled by crimson glass glowed on brackets; patches of crimson glared in the wrinkles of the walls. Carved faces leered beneath the lamps. Each

nose was half the size of its black wooden face. The
eyes looked like globules of oil.

She had just noticed that above her head a gilded
angel hung in chains, his face paralyzed by suffering,
when Guilda appeared. GUILDA MEAKIN EATS LITTLE
BOYS, her T-shirt said. "Hello there. Sorry to keep you.
Two pints?"

Rose's mind felt weighed down. "Two? Why two?"

"One for your husband. He's still here, isn't he?"

Oh God, he must have already left! How long would
it take Rose to find him? But Guilda said, "Yes, you're
all right. Here he is."

Rose couldn't bear a betrayal now—but it was Bill,
his eyebrows glistening with the water he had just
splashed on his face. His smile was both a welcome and
a promise that he wouldn't hurt her. "Ah, just what I
need," he said, reaching for the beer.

She could have agreed, too passionately. Her relief
at the sight of him had robbed her of the strength to tell
him what had happened in the greenhouse, supposing
she had really meant to do so. She paid for the drinks,
slapping down a coin which had twitched from her
fingers, and followed him into the snuggery.

A few people sat in the small dark room, where
colored glass trapped light in webs of lead. Students
were reading the *Socialist Worker:* FASCISTS WIN
BY-ELECTION, the headline said. A gray mass drifted
away from their table, trailing spidery limbs; in each
table an ashtray hid beneath a grille. Hovering figures
with oily faces loomed forward from the shadows,
where the figures were painted on the walls. Hidden
forms were everywhere, reminding her how her world
was changing.

"Shall we get a snack here and have a late dinner?"
Bill said.

"If you like." The change was negligible beside her
problems.

"The thing is, there's something I'd like to try." He

sounded a little defensive. "You remember Hilary, my student with the dreadful boyfriend? After they broke up she went to meditation classes, which helped her nerves a good deal."

"You're trying to say that we ought to go?"

"Well, we could give it a try."

Any hope of peace was welcome, but more was wrong than Rose's nerves. Still, it wouldn't hurt to try; perhaps it might help tone down her perceptions. She could think of nothing else to do.

At her first hint of agreement he called, "Guilda, can we have two pâtés?" Now they would have to wait. Rose glanced about uneasily, at the students who were swapping slogans in lieu of conversation, at two fur-hatted ladies lipsticked by the glow of cigarettes, at a man who had ordered a meal and who kept glancing up hopefully like a lover at a tryst. He was grinding his teeth, which splintered and crunched. No, they were ice cubes which he was chewing.

"I'm sorry I was such a sod yesterday." Bill was speaking low. "After all that you've been through—being mugged, and your insomnia and the rest. No wonder your writing isn't at its best."

The faces on the walls were grimacing. They looked half-engulfed by oily dimness, and unable to move a muscle as they sank. She knew how they felt.

"I've been on edge with everything." Bill tugged a lock of hair viciously back from his forehead. "Did you hear me? I said I'm on edge as well. That's another reason why I'd like to give Ananda Marga a chance."

Ananda Marga, was it? All she knew of them was that they had a vegetarian restaurant on Hardman Street, which seemed to be patronized by somber bearded men and thin, morosely virtuous young people. Her thoughts were in turmoil, yet they seemed to be happening somewhere apart from her.

"I think my writing's suffered too," Bill was saying. "After we've had this session tonight perhaps we can look over the book together and see what we can do.

Maybe we're working too hard when we don't need to. Maybe we need a change of pace."

Yes, it might help to talk about the future—it might help her to believe that she wouldn't feel like this forever, dreading her return home. Would the thing in the greenhouse have harmed her physically or psychically? Perhaps both: it might have been even worse than she'd feared.

"A change of pace, yes," she stammered, desperate to grab the chance, though she didn't know what it might be. "We could do more interviews, do you mean? Were you thinking of Jack's idea that we could go to California?"

"Oh, Christ, no, not more interviews. I'll be glad when that book's over. I think we should work more on what we do best, polish it, try and make it more accessible. My writing too, I mean, not only yours. But Christ, let's try and avoid doing interviews. I still have to talk to this bloody old swine at the National Film Theater."

"Oh, Bill, he isn't supposed to be all that unapproachable—not by people who know as much about his work as you will. I'd go with you if I weren't lecturing." At once she realized she would be alone in the house when he went to London. "I'd even go alone," she said with desperate undefined hopefulness.

"Now, Ro, you know you wouldn't. You don't like interviewing any more than I do. Why, I had to interview Dietrich almost single-handed."

The pub was filling up. University staff looked into the snuggery and nodded to the Tierneys, then withdrew, sensing that the conversation was private. The black leather settle on which Rose was sitting thrust forward arms like snakes with half-human faces, whose lips protruded farther than their swollen noses. She didn't like to touch them; like the walls, the faces looked coated with their age, a dim gluey substance from which she might never struggle free. "Then what sort of change of pace did you mean?" she pleaded.

"Well, it was only a thought. We'd have to talk about it, of course, give ourselves time to think it through. But it seems to me we could afford to give up lecturing and write full-time. Would that make you happier?"

"It might." At least it would give them an excuse to move house, perhaps down South, nearer to publishers. She could feel his concern for her, his willingness to change if it would help, and yet his intentions fell short of her. She was alone in a transforming world.

She gulped her beer, not pausing to breathe. The alcohol seemed to weight her mind a little, prevent it from drifting. "I'd like another," she said.

"Me too. I know how you feel."

Of course he didn't know anything of the kind. She hoped that the meal would be quick, that she would be able to eat it without being sick, so that there would be no delay. The uproar of the pub seemed to be losing perspective, as though overcome by the dimness. The paint on the walls looked like gelatin, coating drowned faces. An unstable, almost insubstantial shape floated uncontrollably out of a table. She was edging closer to the brink of what she had used to believe was reality. Nothing seemed solid enough to comfort her now. Perhaps nowhere was safe.

XXII

By the time they reached Dingle, the rain had stopped. It had pursued them from the bus stop below the Anglican cathedral, a downpour dancing in the side streets that led to the Mersey, leaping from pockmarks in puddles, turning the roof of the bus into a thunder sheet. When Rose stepped down, the air smelled refreshed. She felt a hint of relief.

Still, the evening seemed ominous. Darkness flocked across the sky. As people hurried through the drowned streets, they trod on caricatures of themselves, dwarfed and half-dissolved. Rose felt as though she was trying to shake off a blur of darkness and flesh-colored blobs that was glued to her feet.

Aigburth Road was coated with glistening orange beneath lights like bars of electric fires set in concrete hooks. Traffic lights splashed the road with fluorescent paint: green, amber, red. Cars advanced on fractured luminous stilts, taillights bled on the tarmac. Despite all this, it seemed by no means light enough.

The Ananda Marga address was just round the corner, in Ullet Road. Two Georgian houses with small pillared porches stood united beyond a curved drive. Most of the many windows were lit, but all of them were curtained, noncommittal. A stubby tower topped with a stone spike was full of them; some were barred by wrought-iron balconies. Half a wooden gate leaned against one porch; a Renault patched with wounds of rust was parked nearby. Orange raindrops crawled on the trees and bushes that guarded the building closely.

They couldn't tell which door to use. Eventually they tried the farther porch. The distant muffled bell might have been a stray sound from the road. The silence tightened Rose's nerves. "Come on, Bill. We're already late. Nobody's going to answer now."

"Let's try just once more. I did tell them on the phone that we were coming."

He must have done so before consulting her. That didn't matter, it was the waiting she couldn't stand, the imminence vague and oppressive as fog— But the door opened, without even the warning of audible footsteps, and a young man peered out. He wore an Indian blouse; his hair was tied back by a rubber band.

"We're here for the meditation class," Bill said.

"Oh, really? Come in." He led them through several whitewashed halls and up a staircase enclosed by pale walls. Though he seemed to know exactly where he was going, he faltered at the top. "No, wait—that's Yoga. We'd better try down here."

He hurried them through more pale passages, which looked featureless. Some seemed familiar, some were not; her nervousness was fraying her sense of direction. A door led to another passage, through which they followed him. Surely they were in the adjoining house by now. He knocked on a door and glanced in. "No, that's advanced TM. You want the beginners' class. I wonder where that is? Ah, now wait a minute." He looked into another room. "Yes, I think you're here."

It seemed unlikely. Within the large high white room, on bare floorboards, about a dozen people squatted facing a young woman who appeared to be a nun in an orange habit. Some of her audience were struggling to copy her cross-legged position, others were supple and smug. "I'm Winnie. I'm a shopkeeper," a Welsh woman in a dark suit was saying.

"I'm Gwen, her assistant," murmured the Welsh girl next to her.

"Mother and daughter, right?" The nun's soft voice was American—Rose couldn't be more specific. "Hi, come on in. You called before," she said to Bill. "Thank you, Joshua," she said to their guide.

Rose could only squat in the space the others made for her, and cross her legs deftly. She wasn't at all sure that she wanted whatever was going to happen. She glanced at the others in the semicircle: young women with engrossed smiles, who looked too calm to need this class; a man in a tweed jacket, lanky as a giraffe; a small square red-faced man who resembled a tightly locked box. They weren't very reassuring.

"We're only just begun," the American said. "We've been talking about reasons to meditate. It seems as though most of us need some means to relax, which is fine." She sounded good-humored, even a little unsure of herself. "We're just telling each other our names and a little about ourselves."

"I'm Diana," said the girl next to the Welsh couple. "I'm a teacher." Her face, which looked calm and open as a painting, didn't change as she said, "I had a breakdown."

"I'm a mechanic," said a young man from Liverpool. A permanent beak-shaped frown dug into his forehead between his eyes, dragging his eyebrows together. "I keep starting fights. People get on my nerves too much."

"I'm, er, Robert," the red-faced man said warily. "I'm in banking. I have difficulty sleeping." The self-revelations were advancing too quickly for Rose; when they reached her, what could she say?

"I'm Bill," he said next to her. "I'm a writer. I've had some nervous trouble lately."

"I'm, um, I'm—" Her mind stumbled among the clutter of syllables. "I'm a writer too. I had to take Librium for a while." It sounded dishonest and feeble.

"Okay," said the orange nun. "To start with we need to do some relaxation exercises. We need to be in a state of bodily calm. So first we all stand up."

Some had to lever themselves upright, hands on knees. The lanky man had a giraffe's gracefulness. The red-faced man was massaging one leg; a muffled growl escaped through his cramped lips. "Don't sit the way I do if it isn't comfortable," the orange nun said. "But try it if you can. It helps you find your point of balance."

Something unexpected seemed to be happening to Rose. Had it begun when she'd stammered? Nobody had minded her clumsiness; all of them were nervous, whether or not they showed it; they sympathized with her, they wanted her to grow calm with them. To stand up with everyone else, which at school she had always resented, seemed actually reassuring. Was her nervousness draining away, into the promise of calm? It was too soon to tell.

"First I want to teach you to relax," the orange nun said, fainting—but she had only begun to rotate her head loosely, ear to shoulder, chin to chest, opposite ear to opposite shoulder, head back as though gargling. It was like Music and Movement at primary school, and it cleared the room of the last traces of self-consciousness; even red-faced Robert was lolling his head enthusiastically. As Rose's head fell back she glimpsed the cornice of the ceiling, elaborate and spotless.

They writhed their shoulders to shrug off tension. They bent low from the waist, questing all around themselves for relaxation. They raised their arms and let them droop, in the slow motion of a film that was near to stopping entirely; then they shook their arms limply, to shake out the last of the tension.

"Now I want to teach you to breathe."

It was rather late to learn that, Rose thought. The joke was less defensive than relaxed. Though she was still afraid to believe it, she felt safe. She could sense no threat in the spacious white room, only the hope of peace. Would she be able to take that peace with her, out of the room?

Perhaps she might—for she was learning to inhale peace. She was breathing from her diaphragm. Air seemed to swell the whole of her chest before it reached her lungs. When she breathed out, her chest felt strong and clean. The sensations filled her skull.

There was more. As her chest swelled, the room seemed to fill with peace. Everyone was calm—thank heaven, Bill was—but there was something greater than individual calm; in the room, or very near. Was their shared peace a kind of energy? The more she trusted her sense of it, the more the peace seemed to grow. Perhaps she was helping it. She was shedding her tension like old dry skin, hard and chafing.

"Now we have the best relaxation exercise. We need to lie down flat, hands by the sides."

Rose felt a pang of nervousness. Suppose that position let her drift away? It was the ideal position for astral voyaging, she'd read that in her book. Still, would it matter? She wouldn't panic here, she would be able to control herself immediately. Besides, a ridge between the floorboards was nipping her thigh; that ought to keep her aware of her body. She was dismayed that she needed to be so careful of herself.

"Close your eyes," said the orange nun. "Now I want each of you to experience your entire body. Start at your feet. Feel all the tension in them, in your toes. Make your feet tense. Now let all the tension drain away, into the floor. Feel it draining away. Now your calves. Feel how tense they are . . ."

Perhaps this would be doubly helpful: besides relaxing Rose, it would help her vigilance over her body. "Let the tension drain out of your thighs into the floor . . ." The boards felt softened, soaking up the tension from her legs, which grew luxuriously limp. The American voice was soothing, almost hypnotic. It was filling the room with gentleness and calm. It sounded firmer now, secure in the trust of the group. They were united.

"Let the tension drain out of your face. Make funny faces."

Rose's face relaxed into a grin. She could imagine everyone grimacing obediently—Bill, Robert, even the orange nun. They'd left embarrassment behind. They trusted one another, companions in the search for peace. She wished she could see their faces.

At once she could, below her on the wide floor.

So it had happened after all, despite her vigilance. Their shared calm had robbed her of her sense of her body, of its individuality. Yet she felt no panic. She was buoyed up by their calm, by the sight of Bill at rest, of her own body, relaxed at last. The cool white room was peace made visible. She wasn't afraid to be floating; on the contrary, she felt intensely grateful that she could do so without fear, cradled by the whiteness. Perhaps it was partly relief that she had transcended her fear, but she had never in her life felt so relaxed.

Movement caught her attention. The nun was sitting up. Below Rose she looked small, fragile, pleased by the calm she'd helped create. Rose felt enormously fond of her, and eager to express her gratitude somehow.

"Sit up slowly," the nun said.

Seen from above, the semicircle of figures resembled a flower closing for the night. Everyone had sat up except Rose. She must return before anyone noticed that something was wrong. Of course they would only assume that she was completely relaxed, but she'd better be quick, nonetheless. She had only to think of—

She was still gazing down at it when her body sat up and opened its eyes.

Its movements were jerky, not quite lifelike. It looked like a puppet, trying to parody her—a puppet with a mind of its own, if it had a mind. Its hand scrabbled along the floor to prop it upright, and touched Bill's fingers. He blinked at what squatted beside him, and smiled privately at it, as though the jerking object were Rose.

As he smiled, the head turned to him, nodding a little as if the neck was giving way. Its eyes gazed into his. His smile seemed to falter, to grow puzzled—but he was clearly unaware that whatever was behind the eyes, it was not Rose.

Her worst fear was that she would have to look into those eyes. Her mind seemed to collapse, a husk empty of thoughts. She could only struggle to scream before her horror carried her out of the room, into the boundless dark. The cry burst from her lips as a strangled squeal, which bore little resemblance to her voice.

But she was squatting next to Bill. She could feel her hand gripping his, the trembling of her limbs, cramp in her thighs. Would her trembling shake her out of her body again? "Oh God, oh God," she was muttering. Not until he gasped did she realize that her nails had punctured the skin of Bill's palm.

The orange nun came hurrying over, anxious to help. The Welsh women fluttered around Rose, Robert frowned in the background and grew redder. None of them was any use to Rose; they only oppressed her. She wanted to be alone, to judge how badly she was harmed—alone with this treacherous unfamiliar object, her body. It felt feverish, unstable, perhaps not quite like flesh.

She struggled to her feet. She would have shouldered the worried faces aside if they hadn't fallen back. They couldn't help her, but what could? Alcohol, Librium? "I'm sorry," she managed to say, and stumbled out, hoping Bill would follow, too shaken to care if he did.

By the time she reached the porch, having been neurotically aware of every step she had taken through the houses, her body felt something like hers. Although the vividness of her sensations clung to her like mud, congealing time around her, in a sense this was welcome; it helped her hold onto her awareness of her body.

Outside, sodium lights seared the night. Trees were skinned skeletons of orange metal, plated with oily leaves. "I'm going to see Colin tomorrow," she said at once to Bill. It was the only hope she could offer herself. Her voice sounded thin, shrunken by the night.

"All right." His voice was weary, helpless. They seemed already to have reached a tacit understanding that he wouldn't ask her what was wrong. "Just don't let him use you as a guinea pig," he said.

They trudged along Aigburth Road. Buses lumbered by, bearing luminous airborne heads, dragging blurred veils of light over the pavement. Overhead the clouds were far too sparse; darkness hovered, leading to infinity. Ahead, perhaps both a memory and a premonition, she saw something the color of lard groping out from among vines.

XXIII

"Gladys," Rose said abruptly, "have you been in the greenhouse lately?"

Gladys ducked forward over the teapot she was holding. The jet of tea began to stagger around the edge of the cup, as though seeking a way out. "I watered in there as much as I could," she mumbled. "But it got too much for me."

"So you haven't been in there for a while?"

"I'm sorry, Rose. I didn't mean to neglect it. I know I promised, and now I've let you down. I did try, but I found I didn't really know what to do."

"Don't blame yourself, Gladys. I said I'd help you, and I didn't." Rose fell silent, cursing her own clumsiness.

When Gladys had carried her jittery cup and saucer into the kitchen, Colin said, "Between ourselves, Rose, there's a little more to it. I think the place reminds her of unpleasant experiences in Africa—too much greenery, you see, and the atmosphere. I should have offered to take over, but I've been so busy."

"It's more than atmosphere. Perhaps she senses it too, vaguely." Rose felt in danger of a fit of trembling. "There's something in there. I've seen it," she said.

"Something—? Ah, you mean—?"

"Yes, something unnatural. Something evil."

"This is one of your new perceptions? May I take it that you believe in them now?"

He sounded eager, not at all disturbed by what she'd said. She remembered Bill's warning. "Yes, I have to," she said miserably. "But I don't want to, not when they're like that."

"Forgive me. Of course it must be very difficult for you. Will you come to the window for me and tell me whether you can see anything now?"

Grass gleamed like shards of bone. The panes of the greenhouse roof were blue as a swimming pool, into which a foam of clouds were seeping; the panes which faced her were clear, except where vine leaves stuck to the glass. "No, there's nothing there," she said wearily.

At least, nothing was visible, which meant that she couldn't see what it was doing; she couldn't even see the wooden tubs. Last night she'd lain awake, telling herself that it seemed imprisoned in the greenhouse, their bedroom didn't overlook it, she didn't have to see. Her thoughts had floated aimlessly on waves of bourbon. Their comfort had been pathetically feeble.

"Yes, there is something." She mustn't let him think she was calm. "I can feel it. Everything's rotten in there. Maybe it made that happen, or maybe that's what made it grow. Whatever it is, it's alive, or at least it can move." Every phrase sounded more insane, but it seemed hardly to matter. "I think it's in one of those wooden tubs," she said.

Colin looked sympathetic. "Well, let me tell you one thing we can do. Before today is over, Bill and I will clear the greenhouse out completely. Will that make you feel better?"

"It might." She wished she could feel more grateful—but then she noticed the flaw. "You mustn't tell Bill why you're doing it," she pleaded.

"Of course not. I quite understand. All he needs to know is that things are rotting."

She disliked conspiring against Bill, but what else

could she do? He'd offered to come with her today, as though she were a child scared of the dentist. She'd had to be outwardly firm before he would let her go alone.

"What else is troubling you?" Colin said.

"I don't want to be so afraid. I'm afraid all the time now."

"Of your developing powers, do you mean?"

"Yes, of them. Most of all I'm frightened that they may be attracting the things I see."

"I don't think that's likely, do you? Remember, they're only perceptions, however strange they may seem. We know that observation alters whatever is observed, but not in the way you mean. Really, I think you can set your mind at rest about that."

She didn't see how he could know this, but in any case it wasn't very reassuring. "Are you still afraid?" he said.

"Yes."

"Can you tell me what frightens you?"

The room was bright and thin as shell, no defense against the sluggish movement in the greenhouse. Everything was fragile and partial—everything she'd taken to be the whole of reality. "I'm afraid of being overpowered," she said.

"By what? Do you know? Try and tell me."

"By the things I see. By the things that are happening to me, the changes. And by panic." Her words seemed not to grasp her fears. They drifted away like mist in the sunlight, leaving her fears buried in her, in the dark.

"But do you need to be afraid? Keep in mind that you *have* survived all these things. They haven't overwhelmed you. It seems to me that your inner strength must have grown to cope with them. Many people would have had a breakdown if they'd had half your experiences. May I suggest that what is hampering your inner strength is simply the threat of panic?"

"You're probably right." She had reached the same conclusion last night, as she'd lain sleepless amid the swells of bourbon. It had allowed her to sleep for a while—but as soon as she'd awakened, her fears had been lying in wait for her. "But what can I do?" she cried. "Sometimes the panic is so bad that I can't think. That's when I'm in danger."

"And so you want me to help you."

He sounded so sure of himself that she gasped, "Can you?"

"Well, I can't halt your development. Even if I could, I doubt that it would be advisable." Seeing her dismay, he added hastily, "But I may be able to ease your fear, perhaps cure it."

"How?"

"By confronting you with its source. Don't worry, I don't mean anything actual. I think the source is in your memory. As a matter of fact you more or less convinced me of that, a while ago. I'd like to lead you back to it."

Surely a memory couldn't harm her, yet she sounded uneasy. "How will you do that?"

"Preferably with drugs."

"No. No, I've had enough of losing control."

"All right," he said equably. "You can be conscious while I guide you. It may take longer, but you'll feel safe." He glanced into the kitchen. "Rose and I will need to be left alone for a while." As he drew the curtains he said to Rose, "I'd like you to lie on the couch. Sorry about the cliché."

As soon as she lay down she felt vulnerable, remembering what had happened at Ananda Marga. The dimness blurred her sense of the room. He must have glimpsed her nervousness, for he said, "Don't worry, I'll be with you all the time."

Perhaps that would help. At least he seemed to have an inkling of the dangers she was risking. He sat beside her on a chair and began to stroke her forehead. "Try to relax," he said gently. "Just listen to my voice. Trust my voice. Just relax and let my voice guide you. You will be able to hear my voice at all times, so that you'll know I'm with you. Relax now and drift with my voice. Remember that I'm with you. You aren't alone . . ."

Was he trying to hypnotize her? His voice droned on, his hand caressed; they shared a gentle rhythm. Surely there would be more to hypnosis than that. At least she was beginning to feel safe, and didn't mind closing her eyes. Now his hand seemed enormous, a protective giant's. She felt like a child, secure, uncomplicated, relieved of her responsibilities.

"Now I want you to go back with me." Had he been repeating that for some time? "I'm going to guide you through some of your memories. Remember, I shall be there. If it gets too much for you I'll bring you back at once. Go back now," said his giant whisper beyond his giant caressing hand. "Go back to the last time you were near to panic."

That wasn't fair. He was supposed to be looking after her, not taking her to places where she didn't want to go. But already she was there, hovering in the white room, and beneath her on the floor—

She began to struggle wildly, moaning. This wasn't a memory, it was a moment which had waited for a second chance to overwhelm her. She was alone. His voice had abandoned her.

"Tell me what you see. You must tell me, Rose. Tell me why you are afraid."

Didn't he realize that she couldn't speak? Her mouth was somewhere distant, beyond her reach. His voice had come to her rescue too late. The whiteness had trapped her like amber. Yet in the distance someone was mumbling; she seemed able, up to a point, to control what the mumbling said; yes, its words were some of her thoughts. However indistinct, it was a lifeline. It meant that some part of her was free of the white room.

"I'm outside my body," she managed to say, as far as she could tell. "At a meditation class. We wanted to relax. I've lost control."

"Can you see your body? Where is it, Rose?"

"On the floor. She's telling everyone to sit up. They're sitting up. My body is, when I'm not there. Oh God," the distant voice mumbled, "something's inside my body!"

"Can you return to your body? You must be able to. You can, can't you, Rose?"

"I'm terrified." At the same time she felt oddly detached from her feelings, as though they were projected on a screen, with the distant mumbling as a sound track. "I can't think. I can't, I can't! I've got to scream!" The sound track did so, a wavering squeal that sounded like the cry of someone congenitally deaf, in agony.

"Are you in your body now, Rose?"

"Yes." Bill was staring at her, gasping; she felt her nails pierce his skin.

"So you managed to save yourself, didn't you? Whatever happened, there's no need to be frightened of it any longer. You survived."

That seemed to be true. The distant mumbling had carried away some of her panic. His voice was guiding her toward eventual peace. "Go back now, Rose," he was saying, "to the very first time you left your body."

So that was why the hand on her forehead had felt so large. She was a child, and the hand was her mother's. But her mother had withdrawn; she was leaving Rose, just as Uncle Wilfred and Auntie Vi had done. Her bedroom felt huge as the night. "Come back," she pleaded, but the voice was indistinct, almost beyond her control.

"How old are you, Rose?"

"I'm eleven." The mumbling was slower, for it had to be dredged up from the past in which she was immersed. "I've got a fever. Mummy's left me alone. I don't want her to!" The mumbling wavered, shaken by panic. Something was seeking to reach for her, and she would rather die than know what it was. On the dim chair, her lolling clothes had become a slackly grinning face; shadows clung to the corners of the ceiling, ready to flap down and crawl over her—but the thing that was squirming like a baby somewhere in the dark, eager to reach her, was infinitely worse.

Before she knew it, she had fled. Her body, which felt swollen and swarming with fever, had gone; she still felt light-headed, but in a new and exhilarating way. She was on the stairs, or above them. Below her was her mother. That part of Rose which was observing the memory was shocked to see how young her mother looked—no gray hairs, no stoop, no chalky skin on her fingers—and yet at the same time her mother looked dwindled, weary, older than her years.

"Are you out of your body now, Rose?"

"Yes." His voice distracted her, nagging at her concentration. "Shut up," she managed to make the mumbling say. "My parents are talking. Let me hear."

She was outside the living-room door. She could hardly recognize it, for she was used to looking up, not down, at its higher panels. Through her fascination, which had left panic behind, she heard her father say, "How is she?"

"Oh, George, I don't know. She doesn't seem any better to me. Suppose it's more than fever? Wilfred and Violet dying so soon after that other business—it can't have helped."

"Don't fret, Margaret. We're as capable of nursing her as they were."

"That isn't what I meant. Sometimes I think we've lost her to them. She doesn't think we can take their place."

"Now, really, that's nonsense. She was fond of them and they were fond of her, but there's no need to exaggerate. Whatever do you mean?"

"Sometimes I think she doesn't trust us any longer. She blames us for not stopping her from going out that night."

Rose was sailing away, like ash up a chimney. The

hall plummeted beneath her. But she wanted to hear the rest! "No, not yet," the mumbling complained.

"Where are you now, Rose?"

"In bed." She could hardly summon the effort, frustrated as she was, to add, "It's over."

"Are you frightened now?"

"No."

"All right." He was stroking her forehead, but she knew he wasn't her mother, she couldn't be deceived. His voice grew very gentle. "Now I think we have to go still farther back. Remember I'll be with you all the time. I won't leave you even for a moment. I can bring you back immediately if need be."

Why was he taking such pains to reassure her? She felt a barely perceptible stirring in her mind. "We're going to return to a time in your childhood when you were very frightened indeed," he said quietly. "So frightened that you've almost forgotten it. I want you to keep talking to me all the time. Tell me—"

He must intend his voice to anchor her, to prevent her from plunging into the depths he was revealing. But it was too late. Sudden terror had engulfed her, dragging her down. It was absolutely dark, and suffocated all her senses. She could just hear his dwindling voice: "Come back, Rosalind. Come back. You must hear my voice. Come back." Her terror was a lightless well down which she was falling. Perhaps there was no bottom, only darkness—but something which had made that dark its lair was scuttling upward, rapid as a spider, to seize her.

XXIV

It was twilight, and still the greenhouse was not clear.
A breeze was groping through the heap of refuse by the
wall; that must be why the heap was restless. Its outline
of vines shivered, its bulk shifted wakefully. Twilight
helped obscure the movements in its depths.

Bill and Colin had to carry out some of the refuse in
cartons; stains seeped through the cardboard. Bill held
his carton so gingerly that its contents might have been
alive. Melons lay on the tangled bed of vines like heads,
faceless and glistening. As the heap grew, so its depths
became harder to scrutinize. At least there was a
definite breeze to explain its movements; trees were
nodding above the wall. Rose thought that any of them
could easily become a lair.

She was staring down from the workroom. The
workbook lay open before her, to aid her pretense of
writing. Colin had brought her home, in order to say to
Bill, "I'm afraid we've let things get out of hand in the
greenhouse." Bill had agreed impatiently to help,
perhaps in order to clear the way for the important
question: "Do you feel better, Ro?" As she'd managed
to smile, aware as she did so that the center of peace
which was soothing her was Librium, Colin said,
"We've made some progress, but I think we tried to do
too much too soon."

She must have fainted on his couch. She'd found
herself struggling upward from blackness. The room
had looked dulled, unconvincing, a stage set whose
lighting betrayed its fakery, even when he'd opened the

curtains. Her mind had felt drained: she couldn't remember much, only a plunge into darkness after her parents had said something which she couldn't now recall. When Colin said, "At least we can deal with the greenhouse today," she hadn't known for a moment what he meant. But when he'd said, "There's something still buried in your mind. We must try to reach it soon," the whole of her had clenched, and she'd felt in danger of trembling until she couldn't stop. "For God's sake give me a Librium," she'd pleaded.

He was carrying out the last of the vines and throwing them on the heap. He dodged into the greenhouse as Bill emerged, and she heard a splintering. Bill hurried back to protest, but Colin appeared with an armful of broken wood. "These tubs are rotten," he said. "Best to rip them out and start again."

She only wished he wouldn't disturb them by himself. Dusk was massing like motionless smoke; he wouldn't be able to see inside the tubs. She watched the door of the greenhouse uneasily—but he emerged with a whole splintered tub, which he thrust deep into the pile.

The worst thing—more dismaying, in a way, than the terror which she'd doused with Librium—was that she no longer trusted him entirely. "I'm sorry," he'd said after a while. "I hadn't realized you would be so suggestible. I suppose I ought to have anticipated that. I should have taken it more slowly, been more careful." Didn't that mean simply that he couldn't keep her as safe as he'd promised? He must have been growing unsure of his skills too, for he'd suggested she try acupuncture for her nerves.

The greenhouse was empty now. The panes were clear, except for ghosts of leaves which clung where leaves had been peeled away from the glass. Colin was pouring petrol on the heap of refuse; that was the only reason why parts of it glimmered moistly and were not quite still.

The first whoof of flame kindled the faces of the men

as they recoiled. Flames swarmed up the bonfire, racing for the summit. Vines writhed, crackling; rotten vegetables hissed. Shadows of grass danced, advancing in ranks and withdrawing. The bricks of the wall looked red-hot. The greenhouse panes resembled monitor screens, reiterating images of fire.

Rose had abandoned her pretense of writing, for she mustn't look away from the fire for a moment; she had to be sure that nothing escaped. She felt like a child too young to stay up on Guy Fawkes' Night, gazing secretly from her window. Certainly she felt small and alone. She hadn't dared go closer to the greenhouse.

Gray smoke billowed away from the fire. It looked oily, almost too solid for smoke. It fumbled over the wall and seemed to become entangled in the trees. Part of the smoke came loose and headed toward her: a bloated dwarfish shape, almost formless. A breeze headed it off, and it drifted toward the sky, disintegrating.

Soon the fire was spent. The panes of the greenhouse dulled, switched off. Bill's shadow, which lay twitching on the grass, was fading. Colin glanced up at her, and poked at the tangle of charred skeletons. Fragments burst into flame and collapsed, blackening. Now there was only a low mound that glowed dull red and crawled with ash. Seeds of fire sailed away on the breeze and were extinguished almost before they took flight. Obviously Colin meant her to be reassured—but as the last of the fire sank into gray ash, the night closed in.

XXV

"Written any good books lately?" Bill's father said to Rose.

His voice jerked her out of her thoughts. "Oh," she said vaguely, "we're doing quite well, I think."

His wife was wheeling him through the foyer of the Royal Hotel, past potted plants and a glass case displaying a torso dressed in a suit. They emerged beneath the long awning onto Southport Promenade. The facade of the hotel shone like cream; dormer windows glittered beneath high narrow foreheads. Next to the hotel, the tinted windows of the Kingsway Casino resembled sheets of brass. Beyond the formal garden which bordered the promenade—huddles of bushes, frequent shelters, fat balustrades guarded by lanterns—rowing boats flocked on the Marine Lake.

"I'm glad you two get on so well," Bill's father was saying. "Me and Edna, we had our rows. Her and her argumentativeness." He savored the word as though proud of its length.

"Listen to him. You'd think it was all my fault. We used to get on your nerves, didn't we, Bill?"

"Occasionally, perhaps. Never very much."

"So long as we didn't stop you thinking up your books."

"Oh no, nothing like that."

"That's right. We didn't think so. We always knew you'd make a success of your life."

If they had really felt that way, they had never let him

know. Sometimes Rose wondered how he could have grown from such an upbringing: as a reaction against it, perhaps? She was becoming tense. Soon she would have to sneak a Librium into her mouth when nobody was watching. Not yet, not quite yet. She wasn't addicted yet.

"Shall I push for a while?" Bill said.

"No, I'll do it. I'm quite capable." His mother gripped the handle of the wheelchair as though he were threatening robbery. Was she determined to cling to all she could do for her husband? Their arguments were feebler now, mellowed by age, and she was holding fast to that relief. After decades of squabbling, that must seem like complete stability.

Rose's hand closed secretly around the packet of tranquillizers. Another fifteen minutes, surely she could bear that. But why was she here at all? This time her instincts seemed to have let her down.

All of a sudden, to Bill's surprise, she'd said, "Let's go and see your parents." These days he usually went alone; his parents were wary of Rose, they hid their Liverpool accent as though it was ragged underclothing, they enunciated their words like drunkards, afraid of stumbling over grammar. All this made her nervous. When he'd asked why she was suggesting the visit she could only say, "I feel like a day at the seaside."

Of course she was trying to recapture her childhood. Splashes of the distant beach, spilled from toy buckets, glittered on the pavement. A miniature train full of families of holidaymakers trundled along the far edge of the lake. Beyond it the Irish Sea was just visible, a metallic thread on the horizon of the beach. The waves were barely audible, more like a hiss of sand. What was missing?

Victorian hotels extended along the promenade, interrupted by a stack of boxy flats. How had they changed since her childhood? There was the putting green, where Uncle Wilfred had pretended not to notice when she stole an extra stroke; there was the pier, whose small train carried you out to nothing in particular, a platform above a stretch of sand, above the sea if you were lucky. She remembered Auntie Vi squealing like a young girl on the lake, as the oars splashed her; she remembered monkeys at the Children's Zoo performing slyly for their audience, the giant rolling barrel in the Fun House inside which you were supposed to laugh at your bruises, the model village like a gnome's abandoned settlement. The memories seemed microscopic, beyond the reach of her emotions. Everything looked smaller than she remembered, and less bright. Even the illuminations that festooned the lamp standards looked dusty.

Blackpool Tower was a glinting pin on the horizon. She remembered trips to Blackpool Illuminations, the first sight of the town lit like a Christmas tree, illuminations chasing over their paths to decode luminous pictures all along the promenade, fountains of light—miraculous fireworks—that repeated again and again. That had always been her final treat when she was staying here.

She was there. She could even see the moths, glowing red and green as they fluttered round the lights. Then Bill's mother jolted her back to Southport, sand gritting underfoot, an open bus cruising by. "We always used to come here for our holidays," she said.

They must have brought Bill. Suppose he had met Rose, years before Brighton University? They wouldn't have noticed each other; she wouldn't have said, "You're from Liverpool, aren't you? I'm from Ormskirk." Or had those been her first words to him? Her memories seemed unattached, in danger of drifting away.

"We like it here," Bill's mother said. "It's peaceful, not like the rest of the world."

It seemed less peaceful than inhibited. The holiday-

makers looked subdued, afraid to enjoy themselves too
loudly, awed by the width of the promenade, abashed
by the genteel hotels, the fountains and arcades of Lord
Street. Pinball machines jangled in a different world,
walled in by glass. Postcards dangled, strings of innuen-
dos, on stands outside shops, but the cinemas were
forbidden *Emmanuelle*. Rose felt surrounded by an
odd sense of resignation, as if Southport had once
hoped to be a spa town.

Ahead along the promenade, an elderly couple
emerged from Seabank Road. They were almost a
memory, but their faces were disappointing: the woman's deadened by powder, the man's moustache stiff as
a silver comb—they looked like stylized posters for
British intolerance of nonsense. He carried the *Daily
Telegraph* like a club, ready for use. They stalked by,
their voices creaking.

Beyond Seabank Road, across the flowery round-
about, stood the Promenade Hospital. With its stepped
gables and its pointed turrets it still resembled a
red-brick castle from a picture book. Beside the
promenade, yachts lay like stranded fish, speared by
masts. She'd loved the yachts on the lake, gliding and
dipping.

She'd used to run down Seabank Road, hardly
glimpsing the houses, toward the embrace that was
always waiting. "Shall we give Rosie one of her special
cakes, Wilfred? Oh, I don't know if we remembered to
ask Mrs. Hale to keep one. Yes, we did, I'm only
teasing." Now the street looked faded and undistin-
guished, the ranks of small bare facades, bay windows
cobwebbed with net curtains, old people propped in
garden chairs as though left out to dry.

"Do you ever think of moving here, Bill? It would be
good for your writing."

"What do you know about it, Edna?" His father
thumped at his useless leg with a fist, trying to lever
himself round. Unable to turn, he knocked his head

aggressively against the back of the wheelchair. "He doesn't need anywhere special to write. It isn't like shopkeeping, when you're stuck there with the rates and taxes. Don't go murmuring at me. We'd have been able to manage, leg or no leg, I don't care what you say. All we needed was a bit of help in the shop, and a bit more cash to see us through."

"Yes, well," Bill managed to reply to his mother, "we're all right where we are, I think." Rose heard him snarl under his breath, "Come on, damn it, Christ almighty."

He was muttering to himself too often. She wasn't sure if he meant her to overhear. She understood his anger this time—he and Rose had helped pay for the apartment at the Royal, after all—but she had her own edginess to cope with. She couldn't stand Bill's as well, whatever the cause.

"I'm just going down Seabank Road," she said. "I'll catch you up. I just want to look at where I used to stay."

This was the final betrayal: to use her memories as an excuse to sneak away and take her drug. She hurried downhill, anxious to be out of sight. Stray sand hissed on the pavement, alongside a few trodden shells and the claw of a crab. Beyond the netted windows, families sat at dining tables. Their movements grew stylized, self-conscious, as she glanced at their display. They needn't worry, she didn't want to watch them. Even less did she want them to watch her.

As soon as she passed the last boardinghouse she would take her pill. Her fingers skulked in her pocket, opening the container, expertly freeing the pill. One quick lift of her arm, like her childhood money-box which had fed itself pennies, and she would be safe.

Maybe tomorrow's acupuncture session would help, or maybe she could try to contact Freda at wherever the psychiatric commune was, down South—but that was a last hope, too near desperation to ponder now.

Just let her deal with the present moment, never mind the house where she'd used to stay, ignore whoever was looking out at her, just avoid their eyes and run to the end of the street for her prize, a few hours of tranquillity—

But she couldn't resist glancing up. Gazing down at her from the window were Uncle Wilfred and Auntie Vi.

She was scarcely aware of halting. Everything around her—the street, the intense blue sky, the retreating voices on the promenade—seemed to withdraw almost respectfully, leaving her alone. If she felt surprise or awe, the emotions faded quickly into a sense of absolute rightness. Her instincts hadn't betrayed her in bringing her here, after all. There was at least one place in the world where she might be safe.

For a long time she stood gazing, at Auntie Vi's fragile triangular face made asymmetrical by its rakish fringe of gray hair, at Uncle Wilfred's square jaw which he protruded like knuckles, an aggressive gesture which was quite untrue of him and which his drooping moustache contradicted. Their faces had always looked skewwhiff, worn carelessly, and all the more lovable for that. Now they looked faded as images beneath dusty glass.

But their eyes were alive. They were gazing consciously at her, she was certain. They were welcoming her, willing her to come to them. Her only fear was that if she looked away, the figures might vanish.

At last she strode into the house. It might almost have been twenty years ago: the notice board was patched with posters for attractions at the Floral Hall; the legs of the telephone table still had metal twirls like bass clefs, though the telephone was crimson now. She mustn't dawdle over memories, nor had she time for the woman who was approaching down the hall—but the woman moved into her path and said, "Yes?"

What could Rose say? She had to go into the room

upstairs, if only for a few moments, but how could she explain? I'm just visiting someone, the person on the first floor, I forget the name, no, I stayed here the other week and I think I left something upstairs, there's something wrong in your first-floor room, I'd better help you look—

The woman's face blocked her way, patient but firm. All of a sudden Rose saw that its age was a mask, its lines and wrinkles were simply confusing her vision. "Mrs. Hale! Don't you remember me? I'm Rose. I used to visit my aunt and uncle here."

"Rose?" The net of wrinkles tightened with her frown. "I don't think I remember anyone called Rose." She sounded wary, suspicious.

Perhaps Rose could slip past her, dash upstairs—but there would be no point; the room would be locked. She felt her face grow heavily slack, defeated. Her hand was groping automatically in her pocket for a Librium.

Suddenly Mrs. Hale's eyes brightened. Her wrinkles helped them smile. "Of course, they used to call you Rosie, didn't they? How silly of me. Of course I remember. They used to live in the first floor front."

"Yes." Rose was planning swiftly, while her mind was bright. "I was just passing, and I wondered—is anyone in their room at the moment?"

"Not just at this moment, no. I've some guests arriving later on."

Rose managed not to sigh aloud. "Would you mind very much if I were to look at the room, just to remind me?"

"No, of course not. I'll take you up. Excuse me while I fetch the key."

But Rose must be alone! Just a few minutes alone with them, that was all she asked. Security waited at the top of the stairs, a place where she could never be harmed, but it was for her alone—nobody else must intrude. Her nails felt like fire in her palms.

Mrs. Hale came hurrying back. Keys rang dully in her hand. "We'll have to be quite quick," she said. "One of my girls has had to take her baby to the clinic."

Rose's hands unclenched; they made her think of flowers opening. "Look, I mustn't put you to any trouble, not when you're so busy." She managed to keep her expression neutral, so far as she could tell. "I remember the way up. If you give me the key I'll let myself in."

"No, it's no trouble." Wariness had crept back into her voice. "We just won't have to be very long, that's all."

When she strode upstairs Rose trudged after her, though it seemed pointless. There was the landing, which looked almost as spacious as her memory of it. But she had only memories now. Mrs. Hale had spoiled everything. She was leading Rose to an empty room.

She was speaking as she unlocked the door, but Rose heard only the key. The door inched back, taking its time; it had nothing to offer. The room was open now, spread with sunlight. On the bed something lifted its head feebly as the opening of the door disturbed it: a Scandinavian quilt.

The room was the same odd shape that she remembered, not quite square, though the discreetly patterned wallpaper had changed. She remembered the view from the window—long thin gardens, terraced houses shining like sand. She had no reason to go in, for she could see from the landing that the room was empty.

Yet when she stepped over the threshold, she knew that it was not. Love for her filled the room.

At last she remembered how it had used to feel, to be with people whose sole aim had been to protect her, to make her happy. She had been their only child, and they had treasured her. Even she and her parents had taken each other for granted sometimes, but she had never felt that here.

None of this was a memory. It was intensely present in the room. She was embraced, though not physically. Someone who knew more than she was looking after her. Her protection had been so complete that she hadn't been conscious of it—but she was conscious of it now.

Except for the presence of Mrs. Hale, she would have wept for gratitude. Nothing that had happened seemed to matter now. It might have been twenty years ago; there might have been twenty years between her and the landlady's voice. "I'm sorry," Rose said automatically. "What did you say?"

"I said, they're here now." She was standing at the window. "The couple who've booked this room. They're just bringing in their luggage. We'll have to go down now."

"Oh, can't I just—" But it was no use; she might have been the child of twenty years ago, wanting to plead for something which adults wouldn't understand; there was nobody to speak up for her. "Yes, all right, I'll go," she said dully.

Mrs. Hale closed the door behind them. She hesitated, then seemed to decide to take no chances, and locked the door. She turned to Rose with a smile that denied her suspicions. Then she frowned. "Do you feel all right?" she said, staring.

For a while Rose dared not move. Eventually she found her voice. "Yes, I think so."

"Well, you look happy enough." As she waited for Rose to go downstairs she shook her head once, like a shrug at Rose's eccentricities. "You look as though you'd found a treasure."

"Yes," Rose said, hardly daring to speak in case it went away. "Perhaps I have."

Must she venture out of the house? Mightn't that rob her? As soon as she emerged onto the street she knew she was in no danger. Her smile opened to the sunlight. The sky seemed to widen, flawlessly blue.

"Well," Mrs. Hale called from the doorway, "it was a nice surprise to see you. I'm glad it made you happy to come back."

She sounded forgiving, almost apologetic, but Rose scarcely heard her as she hurried toward the promenade. After the briefest of hesitations, she reached in her pocket. To hesitate seemed disloyal. She dropped the packet of Librium in a wastebin, beside a dead sherry bottle, and strode up the brilliant street. Someone was on either side of her, guarding her. To see them would be superfluous. She knew they were there.

XXVI

Rose woke alone.

She had been dreaming of a struggle in a gray place where boundaries and forms shifted like fog. Everything was obscure: the participants, the reason for the struggle, its outcome. She knew only that one of the combatants was insidious and detestable. Then there had been a glimpse of something leggy that searched for prey. Its web was the spaces between the stars, its substance was far darker, and unthinkable. As she opened her eyes to escape the shadow of the dreams, she felt she was alone.

Not only Bill's side of the bed was empty: the house seemed to be. She began to breathe slowly from her diaphragm, trying to calm herself before her nerves drew tight. Sunlight thinned the curtains, planed the walls; the room was a bright box whose emptiness the furniture could not relieve.

All at once she relaxed. Her guardians were near. She couldn't distinguish individual personalities, but she sensed vigilance. She was being watched over. Bill was at work, but she had no lectures until this afternoon. She could relax.

She drew the curtains and saw the autumn. Mist, a penumbra of the Mersey, lay on the grass beside the promenade. Mist filled the outlines of trees on the far side of the field, like a ghost of light.

Eventually she strolled down Fulwood Park. Slow autumn flames were consuming the green of trees. Leaves tingled in a breeze and fell away like paint flaking to reveal the preliminary sketch of branches. Sunlight nested in foliage, igniting colors. A bird fluttered on a tree trunk, searching for insects—then it fell, for it was a dead leaf. Leaves scraped along the roadway like tinfoil. She felt melancholy, resigned. Were her gifts dying too?

Southport had given her peace. A session of acupuncture—needles pricking like migraine in reverse—had made her peace explicable to Bill. One day she'd wandered in the field beside the Mersey, and had felt ready for a revelation, something that would involve her new gifts to the full. Everything had seemed close and absolutely clear: across the river, windows shimmered, pierced by sunlight; across the railway cutting, bay windows framed tableaux of domestic life. The shapes of grass blades were repeated and developed and transformed like musical phrases, moving in chorus. Sunlight streamed from the sides of a liner, massive yet graceful as a cloud.

But the day had dimmed, and so had her expectancy: not yet, her mind had murmured. Now only pigeons moved in the field, nodding sagely to themselves, wings folded neatly behind their backs. They looked as earthbound as she felt.

She felt almost too secure with her gifts. Her writing and Bill's harmonized perfectly now; she'd found that skill within herself—and yet it felt as though she was imitating him. She was more open to her students and their ideas, more able to guide them to express half-formed, sometimes unspoken, notions. But all this seemed to trivialize her gifts.

She waited for a bus on Aigburth Road. A sodium lamp glowed like an ashen ember. At least her resignation meant that she was adjusting. Perhaps her gifts were only dormant, ready when needed—if Bill were ever in danger again, for example. He would be watched over, just as she was. What more did she want? She didn't care whether Diana replied to her question.

She reached the University well before lunchtime. Students flocked over the paved campus; the younger ones looked as if they were just beginning to find their way. Scarves fished for breezes. Leaves scurried toward Abercromby Square. She must remember to show Jack and Diana the Bishop's Palace in the square, where the single star beneath a window was supposed to have denoted the Confederate Embassy.

When she saw the envelope on her desk she thought at once of Diana, though at first she wasn't sure why. If Diana had written to her at the University rather than at home, what was she anxious to keep from Bill?

No, the letter had been posted in England, in Manchester. It might still be Diana's doing. Rose was all at once eager to open it, yet afraid of being disappointed. The printing of the address was odd: after "Mrs. R. Tierney" the ungainly capitals grew larger and more clumsy. The cheap brown envelope was the size of a thin pamphlet, and that was what it contained.

The paper of the pamphlet was cheap too. Nevertheless, a rayed sun was printed on both pages; its rays embraced each page, through the text. The text itself faded toward the edges, as though fog had seeped into the margins. On the cover, the title stood out black and thick as tar against the printed sun: ASTRAL ARMAMENT. Within, the text was laid out in paragraphs, like an unquestioned catechism.

We of Astral Armament are a group of ordinary people who have discovered extraordinary powers within ourselves.

We believe that these powers are not so extraordinary or so rare as many people think.

We believe that many people have untapped powers, sometimes called psychic powers.

We believe that you have had certain experiences—experiences which you may have told nobody else about—which suggest that you have untapped powers.

We believe that these powers are best developed in a group, to guard against mishaps caused by panic or lack of experience. Perhaps you have already had mishaps which have made you wary of developing your powers by yourself.

We believe that people who have such powers must unite in developing them for the common good.

While we are not a religious organization, we believe that our experiences as a group can help us understand and aid the powers of right which oppose the forces of chaos.

Then the pamphlet's tone seemed to slip awry, and began to sound like an advertising circular: please write if you are interested, attend one meeting, no attempt will be made to force you to join us. Come and look round, Rose thought, no obligation to buy. Finally, rubber-stamped on the page, there was an address in Hulme, a suburb of Manchester.

She knew Hulme. She and Bill often went there to the Aaben cinema, to see films that seldom reached Liverpool. Hulme was a mass of council flats and council houses, which seemed an appropriate origin for the amateurish pamphlet. But could the pamphlet be dismissed so glibly?

She thought not. However they had managed to contact her, it seemed to prove they had something to offer. If Diana had given them the address, Rose was a little annoyed with her, but it suggested that Diana trusted them. Rose had written to her weeks ago, asking whether she knew of anyone who offered psychic training—there had been no help in the Liverpool telephone directory, nothing between Occleston and Ocean except Occomore. On the other hand, if Diana hadn't told them Rose was interested, then the very fact that they knew was promising.

Her intuition couldn't grasp the pamphlet. Any feeling the pamphlet might communicate was lost among its ambiguities. Surely they were anything but "ordinary people"—but perhaps they didn't want to scare away potential members. If they were "not a religious organization," why did they believe, believe, believe? Perhaps they were taking care not to estrange atheists.

Nothing would come of wondering. She had to find out more about them, preferably before she promised to meet them. She wasn't apprehensive, only cautious. An excuse was readily available for her to go and look at the address. She called Bill on the internal phone.

"If I don't see you before, I'll probably see you down there," he was saying. "Oh, hello, Rose."

"Hello. I was wondering if we wanted to see the Chabrol film at the Aaben tomorrow."

"Yes, I should think so. It would have to be the evening, of course."

"Well, quite. Actually, I was thinking that since you're lecturing in the afternoon, I could go down and wander round the shops."

"I wish I could join you." She didn't know if he looked at his watch before saying, "Why, it's nearly lunchtime, isn't it? Are you in your room? I'll come and collect you in a few minutes."

She hoped he wouldn't think it odd that she hadn't waited until lunch to speak to him. As she put down the phone she was doubly glad that it had done its job, making it impossible for him to see her face.

XXVII

"Somewhere in England there stands a small house. It looks exactly like the other houses in its row, and millions of other houses. Yet I believe it is the most evil house in the world. I hope this book will make it clear why I prefer not to state where it is."

That was a good start, Rose thought, in a sense: terse, worded simply, calculated to make you turn the page; a professional's opening. It seemed designed to seize the casual reader at station bookstalls. Still, she could hardly complain about that, for she had picked up the book to read on the train.

Finding that she had half an hour to wait at Lime Street, she had strolled across to the library. She hadn't expected the book still to be reserved for her. Presumably nobody else had asked for it; certainly it took a kind of courage to ask, "Have you *Astral Rape?*"

There wasn't much left of the jacket; someone must have used the flaps for bookmarks. The fragment that clung to the front board said only *Astral Rape*, by Hugh Willis. She turned it on its face while she gazed from the train.

The edges of the landscape were consumed by fog.

The far ends of streets looked burned away, transformed overnight into smoke. The sun was a shrunken disc of glass or metal. When the train left the city the fog advanced, dissolving the yellow fields. The grass looked senile with frost. After a while she reopened the book, skipping the rest of the preface, whose vagueness was no doubt meant to be tempting. Chapter One: *The Priest of Evil*. Oh dear.

"The Victorian Age was an age of social injustice and social reform, of high standards and secret vices, of revolutions both industrial and political, of Richard Wagner and Thomas Hardy, of van Gogh and Jack the Ripper. In England it was a great age of scientific discovery—but it was also the great age of the occult.

"It was the age of secret societies, and of societies which required new members to swear occult oaths and to practice secret rituals and disciplines . . ."

She scanned the rest of the page: the Rosicrucians still flourish; libraries still stock books by Madame Blavatsky, who brought secret Tibetan doctrines to the West and founded the Theosophical Society. "These societies, so far as we know, have done no harm—but one society produced two of the blackest magicians who have ever lived. One of the men was Aleister Crowley, whom newspapers called 'the Wickedest Man in the World'; the other, and worse, is the subject of this book.

"The Hermetic Order of the Golden Dawn—'hermetic' means both 'magical' and 'closed'—was founded in 1887 by the coroner for North-East London, Dr. Wynn Westcott, together with William Woodman, a Freemason and occultist, and Samuel Liddell Mathers, later to become curator of the Horniman Museum." There followed a list of members: The Astronomer Royal of Scotland; the poet William Butler Yeats, who won the Nobel Prize; Oscar Wilde's wife; authors of occult fiction—Algernon Blackwood, Arthur Machen, Sax Rohmer, Bram Stoker; Sir Gerald

Kelly, President of the Royal Academy; Florence Farr, director of the Abbey Theater. On joining the Order, all of them must have sworn "to prosecute with zeal the study of the occult sciences." Rose was beginning to feel that she was in good company.

The Golden Dawn was divided into an Outer and an Inner Order. When a member reached the Inner Order, having undergone a series of ceremonial initiations, he had to take another oath. Among other things, he declared his intention to "attain to be more than human." This must have particularly appealed to an English clergyman, Peter Grace.

It is difficult to find out much about him before he joined the Golden Dawn. Peter Grace may not have been his real name, since no such name can be traced before he joined. Quite possibly his superiors in the church had him quietly stricken from the records; he boasted that they were glad to disown him.

In another age he might have been a visionary. But at this time, when the church found it prudent to appeal to rationality, he was an embarrassment, a throwback who preached fiery sermons on the growing menace of science, which he believed was destroying both man's soul and his world. He especially hated psychiatry—"the thief of man's divine spark."

When he began to claim that he saw visions of the world ravaged by science, and refused to deny them when called upon to do so by his bishop, he was posted to a remote parish where, presumably, he would be less embarrassing. Instead he left the church, and joined the Golden Dawn.

If Grace's progress through the Order was in any way remarkable, no evidence remains, though some of Yeats's poems contain veiled references to

Grace's visions. We next hear of him, having attained the status of Adept, in 1900. Under the name of Pater Luminis—Father of Light—he began to question the aims of the Order. In a letter, he challenges Mathers to direct the Order toward a more positive (as he sees it) goal. "Our aim should not be to become more than human, for we are already that, but to awaken mankind to the conspiracy between science, politics and the churches to reduce man to a subject for experiment, a pawn to be deployed."

In the same letter he describes his visions more fully. "My soul can fly to a place where I am shown what is to come. The place has no boundaries as rooms have, unless I make them. My body must be limited, but there my soul is not, which is as it should be. There I can see what is to come, as it were a picture gallery."

He may have exaggerated in order to impress Mathers, whose leadership he became obsessed with challenging. He felt that Mathers, who claimed to have met the "Secret Chiefs" of the Order astrally, was willfully hindering the Order from researching astral projection. "Is it timidity that gives rise to such lack of zeal," he demands late in the exchange of letters, "or the old trick of the dog in the manger?"

The next several pages explained astral projection. Rose skipped them, though one line caught her eye: "Unsupervised astral projection is definitely not to be risked, because—like some drugs—the experience can release repressed or atavistic material from the subconscious." Her subconscious must be well under control, since she'd experienced no such release.

"In one letter, apparently in an attempt to convince Mathers of the urgency of his proposals, Grace describes a vision fully. 'The conspirators will set men at one another's throats. Men will dig holes in which to be killed. Those whom weapons spare will nonetheless be crippled. From this chaos the nations will build a false order. From this iniquitous division of the spoils, worse misery will proceed. Again men will be set to fight, striking one another down from the air. Men will be driven underground for shelter. Nothing will end this slaughter except devastation, compared to which hell-fire is a taper.' Despite its vagueness, this seems a remarkably accurate prediction of the two World Wars."

Mathers was not impressed; at least, not outwardly. "I shall not tolerate any futher attempts to interfere with the hierarchy of the Order." Already the Order was troubled by schisms; Crowley went so far as to challenge Mathers to a magical duel. Perhaps Grace saw an opportunity to make his bid for leadership. But he failed, even in an attempt to set up his own Temple outside London and to take some members, including Crowley, with him.

Nevertheless, when he left the Order, he gathered a group of occult experimenters about himself in a small country town. At first he named the house where they met the Anubis Temple, though it was an ordinary terraced house. (There was a Horus Temple in Bradford, and the Isis-Urania Temple—the original home of the Order—was simply a set of rooms in a London back street.) Before long, however, he declared that he owed nothing to the Order, for "they are too bent upon their navels to see what needs to be done." He grew fond of boasting that his aims were both essential and unique.

His primary aim was personal immortality.

Whatever he may have told his followers, this aim did not include them. Though he was generally careful to conceal his feelings, he regarded his followers as, at best, apprentices to serve him. It seems likely that the small town where he settled had been near to his original parish, and perhaps some of his followers were parishoners who had sought his advice on occult matters. More experienced occultists joined him in time, attracted by rumours of his experiments, but his opinion of them was not high. Apparently, despite his boasting, he still yearned for the Golden Dawn, perhaps regarding it as a fellowship of equals.

Our knowledge of his experiments comes from that once-famous document, *The Confessions of a Reformed Magician*. Published anonymously in the 1920s, the pamphlet was supposed to have been written by a man who had practiced, in his own words, "black magic" before entering a monastery as penance. It became fashionable to have read it, and for a while copies were eagerly sought, since it was supposed to describe secrets of Crowley's own order, the Argentum Astrum. When someone pointed out that the occult leader described in the pamphlet did not resemble Crowley, interest quickly waned.

But the occultist was Grace, and this is a description of him: "At first sight he seemed a model clergyman: taller than the average, straight-backed and slim. His face always calm, like a blessing. His hair and his brows pure white. His voice so quiet and gentle that one seemed to hear it in a dream. But now I think he stood so straight because he was unbending, and would not stoop to those whom he thought lesser than himself. His was the quietness of one who is careless of being heard, so that one must strain to hear him, as though his words are precious. His eyes were always mild, but their mildness was that of one who knows he will be obeyed. Perhaps they conspired with his words to sway us, his followers. Yet would God allow one to commit evil against one's will?"

Rose skipped a few pages. "Immortality has always been mankind's great dream; alchemists sought the elixir of life; today, surgeons . . ." She was halfway to Manchester, but only a few chapters into the book. "Perhaps there is no evil in the search for immortality—but there was in Grace's methods.

"Immortality of the body he dismissed as absurd. Reincarnation was the key. Yet reincarnation as it was generally understood—to be reborn only to have to relearn the world—was no longer enough. He was convinced that adepts such as himself would lead a revolt against 'Science the Destroyer, and its lackeys, Religion and Politics.' His paranoia was growing, perhaps because his hopes had been betrayed first by the church and then by the Golden Dawn. It seemed to him that since the adepts might be betrayed after their deaths by their followers, the adepts must not die.

"His plan for rebirth was simple and terrible. Since he was able to leave his own body, he believed that he ought to be able to enter another body if its personality could be overcome. A baby's should be no match for him. He grew convinced that in order to succeed, he must will his death on one of several dates calculated by magical formulas. This much we know from a letter to Crowley.

"So—incredible as it may sound, though it is evidence of the hold he had over his followers—he trained some of them in astral projection, in order to discover whether he could enter their bodies while 'empty' and make them behave as he wished."

Rose jerked as though awakened violently. The book snapped shut on her lap. She'd glimpsed her body sitting up in the Ananda Marga circle. Backs of heads swayed against seats, as though a nervous tic had become epidemic. Houses floated, robbed of foundations. The coating of frost seemed to drain the fields of color, to feed its own muffled glow. She wished she could see at least one face.

After a while she began to dodge from page to page. Eventually a phrase caught her. "Then, as if to help him develop his growing power, coincidence gave him a victim even less willing than his followers: a runaway child, perhaps from the nearby workhouse.

"Ill luck must have been abroad that night. Of all the strangers whom she could have turned to in the strange town, why did the child pick Grace? No doubt when the tall man who looked like a clergyman came out of his house and asked if she was lost, she thought she was saved.

"We can imagine more than the writer of the pamphlet dared describe: the child tempted into the house by a promise of sanctuary, only to be seized and gagged by Grace's followers; her struggles as she was surrounded in a darkened room by people whose sole purpose was to terrify her, to assault her with the psychic energy which was their only real usefulness to Grace. Perhaps she saw the man who had looked like a clergyman lying down nearby and apparently becoming a corpse. She must have been frantic to escape—to die, if that was the only way. No doubt it was easy for them to driver her out of her body.

"After a time she ceased struggling, and began to smile.

"The author of the pamphlet never forgot that scene, despite years of trying. The child—no more than ten years old—stood up and stalked around the room straight-backed, as though imitating a favorite uncle. When she began to speak, several of Grace's followers were so appalled that they blocked their ears. It was still her voice, but the words were not hers, nor the tone. Striking a pose which mocked a priest's, but which froze her listeners into attitudes of fearful attention, the child with her piping voice preached a sermon, smiling as the words grew longer and more orotund, that began, 'I am the Resurrection of the Soul.'

"After a while the child began to stride like an actor on a stage, smiling sweetly and declaiming. Grace was pleased with his new toy. Did he grow tired of it at last, or did it collapse, exhausted by the demands he made of it? We know only that the child slumped like a puppet after a performance, while Grace stirred and woke smiling. But the child was dead."

Rose stared from the window. The fog was clearing; houses gathered beside the railway. The colors of gardens looked moistly refreshed. Warrington Station was crowded with stolid reliable faces—but they turned their backs on her when they sat down, and she could see only the tops of their heads, overgrown and inexpressive, not at all companionable. It took her a while to return to the book.

At first Grace seems to have regarded the child's death as a defeat. Perhaps he resented its unexpectedness, or perhaps he had wanted her for futher experiments. Yet before long he was describing it as a stroke of luck—for (he said) it had had the effect of a sacrifice.

He claimed that his experiments, and in particular the girl's death, had attracted beings which wished him to succeed. He conversed with them in his sleep, or outside his body. They had promised him the secret of possessing any body at will. He claimed that others who, in the past, had sought immortality were determined now to be reborn. He called himself "the Leader of the Resurrection."

Most of his followers now considered him to be mad, and it seems obvious that he was. Perhaps the nocturnal meetings in which he claimed to participate, with the dead and with other things, had turned his mind, or perhaps the meetings themselves were only symptoms of madness.

His aims became wilder. Not only did he propose to resurrect "those whose purposes are mine and who have held to them after death"—which might seem to imply a resurrection of the world's most evil people—but he spoke of plans to oust scientists and politicians from their bodies, in order to confound their "conspiracy." All this was only megalomania, but it strengthened his faith that he would succeed, "alive or dead."

He grew obsessed with the idea of his return. "When the conspirators have shown that they can devastate an entire city in an instant, the world may beg to be enslaved by them. But the fire they create will not be their beacon, but their pyre. It will be a sign that we who are more than human are preparing our triumph."

By now his paranoia had grown into an almost psychopathic hatred of anyone who seemed to oppose him—a hatred expressed only by a lowering of his voice, a lifelessness of tone which, the pamphlet says, was as frightening as any aspect of him. "The greatest power in the world is hatred," he used to say toward the end. "You must learn how to hate. Hold fast to your hatred and learn to use its power."

By now several of his followers had deserted him, fleeing not only the group but also the town. Those who had stayed seem to have done so because they feared Grace might find them and steal their bodies in their sleep.

At last he demanded too much of them. One woman gave birth to a child which he claimed for his experiments. He wanted to be sure that the baby could contain his own personality without being destroyed. The mother must have been terrified of him, or mesmerized by him, for on the night he instructed her to, she brought the baby to him.

We can only deduce what happened then. Certainly Grace's followers had had enough, and fled with the baby before it could be harmed. Grace's body was found at the foot of the stairs, its neck broken. Did they hurl it downstairs while his spirit was elsewhere? One thing is certain: they were grateful that his secrets, which he had revealed to none of them, died with him.

One would like to think that at last his followers had listened to their consciences, but this may not have been their motive. According to the pamphlet, the more psychically gifted of the group turned against him because "when he had killed the child, they had glimpsed a horror that began to approach across the web of the stars."

Absurdly, Rose found herself relaxing. Grace, the villain of the piece, was dead. Then why was there so much of the book still left to read? She riffled onward. Houses sank out of sight, swamped by fog.

"Eventually the house was occupied again, despite a vaguely unpleasant reputation which was blamed on Grace's death. Though they had promised to take over the house in the event of his death, his followers avoided it studiously.

"The pamphlet ends with an anecdote. All except one of Grace's followers died childless; it seems they were afraid of his rebirth. One couple, however, bore a child. We have only their word for what happened, and they may have been unbalanced mentally by their experiences with Grace. Quite possibly, terrified of Grace's return, they killed the child.

"The father was acting as midwife, and the mother may well have been confused as to what happened. Nevertheless, they swore that as soon as the baby emerged from the womb, it began not to cry but to scream. Within minutes it was dead. The parents swore—though of course they may have been trying to justify its death to themselves—that the baby died 'trying to speak its name.'"

The fog was crowding forward now, leeching color from the fields. There was nothing solid in it except tall thin shapes full of gaps: trees, or pylons. Her fingernails picked at the pages, twitching them aside. Chapter Nine: *The Undying Threat*.

"My own interest in Grace and his activities stems from two apparently unrelated events: the discovery of a corpse and the death of a middle-aged man.

"Decades after Grace's death, the body of a child was found buried outside the town. The verdict of the inquest was that the girl had died about fifty years before, apparently of natural causes. I am now sure that it was the body of the child whom Grace killed.

"The middle-aged man died shortly after the corpse was discovered. He was found in the front hall of his terraced house, apparently having fallen on the stairs and having been unable to reach the door in order to call for help. His death was attributed to a heart attack. The coroner said that the strain of his exertions must have distorted his face, giving it an expression like that of fear.

"If the yellow press had not reported the case I might never have pursued it. Somehow a reporter traced a friend of the dead man, who said that the man had been growing afraid of the house where he lived. He hadn't told his friend why, but the house 'always had a nasty reputation.'

"At that time I was a journalist who liked to report the supernormal and unexplained . . ."

Was that a canal which had drifted beneath the train, or tarmac, black and glistening? Manchester was near. Her glance raced over paragraphs.

"I think now that the discovery of the child's body awakened something in Grace's house. Perhaps, because he died before he planned to, Grace was less free than he wished, and was trapped where he died. His spirit must have festered there for decades. Who knows why the discovery of the child allowed him to make his presence felt? Perhaps some trace of her terror still clung to her body, and awakened him . . ."

"My first visit to the house hinted to me something of the power that still lurked there. In the living room I found a tattered copy of the pamphlet *The Confessions of a Reformed Magician*. Phrases had been shakily underlined in it, especially one which occurred several times: 'the upper room,' where Grace carried out his experiments. I went upstairs . . ."

"It looked exactly like millions of terraced houses built at the turn of the century, nondescript and rather shabby, with the musty air which untenanted houses have. But it felt unpleasant. My job had made me sensitive to atmospheres, but this was more than an atmosphere. I had the impression that the fabric of the house had changed, as though the walls were rotting within their exterior shell.

"As I reached the upper room I heard something moving inside the walls. It was not a mouse, for it was far too large, and sounded pulpy. I felt that it was groping about just beneath the surface of the walls, trying to find a chink through which it could squeeze out . . ."

Rose turned pages violently. Hurry up, Manchester! She found the book unpleasantly hysterical; it made her feel delirious, on edge—she couldn't tell why. The fog loomed at her shoulder. Well, there was only one more chapter: *The Resurrection of Evil.*

"When I finished writing this book, I thought that was all.

"I went back for a last look at the house. I wanted to be as sure as I could be that I was right not to set fire to it. I believed, and still believe, that to destroy the house might only release what is trapped there.

"I should not have gone back. He was waiting. He knew that I had written this book, and he meant to

terrify me into destroying it. Thank God, I had already
sent it to the publisher.

"Since his death his evil has grown, fed by his
madness and by his companions. Like attracts like after
death. Things deformed by their own evil are his
constant companions. It is as though his corruption has
bred a kind of life.

"I have been to the place where he and his creatures
are festering. He dragged me there, out of my body,
but he could not destroy me. I have seen what he plans
to do to the world . . ."

The book was snatched from Rose's hands. The train
had jerked to a halt. Lights, bleary with traces of fog,
glared in the windows. A crowd of signs repeated
OXFORD ROAD, OXFORD ROAD, OXFORD ROAD; sections of
the words peeked round corners. She stuffed the book
into her handbag, from which it protruded as though
trying to attract her attention. Let it try. She couldn't
think of any reason why she should ever want to open it
again. It had made her feel sick and nervous, and for no
cause. Her dislike for it was close to hatred.

XXVIII

The gray canal into which the steps from the station
plunged was a street. Nearby, on the main road,
headlights collided with fog. High on a tower above the
road a clockface glimmered, a blurred mask on stilts.

Rose picked her way over cobblestones, through an
arch that supported the railway. Darkness clung like
soot beneath the arch. Some of the arches were walled

up, and some of those walls contained doors. Beyond one door, cars were being dismembered. Metal shrieked incessantly beneath the flare of a fluorescent tube.

The narrow streets were closed in by factories and warehouses, a multitude of red bricks interrupted only by ranks of identical windows. Some of the windows looked coated with fog. Bare rooms glared out, their walls oily with paint. She could see nobody in any of the rooms.

She thought she knew where she was going. She was hurrying, though the fog made her feel she was not, and made the buildings look heavy, dark, oppressive. Above a wall tatters of clothing stirred, caught by loops of barbed wire. Beyond the wire a canal was black as treacle, its edges jagged with debris. The sun lay like a tin lid on its surface.

Ahead of her shone a beached liner, a building composed mostly of windows. She turned away, beside a garage above which floated the luminous egg of an Esso sign. Now the windows grew less frequent, and the bricks were closing in. Thick cords that looked drowned dangled six stories, from lofts. A smell of rubber seeped through the fog. Around her was the moaning of machinery, unrelieved except for the slopping of a canal.

The fog was dousing her sense of direction. Perhaps she ought to ask her way. But the streets were deserted, as were the inner courts beyond barred gates, lairs of dim vehicles. Steam hissed from vents in the courtyards. A man peered out of a glass cage within a dark vestibule, but he didn't look encouraging—more like a waxwork left behind after an exhibition, still propped up in the dimness. Was someone descending a fire escape ahead? Rungs were clanking. Yet when she reached the fire escape, there was nothing on it except several stories of identical closed doors.

When she emerged from among the factories, the fog

appeared to be thinning. A yellow forklift truck wandered by like a component in search of its machine. Buses ferried illuminated crowds through the fog; glowing faces sailed over their roofs. She had to squint to make the pillars of the overpass look more solid than the fog.

Beyond a pedestrian subway, in a bowl beneath the overpass, cobbled dunes like scaly backs of buried reptiles supported the pillars. As Rose reached the pedestrian subway to Hulme, a woman struggled out of the dark mouth, dragging a swollen black plastic bag. "Aye, love," she panted. "Go up and turn right. Go straight along for a good bit and you'll come to Partington Street, if they haven't knocked it down."

Most of the streets beyond the subway were crescents, long featureless three-story curves of red brick. Streets which ran straight were cut short by intersections, helped by fog. Whole streets were boarded up, except for infrequent defiantly curtained windows. On narrow strips of lawn, broken saplings leaned against one another. Something like a gravestone said NO BALL GAMES ALLOWED.

Had she been misdirected? Abandoned streets were everywhere, filling the gaps between streets; the farther streets were abstract with fog. Still, she ought to find the place, now that she'd come so far. The effects of the book were fading; perhaps they had been merely the effects of reading on the ill-lit train.

Some of the crescents were mounted with boxy balconies of the same red brick. Their windows were open, but nobody stood gazing. Fog crawled about the deserted rooms. A face moved with her, dodging from window to window of an entire street. She kept reminding herself that it was the reflection of the dull sun.

Where was the main road back to town? She glanced over her shoulder, but there was nothing except layers of streets, some of which might be hulking fog. It was all the fault of the fog, which had robbed her of her sense of direction and seemed to have stuffed her ears until she couldn't hear the guiding sounds of traffic.

Was that the sound of a vehicle? It might be large and distant, or small and close. In a few steps she made out that it was not alone. The hiss of wheels was regular as windshield wipers. She'd found the main road.

She hurried down a street of council houses, two-story concrete boxes jammed together beyond slumped fences and overgrown gardens. Headlamps passed ahead like slow will-o'-the-wisps, beyond a clothesline hanging low as a skipping rope, a pack of cards scattered like an exploded card trick over a tangled garden, a crumpled pamphlet, SQUATTERS OUT in letters half as tall as the house which they defaced, the street sign: Partington Street.

If her sense of direction had brought her here, it seemed to have done so only to disappoint her. The street looked dead. She'd already walked past the address on the pamphlet. Irritably she trudged back.

Perhaps the house was tenanted. The windows were so grimy that she couldn't tell whether the covering within them was newspapers or faded curtains. The garden was humpy mud, covered with stubble and lolling grass-blades. Splintered planks of the fence protruded through the hedge like broken bones. A toy glider with snapped wings stood on its nose in the mud.

If Astral Armament had ever occupied this house, that didn't do much for their image. Still, perhaps that was unfair. If they were devoted to the occult, would appearances matter to them?

She opened the gate, which staggered awry. If they were still here—assuming they hadn't been ousted by squatters—it would do no harm to find out what sort of people they were, and how they had contacted her. As soon as she wanted to leave, she had the excuse of meeting Bill.

The door of the garden shed leaned beside its doorway, like a whore. In the shed the heads of brushes looked swollen with dust on their thin necks. The pale undersides of the house's windows were curtains, after all. There might be a light beyond them, or only the insidious glow of the muffled sun.

When she dragged at the stiff knocker, it almost came away in her hand. Its screws ground in rotten wood. She thumped the door a few times, and waited restlessly. Suppose the knocker had fallen off, landing her in slapstick! Even now it looked ready to drop.

When the door opened she was sure she had wasted her time. The man was middle-aged and shabby. The bent cigarette in his mouth spilled its dandruff over the lapels of his baggy blue suit, whose elbows looked polished. As he frowned up at her, his eyes gleamed warily: did he think she was here to winkle him out of his house? "What can we do for you?" he demanded.

"I'm sorry, I must have the wrong address."

"Maybe you have and maybe you haven't. We won't know unless you tell me what you want."

His dourness amused her. He reminded her of petty men in uniforms; the more minor their responsibilities, the more pompous and unbending they became. "I thought I was sent a pamphlet from this address," she said.

"Aye, you were." He glowered at her from beneath his thick red hair, which overhung his forehead like rusty thatch. "Well, you'd better come in then, hadn't you," he said flatly.

Beyond him was a long kitchen. Uncolored wall cupboards displayed a few cans of food, a torn concertinaed packet of cereal. Metal occupied most of the rest of the wall: a large sink, a larger oven and grill, stained and dull as fog. The room felt cold and empty. On a small table a piece of bread glistened with red jam, which oozed into the serrated gap left by a bite.

The man pushed open a door opposite the oven. The back of his neck looked raw; his hair was chopped off roughly just below his ears. "It's her that you sent the pamphlet," he complained.

His voice was swallowed by the large bare room. Rose saw a rickety desk on which a pile of pamphlets sat beside a rubber stamp and an ink-pad. It was a sketch of an office, a caricature. As in the kitchen, the dim light was heavy with dust.

A young man was advancing from the desk, smiling like a salesman. His hair was tied by a rubber band, and dangled between his shoulders. "This is a surprise," he said in a voice which seemed to fill his chest, emerging unselfconsciously resonant, open as an organ note. "We didn't expect you today."

The shabby man retreated through a doorway at the far end of the kitchen. She glimpsed a small room that looked stuffed with dimness. "I was just in the area," she said. "I thought I'd ask you a few questions before I committed myself."

"Of course." He seemed delighted. "Come along," he said.

He led her across the low-budget office and through another door, into a short hall at whose end she glimpsed the small dim room again. The shabby man was muttering at what sounded to be several people. Perhaps they were a different group, for as she climbed an enclosed stairway from the hall she saw on the half-landing a dusty pile of pamphlets. SQUAT FOR YOUR RIGHTS, the top one said, which she thought was an unfortunate slogan.

The walls of the landing were crowded with doors, which seemed determined to outdo the walls in feature-lessness. Cramped dusty panes above the doors hinted at dimness beyond. The whitewashed walls looked dry, brittle, grown patchily pale with the absence of light. Beyond the ajar bathroom door, a lonely ragged towel drooped from a plastic hook.

The young man ushered her into the back room. "I won't be a moment," he said.

The room was as large as the office below, and as bare. Dust nested in the corners, and in dog-ears of the wallpaper. As she ventured in, floorboards seesawed underfoot, creaking. The castors of a vanished bed had left four rusty stains on the boards.

She pulled open the curtains as best she could; their gliders clung stubbornly to the plastic track. She'd thought the window might be in sight of the main road, but there was only a terrace, nailed shut with boards, beyond concrete paths engulfed by mud. She could hear a murmur of traffic, and was just able to see headlights swimming through the fog at the end of the terrace.

The young man came hurrying upstairs, conferring with someone. She hoped they wouldn't try and induce her to join them. She must keep asking questions, to give them no chance. How many of them were on the stairs? Half a dozen, by the sound of it—the ones who had been in the back room. Surely they didn't propose to hold a meeting now on her behalf.

"You'll admit I was right," the young man was saying with perhaps a tinge of bitterness.

"I hope so," a man said in a voice so exaggeratedly English as to sound snobbish. He strode into the room as though braving a lair. At once the rest followed—the young resonant man, the shabby man, and others—but Rose saw only the man who led them.

"I didn't think you would be tempted," he said. His bald head gleamed with sweat. "I really thought we'd have to come to you."

XXIX

She recognized him immediately. She had seen him before, in Lewis's store in Liverpool, spying on her across the bookshelves. She saw triumph in his eyes, which looked less welcoming than vicious.

She kept her voice level. "I'm sorry, I hadn't realized it was so late. I must go."

Was she hoping that to be matter-of-fact would turn the situation into a misunderstanding, an excess of missionary zeal? His only reply was to close the door and stand against it, blocking her way.

Panic stirred in the pit of her stomach, but she said firmly, "Will you let me out, please."

His followers answered for him. They spread out on both sides of him and began to advance on her. There was an enormous woman in a flowered dress, whose round face was propped on a heap of chins and quivered as she plodded. There was a man whose left cheek was purple, crumpled by either a burn or a birthmark. Another man was very thin; his shoulders jerked repetitively, as if trying to dislodge an invisible burden. Beside them were the shabby man and the long-haired youth, who was smiling faintly, unreadably. They were taking their time. After all, she couldn't escape.

She stood her ground. "I advise you to get out of my way. I'm already late for meeting my husband. He knows I'm here, and he won't wait long before he comes to find me."

A smirk appeared on all their faces. Their uniformity was terrifying. "I don't think so," the bald man said.

Suddenly, instinctively, she appealed to the young man. He looked more human than the others; surely he must have feelings of his own. "What do you want? You aren't going to scare me." She felt a shiver almost reaching her voice. "Why do you want to try?"

He stared at her. His indifference was as easy as his smile had been. The bald man said, "I think you know perfectly well."

But she didn't, nor did she want to, in case the knowledge left her vulnerable to panic. She wouldn't be intimidated. Where was her inner strength? Why was she waiting like a fool for them to reach her? By God, if he didn't stand out of her way she would do something to him that would make him fall aside. She strode at him, ready to claw them if they tried to stop her, ready to club them with her handbag, which felt reassuringly heavy—and the book fell out of her bag.

All of them glanced down, then back at her. Let them have the book, it was exactly the sort of hysterical nonsense they deserved. But some of them were smirking again: the youth with the ponytail, the shabby man. Only the enormous woman looked obscurely dismayed. She could hardly have been as dismayed as Rose.

Yes, Rose knew what they wanted. Only a conviction that she couldn't be trapped so easily had prevented her from admitting it to herself. She'd read of a girl who had been lured into a house by a group fanatically devoted to astral experiments, yet her instincts had warned her of nothing. The influence of Peter Grace was not dead, yet she had had no premonition that she would meet it here.

Panic reached her. As the five of them closed in, she began to back away. The young man kicked *Astral Rape* aside. She heard it slither across the boards. She heard their padding, which sounded as though they were treading a carpet of dust. Dust and fear parched her throat. Their glistening eyes closed in.

They saw her fear. "That's right, you're on our ground now," said the man with the purple cheek. "Not yours."

His Lancashire accent was so pronounced that he sounded like a music-hall comedian or a character in an old British film comedy. What could go on in the mind of someone who talked like that yet behaved as he was behaving?

Rose began to turn. Perhaps she could smash the window and cry for help. But the terrace opposite was derelict, and the fog would muffle her cries, as it was subduing the murmur of traffic. If she jumped from the window, the flagstones of the backyard would certainly break her bones.

"She knows she can't escape," the young man observed.

"Good," the bald man said. "Good. Let me see her."

The semicircle parted for him. Though he hadn't moved from the door, his gaze felt so piercing that he might have been close enough to touch. If only he were! She'd rake his face, make him blink—but she could feel his gaze entering her, stiffening her limbs, slowing her blood. She could only look away and try to plan before her thoughts were shaken apart by panic.

Looking away was useless. Everywhere she looked, eyes were waiting, determined to render her helpless. There might have been a single mind within them. The enormous woman's head was squirming back and forth on its rolls of fat, but her gaze never wavered from Rose.

"We have to do this," the bald man said. For a moment, grotesquely, Rose thought he was apologizing to her. He must be addressing the enormous woman, whose face hardened and seemed to arrest the head on the swollen neck. Rose felt their assault intensify.

They were dwindling her. Their own personalities had been swallowed by fanaticism. They were a single personality, massive and overpowering. Absolute faith and hatred gleamed like metal in their eyes. As she shrank within herself, trying to retreat from their probing, the walls grew distant. The room was a desert, dusty, lifeless, immense.

If her strength had been down here, deep in herself, it was lost. They had infected her with vertigo. There was nothing to which her mind could cling. She had ceased to be aware of the room except as a desiccated void, a vacuum into which she was about to rush. She was trembling. How long before her trembling shook her out into the open?

The bald man stepped forward. They were ready to execute their plan. All at once she was sure what they meant to do: to emerge into the void and capture her.

Images rapid as the events of a nightmare, but far clearer, seized her mind. The woman would rush out of her body like melting fat, gray and suffocating. The young man would be something bland and insidious, featureless as a worm. The shabby man would be harsh as acrid smoke. Perhaps the thin man would be quickest to capture her, a jerking bundle of gray sticks with hands and a skull. The bald man's head looked brittle, and was twitching; would it crack to let him ooze out? Certainly the purple cheek of the Lancashire man was working, bulging. It might only be his tongue that was writhing—but perhaps he would emerge from the discolored flesh nevertheless, like a flood of poison.

Among the shrunken huddle of her thoughts, an idea was struggling to make itself heard. While they were preparing to emerge, their bodies on the edge of trance, they might be unable to capture her physically. If she could move now, dodge through the gap and past the bald man, she had a chance.

Perhaps they had anticipated her ruse, for she could not stir.

Yes, she could. Of course she could. She must. She

had time to remember how to control her body, she'd learned how to merge with it, that was all she needed to remember, that instinctive control. Just let her intuition take over, believe that it could do so, just let it move one muscle and the rest would follow, before the gray things emerged, dropping their bodies like discarded clothing, and dragged her out into their midst—just let a cry reach her throat, a cry of outrage that would give her strength, just let her mouth suck air into her lungs, let her throat which was drowning in saliva form the sound, let her cry out, oh please—

But when the cry came, it was not from Rose.

It was the enormous woman. "I can't," she cried, shaking her head; her face wobbled. The interruption gave back to Rose her awareness of the room—a large dusty room, that was all. The woman blundered out before the bald man could stop her. The floorboards rumbled like a bowling alley.

When Rose's fist clenched, she realized she could move. The eyes, which had wavered momentarily, turned back to her, united in a single paralyzing glare. It had changed somehow; it was more violent, more determined yet less powerful, more— All at once she knew: they were afraid.

By God, so they ought to be. Already one of them had fled—and of course, they hadn't been expecting Rose: very possibly they had planned to overwhelm her in greater numbers than had happened to be here today. Let them try to overcome her now! Her power was coursing through her, the power they must have planned to capture by trickery, by paralyzing her thoughts.

They were glaring at her. They looked absurd and pathetic, a few grotesque figures isolated in a room that hadn't been cleaned for months. They might have been overgrown children, trying to outstare her, or dusty dummies abandoned in a loft, their eyes incapable of movement. They looked dwindled from her first sight of them, and she couldn't understand how she could ever have been afraid: of a sly youth with a ponytail, a man with elbows that looked oily, a music-hall failure who was trying to ignore one side of his own face, a man who could only shrug, a poor man's Yul Brynner? Come out and fight! her mind was mocking them. She was possessed by a fit of laughter.

Abruptly she tired of them. They weren't even worth mocking. They looked as if they wished they dared to back away. Yes, they were like dummies, their eyes too cheaply manufactured to contain individuality. All their faces looked beaten, exhausted.

When she strode toward them they winced back. Only the bald man tried to hinder her. "Get out of my way," she said coldly, and experienced a surge of hatred: she'd asked him to stand aside before, and he hadn't deferred to her; this time she wouldn't waste words. The slap seemed to fill the room. He staggered back, his cheek almost the color of the disfigured man's. The tingle of her palm was intensely satisfying.

She marched downstairs. Dust swarmed about her face. She wrenched open the front door, challenging anyone to be there. The fog was clearing; patches of grass shone as though it were spring. She stood outside the lolling gate and stared back at the windows as she breathed out the derelict smell of the house. Faces peered through curtains upstairs, then flinched back. So they should. She turned unhurriedly and headed for the main road.

XXX

Rose had nearly reached the cinema when she began to smile.

Of course, she knew why she'd had no premonition: because there had been no need. She was stronger than they were—far stronger than she had been the night they had shaken her out of her body to drag her into the river and beneath the earth.

She was sure that was who they were. She had seemed to be dragged beneath the earth for hours, no doubt so that she wouldn't be able to locate them. The bald man must have sensed her powers before she had; that was why he'd followed her in Liverpool. Well, they knew now that she was more than equal to them.

She strolled among the council houses. Twilight and returning fog made concrete indistinguishable from the gaps between, but she wasn't lost now. Had it been the weather which had robbed her of awareness of her guardians? At least they hadn't withdrawn from her because of the distrust her panic had caused her to feel, her sense of having been betrayed. She felt watched over now, secure—secure enough not to let Bill suspect that anything had happened today.

She was smiling when she met Bill. He stood beneath the marquee of the cinema, among three-story crescents that looked overgrown with balconies and harsh protrusions—crescents drowned in the fog and covered with artificial coral. Light from the foyer smoked around him. He peered out of the blue hood of his windbreaker, one finger poking his glasses higher on his nose, as if that would clear the fog from his eyes.

When he saw her he smiled widely. He thought she was smiling at him. Her expression wavered before she realized that it didn't reveal its source.

"You're late." He added quickly, "It doesn't matter. We would have been too early—I read the times wrong. What have you been doing?"

"Oh, just exploring."

"Is that all?" The remark wasn't quite casual; he sounded as though he would welcome reassurance.

"Yes, that's all. What did you expect?"

"I don't know. You just seem—I can't put it into words. Changed, but that doesn't quite express it." He was becoming more unsure of himself as she continued to smile at him. "Anyway, you know," he stumbled on, "if there's anything you want to tell me . . ."

"Of course I would, but there's nothing of the kind."

"All right." In the time it took him to nod once, a frown appeared and vanished. Was he faintly aloof as he held open the foyer door for her, or did her secretiveness make her feel that he ought to be?

As they went upstairs to the largest of the four units into which the cinema had been divided, he said, "There's a letter for you from Diana."

"Oh, yes." She'd delay reading it until he was out of the way.

A block of people sat isolated by the auditorium. The numbers of the Tierney's tickets added them to one end. Curtains stirred sleepily on the blank screen. "Here you are," Bill said, taking the letter from his briefcase.

Good God, was the envelope open? No, a stray shadow had appeared to gape beneath the flap. As instructed, Diana had addressed the letter to Rose alone. Rose was opening her bag to stow the letter out of sight when he said, "Aren't you going to read it?"

"Yes, I will in a minute. Have you got a program?"

"No. We can pick one up on the way out."

"Would you mind very much getting one now?"

"The film will be starting in a minute." When she continued to smile at him, he grumbled, "Oh, all right," and hurried away.

She ripped the envelope open so violently she thought he must hear—but the double doors were closing behind him. Beside them a face and the eye of the projector peered through a miniature window. She read hastily, squinting through the dimness, to be finished before the film began.

Dear Rose,

Sorry I don't know anyone in England who could help you develop your powers. I wish you could meet my occultist. He is very interested in what we found out in Munich. In fact he thinks that the present interest in Hitler, all the books and films, may be an omen.

I guess you read *Astral Rape* by now. What did you think? Did you know Hitler hated psychiatry just as Peter Grace did? He called it "Jewish medicine." Speaking of which, maybe you know Hitler always suspected he had Jewish blood, so he had his blood drained by leeches and then later on by a surgeon, Doctor Morell. Remember it says in the letter we were given in Munich that he thinks his flesh is poisoned. That would be a strange thing to put in if the letter was a forgery, right?

Jack has kind of lost interest, but I really think you ought to write this article, it may be important. Here are some more things I found out. You know Hitler was hung up on conquering time. He never wore a watch and wouldn't let anyone wind his clock. He used to talk about resurrection a lot, and he believed there was an elixir of youth, he wanted to send an expedition to India to find it. You know he used to hate the moon? When he was 35 he said to Hess, "It is something dead and terrible and inhuman . . . It is as if in the moon a part of the terror still lives which the moon once sent down over the earth." It sounds like he was talking about some kind of occult force, and remember Dietrich said he was supposed to have called up something he was scared of.

Then he once said, "I have to attain immortality even if the whole German nation perishes in the process." I keep reading one thing about him, that he planned all he was going to achieve when he was young and then achieved nearly all of it. Maybe he achieved more than people think. What I just quoted sounds like the way he wanted Germany destroyed at the end, doesn't it? And right at the end when they said he was senile, his eyes were still alive. See, he could stay alive when they thought he should be dead.

One frightening thing I saw in a book is a painting by a guy called Franz von Stuck, who was Hitler's favorite artist. It's called *The Wild Chase*, and it shows the god Wotan hunting on a horse with hounds. He's got a head hanging from his sword and there are things like corpses running around him howling. Only his face is exactly like Hitler's, even the moustache and the forelock. That's why I find this idea about new omens a bit frightening, because *The Wild Chase* was painted in 1889, the year Hitler was born! My occultist says that if there were more people committed to destroying everything that's left of Grace then we wouldn't need to worry about what might happen by mistake if people start experimenting.

Jack and I are disagreeing over a few things, but I hope that's just a process of adjustment. Anyway, we'll see you October 27 or 28, I can't say which yet. I'll try and call you to let you know. Jack has a lot of work right now. It'll be good to see you, and I hope you'll be able to help me develop my gifts too, which I'm trying to bring out again. I find them very exhausting, as most people do, though I guess you don't.

Love,
Diana

Rose stuffed the letter into her handbag. What a mess of incoherence and non sequiturs! Diana must have been in a hurry. At least Rose was glad that Diana had had nothing to do with Astral Armament. And today had convinced Rose that what was left of Grace was hardly worth noticing. Perhaps the letter would make more sense on a second look—but here was Bill with the program.

As she pretended to read it he said, "Can I see Diana's letter?"

"I'd rather you didn't. Diana asked me not to show it to anyone. Female topics." She felt frustrated, both by the lie and by having to be so banal.

She could tell that he was thinking: not so long ago you'd have shown me anything. It seemed childish, embarrassing. She could only take his hand to compensate for her disdain. She was glad when the darkness closed over his face.

After the film they walked into Manchester. Orange fog loomed beneath sodium lamps. Beside the main road, tracts of land looked built upon by fog. "I saw a book today while I was browsing," Rose said. "*Cinema Plus*. It's about film techniques that didn't last, 3-D, Cinerama, and so on. It reminded me of all kinds of things that I'd forgotten."

"Yes, that's a nice book. I saw it in Liverpool recently."

Of course that was where she had seen it. Perhaps it was less risky to keep silent. Her thoughts felt waterlogged, as the night looked. Fog led her over the pavements, its track glistening. Her footsteps sounded padded.

In the Indian restaurant, a waiter who seemed both slavish and determined insisted on taking their coats.

The restaurant was quiet as a temple, except for Muzak which hovered discreetly at their shoulders. Waiters served them with ritual movements, as though presenting offerings to gods. Rose rather enjoyed their attentions, but could feel that Bill thought they were too servile.

"Jack and Diana are coming on either the 27th or 28th," she said after the first course, hoping that would make him feel less excluded from the letter.

"Can't they be definite? Well, I suppose he's busy. Still, it doesn't make things any easier for you. I wish I didn't have to leave you to entertain them by yourself."

"Oh, I'll enjoy it, don't worry." She would have more chance to tell Diana whatever she had to tell. "I just hope your interview goes well, then we can put *Rediscoveries* together."

"Yes." He was refilling their glasses with Riesling. "Listen, we must get *The Meanings of Stardom* into shape, I know we haven't got a deadline, but still, we've never been this late before. And we did say we'd try and think of a better title."

"I know." For the first time the writing of a book had outstayed the summer holidays. "I'm sorry."

"Christ, it's nobody's fault. It was just a messy summer, that's all."

Over the main course and another bottle of wine he told her, "We were playing at television production today. The staff showing the students how to go about it, and being a lot more self-conscious, as usual. Jim Logan looked as if he was having his picture taken by the police, Maurice sounded like Peter Sellers parodying an elocutionist, Hannah's legs seize up if she even thinks she's being filmed, so she comes on like John Cleese . . ."

"As usual"—that was just the trouble: she'd heard it all before, last year and the year before that. She tried to seem interested, but wasn't sure that he was convinced. Again her smile was a mask.

Abruptly, halfway through the second bottle, he

said, "Listen, if there's something about me that's getting on your nerves or bothering you somehow then you must say, you know. I think it's healthier to bring these things into the open, don't you?" He glared at a waiter who had begun to circle them attentively, mothlike. "I mean, I have tried not to be so monolithic. I don't know if it shows."

"Really, Bill, I don't know how you could improve for me," she said ambiguously. Was he tempting her to criticize him so that he would have an excuse to discuss her, to probe for her secrets? "Just so long as you're there when I need you," she said.

"I don't think you need worry about that." He laid his fork beside a demolished mound of rice. "I was thinking—just thinking, I mustn't be more definite than that—maybe if this interview goes well, we could talk to Jack about the Hollywood idea. Possibly as I gain more experience I'll feel more relaxed with interviewing. Are you still anxious to go over there?"

He was working so hard to reach her, and yet she could only feel cramped: there were so many subjects she had to avoid, so many secrets to be kept from him. She reached for his hand and squeezed it. "We'll see," she said.

When he'd drained another glass of wine he began to quote bad lines from films. Was he trying to cheer her up, or himself? "'Only a miracle can save her,'" he quoted. "'I'll do my best.'" His voice oppressed her, chafing her nerves. Though she responded mechanically, she felt she'd outgrown the humor long ago.

At least the rocking of the train was noisy, and gave her an excuse not to talk. Sleeping commuters swayed on the edge of their seats, suspended by dreams. Rose watched distant sodium lights, embers in the ash of fog. Scattered lit windows resembled stamps, pictorial or blank, left half-consumed in the ash.

In Liverpool, buses lumbered timidly through the fog. Spikes of light protruded from the trees of Fulwood Park. The living room was chill; soon they would have to begin making fires. Perhaps they ought to think of central heating.

Bill heated milk while she spooned chocolate out of the can. They stood in the kitchen, warming their hands round the potbellied mugs. Gazing at her across the table, he said, "Are you tired?"

He wanted to make love. "Turn on the fire upstairs," she said.

As she climbed the stairs she heard the hiss of the gas fire, a shrill wind, incessant and monotonous. The heat of the flames hadn't yet reached very far beyond their cage. Perhaps he would warm her.

But he seemed aloof. As he spread her on the bed she felt more like an anatomical specimen. Though his caresses were urgent, she thought he was less eager to make love than determined to possess her. She trapped him gently, stroking him order to soothe him into awareness of her.

She'd managed to communicate her needs, to an extent. His mouth explored her body, but impatiently. She could feel him willing her to respond, and therefore she felt very little. When her genitals stirred, the reaction seemed separate from her, an uncontrolled convulsion, a nervous tic. How could she respond wholly to him?

She was letting her mind get in the way of her body, that was all. She needed to let go of her doubts, to trust her instincts. Perhaps sex had something in common with her powers. Bill was lowering himself onto her body. The gas fire hissed as though it saw a villain. It all seemed faintly absurd: he was frowning, determined to pin her down with his penis, impale her until she capitulated to him—but these thoughts were treacherous. She had only to feel, to love, to let go. She closed her eyes.

Sensation flooded her at once. She felt pierced with light. At once she was moving with him, riding the waves of light and warmth that were radiating through her. Good Lord, how long had she been capable of an experience like this? It was like her flight above the clouds.

Her thoughts were dissolving, her doubts had been washed away. She'd had only to trust her intuition. Now she was nothing but the surging of the waves of light and ecstasy. The waves reached her lips, parting them in a wide smile. She opened her eyes.

A shudder convulsed her entire body. Her arms jerked, levering him away from her. She cried, "Christ, who—"

She stopped, because it was only Bill—but she was too late. She felt him dwindle within her. As soon as he could, he recoiled. Before he turned his back she had time to glimpse his face, locked into itself by her rebuff.

Her ecstasy had blinded her, her pleasure had been so intense that she'd forgotten momentarily who he was; but how could she expect him to believe that, when she wasn't sure that she believed it herself? She lay inert and heard him masturbating in the bathroom.

Eventually, when she heard him emerge, she went to him. He stood aside as though they were strangers on a hotel landing, and wouldn't look at her. She felt too depressed for tears. When she turned out the light he lay beside her like stone, tolerating her arm about his waist. At last he softened, because he was asleep.

XXXI

The train plunged into darkness. The platform, laden as a lifeboat, sailed away. Lights flicked past, quick as afterimages, on the walls of the roaring tunnel. Abruptly the walls were daylight. The Mersey, an expanse of wrinkled slate, paralleled the railway. Beneath a sky like white tissue paper, ships and warehouses were attended by bony cranes. In the diffused light everything looked sullen, introverted, not quite real.

Rose stared out of the window. At least that gave her a chance not to think. Railway lines bunched under bridges, then frayed into sidings. Patches of grass clung to the stone banks of the cutting, which were the color and almost the texture of soot. At Aintree the banks fell away to reveal a jungle of metal pipes. Beyond Old Roan, fertile fields were divided by canals. Identical houses gathered together for company or reassurance. Outside Maghull, sheep bowed their heads to the grass, hardly moving. Banks of red stone towered over the platforms of Aughton Park. Above the banks, as if to herald Ormskirk, cocks were crowing.

As the train slowed, Bill stood over her to take down the overnight bag. "You look happy," he said.

"Well, we haven't stayed here for a while."

Was he frowning to himself because he thought she would rather be with her parents than alone with him? She must make sure he didn't withdraw from her again. Their sexual misunderstanding had shown her how vulnerable their marriage was.

No, it had been more than a misunderstanding. She'd concluded that her momentary lack of recognition had been a symptom of her growing disillusionment with him. Well, she had no right to feel disillusioned. He was doing all he could to make sure they didn't drift apart.

Though he hadn't referred to the incident since that night, his gentleness and concern for her had themselves been a response. They'd made her feel intensely ashamed. When he'd said that her parents had called and that he'd agreed on her behalf to visit them, she was glad. Perhaps a night here would help their marriage regain its balance.

The Wigan Road was a mass of released schoolchildren, an almost uninterrupted parade of blue. They overwhelmed the pavements, and nearly deafened Rose. Despite the crowd, she stayed on the far side from the shops, and hurried along the block. Could she smell the butcher's through the stench of traffic as she passed the shop? How could it smell so old and rotten?

She slowed when she came in sight of the hospital, which had once been a workhouse but now looked more like a village. Was Wendy on duty today? Climbing Tower Hill, she wondered how many hundred times she must have walked down the hill with her parents or Wendy. In winter it had been a frosty slide, with the Wigan Road lying in wait at the bottom. In autumn she'd tramped through drifts of leaves, which had sounded like the cereal she had just eaten in the mornings. When she was little she had wheeled a doll's pram up and down the hill, and the destinations of the lorries on the Wigan Road had been unimaginable, other worlds. She was glad of these memories. She hadn't lost her sense of herself as she'd used to be.

When her mother opened the door she looked startled. "Oh, I thought you weren't due for an hour."

"Don't tell me Bill quoted you a twenty-four-hour-clock time."

"I'm afraid I did. Sorry, Margaret. We of the jet set go in for these newfangled things," he joked rather self-consciously.

"Well, does it matter? Can't we come in?"

"Of course you can, Rose. What a thing to say!" But as she stood back, the wrinkles of her forehead seemed to deepen. "Your father's just back from an auction," she said.

The dining table was covered with stamps, like an expensive parcel. The overhead lamp had descended its cord, spiderlike, to keep him company. "Oh hello, er, Bill," he said without looking up. "Hello, Rose."

"Shall we keep out of your way? We don't want to send your stamps flying."

He glanced at his wife before answering. "No, stay

and talk to me, Bill. These can wait until I can examine them properly, at the shop. I was just glancing over them."

That looked unlikely, but he was clearing them away. "Are you in the kitchen?" Rose asked her mother. "I'll come and talk to you."

"No, Rose, I don't want interrupting. You know how it is, two women in one kitchen."

Rose had felt like that in her first lodgings, but she and her mother had happily shared. Perhaps sensing that Rose was hurt, her mother said, "I think your father's ready for a game."

"Yes, what about a game of croquet?" He was almost quick enough to make it sound like his own idea. Was Rose's mother preparing surprises in the kitchen? Was that what hid behind her smile?

Her father handed Bill croquet hoops to stick into the lawn. "The only drawback is, we've lost some of the croquet balls. We'll have to use—oh, dear me, what are those things? Good God Almighty, what is the damned game called? Boule, that's right, boule."

Perhaps that was why her mother was anxious: more words were deserting him. Not only his speech but also his game was more erratic than it had used to be. Once he would have used his knowledge of how the lawn tilted to win, but now, even when Rose left him chances to croquet, he missed them.

He spent most of the game talking to her. "Remember the days we used to spend at Martin Mere? They've bred some rarer birds since you were there. Do you recall the time we took you out to Appley Bridge? You remember, that's where Skull House is, where the skull is supposed to return if they try to get rid of it. You wanted to wait outside all day in case you saw it going in . . ." Was he making sure he hadn't lost these memories?

The meal was plain but delicious, like all her mother's cooking. A Mozart string quartet played in the background. It was very much like Bill's and Rose's first dinner here. What books were they planning? What did they think of the state of the world? Did Rose remember old Mrs.———did she remember young——— The chat was bright as the lights, and flashed as the cutlery flashed. Cutlery and china rang like bells.

But the light seemed unrelenting, and the sounds were growing shrill. Her mother's surprise hadn't been the dinner, after all. It hid beneath the conversation, making everything seem brittle. Rose wasn't sure that she would like it when it came.

She helped her mother clear the table. As soon as they reached the kitchen, she said, "Look, mummy, I can't stand this. You keep wanting to say something. What is it?"

"Oh, Rose." Her mother was biting her lip, struggling not to turn away. "Let's leave the washing-up for now and let your father give us both a drink."

"I don't need a drink."

"No, but I do. Oh, don't make it more difficult for me, please."

The light had been switched off above the dining table. At that end of the room, the Mozart quartet fitted notes together in the dark, precisely, neatly, perfectly. Bill and her father were chatting on the sofa, surrounded by muted light. When they saw her mother's face they fell silent.

The silence persisted while her father poured drinks. Bill was gazing at his toecaps and tugging at the remnants of his moustache. He must have sensed that family matters were imminent.

Rose's mother set her drink down carefully, untouched. Perhaps she'd had to know that it was there when she needed it. She gazed determinedly at Rose. "Rose, there's something I haven't been able to talk about ever since you were a little girl. I want to ask you about it now."

"Well, go on."

"Don't sound like that, or I won't be able to."

Rose was convinced she hadn't spoken harshly, but her mother was shaking her head, closing her eyes tight in her nervous way. Eventually her father said, "I'm sure you must remember, Rose. It was the night you went to see that awful film with Wendy, the rock-and-roll thing."

"But she didn't go and see it, George. That's the whole point."

"Didn't she? No, that's right, you didn't, Rose. But it was the night Wendy was supposed to be taking you, that's what I meant to say."

The confusion was frustrating Rose. "Are we talking about *Rock Around the Clock?* One of my childhood mistakes? I did see that with Wendy."

"No you didn't, Rose." All at once her mother was near to angry tears. "You're thinking of some other film you saw with her, another time. You know which night we're talking about now."

"Yes, certainly I do. And I remember seeing that film." She couldn't remember details; films like that were indistinguishable. "I saw it with Wendy at the Pavilion."

Her mother had drawn back, closing her eyes, as though Rose had struck her. Her father was frowning. "Rose, why are you still carrying on like this? Shall I tell you where you were?"

Rose shrugged helplessly. "I know where I was."

"Then you know that you weren't at the film. You were playing at séances. Wendy took you to Richard—oh, what the devil was his name? It doesn't matter. He lived on the Wigan Road near the bus station. He'd involved a whole group of people who ought to have known better. All of them were older than you."

"You've mixed it up with another night," Rose said. "Anyway, I must have found the séance hopelessly disappointing, because I don't even remember—"

"Oh, don't say that, Rose. You know you do." Her mother's hands were clenched in her lap, crumpling handfuls of her skirt. "The little swines locked you in by yourself. You haven't forgotten that, have you? She was so sorry afterwards, the little bitch, saying she hadn't meant to. I never forgave her for that. Do you know, the last thing she said before you went out that night was that she promised to look after you. And Richard, he was just as bad—breaking into a house where someone had died. I wished I could have got hold of him! You were well rid of all of them, that was the one good thing that came of it. Thank God, it wasn't long before you went to grammar school and made new friends."

"Mummy, why are you upsetting yourself?" Rose tried to take her hand, but it was fastened immovably to her skirt. "I don't know who told you all this. How long has it been worrying you? Believe me, it never happened."

"Oh, all right. It never happened." Her mother sounded exhausted, hopelessly. Abruptly she made a last effort. "Rose, it wasn't the others who found you, have your forgotten that? It was Richard's parents. They wouldn't lie, would they? God only knows how long you were left alone in there. You wouldn't speak to anyone when you came out, and I don't blame you, poor child. I know how you must have felt—don't you think I felt it too? We sent you out with that treacherous girl when we should never have trusted her. I don't wonder you blamed us. We sent you to stay with Wilfred and Vi, and that seemed to buck you up. But oh, if you'd only said just a few words to me, even that you blamed me for not looking after you—"

She was weeping. Rose couldn't feel much sympathy; the whole thing made no sense. The names of her aunt and uncle had made her feel protected, but the rest was confusion. She could only say, "This really isn't necessary. You're upsetting yourself for nothing."

"Oh, all right. It's nothing." Her mother was stemming her tears, digging her knuckles into the corners of her eyes.

"Margaret, isn't there another possibility?" Bill sat

forward as though to cut Rose out of his field of vision.
"Perhaps the experience was so traumatic that she
really can't remember."

"Oh no. No, I won't have that. There's nothing
wrong with her mind."

Her father stood up. Was he towering over Rose to
make her feel small, a child again? He needn't bother
trying. No, it was only that the Mozart had ended. A
thin monotonous clicking came out of the dark, the
sound of a trapped insect.

As her father released the needle from the central
groove he said, "As a matter of fact, Margaret, I've
often thought what Bill's suggesting. I didn't mention it
because I knew how you'd react. But really, Margaret,
everyone loses a few memories. God knows I have, but
that doesn't mean there's anything wrong with me. Do
you know, I think if Rose went to a doctor the whole
thing could be straightened out with no trouble at all."

"Look, I haven't left the room, you know. I'm still
here," Rose said angrily. "What whole thing? What
exactly do you mean? There's nothing about me that
needs straightening out so far as I'm concerned."

Suddenly Bill and her father seemed overcome by
clumsiness; all at once they couldn't look at her or at
each other, only at their limbs which had grown restless
and unwieldy. "Yes, there is," her mother said, glaring
at the men for leaving her to say so, "whether you like
it or not. You've been behaving toward Bill exactly as
you used to behave toward us—ever since what happened to you in New York."

When Rose eventually realized what her mother was
saying, she knew why everything had seemed brittle
and false. She stared at Bill until he had to look at her.
"You knew about all this in advance," she said
accusingly.

"Now don't go blaming Bill for everything."

She stared at her mother, who was rallying. Her
father was gazing embarrassed into the surrounding

dark. "You set this up between you," Rose said. "How long have you been discussing me behind my back?"

"Oh, Rose," her mother said, "don't make it sound as though we've been plotting against you."

But that was exactly what they had been doing. A nerve twitched beside Rose's lips; if she spoke it might drag her speech awry. The room was growing distant as an old film, its perspectives flattened, its surface sparkling with threats of migraine.

Her mother assumed that her silence was stubbornness. "Now just you listen to me, Rose. Bill had to talk to someone about all this. Who else could he talk to?"

They must have planned over the phone how to get the better of Rose. It was like a mockery of a birthday surprise. "If anyone says another word about this," she managed to say, "I'm leaving."

"Oh, Rose, don't be childish. We're only doing this because we care about you. We have to get to the bottom of this for your own good and Bill's."

"That's all," Rose said coldly. "I warned you." Her nerves were drawing tighter, tying her into herself. Before anyone could stop her she strode into the hall, grabbed her coat, and elbowed the front door shut behind her.

She hurried toward the railway station. She was a shrunken point of hatred, intense and self-consuming. Perhaps most of all she hated Bill and her parents for making her feel this way, for betraying her to emotions which she'd had under control since childhood.

As she passed warm bright locked-up rooms, she coaxed herself out of the depths of her mind. She didn't need Bill or her parents; she was watched over. But she shouldn't become too dependent on the unseen—nor was that necessary, for she had her inner strength. She needn't trust anyone ever again, and she didn't think she was likely to do so.

Ahead, at the Ribble bus station, the engine of a bus was thumping regularly. In five minutes she would be at the railway station. She hoped there would be a train about to leave, but if she had to wait and they followed her onto the platform, it didn't matter; nothing they said would make her go back to the house.

The thumping was not the sound of an engine, for there was no bus in sight.

She stared along the deserted road. An empty bench sat outside the bus station. Traffic lights climbed, compelled to race, only to fall again; the red light stained the statue of Disraeli like blood. The last terrace of the Wigan Road was the color of mud, and soaked up the light of the streetlamps. One of the downstairs bay windows was lit. From beyond it came the thumping.

That wasn't quite the word. The sound was heavy and regular: chunk, chunk, chunk. She mustn't dawdle, mustn't waste time struggling to remember where she'd heard that sound before; she must hurry past it, before she was too afraid to do so, for it was coming from the shop where darkness and the smell of blood reached for her.

Suddenly she relaxed, although she continued hurrying. Of course, the shop was a butcher's; that explained the sound. She could see the butcher now, a stout red-faced man in a striped apron. On a slab which glared like the fluorescent tube above him, he was chopping meat: chunk, chunk. That explained the smell of blood that tinged the air, she had only to hold her breath as she passed—but all at once she was dizzy, in danger of stumbling, for she'd realized that the butcher's stood next to the house where Richard had lived.

Something had happened there. There must have been a séance, after all. It couldn't have been the night she'd gone with Wendy to the film; she remembered that night, her father trying gently to dissuade her, *The Magic Flute* backing him up. It must have been another night. She thought she was near to remembering, but she mustn't; her mind felt like a thin shell holding down an upheaval of panic. Please let her pass before it overcame her, please!

She was running. The stout man's arm rose and fell, rose and fell, like the arm of a fairground puppet; the cleaver chopped, chopped. His bright apron was stained red. The smell of blood grew in her nostrils, it was muffling all her senses, closing in like thickened darkness. In that darkness something was writhing, growing.

She tried to stare ahead at the traffic lights, which were descending their sequence again, an intolerably monotonous phrase. Nearly there, only twenty more steps, maybe thirty, nearly there—but her head was dragged around, and she was staring at the lightless upper window. Were the curtains about to separate? If part of a face peered through, would it be recognizable as such? She faltered, for she seemed to have forgotten how to move her legs—and then she was running wildly, past the lights, across the path of a screeching car. Shouts pursued her, but she didn't look behind her until she reached the station. Whatever happened, she would never come back here again.

XXXII

"I won't go to London," Bill said.

He'd set down her coffee to close to the typewriter. Now he stood like the mug: stolid, intrusive. Rose pushed the coffee aside, murmuring, "Thanks." Without looking up from the typewriter she said, "Of course you must go."

"No, I think it's better if I stay with you."

"Well, I don't think so. What is this, Bill, some kind of emotional blackmail?"

"Nothing of the kind. Can't I just be anxious to look after my wife?"

"I can look after myself perfectly well." She found his concern oppressively patronizing. Why, she could gaze from the window while the keys chattered beneath her fingers; she could watch the late afternoon light creeping out of the garden and leaving a sediment of shadows, she could look at the stain which the bonfire had left on the wall, an oily black silhouette which raised its unequal arms as its head smoldered and collapsed. That didn't affect her at all. "You must go and interview this man," she said. "You don't want to spoil our book." The typewriter's bell rang, as though at the end of a round.

"Well, can't you—"

"You know I can't come with you. I have important lectures, and besides, I need to be here for our guests. I'll have plenty to talk about to Diana." After a sly pause she added, "And Jack."

He turned away. He couldn't answer that without a full-scale row. In a moment he turned back. "All right, then I'll just go down for the day to interview him. I'll catch the last train back."

"You know quite well that you need to see his films. You must go down early and stay overnight." He was about to disagree, but she said, "Look, Bill, don't annoy me. I'm trying to finish this chapter. If you really care how I feel, just leave me alone."

His descending footsteps sounded tentative, dissatisfied. He'd set thoughts jostling which she had had under control. Before she could continue typing the final draft she must clear her mind.

He'd done the same at Ormskirk station. She had just achieved a kind of peace, founded on her relief at having passed the shop on the Wigan Road, when he had appeared on the platform. "Come back with me,

Rose. You've upset them badly. Please come, I haven't brought the bag." He'd seemed to feel that would sway her. She had turned away, for he'd looked like an amateur performer on the empty stage of the platform: clumsy, inept, embarrassing. The banality of the scene had infuriated her; he was keeping her away from her thoughts. When he'd insisted on following her home she had gazed resolutely out of the window, trying to resolve her insights.

They must have held the séance in the room above the butcher's shop. That was why the window seemed so threatening. Had that been where she'd acquired her powers, which then had lain almost dormant until recently? The séance must have touched them off. That was all she needed to know; she was strong enough not to remember what had happened in that room, and she would never go back. That must have been the memory which Colin had almost reached. No wonder her gifts had at first been associated in her mind with panic.

She was smiling to herself, eyes closed, and nodding. She was calm now. Her fingers were eager to scurry over the keyboard. Before they could do so she heard movement behind her, in the room.

Bill had returned, rather timidly. "Listen, Ro, there is one thing I should have said before." His hands rested on her shoulders, but he was gazing shamefaced at the trees, where dimness was returning to its nests. "I realize now why that séance at the Hays' upset you. I'm sorry, I should have taken your feelings more seriously."

Did he think that made everything right? That wasn't what he should be apologizing for. "All right, Bill," she said indifferently. "Thank you."

She felt his hands slump, then withdraw from her. Perhaps he genuinely didn't realize how much his behavior had hurt her; perhaps he'd convinced himself that because he'd meant to act for her good, that was all that mattered. Trying to be generous, she said, "It is all right, Bill, really. You needn't worry about me. As a matter of fact, I think we might benefit from a couple of days apart. It'll give both of us the chance to think things over."

He was gazing warily at her. He must be sure now that she wanted to get him out of the way so that she could be alone with Diana. Everything about him at the moment chafed her nerves. "Oh, go on, Bill," she said wearily. "Just go away, please."

He assumed she meant immediately, which, apart from the other meaning, she did. He tramped downstairs, each step a phrase in a tirade. With a sigh that mingled relief and resignation, she glanced out of the window, into the peaceful, almost sourceless light, and saw a gray naked dwarf pressed against the inside of the greenhouse. It seemed to have no face or hands, only wads of lard-colored flesh.

She had recoiled from the desk, which rocked dangerously, almost spilling the typewriter, before she saw what the figure was: a stain on the glass of the greenhouse, only now revealed by the way the light was falling. Nevertheless its presence was unbearable. She hurried out into the garden.

The shape was more than a stain. It looked like mold, which had grown in the place where a dwarfish shape had pressed itself against the panes. Mold must have grown there since the greenhouse had been cleared. Mightn't it simply have formed where vine leaves had clung to the glass? But its shape looked too definite to be explained away so easily.

She poured disinfectant into a bucket of boiling water. While she was fetching a scrubbing brush, Bill looked into the kitchen. "What are you doing?"

"Cleaning windows." Impulsively she demanded, "Can you see that?"

He peered toward the greenhouse. "Yes, of course. Why shouldn't I be able to see it?"

"What does it look like to you?"

"Mold, I should think. Why on earth are you asking all these questions?"

"It's all right. I just wanted to know." She could think of nothing else to say. "No, I want to do it," she said when he offered to clean the panes.

The grayish substance felt like gelatin, and squeaked as she scrubbed it away from the glass. Twilight had already massed oppressively within the greenhouse. Furiously she rubbed the last trace of the outline from the panes, and hurried out of the greenhouse, carrying the bucket. Large patches floated on the surface of the water, like scum. When she emptied the bucket down the curbside drain, they clung glistening to the bars of the grid.

As she returned to the house, for a moment she was tempted to tell Bill that he was right, he oughtn't to leave her alone here. That would be childish, an unforgivable betrayal of herself. She must have the courage to trust her own strength. But she couldn't help wondering, until she controlled her thoughts, how recently the marks on the greenhouse windows had been made.

XXXIII

Rose was glad to emerge from her office, though the corridor was dim and the Henry Moore figures on the wall were faceless. The morning's tutorial had been disappointing; because the students had read all the major analyses of *Psycho,* they'd found nothing new to say. They should be more lively tomorrow, when she showed them Bergman's *Hour of the Wolf.*

Wind was hunting among the concrete blocks. Taped saplings tugged at their collars. On the back of Abercromby Square, quivering ivy made the wall appear to shudder. Perhaps the wind would blow away her tension, if that was what it was. All morning her skull had felt heavy and irritable. Perhaps once she met her mother her tension would be resolved.

Bill had left this morning for London. Last night, when her mother had called, Rose had suspected at first that she meant to keep an eye on her in Bill's absence. But her mother had sounded both apologetic and offended, and Rose didn't think she had been hiding a ruse. "I hope we can still meet for lunch occasionally. Anyway, you'll want me to return your bag that you left here."

Winds carried Rose downhill. Clouds like scraps of paper raced across the sky, their edges fluttering. The spiky massive crown of the Catholic cathedral appeared to be floating away. At the bus stops children lay in wait, accompanied by hooded figures with faces of crumpled newspaper; outside Chaucer's Tavern two children were demanding, "Penny for the guy" on behalf of a pink teddy bear as big as they were.

Rose dodged through the lunchtime crowds to Watson Prickard's. The restaurant was in the basement of the store. Fronds of neckties hung from stands; empty school uniforms were lined up like a rank of multiplied reflections. In an alcove guarded by toy pigs and monkeys, figures in white coats flourished razors over men in chairs.

As she went downstairs, past a huddle of virgin suitcases, she saw her mother at a table near the stairs. She was talking to three men. Who were they, and what were they doing here?

"I'm glad you've come, Rose." Her smile looked a little relieved. "I was just telling these gentlemen about your books."

They were only businessmen, in identical dark suits: two middle-aged men and a younger, who kept blushing and agreeing with whatever anyone said. Perhaps one of the men was his father. "Oh yes, certainly, I will," the young man said hastily when Rose's mother asked him to keep their places.

The two women joined the queue. Beneath the low ceiling, lights hovered just above circular tables. Small blue pyramids of menus announced "True Scandinavian Gourmet-style Smörgasbord." On the counter an artificial lobster guarded the fish courses; a chunk of herring had escaped its bowl. A mother was hurrying her child onward: "No, don't touch that. No, you don't want any of those. Not that one, no, you'll be sick." The eyes of hardboiled egg stared out of slices of pie.

"Did you have a good morning?" Rose's mother said.

"Oh, tolerable, I suppose. My students knew all about *Psycho* but didn't have any original ideas. Except one suggested that the fly on Anthony Perkins's hand was a symbol of how he was rotting away from within. My God, listen to my choice of lunchtime conversation!"

But her mother was glad she was chatting so freely. "It must be difficult for them sometimes. I never used to realize how much of a strain it was to study properly—for you, I mean."

"At times it was. I didn't tell you because I didn't want to upset you."

"I might have been upset, that's true. I used to be silly about things like that. I suppose I underestimated your ability to cope. Well, I'm not like that now. Better late than never, don't you think? You see, Bill was telling us how his mind used to behave strangely near exams."

"Oh."

"Yes, he was saying that he used to have lapses of memory. Once he lost a whole morning before an exam, and to this day he can't remember what he was doing. He told us this after you left," she added quickly, as though that removed any taint of conspiracy. Rose was thinking bitterly that her mother could accept the idea of mental lapses now that she knew they happened to Bill, stolid sensible Bill, as well as to nervous untrustworthy Rose.

"You don't know how that helped me, Rose, to be able to accept that. You see, ever since I heard that little bitch had locked you in that room, I was afraid it might have harmed your mind. Don't you remember how you used to scrub yourself, as though you could never get clean? I was so afraid I couldn't bear to think of it. I preferred to think you hated me."

"Look, mummy, let's change the subject, if you don't mind." Her mother was leading the way back to the table, and Rose was damned if she would get involved in a family argument before strangers.

"Please give me this chance, Rose. Let me get this off my chest." She couldn't be heard by the men across the table, the young man hurrying to say, "Yes, you're right, of course," the others joking loudly, perhaps to stave off thoughts of the afternoon. Behind Rose, secretaries were gossiping low; she could hear only the hiss of sibilants. "I lay awake all night after you stormed out, making myself think sensibly," her mother said.

If Rose refused to listen, her nerves would only draw tighter. "Well, get it over with," she said.

"I only wanted to say that Bill showed me I needn't have worried in the way I did. It was my fault, I just made things worse for myself and for you too, I suppose. Rose, do you really and truly not remember what happened the night that Wendy took you out?"

An underground train passed like a hint of an earthquake. "Yes," Rose said wearily, "I really and truly don't remember."

Her mother reached for her hand beneath the table. For the moment she seemed unable to speak, and was squeezing Rose's hand to help herself restrain her tears. Embarrassed and somewhat annoyed, Rose glanced away, at a woman who was advancing purposefully toward her. At once the woman turned her back on Rose, then faced her again, not quite looking at her.

Eventually Rose noticed the price tag dangling from the dark staid suit the woman was modeling.

"You can't imagine how much better I feel," her mother was whispering. "When Bill rang and I told him a little about that night, I wasn't sure at all that I'd done the right thing. And when you came to see us, I was so afraid to talk about it. I didn't know how you would react." Her whisper was quivering, threatening to jerk louder. "Will you forgive me now that I've been honest with you?"

Rose was most aware of the ache in her own grasped hand, but some of her mother's feelings had reached her. She'd struggled to come to terms with the way Rose had changed, though she was already burdened with Rose's father, his disintegrating memory, his growing irritability. However annoying it had been for Rose, her mother had acted out of love. "Yes, mummy," she said softly. "Don't worry. There's nothing to forgive, really."

Her mother relinquished her hand after a final squeeze. Rose felt strange; it was as though the barrier which had fallen from between them had changed her perspective entirely; she felt intensely close to her mother, but it was more than that. When a train passed, the floor seemed to shiver. Yes, that was rather like what she was feeling: something had shifted, or was about to shift; she felt dizzy, close to an edge. Her mother was smiling with relief, closing her eyes, relaxing at last—

The sounds of the restaurant withdrew from Rose, and she was gazing down on her mother's face.

Her own position hadn't changed. It was her mother who was lying down, eyes closed, face calm: too calm. Around Rose, everyone was dressed in black. Silence muffled them like crape.

Rose's fork dropped on her plate. The sound cut through her trance. Nobody was wearing black; the secretaries were multicolored, perfumed like an artificial garden; businessmen whose heads poked through gray hair wore gray; women with powdery faces, whose hair looked supplanted by neat caps of fur, sat guarding their half-consumed meals. "Oh, look at me, Rose," her mother rebuked herself, "keeping you from your lunch. You've eaten hardly anything."

Even worse than Rose's glimpse was the fact that she had no idea when it would happen. She forced herself to eat, to convince her mother that nothing was wrong. All of her movements felt intolerably ponderous; her arm dragged the fork to her mouth, her jaws chomped mechanically, chomped. The crowding grains of rice seemed endless. They'd been refrigerated, and it was like chewing ice. Her head was a hollow as a cave, filled with the sounds of her chewing. She had to hold the fork well away from the plate, in case it betrayed how her teeth were trying to chatter.

She was alone with her glimpse. She couldn't tell her mother, who would either think that Rose's mind had been affected after all or, worse, believe her. She couldn't tell her father, who would be bewildered and upset and powerless, assuming there was any chance of his believing her. There was nothing at all that Rose could do. Never before had her powers made her feel so lonely.

She had to follow her mother back to the counter, for they never had only one helping. Dressed rice glistened in bowls. No, it didn't resemble nests of eggs; no, the grains weren't stirring restlessly, it was only her nerves—but she had to restrain herself from fleeing.

Women with price tags were turning like music-box figures, sluggishly pirouetting. Rose gazed at them, for they gave her an excuse not to be eating. Cigar smoke crept across the table from the businessmen. A train rumbled, and she was sure the floor quaked. Everything—the gatherings of diners, the elaborate blurred sound track of conversations—seemed unreal, an appearance that threatened to give way to another glimpse.

"Can't you eat any more, Rose? You'll make me feel I shouldn't be eating."

"You go ahead, mummy." Rose hid her clenched hand under the table. "I'm not very hungry today."

"Oh, I hope I haven't upset you." She was whispering. As Rose strained to hear, the sounds of the restaurant receded. "I couldn't have borne keeping it to myself. We understand each other better now, don't we? Just think, I need never have felt that you blamed me. It was just that you seemed so changed after that night, I hardly recognized you. And yet you couldn't really have felt betrayed, since you didn't remember. Oh, I'm so glad it's over, Rose."

Rose was hardly listening. In fact she did feel betrayed deep down, if only because her mother was harping on the subject—it wasn't quite a memory. Her feelings were wasting her time with her mother, when she didn't know how long was left. Oh, surely she needn't think that; was there no other interpretation of her glimpse? She wanted to cling to her and never let go, before her mother drifted away. But her mother was smiling. She was closing her eyes.

Rose reached out to stop her, but it was too late. They were surrounded by figures in black. Bill looked abashed, Rose's father looked stunned, his eyes empty of tears, of everything. Her mother's still face hovered in the silence. Were present and future about to merge?

"Try to eat just a little more," her mother said. "You'll have me worrying."

It might be worry that would kill her. Rose forced more food down, hardly noticing what it was. If necessary she could retreat to the Ladies' and make herself sick. She was feeding a hole in a stiffly cheerful mask. Beneath the surrounding conversations, an ominous rumbling advanced.

At the cash desk her mother said, "I'll pay. No, I want to." Somehow her words sounded unbearably final, a last treat. Beyond the stairs a man reclined, exposing his throat. A barber stooped toward him with a razor.

Halfway upstairs Rose seized her mother's hand. "Mummy, please take care of yourself." They were the least adequate words she had ever spoken.

"Oh, I'll be all right. You take care of yourself, that's more important. I can feel how tense you are." She halted in the shop doorway, holding Rose's hand. "I must rush. Give me a ring soon, or come to see us. Let's try to see more of each other."

Rose watched her mother as she was engulfed by the crowd. Her head bobbed among the others for a while, then vanished. Rose's fists felt like weights at her sides. Oh God, she must see more of her mother, see her whenever she could—but for how long?

XXXIV

On Aigburth Road, wind was doing its best to direct the shoppers, but failed to throw Rose under a car. Layer on layer of dark cloud piled up like sediment at the horizon. Against the sky trees glared, bunches of frayed rusty wire. Birds were scraps of light high overhead, in danger of being blown out. Above a church doorway a Virgin and Child were caged by wire netting, which rattled as though they were trying to escape.

Her clothes dragged her into Fulwood Park. The wind made them as strong as she was. Dervishes of leaves were dancing in the road; above gateposts, the green pelt which covered the faces of stone lions was quivering. As she came in sight of the postbox, whose nest of grass was twitching, an unfamiliar car was emerging from her drive.

Oh God, what was wrong? She tried to run, but the wind was like water. Before she reached the postbox, the car was cruising away from the house.

She struggled into the roadway, to wave the car to halt. But they hadn't been looking for her, after all; they were the newspaper editor from the Hays' party, the magistrate in a sweater set, one of the young people who seemed to have seen the world.

When she let herself into the house, it sounded hollow. The sound of the wind was everywhere, the sound of loneliness, of insubstantiality. Furniture sat emptily. The porcelain Chinaman reached out to his companion, a dark corner. The presence of her guardians seemed as weakened as his.

Wind persisted in snapping the letter box. She resisted an urge to make sure there was no letter, though she couldn't help feeling that someone was trying to get in touch with her. Could it be Diana? But Rose would see her tomorrow or the next day. She mustn't phone her mother, not yet. If she yielded to that compulsion so soon, it would never leave her alone.

She sat in the empty living room. The way she felt, the name of the room seemed a cruel joke. Eventually the wind dropped, the light began to fail. The silent barren gloomy house felt like her mind.

She was in the kitchen, gazing blankly at the first stirrings of bubbles in the percolator, when the phone rang. Her start was so painful that moments passed before she was able to run along the hall. The ringing seemed too quick for her. There were far too few of her steps to each pulse of the bell.

When she grabbed the receiver, she heard an urgent chattering of pips. If they weren't fed the connection would break. At last a coin dropped. "Here I am at the National Film Theater," he said.

It was only Bill. She needn't have run, after all. "I've

been offered a viewing of one of our friend's films," he said. "That ought to help our interview. NFT2 has a season of Eastern European cartoons—you can probably hear the audience trooping in. They look suitably serious. Two hours of men being chased by the letter K, guns turning into flowers, you know the sort of thing. Next month there's a season of Nazi films."

Her fist clenched on the receiver; it felt as though the plastic might crack. Her mother was near to death, there was nothing Rose could do, and now she had to listen to him, driveling on about films. Least of all could she tell him. "Oh, can't you shut up for a minute?" she blurted.

"What's wrong?" he said after a pause in which she heard film buffs chattering. "Do you want me to come home?"

Nothing was wrong that she could tell him. "You're the last person I want to see at the moment, Bill."

"Oh, really." He sounded less angry than hurt. "You make me feel I shouldn't have phoned."

Something odd was happening. She felt as though her voice was beyond her control; it didn't matter what she said—nothing mattered, not when she was powerless to save her mother. Yet she had an odd sense of power: she was free to say what she liked to Bill. "For God's sake don't pretend you're concerned about me, Bill. You're concerned about yourself."

"That's a fairly rotten thing to say."

"Why? Because it's true?" He sounded insufferably false to her; she would drive him out from behind his pomposity. "You know damn well you only phoned to reassure yourself."

"How the devil do you make that out?"

Before she could reply, the pips began to clamor. She had a momentary sense of being given a last chance, which she didn't want. His anger made him seem utterly banal, contemptible. She felt possessed by her voice, eager to continue the attack.

She heard the coin drop. He'd bought himself more

of the truth, and by God, she would give it to him. "How the devil do you make that out?" he repeated like a retake of a scene.

"The only reason you phoned so early was to convince yourself I'm all right, so that you can forget me for the rest of the evening. I don't think you realize how incredibly selfish you are."

"Selfish? You're calling me selfish? Jesus Christ—"

"Don't shout, Bill," she said, grinning to herself: there he was, driven out from behind his disguise. "People can hear you."

"Can they? Well, fuck them, then. Don't you try to force your Ormskirk correctness on me. You don't want to hear about my feelings, do you? You're too busy with your own. That's why I had to turn to your parents. That's supposed to show how selfish I am," he shouted, "is it?"

He'd slurred a few words; she realized he must have been drinking. "Oh, very much so, Bill. Shall I tell you why you felt you had to turn to them? Because I'd threatened your masculinity. The only reason you've ever been worried about me is that you're afraid I'll disturb your routine."

"And just who did you think I was that night," he tried to outshout her, "when you thought I was someone else?"

"You wouldn't believe me if I told you. I don't know why that worries you so much. All you want is someone to masturbate into."

Before she knew it she was laughing uncontrollably. She'd glimpsed him as he must seem to the crowd at the National Film Theater, a wild-haired pompous rumpled man, ranting into the phone, oblivious of everyone. Through her laughter, which she hardly recognized as hers, she heard him say "Hello" distractedly to someone.

He sounded abashed and friendly, trying to pretend that he hadn't been shouting. Abruptly Rose tired of him. "Whoever that is," she said, "why don't you go and bore them instead of me. They'll be someone else to whine to about me."

As soon as she slammed down the phone she was furious. No doubt he was already on his way to get drunk with whoever he'd met. No doubt he would drink until he felt comfortable, until their argument seemed just a tiff, a breakdown of communication, an outburst of insults· Rose didn't really feel. Nothing would ever change him, nothing would make him less stolid and self-satisfied. She might as well not have saved him on the stairs in Aschheim, for all the impression that had made on him—

All at once the room seemed to brighten, to snap into focus. She had overlooked something. Had there really been so little reason for her despair? Dared she dismiss it so completely? But she felt she'd found the truth now, and she had to trust her feelings. She must go out; the house was too small to contain her sudden optimism.

A few dazzling wisps of cloud floated at the zenith, leisurely as dreams. The sky was turning into intensely luminous stained glass. By a transformation impossible to perceive, the deep blue of the zenith shaded into the chalky tint of the horizon. The colors of the field withdrew into themselves, preparing to shine in the twilight.

She stood there, reflecting, until it grew dark. She could see no flaw in her intuition. She'd saved Bill, which meant her premonitions could be headed off— but it didn't follow that she had to intervene. Chance could save her mother, and it would: otherwise, why was the premonition already less intense?

Breezes crept up from the river. Above the lamps of Fulwood Park, bare lurid branches were writhing. Beneath them, leaves rattled like beetles across the stages of light. She must get in touch with Bill as soon as she could. Though she was appalled by the things she'd said to him, she could feel nothing but hope: surely he would understand that she hadn't been herself. Everything would be all right now. "I know you're there," she said gently, to make up for her doubts of her guardians. "I know you'll look after me."

A breeze reached out of the dark for her. Her nostrils twitched; then she retreated quickly into the house. Shivering, she locked and bolted the door. Close by in the night, something was rotting.

PART FOUR

THE HIDING PLACE

XXXV

Rose hurried out of the Center for Communication Studies. The cellar was a hive of television monitors, humming and flickering. The world looked transformed by the late afternoon. The concrete buildings burned sullenly, engrossed in their own colors. On the shaved lawny mounds each blade of grass glowed separately, glazed by the light. The ivy on the backs of Abercromby Square was a frozen cascade of orange flame. The sky was icy crystal, a bottomless deep blue blending imperceptibly into pale green. She wanted to be home, to sort out her thoughts.

Most of her students had admired the Bergman. Some had argued that it was too serious, that good horror films worked subversively, hiding their real themes beneath a conventional surface. Rose had thought that both an oversimplification and a sloppy use of language, but she hadn't been entirely in control of the discussion. The film had disturbed her in the wrong way.

And yet it was only that Bergman used a scene from *The Magic Flute*. The sense of a memory struggling to surface—childhood, Ormskirk, her parents. *The Magic Flute* playing, the night all around—had made the viewing room feel like the subterranean cell which it was. She'd smelled the earth that pressed against the walls. Of course it was one of her father's favorite operas, and she knew why she couldn't put her parents out of her mind.

Once she had locked herself in last night, she had called her mother. They had chatted inconsequentially for a while, restraining their concern for each other to a bearable level. Though everything had seemed to be all right, Rose had dreamed of her mother in vague danger. Perhaps the dreams were only the fruits of nervousness, but she'd kept waking in the indifferent dark. Yesterday, had she been too eager to believe that her mother was safe?

She hadn't been able to reach Bill at the National Film Theater, nor at his hotel last night or when she'd woken late this morning. Perhaps he had been refusing to speak to her, and she could hardly blame him; it had been grotesque of her to expect an instant reconciliation. Her insomnia had given her ample time to recall everything she'd said to him. Even though she had been distraught, how could she have said such things? It was as though someone else had said them.

To make her even more nervous, this morning someone had called her while she was on her way: "a writer," the University switchboard had said. Bill was the only writer she knew. It must have been Jack. Now she would have to wait until she reached home to call him—she couldn't very well call New York from the University.

Could Jack have been calling from London? She paced impatiently around the bus stop beside St. Luke's Church. Pigeons like restless corbels wandered the jagged edge where the blitzed roof should have been. Through the high arched windows she saw the darkening sky framing the glint of a star. The star made her think of a vanishing point glimpsed across unimaginable gulfs of space.

In Fulwood Park, twilight settled on the villas. Hedges stirred like hatching swarms. Her house looked dwarfed by her nervousness. At least the air smelled only of salt.

The house felt colder than the road. The rooms were stone boxes. Her movements sounded intrusive and unreal, which was how she felt. The dimmer switch woke the dining room gently, the Victorian suite sat forward from the shadows of the living room as she switched on the light. Everything looked vivid as a photograph, and as aloof from her.

She couldn't get through to Jack. The house magnified the whirring of the dial. She poured herself a bourbon to help her relax, then she tried again. This time she made sure of the number she was dialing, but there was no response except the tolling of the bell.

Nor could she reach Bill. Was he still punishing her? Surely he must have realized by now that she had been horribly on edge; how else could she have been so cruel to him? He ought to phone her to find out what had been wrong. He was being crueller than she had been.

She didn't intend to brood. Things must work out eventually. The bourbon was mellowing the house, and she refilled her glass. No doubt Jack had only wanted to confirm that they would arrive tomorrow. She rapped the sideboard with her empty glass. "We'll have a fire," she said.

The coal-bunker stood against one corner of the house. She hadn't realized the twilight had darkened so swiftly. She pushed the kitchen door wider, to spread its fan of light. The scraping of her shovel echoed harshly round the garden, making her aware of the high dark walls, the looming greenhouse which looked fattened by darkness.

Soon the fire was blazing. Chairs danced with their shadows. She left the room at play with the firelight, one shadowy pace forward and one pace back, while she cooked herself dinner. She drew the curtains, for the sight of herself hovering outside in the dark and imitating her was rather disturbing.

She couldn't be bothered to cook anything more than an omelet, for she felt relaxed almost to the point of sleep. She ate by firelight and watched the transformations of the fire. Mysteries of flame were enacted in incandescent grottoes.

"Do you know, I haven't listened to a record for ages." Anything but Shostakovich, whom she found intolerably depressing. When she'd washed up her plate she played Janáček's Mass, whose jagged, primitive, almost pagan rhythms were interrupted unpredictably by episodes of tenderness or yearning. The fire provided a light-show, alternating warmth with violence.

She'd begun to doze when the thin chill stream of sound crept out of the speakers. The choir was singing *Kyrie Eleison,* Lord have mercy on us, and the violins were emitting this unmoved response. There was no mercy, only the sound of the endless indifferent void.

When she lifted the needle, the sound continued creeping through the house. Of course that was an echo in her mind, and she knew how she could drown it out. She switched on the light, to halt the stealthy firelit movements of the door. Never mind Bill, who could be anywhere. She knew who she wanted to hear.

A distant phone began to ring. She imagined wires stretched across the dark countryside, quivering in the night wind. Suddenly there was no ringing, only a voiceless whispering. "Yes, who's there?" her father said.

"Hello, daddy, it's me."

After a distinct pause he said, "Is that Rose?"

"Yes, that's right." Who else could it possibly be?

"Oh, hello." They hadn't spoken since that night in Ormskirk, and he still sounded uncomfortable. "Well, what can we do for you?"

Since he put it like that, there was only one question. "How's mummy?"

"Oh, satisfactory enough, all things considered. Can't complain. And you?"

She'd never heard him speak so oddly of her mother. "I'm all right, thanks," she said, wondering how to rephrase her question.

"And the rest of it?"

"Bill's fine." The conversation seemed to have slipped out of focus. Her voice sounded small in the empty house.

There was another silence. "What was that you said?"

"I was just telling you that Bill's all right too."

"Bill, your husband."

What in God's name was wrong with him? "Yes, who else could I mean?"

"I'm sorry, I thought you were talking about bills." He didn't sound apologetic—rather irritable, even suspicious. "You still haven't answered my question," he said.

She was beginning to feel afraid. "I don't know what question you mean."

"About your situation. How is your situation?" He sounded close to anger, as if he felt she was manipulating him somehow. She was speculating wildly—did he mean Bill's absence or her flight from Ormskirk?— when he said irritably, "Your financial situation."

Despite the loudmouthed fire, the room seemed abruptly cold. "You didn't ask me about that," she said in despair. "But we're quite comfortable." She had to get rid of the subject before she could be reassured about her mother.

"I don't understand. What else have we been talking about?" He sounded resentful. "What did you ask me to begin with?"

"I asked after my mother."

"Your mother—ah, I see. I thought we were talking about money."

So that was why he was uncomfortable: he was growing deaf as well as losing words. He hadn't even recognized her voice immediately. She wished they could share laughter, but he sounded too frustrated.

"Well, how is she?" she demanded, unable to bear the silence.

"Why, she's perfectly well. You don't want to speak to her, do you? She's just in the bath."

"No, don't disturb her. So long as she's all right. Give her my love."

"I will do. Was there anything else? I'm just in the middle of watching a show."

"All right, daddy. Goodbye." She was gripping the receiver as she might have clung to his hand. "Tell her she can call me later if she likes." The click came before she'd finished.

When she'd put down the receiver the entire house sounded like a dead telephone, or would have if she hadn't controlled her imagination. Should she relax in a bath? As her mother stood up in the bath she slipped, knocking a radio into the water, an electric heater. Nonsense, she would never be so careless.

Rose marched upstairs. Beyond the bathroom, a half-typed page drooped in the typewriter. She ought to be working. She typed a few pages, the head of the Anglepoise lamp close to hers. But a herald of migraine, like a spider composed of bright shards of glass, crawled over the type; her face peered uneasily in at the window, a suspended glowing mask without ears or hair. When she wrote an afterthought, her handwriting hardly resembled hers.

This was ridiculous: she must have a bath, since alcohol wasn't sufficiently relaxing. Water poured into the bath with a muffled roaring. She went downstairs for a few minutes in case the noise should blot out sounds—but it couldn't deafen her to the phone, and what other sounds could there be?

She lay in the bath and watched her limbs waver with the lapping. Condensation crawled over the window; it looked as though the translucent bumps of the frosted glass were hatching. She washed herself gently, anxious not to make too much noise. When she climbed out, her face in the wall-tiles looked distorted, drowned in blackness, almost unrecognizable. But she felt far more relaxed, she knew she was smiling peacefully without having to check with the mirror—

Something was moving in the house.

She dragged her bathrobe about her and tied it viciously, then she made herself open the door. The landing was bright and deserted. Paint gleamed like ice on the closed doors, and made them look treacherously thin. The sound had seemed close. It must have been in the spare bedroom—a faint tentative shifting.

When she managed to ease the door open and reach into the dark for the light-switch, there was nothing. The bed, which she'd made up for Jack and Diana last night, was featureless as untrodden snow. She stooped quickly, but the carpet beneath it was bare. Perhaps the noise had been at the Hays', or perhaps it had something to do with the light bulb, which looked dim. She must remember to replace it tomorrow.

She checked the other rooms cursorily, then she went downstairs. Had she sweated out some of the alcohol? She poured herself another bourbon to put her in the mood for the Marx Brothers, but the bourbon wasn't enough; their rapid patter seemed nerve-racking, their routines were inane simian antics in the cage of the television.

She wasn't being honest with herself. She would laugh if she dared, but her laughter seemed too loud in the empty house. She could hear how it resounded through the rooms, she could imagine how it might attract an audience which would gather outside the living room, would wait silently for her to open the door—

She switched off the film. Its noise could attract attention too. Now the silence seemed unnatural; she felt as though she was trapped in a glass case. Yet she couldn't quite make herself speak—because she was afraid that her guardians had left her alone, or that something else might answer?

Damn Bill, why didn't he phone? Eventually, though

it meant standing by the door to the hall, she rang the Bloomsbury Center Hotel. "No," a Latin male voice said ungraciously, "his key is here." She would be far better occupied in trying to sleep. She wrenched the hall door open curiously, and confronted nothing.

She had to check that doors and windows were secured. She scurried through the rooms, hating herself and her paranoia, wary of turning her back on the rooms in order to check the windows, scrutinizing the reflections of her surroundings as obsessively as the catches. Behind her in the spare bedroom, she was sure the light was dimming. Its reflection made her think of a bulbous spider on a thread.

When she found herself beginning to repeat the patrol, she made herself calm down. She must be exhausted, or in danger of migraine; the edges of her vision seemed grayish and faded, like the border of an imperfectly preserved film. She poured herself a last large bourbon and sat gazing into the fire, but not for very long, for all the shapes looked deformed and unstable. Flames struggled to leap free of crumbling figures. Having gulped the bourbon, she clipped the fireguard into place and strode upstairs.

The bourbon was working, after all. It drew her down toward sleep at once. She lay in the middle of the bed, her head resting in a valley between pillows. The emptiness on both sides of her felt luxurious rather than isolating. Her fears were drifting away like scum on water. She sank into a bath of sleep.

She lay in one of a rank of beds. The air was full of crying. Someone was bringing her a wrapped bundle. Everyone else in the beds had one. The bundle was struggling feebly. As the nurse unwrapped it, it began to cry, and Rose saw that it was a baby.

She jerked awake. On both sides of her the bed felt very cold. Why in God's name had she dreamed that? Never mind, it didn't matter, there was no point in remembering—but sleep was out of reach, and there was nothing with her in the dark except her memories.

She'd felt numb. Everything had felt drained of life, because she was unable to give life. "I'm sorry. I wish I could give you more hope, but I think that would be cruel. You're too intelligent to be deceived, in any case." The doctor must have meant to soothe her, but his voice had seemed toneless as the hospital tiles. "I'm sorry. I'm truly sorry." Had he repeated himself so often, or had that been her mind? The worst of it had been that she'd lost all desire for Bill; her genitals had felt paralyzed and raw. When eventually they had made love she'd felt repelled by the mindless gulping of her body, the pointlessness of the reflex; her body was useless, hollow. It must have been only a matter of weeks before he'd coaxed her back to normality, but they had seemed endless. Everything had seemed leaden as four in the morning.

It must be close to that time now. She peered irritably at the digital clock. Its angry colon pulsed away the seconds. Yes, she was right, and she must settle down to sleep. Wakefulness was least bearable at this hour.

Surely she ought to be able to sleep. There must be pleasant memories which would help her drift away. Why was she unable to remember anything, or even to think? Why was she aware of every sound in the house?

There was no way of avoiding what, deep down, she already knew. She was listening for the sound which had caused her dream.

At first there seemed to be nothing: only the rodent squeak of the letter box as a stray breeze tried to slip in, the fall of a single drop of water which must have been gathering silently on the lip of the tap for minutes, the restless flutter of a bird on the roof.

Then her arms grew stiff at her sides, her nails dug into her thighs. She lay absolutely still, willing herself to be mistaken. She felt rage almost as much as fear; why couldn't she be left alone? But it was no use.

Downstairs a baby was crying.

Reluctantly she crawled out of bed. The sound

couldn't be in her house. How could it be next door? Of course it could, if the Hays had guests who had a baby. But when she crept onto the landing and grasped the banister, which was chill and unyielding as metal, there was no doubt that the sound was rising up the staircase.

She trudged downstairs. Her clutches at the banisters counted her steps. Perhaps if she took enough time, the crying would vanish—but it went on and on, beyond the living-room door. It seemed to fill the house.

When she reached the door, she couldn't touch it. She felt sick, dizzy; her dismay was a lump in her stomach. She dared not speak aloud for reassurance. She knew she must brave whatever was there, but her fingers flinched inward as though they were burned. She had to shove the door with her fist, and then punch the light-switch, because her hand wouldn't unclench.

Though the crying was very close, the room appeared to be deserted. She was grinding her knuckles against the doorframe. Furniture stood, emptily stolid. Books, objects which seemed to have nothing to do with her, pressed together on the shelves. The curtains hung still as the walls.

But there was movement at the edge of her vision. She had to dig her knuckles into her jaw before her head would turn, toward the hearth. She stared appalled at the fireguard. Beyond the mesh, something moved weakly.

For a moment she was frozen, then a different kind of horror compelled her forward, sobbing. She fumbled wildly with the clips of the guard. As she did so, the crying behind the mesh ceased. The only sound was the rattle of the fireguard as she threw it onto the hearth.

In the grate was nothing but half-consumed lumps and ash. Only the sudden draft made the gray mass appear to stir feebly, as though trying to raise itself. Nothing was struggling to crawl out from beneath the ash. She was gazing at the remains of a coal fire, a small hole in the embers that collapsed inward as she watched, two sockets above it which were tinted unsteady pink by a last glow, which flickered feebly as they crumbled.

She staggered back. Her entire body felt crippled with horror, clenched like a dead spider. Her mind was shrunken within it, unable to think. Could she flee next door? But she might have to wait out there in the dark for minutes before anyone answered her—and besides, though her concern seemed grotesque under the circumstances, she didn't want to startle Gladys in the middle of the night. Too dark, mustn't wake Gladys, her mind was repeating inanely.

She managed to unclench her hand sufficiently to pick up the phone. Her fingers stumbled over the dial, scrabbling at digits. Was the whispering the restlessness of electricity, or was it in the fireplace?

At last something clicked into place; a distant bell awoke. She must have waited at least a minute before a hostile Latin voice, probably not the same one, answered. His tone was unimportant, all she wanted was to get past him. "Mr. Bill Tierney," she pleaded. "Room two-seventeen."

There was a prolonged whispering pause. In the fireplace, something shifted or fell in on itself. She had to hang onto the receiver with both hands to prevent herself from fleeing. Eventually the voice returned. "No, he is not in. His key is here."

"But he must be!" Was she sobbing? She couldn't tell. "Have you tried to call him?"

"No," the voice said with no variation whatsoever, "he is not in. His key is here."

"Please ring his room at once and make sure." She could hear the plastic of the receiver creaking in her grasp, and feeble movements in the hearth. "Please do as you're told. This is very urgent." Each moment of waiting made her less sure what speaking to Bill could achieve.

This time the pause, though it was occupied by gray shifting in the fireplace, seemed too short. "There is no reply. You see, I told you, he is not—"

Perhaps the man had only pretended to call Bill's room, but there was nothing she could do. She let the receiver crash onto its cradle. No doubt Bill had gone home with someone he'd met at the NFT. To punish her further, he hadn't let her know.

She made herself step forward again, to clip the guard into place. Her cramped hands were shaking, her skin felt covered with crawling ash, her eyes were wounds. She looked away as she replaced the guard. A nerve pulled her mouth awry, as though she was mocking herself. What possible use was the guard?

She was too exhausted by fear and disappointment to hurry upstairs. She had no sense of her inner strength, and little sense of herself. If anything more was lying in wait for her, there was nothing she could do. In the bedroom, she thrust a chair beneath the doorknob: another absurd defense.

She lay on the bed, awaiting dawn. Once it was light outside she might be able to plan, but now she could only be on her guard against the dark. The light in the room looked seedy, dismal. It weighed on her like fog, insubstantial but chilling. It congealed time. When the inflamed pulsing of the clock reached sixty, that was only another minute consumed.

She slept before she knew, and woke cold and aching. Her mouth was rusty. Though the light in the room still looked thin and shabby, it was sunshine. Good God, it was almost nine o'clock. She knew at once what she wanted to do, but had she time?

XXXVI

The silenced world rushed by. Rose was surrounded by a muffled uproar which resembled an incessant wind mixed with sounds of knitting. Trees sailed past, mostly bare. A few leaves like aged paper filled with light, then dimmed. Shocks of evergreen leapt up. Streets were conveyor belts in a toy factory; a few dolls pottered in gardens. She felt safe.

"Good morning, ladies and gentlemen," said a voice encased in static and breath. "This is your guard speaking. This is the 10:04 to London Euston, due to arrive at Euston at 12:44 . . ." As soon as she had left the message that she wouldn't be at work today, she'd felt a surge of relief. At last she was sure of what she was doing.

She would know what to say to Bill when she saw him. Surely he must forgive her when he saw how she was. If she had to wait for him at the hotel, she would be safe there. Besides, she needed time to contact Jack and Diana at Heathrow, to make sure they would be riding home with her tonight, while Bill finished his work. Everything was on her side now.

The train was speeding through explosions of color, of sunlight and silver branches, beneath the slow efflorescence of the sky, gray and white and less frequently blue, above sudden breathtaking falls of slopes and leaps of grassy banks. A meandering river carved from a mirror snatched her gaze toward the horizon, and now the view was a parade of landscape paintings, Constable and Stubbs and a field that displayed cows in an assortment of postures. She felt cradled, drowsy.

A grille announced Crewe Station, which looked faded and dusty. It reminded her of hours spent waiting on the bare gray platforms, stranded between Brighton and Liverpool, night winds roaming the station and rattling signs, the insect hum of trolleys drawing their segments behind them under lights that looked yellowed by fog, the oppressive silence of the surrounding town. She'd used to feel she was adrift on a dim raft in the night.

The train moved off as she returned from the buffet car. In the first-class carriages, businessmen talked guardedly or dealt papers from briefcases. Near Rose, men played poker at a table which beer had turned into a skittle-ground. An overcast paced the train; the horizon doled out a strip of indirect lighting on which a frieze of lemony clouds was sketched. She uncapped her plastic cup of coffee and watched the landscape's procession.

A shower pelted the windows. Dozens of raindrops trickled doggedly backward over the glass in slightly jagged lines. Now the shower had passed and the landscape was brightening. Shadows washed over the fields, drained swiftly into the ground, welled up elsewhere. Yes, that was how it had been in the Lakes.

During their Lakeland honeymoon, she and Bill had made love on a fell. The wind had shoved puritanically between them and made a hoot of their kisses; rain had doused them like a boy scout's cure. They'd chosen another day more carefully and had remembered to take a blanket. Heather had lapped in breezes, light and shadow had played like huge cats on the massive slopes. She'd sneezed through the rest of the honeymoon, but that afternoon had been worth it, her afternoon alone with Bill above the world.

Too many of her memories were fading. She and Bill must share them, revive them. Soon they would, she knew they would. However vicious her outburst had been, it couldn't have killed their marriage. There was a multitude of memories to share—if only she could think of them.

Of course they seemed fragile. She was rummaging too roughly for them, that was all. She had only to relax, let them flow. Nothing loomed over them but the overcast and her sense of guilt. No wonder they felt distant and dull.

The platforms of Nuneaton whooshed by like rockets. Still more than an hour to London. A train shot past, bearing a streetful of parked cars. Without warning she remembered New York: in a sense they'd begun to grow apart there, when he had been so surprisingly hostile to Diana and her Tarot. That had foreshadowed their own disagreements. She was trying to recall his Tarot—but it didn't matter now; his reading had come true, and Rose's had been a mistake.

But had his reading come true? Not in New York, surely. In any case she was thinking of the second interpretation, which Diana had made up to calm him. But Diana had told the truth the first time: occult influences, someone close to Bill who was involved in the occult, conflicts arising—

And then death. Death in strange surroundings, away from home.

It needn't be the death of a person, Diana had said so. So much had happened since the reading that surely its predictions had already come to pass, even if she couldn't think where. Worrying would only make the journey interminable. She must think of something else.

Factory chimneys like inverted concrete tumblers appeared to be sucking in the overcast rather than expelling smoke. A section of night closed moaning over the train, and it was minutes before she was out of the tunnel. It trapped her with her thoughts: apart from Bill, all she could think of was the crying in the fireplace. The tunnel gave way to glittering fields,

gleaming trees, but she was closed in by her thoughts.
Why was she clinging to her Lakeland memory as
though it were a charm?

Her memories were exhausted, as she was; that was
all. But suppose her outburst had made Bill desperate,
uncaring? He had already been drinking—where might
he have wandered, what might he have done? Less than
an hour to London now—God, almost an hour. She
wished she could race ahead of the train, but she was
weighed down by her body, caged in her head, which
felt padded and ponderous.

Might another coffee help her waken? The aisle
swayed, nodding corners of seats at her. An empty
bottle rolled beneath seats, eluding would-be captors.
Children were strewn beside their parents. Gray skeins
of smoke twined toward the ceiling. She groped back to
her seat, gripping the lidded cup in one half-scalded
hand. Where had Bill gone last night? What had
prevented him from calling?

She gulped the hot coffee, hoping the pain would
distract her. A whiff of ozone from the brakes reminded her of the seaside, but that wasn't especially
reassuring. If she was being watched over, the presence
was very vague.

The train was slowing. That was why she could smell
the brakes. It halted near a group of men in orange
waistcoats who were picking at sections of line. After
five minutes passengers began to mutter complaints,
muted as drizzle. Rose gripped the edge of the table;
one nail sank into a limpet of chewing gum and
recoiled. If the train didn't move soon, her nails would
break.

Ten minutes. Eleven. She felt as though her mind
was boiling. As much as anything, the inhibited murmur of passengers frustrated her: don't make a scene,
nothing we can do, ignore the problem and it may go
away. Her nails dug into her palms. At least the pain
was tangible.

Eventually a train inched past on the adjacent line.

Rose's train stood a few minutes longer, apparently to make sure nothing else was on the way. At last it moved off, intolerably timid. The landscape began to roll slowly as a record winding down.

Once the train gathered speed the grille kept making a sound like the parting of metal lips, but announced nothing. As soon as the Euston arrow sailed by she was hurrying toward the front of the train, dodging a fall of bottles from the card table, edging past businessmen who were folding papers carefully as a chambermaid folds sheets, almost tripping over an ambush of children. Nobody must reach the Euston phones before she did.

Before the train had stopped she was running up the slope toward the ticket barrier. A giantess's voice announced messages for passengers from Liverpool. Beyond the barrier, in a white-tiled space like an enormous hospital corridor, people stood scrutinizing the new arrivals. She pushed between them, to the phones.

All were in use. In front of her, in an alcove that clung to the wall, a businessman was arguing patiently into a phone and tapping regularly, calmly, on the floor with the tip of his umbrella. Latecomers crowded around her, staking their claim to the nearest alcove. By God, she was first; she was entitled to the first available phone. Was she wasting time while she could be on her way to the hotel?

The businessman emerged, twirling his umbrella. She ran into the alcove, knocking him aside, and dialed feverishly as she rummaged for change in her purse. Now the bell was ringing, ringing, unhurried as a pendulum: ringing, ringing—

"Bloomsbury Center Hotel," a girl's voice said.

Rose rammed in the coin to silence the pips. "Bloomsbury Center—"

"Yes," Rose said, desperate to get rid of the girl, to hear Bill. "Mr. Tierney in two-seventeen, please."

"Two-seventeen. Two one seven." Perhaps she

couldn't think of any other variations, for there was a lingering silence. "Yes, I understand his key isn't here," she said eventually. "I believe he came in earlier."

Oh, thank God. "Will you call his room for me then, please?" Rose said, keeping her temper.

Presumably the silence meant that the girl was obeying. The hubbub of Euston tried to flood the alcove. Rose rested her elbow on the spines of a rank of directories, until they tilted alarmingly on their hinges, giving way beneath her. Was that the sound of Bill's receiver being lifted? No, it was the beginning of the pips, crying to be fed. She thrust in another coin. It was a small price to pay for reassurance.

At last the girl returned. She sounded annoyed. "He's supposed to be in his room," she said like a matron complaining of a stray child. "But he doesn't reply."

XXXVII

Rose ran through Euston. A multitude of people tried to block her way, as though she were a thief. Luggage lurked near them like dogs, ready to catch her feet. The giantess's voice reverberated overhead. It sounded like a caricature of disinterested efficiency, appallingly bland.

Commuters were trooping down a staircase to queue for taxis. Would it be quicker to go by train? Her feet slithered on the tiles as she wavered desperately. She turned and ran toward the Underground.

The escalator stepped down leisurely, creaking. As she clattered down, some of the treads were not quite where she expected them to be. She was hearing everything she'd said to Bill over the phone. How could her voice have been so cold and cruel?

The ticket booths were besieged. Scrabbling in her purse for change, she struggled through the crowd to the machines. A machine considered her coins for a moment or two, then emitted a yellow ticket. The barrier snatched the ticket and pulled in its elbows to let her through. At once she was running. Piccadilly Line, Piccadilly Line—

The escalator looked clogged with people, but she ran down so violently that everyone retreated to the right-hand side. The crawling rubber banister stuck to her sweaty palm. Beyond a corridor two girls were scurrying aboard a train which seemed about to close its doors.

Rose hurled herself forward, into the last compartment. All right, she was aboard now, please don't let it wait for anyone else, they could catch the next one—

When the doors edged shut, one pair recoiled. At once their neighbors opened. The first pair closed, but now the second made them falter and reopen, a vicious circle of infectious yawning. Rose wavered on the edge of her seat: could she dodge into a compartment which would be closer to the exit at her destination?

The doors were shut, and the platform was slipping away. The lit mouth of the tunnel dimmed as it dwindled, then went out like a spent match. Why was that glimpse so dismaying? She felt sticky and feverish. The sphincter of darkness, and the muffled light of the train, seemed almost unbearably suffocating.

The train dawdled at King's Cross, yawning repetitively. A hidden face broke through another on a torn poster. Rose's heels were trying to spur the train onward, but only earned her a pained glance from a Pakistani student. Let him frown, he didn't know how much she was suffering. Nevertheless his rebuke flooded her with a wave of prickling.

As soon as the doors opened at Russell Square she

was on the platform and running. On the opposite platform she glimpsed the WESTBOUND sign, which Bill had said sounded like a Randolph Scott movie. No need to cling to that memory as though it were precious. Surely there was no need.

A lift was lowering itself like an obese person, groaning over the task. She couldn't face the emergency stairs, one hundred and seventy-five of them; she trudged into the lift with the rest of the shuffling crowd. All at once, now that she was so near, she was less eager to arrive.

Outside, the sunlight seemed unreal. A truck with a jointed yellow arm brandished a man at a streetlamp. A car with a propellor drove by—no, with the foot of an office chair protruding from the boot. An old woman stumbled across a pedestrian crossing; as she gestured the traffic to wait she looked as though she was swimming. Everything looked bright but meaningless. Rose wanted to be seeing it with Bill.

She made herself hurry down the street beside the Bloomsbury Center, which resembled an apartment block with an awning. None of the multitude of windows told her anything. The foyer was crowded with faces beyond faces: men whose overcoats draped them like cloaks, an Arab family seated on red chairs, Africans with ritual scars; nobody she knew, no Bill. She struggled to the Reception counter, though that cost her another wave of prickling, and demanded, "Did you get an answer from two-seventeen?"

The girl frowned prettily. Of course she was only one of several. "Were we calling that room for you? Shall I try them now?"

"Yes, please." But as soon as the girl reached the switchboard Rose found she couldn't bear to wait. She ran for the lift, which was opening.

A German family followed her, and held open the doors for another family. Now the lift was packed, but other people hurried forward, calling "Wait!" Rose was crowded into a corner. She closed her eyes, for the walls were red and raw as a peeled tomato.

Eventually the lift moved. Two small boys were playing with the buttons. "Don't do that, please," their mother said ineffectually. The lift opened at the first floor to display the Happy Casserole Restaurant. Rose felt raw as the walls, and prickling.

When the lift halted at the second floor the mother said again, "Don't do that." "This is mine," Rose said, but nobody heard her. Beyond the crowd the doors were closing. "This is my floor," she called, struggling forward. The boys hadn't halted the doors. She shouldered forward and, knocking one of the boys aside, squeezed through the closing gap. A chorus of shocked exclamations sailed upward.

Several children loitered near a soft-drinks dispenser. A little girl was poking a shoe-polisher with her toes, as though it was a dog reluctant to play. She looked ready to start wailing. Arrows pointed to rooms: 201–226, 227–263. The nearest child flinched back as Rose strode past him, to the left.

The corridor was stifling. Even the swinging of fire doors seemed to create no draft. The pattern of carpet throbbed and shifted; her eyes felt caught in tightening loops of wire: 213, 215. The doors were an identity parade; except for its number, 217 was indistinguishable from the rest. It challenged her to guess its secret.

Her fist felt like a club studded painfully with nails. Her knocking skinned her knuckles. It hovered in the stuffy corridor, and seemed to fall into an empty room.

After a pause she heard footsteps: light, quick, stealthy. They weren't Bill's. Were they in an adjacent room? No, of course it must be a chambermaid. It wasn't an intruder creeping about, having finished his task. It wasn't a bald man.

Suddenly the bolt was drawn on the far side of the door. As the door moved inward, light slipping over it like oil, she felt in danger of breaking. But at last the door was open, and she was face to face with Bill.

She didn't break, but she felt ready to collapse with relief. Her tension had propped her up, had given her a kind of sleepwalking vitality within which she could hardly think or feel. When she went forward to hug him, she was almost falling.

For the moment she couldn't speak, she could only cling to him. Though he looked startled and anxious, he didn't seem to hate her; nothing else mattered. Having kicked the door shut, he was backing down the hall, past the bathroom. The slam of the door seemed to worry him somehow.

They were still embraced, and were moving like a confused pantomime horse. In the bedroom the suitcase she had packed for him lay open at the foot of the rumpled bed, and surrounded by strewn clothes. He was always untidy in hotels.

She stood embracing him beside the devastated bed, which was silently rebuked by its tidy twin. "Oh, Bill, you don't know how glad I am to see you."

"Oh, are you? Oh, good."

Someone moved in the adjacent room. "Have you been traveling all morning?" Bill said into her ear. "Would you like a drink? I was just about to go down."

"Oh yes, I'd love one. Let's go to the Friend at Hand. But the very first thing I must have is a wash."

"Must you? Ah, well—"

The muffled movements were not in the adjacent bedroom at all. Someone was in the bathroom.

For a moment Rose was prickly with apprehension. Was someone hiding in there, having threatened Bill if he gave them away? What nonsense! "Who's in the bathroom?"

"Oh, you know her." He disengaged himself from Rose in order to pick up his jacket. "Hilary, who used to be my mature student. I met her at the NFT."

Of course, she often came to London for the films; she'd said so at the Hays' party. Though she was a relief, Rose couldn't help resenting the intrusion; she and Bill needed to talk freely. Rose knocked on the bathroom door. "Can I come in?"

"Yes, please do." The bolt snapped back. Hilary was wearing Bill's bathrobe; her long blonde hair tumbled over the rough cloth. She looked flushed, bright-eyed, very young. "I'm staying with some friends," she said. "They haven't got a bathroom, or rather the bath doesn't work. Your husband said I could come up here for a bath."

Come up and see my bath, Rose thought with a secret smile which she would have liked to share with Bill. "Oh, I know exactly how you feel," she told Hilary. "Have you finished washing?"

"Yes, go ahead. You don't mind if I get dressed while you're here?"

"No, of course not." Rose rubbed a space in the steam on the mirror, to judge how worn she looked. Not too bad: nothing that a wash and a touch of makeup couldn't improve. The taps washed away pimples of water from the sink. She would have to tell Hilary that they wanted to be alone. She scrubbed her face vigorously and groped blinking for a towel. It didn't matter which one, all of them were folded neatly on the rail, clearly unused—

As she looked up, praying that she was letting her thoughts run away with her, she met Hilary's gaze in the mirror. At once the girl looked away. Yes, she'd said she had come up here for a bath—but though there had been drops of water left in the sink, there was none in the bathtub.

Rose reached out miserably and fingered each of the towels, then she advanced on Hilary. The girl stood against the shower curtain, naked except for her panties. Her nipples were very dark. Rose had always been ashamed of her own, which she thought unpleasingly pale. Hilary looked unsure whether to flee as Rose stretched out her hand and touched the long hair timidly, almost a mockery of a caress. Like the towels, her hair was absolutely dry.

XXXVIII

If Rose felt anything besides shock, it was a lingering hope that she might be mistaken. It vanished forever as soon as she confronted Bill. When he saw her expression his face seemed to sink into itself, to grow smooth as water, trying to hide its depths. Only his eyes flickered with dismay. He began to step forward, hands vaguely outstretched, but her look made his hands droop at his sides. He looked like a guilty schoolboy who was learning resignation. As she stared at him neither of them able to move, the migraine began.

Something like a bright tear appeared in his left eye. At once it began to sparkle and expand, as though the lens of his glasses had shattered. Within the spreading rim of unstable light, his face lost perspective and focus. It became an object without meaning.

She hadn't suffered a migraine all year; this one would be worse for the respite. She was tempted to slump on the bed, to burden them with herself—but by God, she wasn't going to let them think they'd upset her, for apart from a lingering defensive disbelief she felt only rage, not least at their having given her the migraine. She turned, half-blind, and stalked out of the room.

The rim was composed of large vibrating segments now, which jangled against one another as they grew. It dragged the corridor out of focus and made it appear two-dimensional. She could hardly find the button on the wall between the lifts.

She'd groped her way into the lift and was fumbling at the ground-floor button when he elbowed the doors aside. "Ro, I'm sorry. Let's go somewhere I can talk to you. Don't make up your mind until you know everything. I'll be honest with you, I promise."

She didn't want him to be honest, she'd had enough of the truth. She closed her eyes, for the walls of the lift appeared to be oozing crimson. "Go away," she said tonelessly.

"Don't do that, Ro. Don't close me out, not now. Christ Almighty, why do you think this happened at all?"

He was advancing toward her, a clumsy repulsive tormentor in the cramped raw box. The doors stood aside like obsequious waiters, displaying sounds of the Happy Casserole. "Will you get out now, please," she said.

When the doors closed he was still with her. "Ro, we once talked about situations like this, if you remember. We agreed that screwing someone outside a marriage could be a kind of safety valve."

Her temples were pounding in time with the vibrating shards of bright glass. "I'm not listening. I can't hear you."

"Oh Christ, don't make more of this than it deserves. It was like masturbation, only even more depressing. I was wishing I hadn't done it before it was over." He was punching the wall of the lift in frustration. "There's no point in acting like this. For God's sake look at me at least."

"If you follow me out of this lift I'll scream." She raised her trembling fists, both to ward him off and to show that she meant what she said. "I'll scream until you go away."

The hubbub of the foyer closed around her, thick as glue. The carpet looked twined with neon; the crowd resembled cardboard figures. Was that an empty seat near the door? Her head was buzzing like a defective sign. God help Bill if he came near her.

She lay back in the chair, eyes closed. Drafts from the door battled the heat of the foyer, and made her feel at the mercy of fever. Within her eyelids a gray blank was surrounded by flickering. "I'll be all right," she would tell anyone who tried to help. "I just need to rest. Don't bother about me. I don't need anyone. Piss off and leave me alone."

Whoever was sitting beside her was called to a taxi, Rose was alone with the monotonous incomprehensible mass of sound, suffocating as plush. A piercing painful buzz linked her temples. The flickering was fading, giving way to the most unpleasant phase, during which she hated to open her eyes.

Someone else sat down beside her. In a moment she heard a whisper. "Mrs. Tierney," it said.

Rose opened her eyes to glare Hilary away. The foyer was a single flat plane, crowded with restless melting blobs which only her intellect told her were people. Hilary's face was a dull pinkish mass in which moist objects shifted. Rose shut her eyes tight. She hadn't even the energy to order the girl to move.

"Can I speak to you, Mrs. Tierney?" Hilary's voice was full of contrition, and worse, of concern. "I don't want to complicate matters, but I can't go away without saying this. Your husband looked so worried when I met him that I had to ask him what was wrong. And then when he told me, I really felt I had to comfort him. Only comfort him—I mean, I'm sure nothing else would have happened if I hadn't been lonely myself. Shall I tell you something? I'm certain he was thinking of you all the time, not of me. I wouldn't want you to think this has ever happened before. Mrs. Tierney—I know you'll think I'm the last person to advise you, the last person you want to listen to, but what I wanted to say was this. When you've had a chance to think things over, when everything's calmed down a bit, you must let him tell you his feelings that he had to tell me."

It seemed less of an effort to let Hilary drivel on than to tell her to go away. Rose retreated into the perspectiveless gray. After a time, perhaps believing that Rose was asleep, the girl left her alone.

Eventually Rose could see, after a fashion. Her eyes seemed uncoordinated, though it was not quite like seeing double. She stared at her watch, whose seconds throbbed like her skull. She would be too late to meet the plane at Heathrow. "Bastard," she muttered, dismaying an old lady.

Might she catch Jack and Diana at Euston? She stumbled out and hailed a taxi. The journey made her feel as though her guts were slopping from side to side. When she clattered up the escalator into the deafening white-tiled concourse, the first train which they might have caught had just left.

At least there was a chemist's. She swallowed three aspirins without water, and cursed Bill for the taste that clung to her mouth. The least thought of him produced a wave of hatred so intense that it frightened her. She hadn't known that it was in her to hate anyone so much.

She had almost an hour to wait for the next train. She couldn't bear standing in the cold white vault, amid the meaningless swarming of the crowd, beneath a sky that looked like grime coating the windows. Everything scraped her nerves—the clicking of indicators as they dealt details of trains, the huge inescapable efficient voice, the sign of a shop called LONE WOMAN. Where in God's name was that? It must have been a newspaper headline which someone had carried by. There was another glimpse, THE UNLOVED: a book on a bookstall, a poster for a film, an early symptom of a breakdown? By God, she wouldn't break down; he wasn't worth it. She would grow used to being alone, starting now. As she headed for the bar her lips were trembling, plucked by the restless nerve.

She paid for a beer and carried it to a table that was like a dull red tree stump. She seemed to be performing all her actions in the third person. Shock or migraine had jumbled her perceptions. At least she had the drink and her hatred to keep her company.

Men stood at the bar as though ranked at urinals. A fruit machine coughed up a few coins. She tried to withdraw from her surroundings, and all at once seemed to succeed, too well: the edges of her vision appeared to fade, as did the sounds of the bar; for a moment she didn't know where she was. Was this exhaustion or an aftereffect of migraine?

Faces bobbed past the window like clumps of balloons. Some peered at her. At last the train was announced. Though Jack and Diana could hardly have boarded it without her noticing, she searched its length before claiming a seat close to the ticket barrier. Surely they must take this train—or were they trying to phone her at home, to tell her their plans?

A pregnant woman with a baby in her arms squeezed into the seat next to Rose. When the train moved off, Rose hadn't seen a face she knew. After the interminable wait at Euston, she had now to suffer nearly three hours on the train.

The sky had brightened, but was stained by the grubby window. She knew it was a bright shell over infinite darkness. Muffled landscapes sailed by. Distant trees resembled stitches struggling to pull free of the sky.

Twilight gathered liked scum. The world looked drowned, an endless parade of feeble lights, of shapes that might have been composed of smoke. A few premature fireworks flew up. Their sparks clung to her eyes.

She kept seeing the rumpled hotel bed, the untidy suitcase. She'd packed that for him. He was making her think these banal domestic thoughts, dragging her down to his level. She cursed him. Her shouts resounded through her mind.

The window cracked like shell, releasing a flood of water over her arm. Before she could recoil, her arm was cold and wet, but there had been no water and no crack, only a reflection of passing lights. Exhaustion was sneaking her toward dreams. She fought to stay awake, for she didn't want to waken here and remember all that had happened to her.

She ought to have suspected. Of all his students, he was always mentioning Hilary. He had always admired her. When Rose had called him before going to Manchester, had he been talking to Hilary? "I'll probably see you down there." Had he used Rose's outburst as an excuse for betraying her? But whatever he might have said to Rose, she would never have betrayed him. At least she knew now what his Tarot had meant. If his reading had only just been fulfilled, perhaps her own fulfillment was still to come. The words seemed caught in the clicking of the wheels: mental alienation, burial, darkness, terror—

She woke. Beside her a baby was crying. She was barely able to restrain herself from hitting out blindly. Then she realized she wasn't at home. Her body felt hollow and cumbersome; a long tunnel clogged her ears with air. Abruptly she couldn't bear the oppression, she had to release some emotion somehow. As soon as the glowing "engaged" sign went out, she made her way past the drowsing mother, the sleeping baby.

She sat on the lidded toilet and tried to cry, but her tears were few and deliberate. Each one made her hate Bill more for causing them. They were no relief; masturbation could hardly be more depressing. That reminded her of him too. She unbolted the door and stumbled dully out.

The train lurched, hurling her into a businessman's raised newspaper. Did he think she was drunk? It didn't matter: let him think she was clumsy, drunk, rude. No, by God—Bill hadn't destroyed her yet, she still had her dignity. "Sorry," she said, and the businessman responded, "Driver's fault, not yours."

She slipped past the dozing mother, whose husband was cradling the baby now. No, Bill hadn't robbed her of her strength. Nobody had seen how she felt, and nobody would. It would pass eventually. In time she would be grateful for her freedom from his interference. If only she could feel that soon—if only her sense of her future would cease to slip away!

The train was slowing. Her double face, multiplied by two thicknesses of window, peered in from the night. Dark platforms were approaching, scattered with luminous plastic hyphens which said CREWE. She closed her eyes, trying to forget where she was. Crewe felt like desolation.

When she woke, the train was emptying. She felt isolated by silence; the limits of her vision were faded, gray; for a moment she thought blindness was closing in. Now she could see, though dimly, and the retreating passengers were accompanied by sounds. Why was everyone leaving the train at Crewe? Because this was not Crewe but Liverpool.

She staggered onto the platform, and at once was shivering. Porters descended on the train like vultures, carrying off abandoned newspapers. Without warning she was convinced that Jack and Diana had been ahead of her, either on this train or on its predecessor.

She ran toward Central Station. The pavements were sprinkled with frost like dandruff; ice coated the roads. On Lime Street pinball machines were jangling, a man slumped in a doorway beside Yates's Wine Bar. Football fans roamed, besieging cinemas and pubs.

A bored girl, sealed behind glass, spun Rose's ticket and change out to her on a plastic turntable. She seemed no more distant than anything else. Nothing moved on the underground platforms except destination indicators and a few students, returning to the Aigburth halls of residence. Rose couldn't help disliking them.

She paced restlessly. Jack and Diana were probably in Fulwood Park by now. Oh, let the train come before they went away! The platform was covered with cigarette butts like trampled grubs. The board announced the "semifast train to Ormskirk"; once she would have laughed. The students were giggling, giggling.

At last a stubby train arrived, and moved off almost as soon as she'd boarded. Darkness gulped the lit platform. She glimpsed an unlit train lurking in a side tunnel, then there was only dark in which her train's sparks illuminated nothing. She had a glimpse of sodium lights across the Mersey, brief as a blink between dozes. She mustn't fall asleep now, she was nearly at St. Michael's. Indeed, the train was slowing.

She panted up the precipitous steps. The station smelled of new paint; the doors were luminous green, sickening. She hurried out, one hand masking her face from the smell. She would be all right once she was home—once she saw Jack and Diana.

She ran through the side streets, beneath white fluorescent teats which dangled beneath lampshades, past detached houses encrusted with pebble dash and whitewash. Trees stood frozen by the light. St. Michael's church chimed a quarter. A dog began to bark a warning.

Framed by the last streetlamps, the entrance to the shortcut by the Mersey looked very dark. She felt uneasy, but it didn't matter; nothing mattered now. Good God, how much more uneasy would she feel if she used the main road, almost twice the distance, and missed Jack and Diana?

She had no idea what she would tell them about Bill. The truth would be embarrassing for them, agonizing for her. Perhaps she would break down then, after all. The main road would give her more time to prepare her story. Yes, and more time for them to decide not to wait. Impatient with herself, she stepped onto the dark path.

XXXIX

The path was frozen hard as concrete, though less even. It looked like a barely visible trail of fog. Webs of branches shifted overhead, entangling the sky. Between the trees she made out elevated coils of barbed wire, guarding the Esso petroleum bunkers. The wire jangled faintly, restlessly.

The path was descending slightly, between banks obscured by ivy. A rustling in the leaves paced her: only a breeze, which slipped into her pockets to freeze her hands. Over the swarming of leaves and the vibration of the wire, she heard buses on the main road. They sounded very distant. She hated Bill for making her grope along here alone in the dark.

Still, she knew her way. Only exhaustion and the remnants of migraine were making her uneasy. The last few shriveled leaves hung batlike from twigs. An overgrowth of ivy made the outlines of trees appear to be crumbling. The sounds in the banks of ivy had moved ahead.

A stone like a petrified tree stump marked the point beyond which the path descended more sharply and bushes closed in, blotches of oppressive darkness. The path grew rougher, hummocky and unyielding. Bushes nodded, hissing, as she stumbled. At least she could see the constellations of sodium shimmering on the far bank of the Mersey. They were a promise of light, though they made the trees which framed them seem unstable, made a hump on a tree trunk appear to shift.

She hurried deeper into the dark. Soon she would be in the open, where she ought to feel less uneasy. It had only been the antics of light which had made the hump appear to stir watchfully, like a spider alert for prey. She glanced back to reassure herself, but it was no use; the trunk which she thought had borne the hump looked bare. She must have mistaken the tree. They were indistinguishable in the dimness.

Here was the darkest section of the path. Her feet became trapped in the ruts, almost hurling her into the brambles. Take it slowly, no need to run, she would soon be out of the worst of the darkness. She could see the long concrete building beyond the barbed wire, its waste pipe reaching down to the Mersey. Once she ducked beneath the pipe she would be nearly in the open.

She had almost reached the pipe when she heard a large but stealthy sound in the depths of the brambles. It wasn't among the brambles themselves; it sounded muffled by metal, which creaked and scraped. She faltered, hands struggling in her pockets. Then she made out the car parked near the path. Of course, there must be a couple necking in the car, unaware of her or hushed now that they knew she was there—

But the car was a wreck. It lacked windows, doors, seats. Why, she could hear its rust as it shifted. Nobody could think of using it as a refuge.

Then the sound must be an animal's. A dog must be wandering near the rubbish tip—it was the sort of thing one expected of dogs. She mustn't dawdle, mustn't give her imagination time to gather, or she would never be able to go on. Above her, trees squeaked with a sound like burdened ice; they looked like cracks in the sky. Cursing Bill for leaving her alone with her fears, she ran past the car, the faint bulky fumbling.

At the pipe she faltered again. She would have to bend almost double to squeeze under. Climbing was impossible. Suppose that as she stooped beneath it, momentarily helpless, something pounced?

Bushes, banks of earth, concrete, loomed around her. Distant buses murmured, reminding her how far she was from anyone. But she wasn't so far from Jack and Diana; while she was wavering they might be deciding not to wait. "Oh Christ," she whispered, afraid of being overheard. With an effort that made her fists tremble, she ducked beneath the pipe.

As the view behind her stood on its head—the dark overgrown hollow, the dim latticework of trees—she glimpsed something thin, with spindly limbs, which started up from the brambles and scurried into the branches overhead.

A convulsion jerked her erect, until the pipe seemed to grab her by the scruff of her neck and force her head down, jarring an ache into her skull. For a moment she was caught, helpless, struggling, about to disintegrate into a fit of screaming. Then she was free and clinging to the pipe while she glared wildly about at the dark.

There was nothing, only the trees waving gently like insect feelers against the muddy sky. Surely that was what she'd seen, and her imagination, confused by the inverted view, had done the rest. She had seen nothing directly; the glimpse had been too brief, the movement too rapid. Just let her creep out of the enclosed hollow, into the open where she would be able to see there was nothing. Just creep through the dark, carefully so that the path and the invading undergrowth didn't catch her feet, quietly so that she didn't draw attention to herself—no, so that her sounds wouldn't startle her and feed her imagination—

She had taken only a couple of steps when she heard something scuttle along the concrete roof ahead of her.

She backed against the pipe. Her guts were melting, attacked by the acid of fear. Her stiffened limbs felt as though any movement would snap them. As she stared raw-eyed at the dimness, she glimpsed a thin shape leaping from the roof to cling to a tree. At once it was scuttling from tree to tree, fencing her in.

In a moment she might see it clearly, and then she

would begin to scream. Once she began she would never stop. Her impressions were growing: it was like a nervous hand, fumbling rapidly over the trees, as though eager to reach through the bars of a cage for her—or perhaps it was more like a spider, weaving back and forth over the trees, building a web around her. It knew she was trapped, which was why it was taking its time. For a moment she sensed that it was dangling overhead, ready to fall on her, to seize her with all its limbs.

Perhaps there was another reason why it was biding its time: it was enjoying her panic. At once she yearned not to have had that thought. Yes, the thing in the dark was waiting until she was ripe with terror before it fed—except that feeding, however dreadful, was more natural than what it was going to do to her.

Her whole body was shaking. It felt as though it was disintegrating into uncontrollable fragments, each of which was shivering. Her mind was utterly helpless. She was aghast at her feelings, which were far worse than despair. Part of her welcomed her helplessness, yearned to be taken. It was as though she'd discovered a pit in her mind, alive with corruption.

Again she heard the scuttling on the concrete. It had encircled her now, and was ready to seize her. She would rather anything than that—she would rather die than have the pit widen in her mind. She struggled with her jerking hands. Her mind was barren, she had nothing but savage instincts. Perhaps she could rip open her jugular with her nails.

Suddenly the barbed wire began jangling. It was vibrating wildly, as though it had captured a victim. And by God, something was struggling: she could almost see it, a gray scrawny bulk tearing at the barbed coils, flailing its limbs. "You're caught now, you bastard!" she screamed, and was appalled at how little sanity remained in her voice. Sobbing, she ran out of the hollow into the open night.

Long slopes glimmering with grass extended round

her. The Mersey looked solid as a dim road; the far bank seethed with orange lights. Litter had swarmed up from the tip, and clung rustling to the occasional bare trees, crawled flapping through the grass. The litter made the path, which at best was only a dark trail through the whitish grass, more difficult to follow.

She ran, trying desperately to concentrate on the path. A whitish patch rose screaming and broke into seagulls. The ground was full of chunks to trip her. Twice she almost turned her ankle. She could no longer hear the jangling of the wire, only the incessant struggling of the litter—or was that all that was moving around her?

She kept glancing behind her as she ran. Her ears seemed muffled by her breath, which was shivering. Slopes glimmered on all sides of her, lifelessly pale. There was no sign of pursuit; nothing moved except litter, which looked crippled. If the thing managed to tear itself free, it would be injured and therefore crueler. She stumbled onward, sobbing.

Had she strayed from the path? Beyond the Esso land a few streetlamps glinted, appallingly far; they looked even more distant now. She was running toward a patch of land that was paler than the grass. Wasn't it part of the path?

When she grabbed a brick and hurled it, she heard the ice shatter like thin glass. The brick squelched into the ground beneath. God, she was straying toward the tip; flocks of litter surrounded her now. The breaking ice had sounded very loud. Perhaps it had betrayed where she was.

She clambered up the slope and found the path. Lights shone on both sides of her: beyond the enclosed land, beyond the river. They were far too distant to illuminate her way. She could only stagger along the dark path, hearing the ice squeak and snap underfoot in the ruts, stumbling over rubble.

Though the slopes looked bare, she was sure that the

thing was pursuing. The wire was ominously still. She thought that her pursuer was dragging its body forward, what there was of it, with its great eager hand. Its determination was hideous. Was the thing really shaped like that, as her instincts told her it was? By the way her mind recoiled she knew it was worse.

The path was turning. She was close to home, though by no means close enough. She had to follow the path, though it had become a narrow rut which made her feet feel shackled; her sense of direction had fled. Besides, if she struck out across the field the icy shell of the ground might give way, plunging her into softness. She was almost at the railway cutting; streetlamps glared across, interrupting the frieze of lit windows. Surely light was on her side. Once she came close to it she would be safe.

But even the light was unhelpful. It dazzled her; she couldn't see her way. Never mind, so long as she ran parallel to the lit street she would be on the path. She could see the lights of Fulwood Park now, half-choked by the hedge. She was past the first railway bridge, whose barrier of planks was creaking, rattling in the wind. One more bridge and she was home.

She was running and at the same time groping in her purse for her key, to have it ready in her pocket, just in case—in case of what, in God's name?—when she halted, gasping. She teetered on the edge of a rut; one heel broke through ice and dug into mushy ground. The thing hadn't pursued her, it had headed her off. She knew that it was clinging underneath the bridge ahead.

Before she was aware what she was doing, she was trudging toward the bridge. Perhaps if she gave herself freely, the horror might be less unbearable, or at least more quickly over. There was nowhere she could hide. Glaring light filled her eyes. At least she wouldn't see the thing when it reached for her and dragged her into its lair beneath the bridge.

Without warning she cried out, a sound like an

animal's choking death-scream, and fled toward Fulwood Park. She was fleeing the depths of herself as much as the thing beneath the arch. "Please, oh please," she was sobbing. Please let Jack and Diana be waiting to take care of her. She seemed no longer able to do so herself.

White light spread through the hedge. The lurid ground resembled a cage, barred with elongated shadows. She was stumbling into a cage. Somehow she had managed to fumble her key out of her purse. It felt like a wound in her fist. Now she could see the road beyond the gap in the hedge: the dangling white lamps seemed violently bright; the walls, and the grass of the pavement, looked deadened, unreal. It didn't matter, light was all that mattered. She stumbled out of the cage of shadows into Fulwood Park.

She had just reached the stage of light when something touched the back of her neck. It was soft, moist, atrociously cold. Perhaps it was a finger, but she thought that was how congealed slime must feel. Was it thrusting her forward or caressing her? Certainly its touch was intended to hint what it had in store for her.

She had no breath left to scream. She could only stagger along the bright roadway toward her gate. Her swaying shadow looked unbalanced. Perhaps she was, too, perhaps she would fall into its arms. If another shadow appeared beside it she was lost. But there was only the glaring road and her empty gateposts: no sign of Jack or Diana, no sign of her house or the Hays', only a single dark old building where they ought to be.

Her mind was about to crack open, to let everything pour in, when she saw that she'd been partly mistaken. The twin houses were there; they were simply merged by their own darkness. She ran forward blindly, key outstretched. The front door opened a little, until it was blocked from within.

She thrust against it, sobbing or screaming. In a moment the obstacle retreated. It was only a package that had been wedged against the door. She fell into the hall and slammed the door behind her. Her pulse shook her body. Locked in, locked in, locked in, it seemed to be intoning. Thank God, she was locked in.

XL

For a while she could only slump, palms flat against the wall. Her pulse made the wall feel soft and throbbing. Even if something had begun to scrabble at the front door, she would have been unable to move. The door shifted, but that was an aberration of her vision, gradually subsiding.

She was safe now. She had only to wait for Jack and Diana. If they had despaired of her and booked into a hotel, she could join them there as soon as they phoned—please let them hurry up and phone! She turned the packet over with her toe, so that she could see what it was. The handwriting on the front was Jack's.

Why would he have written so soon before they were coming to visit—if they were coming to visit? When she stooped dizzily, the house staggered too. She wrenched open the packet. Inside was a paperback reprint of *Shared Nightmares*, carrying a photograph of herself and Bill, all smiles. Both the title and the photograph seemed vicious jokes. She hurled the book at the stairs.

Apart from the book, the wrapping was empty. She crumpled it in her fist as though that would give her strength. Then she saw a note protruding from the book. Apart from mentioning the reprint, Jack said that he and Diana would arrive today.

No sound would have been capable of expressing her relief. She stood, eyes closed, rocking herself like a cradled baby. She would come to no harm—if the house was safe.

This was idiotic. Last night she had checked every lock and window; since then she had touched nothing but the front door. Nevertheless she felt compelled to patrol. Surely that was no trouble when it would ensure her peace of mind.

She made for the kitchen. She had to grope along the walls in case her legs gave way; they felt fractured by her nerves. The fluorescent light twitched, twitched. Oh God, was the back door ajar? No, that was only the effect of the flickering.

All the downstairs windows were shut tight, yet the house was barely reassuring. It contained no memories; it seemed indifferent to her as a waiting room. Bill had robbed her of her home.

As she went upstairs she grabbed the new paperback, which she shoved into the wastebin in the workroom. The first draft of *The Meanings of Stardom* lay on the desk. What would they do about things like that? How would they divide the spoils of their plundered marriage? The problem seemed both infuriating and dispiriting.

Yes, the window was shut. So was the bathroom window. She mustn't speculate about what might be outside, only remember that it couldn't get in, whatever it was, whatever they were. There was nothing out there except silence like held breath, though perhaps whatever was outside didn't need to breathe.

Her reflected face slithered over the black tiles, an unformed mask of putty. Who was that peering out of the mirror? Good God, it was just her reflection—but her face made her obscurely nervous. She hurried out of the bathroom, switching off the light as she went.

Clinging to the banister as if it was a crutch, she reached the spare room. Of course the window was shut; did she have to go in to make sure? But why should she be afraid to venture in, just because she'd thought she had heard movement in there last night?

There was no doubt that the light was dim, but that was no reason to suppose that it would fail while she was in the room. Would she rather be unsure about the window? She urged herself forward. The light bulb looked grayish, as though a substance was forming on its surface or within. It must be dust, however it had gathered.

The window was unquestionably shut. Now could she please stop being idiotic? She hurried out of the room, slapping the light-switch angrily. Some of her strength was returning.

In the moment before darkness fell, she glimpsed the bulb from the corner of her eye. Something larger than a bulb, and gray, appeared to be dangling from the cord. Perhaps it had a face.

She slammed the door and stood trembling. She mustn't let her imagination take hold. What she needed was a drink to hush her fears or stifle her perceptions, it didn't matter which, until Jack and Diana arrived. Oh, please let that be soon!

She hurried into the bedroom, giving herself no more time to think—yes, the window was shut, the double bed lay sealed by its blankets, a mockery of marriage— then strode downstairs to the bourbon. Should she make a fire? But the ash in the hearth was stirring feebly in a draft. She grabbed the bottle and retreated.

She couldn't wait upstairs; she would be too far from the phone. The kitchen overlooked the greenhouse. Eventually she took refuge in the dining room; at least the room was neutral—the curtains obscured the view of the back garden, the greenhouse. It was almost the only room in which she could bear to stay for any length of time.

Though the bars of the gas fire looked molten, its warmth seemed withheld from her. The Victorian vignettes embroidered on the dining suite had turned nauseatingly sentimental. No doubt they had always been so. Only her marriage had prevented her from realizing it. Perhaps they summed up the marriage.

She poured more bourbon into the tumbler until it was half full, and gazed down at the bottom of the glass, which was magnified and wavering. It made her feel dizzy. She gulped a mouthful to get rid of the wavering.

She needed to rest her eyes; the edge of her vision was fading again, the gray seemed to be closing in; whenever she let it occupy her attention she began to forget where she was. Perhaps by the time she'd rested her eyes the phone would ring—or better, oh how much better, the doorbell.

She closed her eyes. Sparks sailed up as though her head was burning; dim patches floated up like smoke. Was the gray retreating or expanding? She couldn't tell. Just keep her eyes closed while the traces of migraine faded. Just let her rest, she was so exhausted, drained of everything except a yearning for comfort. The bourbon was helping her doze, just for a few moments, a few moments couldn't matter. She didn't realize she had been asleep until Bill loomed over her.

Instinctively she reached out. Thank God, she was safe now. Then she remembered. By God, he'd better stay away from her; if he dared touch her— Her eyes opened stickily. She was alone in the room.

A moment ago she had not been alone. Someone or something had been very close—outside the window, or inside the house? What might be waiting for her to part the curtains, knowing she would have to do so? What might be eager for her to open the door into the hall?

A worse fear released her from her panic—that when the phone rang she wouldn't dare to leave this room. She flung open the door. The hall was empty. At once she began to hurry about the house, switching on all the lights.

The fluorescent tube flickered like migraine. Paleness moved in the greenhouse, but it was only the reflection of the light. In the living room she turned the switch as far as it would go. The bulbs spotlighted the phone, which was silent as a stuffed perched bird.

She stayed out of the workroom as she switched on the light. One glimpse of the greenhouse was enough. Nor was she anxious to see her face sinking into the darkness of the bathroom tiles. She tugged the light-cord and hurried to the spare room. Leaning hastily through the doorway, she knuckled the switch.

The room seemed to spring erect like a folding picture in a child's book. She had no time to see anything, however, for the bulb burst immediately. As the darkness flooded back, she heard something plump to the carpet.

If the thing in the trees had dropped toward her, it would have sounded very much like that. Was it hobbling rapidly toward her? Nothing had appeared when she slammed the door and stood clinging to the knob.

She was still holding the door shut, and wondering desperately how she would ever be able to let go, when the phone rang.

Could she let go? She could feel nothing but the doorknob, which had grown enormous, overwhelming her thoughts. It was a burden she dared not release. She'd forgotten how to move her fingers. Though the phone was ringing patiently, its patience was by no means inexhaustible.

When she wrenched herself free, the door rattled. She mustn't look back. Halfway downstairs she was convinced that the phone would fall silent before she reached it. As she ran into the living room she collided with the edge of the doorway—but her arm could still reach out and grab the phone.

For a moment both her relief and lack of breath made her unable to speak. Upstairs the door was silent, as was the rest of the house, except for a faint scampering like mice. "Rose Tierney," she said at last.

"Hi, Rose."

It was Jack. He sounded close as the next room. Oh, thank God. She was able to sound as though nothing was wrong. "Did you come before and have to go away? I'm sorry."

"Well, no, that's okay. Uh—"

Nothing was wrong. The scampering was only the start of rain. "Aren't you in Liverpool?" she said nervously.

"No." He seemed obscurely resentful. "That's why I'm calling."

It didn't matter, she could arrange to meet them downtown, wait there for them. "When will you be arriving? Do you know?"

"Well, that's just it, Rose. I guess we won't be. Diana's sick."

The phone was beginning to thump her ear repetitively, because her hand was trembling. "But where exactly are you calling from?"

"New York. We didn't leave."

She could think of nothing to say. Her mind was walled into itself. Eventually she heard herself say, out of desperation or pleading, "So you won't be coming at all."

"I'm afraid not, Rose. I'm sorry. I did try to call you several times today."

Her mind was jumbled, cluttered. The sound of rain had merged with the static of the phone, a single hiss which enclosed her. She couldn't think coherently, only hang onto the phone, desperate for someone to talk to. "Did you call me yesterday at the University?" was all she could think of to say.

"No, I wouldn't know the number. Maybe Diana did. No, she wouldn't know it either."

He'd reminded her of the question she ought to be asking. "What's wrong with Diana?" Perhaps it wasn't serious, perhaps she could persuade them to come after all—

"I guess she had a breakdown."

"Oh, I'm sorry." That was inadequate, but there

wasn't much room amid her fears for either understanding or sympathy.

"Yeah." His resentment was emerging. "It was all
this occult bullshit she was into."

"In what way? How?"

"Christ, I don't know. I don't understand that
garbage. I wish she'd never gotten into it. You might
have understood it better, what she was trying to say."
He sounded as if he blamed Rose. "She tried to get in
touch with you."

Before Rose could speak he said angrily. "You ought
to have seen her. She'd been down to see this prick in
the Village, the guy who encouraged her in all this
stuff. Don't ask me what he told her or what happened
after that. You never went to Bellevue, did you? Well,
she looks like some of the patients they have there. All
I know is she tried to call you and when she couldn't she
tried to get in touch with you some other way. You tell
me what that means if you can. This occult garbage
finally fucked her up, that's all I can see."

Perhaps the way Diana had tried to get in touch had
harmed her. If so, Rose was partly to blame. She
mustn't succumb to guilt yet, mustn't let him shame her
into not asking. "Jack, did she say what she wanted to
tell me?"

"I told you, some kind of occult stuff. Why do you
want to know? Is it for this fucking article she was
helping you write? Jesus, I wish she'd never had the
idea."

"No, Jack, I simply want to know because she
wanted to tell me." Rose wasn't sure that reasonable-
ness would work, nor that she could keep it up.
"Besides, it might help you understand what's going on
in her mind."

"Yeah, well, I don't think so. Even her friend who
works in Bellevue is having trouble with that. I guess I
should leave it to him." Nevertheless he sounded
calmer, persuaded of her concern for Diana.

"What she said was all mixed up," he said eventually. "I couldn't make any sense out of it. A lot of mystical stuff about grace and a girl who lived someplace near you with a strange name—what was it?—yeah, I remember, Ormskirk."

Rose felt as though he'd grabbed her stomach. "What girl?"

"A girl called Grace."

Yes, she was gripped by her stomach, and the grip was squeezing. It was making her lose control; she wouldn't be able to stay calm—her questions would grow too violent, they would alienate him. "Do you recall her exact words?" She managed to confine her violence to her grasp of the receiver.

"I told you it was all mixed up. The stuff she was researching got to be too much for her somehow." For a moment it seemed he would refuse to say more. "She kept talking about Hitler, how Hitler couldn't succeed without grace. Then she got onto some kind of *Exorcist*-type stuff, about a guy who could possess other people's bodies without their knowing. Maybe his name was Grace too, I don't know. She kept saying the people who followed this guy were frightened of him because he could get into their bodies and they'd never know. Then she started saying Grace had to be stopped, that maybe you could go to Ormskirk and try. I guess some of this stuff was what she researched and the rest was just delusion. She used the word Grace in so many different ways I couldn't follow her."

Of course it had meant the same name every time. Rose stared in front of her, at the cold deserted room. "Listen, I have to go," Jack said abruptly. "Maybe she needs me, though I don't think she even knows me right now. I'm sorry you've been let down. Maybe we can visit with you both another time." His voice, which had been harsh, grew faintly solicitous. "Let me tell you, Rose—forget about writing that article. Don't get into this occult shit. It can't do you any good."

XLI

Rose let the receiver drop into its cradle and slumped against the doorway. Her mind and her body felt paralyzed. Around her a fusillade of rain shook the windows. It sounded as though the house was cracking. She was afraid to use her mind. She didn't know how painful it might be.

At last, gingerly, she began to think. Jack's call had left her alone—yet perhaps it had helped her, only just in time. Perhaps what had happened to Diana was a warning of what might happen to her.

Diana's message was too garbled to be comprehensible. The reference to Ormskirk must be a coincidence—Diana didn't know that Rose had lived there. Presumably Diana had found another reference to Grace, less cagey than *Astral Rape*. None of this mattered. It had nothing to do with Rose.

No doubt some of the message had been a product of Diana's mental state. That was the important point: Diana was unbalanced. Her belief that nobody was given more to suffer than they could bear hadn't been true for her. But then why should it be true for Rose?

There was no reason to think so: no reason to believe that her mind had survived intact.

It was as though a door was creeping open in her mind. She couldn't tell what lay beyond, but she couldn't close it now. There was no point in avoiding the truth: since being mugged in New York, she had been behaving more and more as though she was mad.

At once her memories were interlocking. The way she'd written to Diana of her experiences as though she was describing someone else's—wasn't that a symptom of schizophrenia? Why, recently she'd felt as though she was acting in the third person too. And what about her paranoia? Surely nothing but mental illness could have made her so unaware of the way she was withdrawing from everyone, retreating so deep into herself that she was in danger of never emerging.

She couldn't stand much more of this. Her thoughts were bullying her into denying all that she'd taken for granted about herself. Her personality felt fragile, insubstantial, almost nonexistent. Maybe she could suffer her thoughts more easily if she had another drink—but good God, that was a symptom too: she was becoming an alcoholic.

She had pushed herself away from the doorframe, but there was nowhere she could go. She stood in the doorway, supported by nothing. She knew nobody to whom she could turn for help.

Or did she?

She couldn't go next door. For one thing, she hadn't heard Colin or Gladys come home. She couldn't bear to seek reassurance only to find nobody. Besides, the only way Colin could help would be to probe for the memory which had terrified her. She couldn't face that terror again; in fact she wished she hadn't thought of it—the memory felt like a dark pit, lurking somewhere in her mind, a pit whose edge she must avoid at all costs.

But there was an alternative to Colin. There was Freda, who worked in a psychiatric commune down South. The commune didn't force people to accept treatment. Freda maintained that the commune helped those who turned to it for aid—they weren't known as "patients"—find their own way back to reality.

Nevertheless the prospect was dismaying. The commune had sounded like an interesting experiment, stimulating to discuss, but she had never expected to have to visit it herself. No wonder Bill was screwing someone else; he couldn't stand living with Rose, who didn't even know she was going mad. It must have been her madness which had made her so cruel to him.

Perhaps just to tell Freda everything might be enough. At least she had a definite motive for leaving her comfortless home. She couldn't talk to Uncle Wilfred and Auntie Vi now. To do so might be just another symptom of unbalance.

Wasn't she being untrue to herself? Hadn't at least some of her experiences been real? Perhaps, but too many seemed like mental aberrations; she couldn't distinguish them from the real ones, if any. All her memories seemed unreal. She thought of the group she'd encountered in Hulme. How soon before she ended up like them?

Perhaps her fear of Colin had been a fear of admitting her own mental state. Why, she had been frightened of Diana's medical friend: that must have been the first of her symptoms. Thoughts of Colin made her aware of the dark pit waiting in her mind. She must go to Freda.

She gasped, because she'd realized something else must have been a delusion. She had glimpsed her mother's death because she had felt betrayed by her parents and Bill—because she was wishing her dead. Her mother was in no danger after all.

The door in her mind seemed to have opened wide, releasing a flood of light. She was sure she was on the way back to health. She only hoped she still had Freda's address.

In the dining room her handbag lolled drunkenly on the floor, guarded by dregs of bourbon in the glass. She rummaged for her address book. Yes, thank God, here was Freda, in Devon. Would there be a train tonight? If not, Rose could stay downtown in a hotel.

She was heading upstairs to pack a case when the phone rang.

She hesitated irritably. She felt as though someone

had interrupted her halfway through an inspired paragraph. If it was Jack, he was too far away to be of any help.

Not knowing who it was might be a worse distraction. She hurried down and snatched the receiver. "Is that you, Bill?" she demanded.

That sounded almost like a plea, which infuriated her. There was no reply except static, as though the downpour outside was leaking through the phone. She listened a few moments, then slammed the receiver into place.

The call had confused her. Her purpose, which had seemed beautifully simple and direct, was interrupted, jumbled up with thoughts of Diana's message, of the memory Colin had almost reached. She must ignore everything but the need to leave as quickly as possible. Striding upstairs, she hurried past the closed door of the spare room.

Her double bed looked flattened, lifeless, a wiped slate. Never mind that, now or ever. She was ashamed of her plea to the phone. But as she reached down a suitcase from the top of the wardrobe, she was intensely aware of the bed and of everything else in the room, vivid as the moment of a flashbulb. It was as though her mind was clinging to her surroundings in order to hold her back from the pit of her memory.

As she carried a dress to the case, she felt as though it was an empty skin with which she was dancing. Everything was too intense. Sweaters took their places in the case, their broken arms folded on their chests. Shoes nuzzled each other in a hollow parody of a sexual position. Rain was patting the windows, scurrying over them. Of course it was only rain.

Suddenly she couldn't hear the rain. It was a momentary lapse, like the flash of a daydream. Surely it was as trivial, a moment's failure of attention, yet it made her nervous. Perhaps it was another symptom, for during that moment the edge of her vision had faded, the grayness had closed in.

She must concentrate. The bathroom, yes, the bathroom. She should collect her toiletries before she forgot. The frosted glass was crawling with rain; it looked as though the window was melting, giving way. She crammed makeup, toothbrush, deodorant, toothpaste into the pouch. Around her in the tiles, vague faces were struggling in darkness. She zipped the pouch shut and came face to face with the mirror.

She stared, dismayed. The face was intensely present, the almost perfect oval sprinkled with freckles like a seasoning of flaws, the frame of long black hair, the small mouth that looked in danger of twitching uncontrollably, the blue eyes too wide and bright. It looked unreal as a mask, and she couldn't recognize herself in the eyes; she couldn't grasp that the face was hers.

Her alienation was worsening. She hurried herself back to the suitcase, past the closed spare room. She mustn't hesitate for anything. Ignore her bedroom, whose vividness seemed almost solid, a medium through which she had to struggle. Don't think, just act, get out—

What was she doing? She was halted halfway between suitcase and wardrobe. Was she unpacking the clothes she was holding? Had she been distracted from hanging them up? Oh Christ, the gray silence had almost overcome her; for a moment it had robbed her of awareness. It must be the worst symptom of all.

She was packing the case, *packing* the case. The phrase echoed, inane and nerve-racking, in her skull. Never mind, it helped her concentrate on what she was doing, ignore everything else. She grabbed handfuls of clothes and stuffed them into the case, as much as it would hold. Never mind tidiness, speed was everything now. She must catch a taxi, to reach the train as soon as she could—soon, please soon! Once aboard the train she would feel safer. At least the driver wouldn't forget where the train was going.

The case was full now. Had she forgotten anything? If so, it couldn't be helped; she mustn't dawdle, in case the gray silence overwhelmed her. It was all right, she could still hear the rain, scuttling over the windows. Just let her concentrate on that while she locked the case.

The case was locked, the handle was solid in her hand. Surely its weight would hold her attention. She had only to carry the case downstairs and then the onslaught of the rain would be impossible to ignore, would keep her mind from drifting. She hefted the case gratefully. Its heaviness was satisfying, a weapon against the treachery of her mind. She'd needed reassurance, something to which she could cling.

"You're far too late," a voice said.

It was toneless, soft as a marsh. It didn't sound alive in any way. Though she had never heard it before, it was coming from her mouth.

XLII

The suitcase fell from her hand. It must have made a sound; it must have shaken the floor underfoot. She was aware of nothing but the inside of her skull. Her brain felt like a hatching egg, from inside which a maggot, or something worse, was squirming.

Like a radio which continued talking whether or not there was anyone to hear, her thoughts were still babbling rationalizations. She tried to cling to them as though they were hopes. She'd failed to recognize her reflection, why shouldn't the same thing happen with her voice? It was only alienation, she was rejecting her voice because it expressed her fears, the condition was curable, perhaps after all she couldn't bear the delay before she met Freda, perhaps she ought to go next door for help—

She'd forgotten why she was avoiding thoughts of Colin. The memory which he had almost released was lying in wait in her mind. It seemed to need only that thought to unbalance her into the pit. She felt like a terrified child alone in darkness. She cried out, hardly aware of what she was saying: "Uncle Wilfred, where are you? Auntie Vi—please—"

She was answered. She felt the presence which was watching over her come clear. It was only one. It was neither of her relatives, but she knew it all too well. It was old and sly and utterly ruthless, and had deceived her effortlessly. It was the thing which the Hays' séance had awakened in the dark.

Her mind gave way. The dark pit opened, and she was falling helplessly, dwindling. Her consciousness shrank until it was small as a terrified child's. She was ten years old, alone in the dark.

She was not quite alone. The others had fled, frightened of the groping they'd heard ranging softly and insidiously within the walls. It had spoken to them through their séance. It was everywhere in the room, perhaps everywhere in the unlit house.

But its physical form, whatever that might be, was no longer trapped in the walls. The séance had set it free. She had touched it through the dusty sheets of the bed, a thin flabby limb. Perhaps her touch had awakened it fully, for it had got out of the bed.

By the time she reached the door she was too late. The voices on the far side of the door had no idea what was happening to her. They thought she was only trapped in the room, in danger of nothing but panic. They would let her out eventually, but they weren't especially concerned. She was younger than they were, after all—less worthy of consideration. She tried to cry out, to tell them what they'd closed in with her, but her breath could only suck in smells of dust and something older, far less clean.

The voices were retreating, sinking into the dark of the house. She was absolutely alone, except for what had risen from the bed. She clawed at the door, but even when she hooked her finger in the hole where the doorknob should have been, the door wouldn't budge.

A pale distorted shape was creeping about the room, slithering over the shabby furniture. It was the stray light of a car, which must be turning outside in the road, for the light managed to reach the door in front of her. Her shadow leapt up, small and wavering. It was alone.

Was that reassuring or more terrifying? Before she knew, something cold and flabby, a body which felt not quite formed, fastened on her from behind.

If she could have screamed she would have done so. Perhaps it would have brought her no help, but at least it would have convinced her that she was still herself—for the thing which had fastened on her was seeping into her body.

She couldn't move or cry out, only writhe inside herself as she felt the parasite within her body, oozing up toward her brain. It burrowed deep into her brain, like a worm into an apple, and hid there, beginning at once to wipe out her awareness of it. Before long her mind was unnaturally calm, peaceful as the surface of water into which something dreadful had plunged. Its depths were invisible to her.

But they were no longer invisible, and they explained too much. She knew why she hadn't been able to speak when the adults had let her out of the room—because the parasite was still in the process of hiding from her. No wonder she'd forgotten what had happened, no wonder her mother had thought she had changed overnight. No wonder she had felt compelled to scrub herself obsessively: though she hadn't been consciously aware of what was inside her, some part of her mind had been.

Frightful as these memories were, they were only

memories—but the parasite had been inside her ever since. It was inside her now.

She began to stagger about the bedroom, clawing at her skull as though her nails could reach in and drag out the parasite. Perhaps she could smash her head against the wall; her skull felt thin as eggshell, eaten away from within. She could feel the parasite inside it, heavy and soft and swollen. It drove her into frenzy. There were scissors in the bathroom—no, in her suitcase. Perhaps she could operate on herself with those, gouge out the cancer.

No, she could do none of these things, for her body was no longer hers. It stood like a tottering dummy beside the bed, and began to tremble uncontrollably. Any moment now it would have to collapse on the bed and lie there shaking.

She knew what would happen then: she would be shaken out of her body. Perhaps this time she would not be allowed to return. What things would have her at their mercy then?

She began to struggle inwardly. Her efforts were pitifully feeble—and all at once she knew why they were hopeless. She had no strength to pit against the thing in her skull because her growing strength had not been hers at all. Neither had her developing powers. They had belonged to the parasite, they had been symptoms of its growth.

She tried to move her feet. If she could only reach the stairs perhaps she could hurl herself down, destroy her body. Hadn't that worked once before, decades ago? But her legs, and the rest of her, could do nothing but tremble. Her thoughts were shaken to pieces. She was aware of nothing but her epileptic shuddering.

She was lost. The gray was closing in upon her vision, pressing against her eyes as though they were filling with fog. The sounds of the downpour outside were fading. She couldn't hold onto a sense of her body, for it wasn't hers. Was she screaming inwardly, pleading with the impersonal powers which had intervened before on her behalf, on the flight home from Munich? Clearly that was not the way to appeal to them, for there was no response. Except for the swollen movements in her head, she was utterly alone, at the mercy of the gray silence.

All at once she realized that the gray was not an absence at all. It was a place, far too close to her surroundings and at least as real: a different state of being. That was where she would be kept. No, please no—but the only opposition she could manage was a thin dwarfed shriek. Her sense of her body was already too distant to recapture; nothing she'd believed to be real was to be trusted. The sounds of rain were gone. She couldn't feel her body. She was no longer in her room. The gray closed in.

She was no more than an intense point of despair. She couldn't move or even think, only experience. The gray suffocated all sense of herself. She might have been deaf, blind, completely senseless, except that she could feel the gray. It felt like being buried in lard.

Now her senses were creeping back to torment her. Whatever the medium was that had engulfed her, it was changing slowly. Shapes were becoming visible, though she could hardly be perceiving them in any normal way. They seemed a cruel parody of reassurance, for they were everyday objects, formed out of the gray substance: an empty bed, a table, a dressing table with a mirror like unbroken scum, the walls of a room. None of them seemed quite solid or stable.

Suddenly she recognized the place they were parodying. It was the upper room in Ormskirk. Some details were missing; the walls were blank, no door or windows. She couldn't struggle physically or mentally, only float trapped in the gray and wait for a shape to form in the empty bed, to rise on its thin flabby limbs.

But the walls were shifting. The furniture began to melt, and then was indistinguishable from the gray. She was in an octagonal vault whose walls were swarming with magical symbols. Though she understood none of them consciously, the symbols were intimidatingly awesome.

She remembered this place too, though it was not her memory. It was the vault into which novices were led for initiation into the Order of the Golden Dawn. Now she had to admit the identity of the dead thing which had taken refuge inside her body. The knowledge was eating away what remained of her sense of identity. The parasite was Peter Grace.

And this gray unstable place was where he had festered after his death, until she had provided him with a refuge. It had taken shape from his memories and frustrated desires. It was as though she was trapped in his mind. There could be no escape from that.

Again her surroundings were changing. Now the room was long and high and dim. Ranks of objects filled it: coffins? No, they were benches—pews. It was a church. Ahead of her was the pulpit, the altar, a window in which vague forms were embedded. Grace must have preached here, until he had been suppressed. This was where his hatred had begun.

Now she could see that hatred. The church was a parody, detailed and vicious. The pews and the pulpit resembled gray fungus, covered with glistening bruises. The pillars looked swollen, syphilitic. The cross on the altar drooped impotently. Within the mockery of a stained-glass window, great figures pranced and grimaced. Their tarnished halos were crumbling. All the figures were defecating and masturbating.

She was trapped in the abominable church, unable even to avoid perceiving. Perhaps she was here for good. This must be his favorite memory, for though its outlines were not quite steady, it was growing increasingly vivid. She was alone with it, all the more helpless because it was at least as solid as she was: perhaps more so.

No, she was not alone. Something was in the pulpit. It was struggling to raise itself, with grublike movements. Eventually its head appeared, nodding feebly over the pulpit. It had no face, only a wad of gray.

It must have gone into the pulpit to try and make her out, for now it clambered down and began to pad toward her. It looked worse than it had sounded in the greenhouse. It was dwarfish and rudimentary, and seemed almost mindless. Perhaps Grace had created it out of the gray, for companionship.

It took a long time to reach her, turning its head back and forth as though snuffling. Perhaps to express its satisfaction, the surface of the soft head writhed like a grub. It began to paw at her with the unequal wads at the ends of its misshapen arms.

So she had a body, or at least the sensations of one. She felt composed of the gray substance too. Worst of all, part of her enjoyed the attentions of the faceless thing. That must be the part which Grace had tainted.

After a while the rudimentary creature hobbled away. It wasn't leaving her alone, only making way for its companion. She became aware of a shape that was squatting on the altar. It was a baby, almost as large as a man.

It climbed down and waddled toward her. Its skin, or the gray surface that resembled skin, was wrinkled and sagging. Though it looked like a baby, it was old. Its fat seemed to flop about inside the skin. Was this the baby which Grace was supposed to have killed?

When she saw the eyes in the senile yet babyish face, she knew that was the truth. Though the eyes contained a baby's single-minded hunger, they were old and sly in an appallingly retarded way. This had been a baby, and it had developed here in the nightmare church.

The baby plodded up to her and pressed against her. She felt dreadfully naked. The features of its face lolled within the skin, and seemed in danger of flopping loose as tripe. Its lips resembled a swollen slit in dough. Its flaccid penis could not quite enter her. Part of her was urging it to try harder.

When at last the baby waddled away, she knew there was one more horror yet to come. Its torments were more skillful, for it seized her from behind. Were they giant fingers that were roaming over her, or numerous spindly limbs? One moment they felt like cold swollen worms, the next thin, clawlike. She could tell that it was reveling in her paralyzed voiceless terror and revulsion. Perhaps it was paying her back for its struggles with the barbed wire.

Suddenly she realized what it meant to do. It would be far worse than rape. It would thrust deep into her and then change shape inside her body. Her terror shrank into itself, growing unbearably intense.

Without warning, and without her having glimpsed its shape, the scuttling was gone. Her terror had satisfied it for the moment. After all, it had the rest of her life to play with her, and that would be eternity— eternity spent in the fungoid corrupt church.

But another change was taking place. A glow had appeared on the altar. Could it be a sign of the impersonal presence which had saved her from a far less dreadful plight? No, for the light was dead; it might have been hovering over a marsh. The gray helped it coagulate. It became a face. Only one face could manifest itself above that altar: it was Peter Grace.

The face was long and thin, delicate as a skeleton. Once he must have looked the perfect clergyman; now his calm was that of a mask. His hair and brows shone like snow, but the brightness of his flesh looked lurid, polluted. His face was enormous, larger than the altar, and his eyes— She could shrink no farther into herself.

The eyes in the giant mask were telling her that she was helpless. She had been his puppet ever since the séance in Ormskirk. He'd bided his time, for he had enjoyed wearing her body. He'd gained a taste for that pleasure when he had inhabited the child whom his followers had terrified. It was a perversion far more profound and delicious than rape.

Now he was ready to realize his dreams, which had festered with him since his death. Perhaps she was incapable of bearing the full knowledge, for she could only glimpse hints. All life would be his playthings. He hated the living, since their world had been denied him for so long. He and only he deserved to live. He would bring a new kind of birth to the world. Perhaps, after all, the dead who felt as he did could join him; they deserved their revenge too. Perhaps they would preserve the world, at least for a while, as a toy.

His confiding in her showed her how helpless she was. She could do nothing to prevent him, that was the only fact she could trust. He was going to return her to the world for a little while, so that she could suffer from the knowledge that he was able to bring her back here whenever he chose, and for good. She would be the first to suffer as he had been made to suffer.

The gray withdrew abruptly like swift fog. She was lying in something hot, swollen, flaccid, sticky. For a moment she seemed to be half in it, half out, then it had trapped her. It felt bulky, repulsive, suffocating. Yes, it was her body.

She was lying on the bed. She heard rain, a clean sound which couldn't reach her. At some point she had vomited. She lay, for movement would achieve nothing. Perhaps if she lay absolutely still she would cease to exist, or at least lose consciousness. She mustn't remember, mustn't anticipate; it was best not to think at all. That felt almost like relief—at least, as much relief as she was ever likely to experience.

Even when she heard Bill wandering about downstairs, that seemed no reason for her to move. He was too late, but she couldn't hate him for that; in fact she felt nothing at all about anything. Was he looking for her, or had he already been upstairs?

A last faint emotion remained to her; a dread of being alone. He couldn't help her in any way, but his presence might be comforting; that was the most she could hope for. Suppose he had already tried to wake her and assumed she was ignoring him? Suppose he was about to leave?

She tried to call out, but could make no sound. She struggled to clamber off the bed. Her body was an awkward dummy which she was trying feebly to wield; its connection with her seemed very tenuous indeed. Somehow she managed to roll it to the edge, from which her legs dangled. Presumably the dull sensation was that of her feet touching the carpet.

Now she had to stand up. Even when she did so, clinging to the headboard, her legs felt like rubbery stilts over which she kept losing control. She staggered to the door, less walking than overbalancing.

Her lack of balance carried her along the landing. She supposed that the hand which was grabbing the banister, preventing her from falling headlong, was hers. Her clumsiness seemed deafening. It made him look up from the foot of the stairs.

But he was not Bill. He was bald, and he had a carving knife.

XLIII

She could feel no fear. Probably she had none left. As a threat he seemed trivial, merely human. As a human being, any human being, he made her feel less alone. She had no idea what he wanted, nor was she capable of caring.

They confronted each other the length of the stairs. His head was a gleaming helmet of skin; she thought she could see beads of sweat welling up. His brows glistened with rain or nervousness. If his frozen gaze

meant to dominate her, perhaps it might succeed. She
no longer knew anything about her mind.

When she stumbled forward onto the stairs it was
neither from choice nor from obedience; she had lost
her balance. Her spongy hand slithered over the
banister, and managed to grab. With each movement
her body felt more revolting. Her flesh wobbled and
churned inside the thin bag of skin. She could feel her
packed innards, wet and raw.

As she moved, he raised the knife. Its gleam was no
more metallic than his eyes. Perhaps he might be
welcome, after all. He looked capable of performing
for her the act which she might not be able to perform
for herself.

She had only to let herself stumble downstairs. She
did so, clinging moistly to the banister. She would have
let herself fall, except that the fall might not kill her.
She kept her eyes on him, inviting him to be quick.

Beside him a patch of the carpet looked wet and
quivering. The gray church must be seeping into the
house. No, it was only rain, pouring through the pane
which he'd broken next to the lock. Absurdly, she
resented the vandalism. She let herself stumble faster.
She mustn't be tempted to cling to life.

He was backing away toward the door. No, he
mustn't leave her! If he knew what she was, what she
had harbored and suffered, he would kill her at once, if
only to put her out of her misery. Perhaps she could tell
him—but her mouth was twitching so badly that she
couldn't speak at all.

Was that shock, or was she prevented from speaking?
She couldn't tell if she was alone in her body; after all,
she hadn't been able to tell before. It didn't matter
now, all that mattered was that the man with the knife
could release her.

She staggered toward him, trying to look pleading.
She could express nothing with her face; it wasn't hers.
Perhaps that was just as well, for he might misunder-

stand the plea. She stretched out her jerking hands, and hoped she looked menacing. He would have to defend himself.

The closer she came to him, the more absurd he seemed. He had obviously never used a knife as a weapon before. He was brandishing it at her, yet he was holding it as though to deny its presence. He looked desperate to overcome her without using it, to stare her into submission. His forehead was a mass of droplets, whose trickles made his left eye flinch.

Stumbling toward him, she felt unreal. She couldn't believe she was going toward the point of the knife, and perhaps that helped her advance. The absurd blinking man was raising the knife as though it was an embarrassment he wished he could throw away. He would have to act now. He had no more room to retreat.

He moved without warning. The knife pecked down. The violence of his movement startled her, expected though it was, and made her lose balance. She stumbled aside, clutching at the wall. She felt the edge of the knife slash her dress and graze one nipple.

She recoiled, gasping. Death might be desirable, but being hacked to death was not. In that moment she realized something infinitely worse. Might death simply trap her forever in the gray church?

The realization came too late. She had inflamed him now. Fanatical determination widened his eyes. He lunged at her with the knife. She was barely able to stagger aside, and she knew she could not maneuver. He had far more control of his movements than she had of hers.

She stumbled toward the stairs. She couldn't grapple with him: much of her strength had not belonged to her, and its withdrawal had robbed her of faith in her own. A few pointed shards of glass lay near the front door, but she could never reach them. Hindered by her body, she dragged herself upstairs.

He was clattering upstairs behind her. She could hear

his eagerness to finish her off. As she glanced back dizzily, the knife came swooping toward her legs. When she felt the impact, so violent that she almost toppled backward onto him, it took her a moment to realize that the blade had struck deep through the carpet into the stair.

He was wrenching at the handle with both hands. Oh, please let the blade snap! She heaved herself onto the landing, hand over hand along the supports of the banisters. Where now? If only there were a telephone upstairs!

She heard the twang of the knife blade as it pulled free. She saw it flash as he came striding upward. Oh God, which room contained potential weapons? She might have stunned him with the typewriter, but he was between her and the workroom. Could she scream from a window? The spare room was nearest, it faced the road—She had grabbed the doorknob before she remembered the burst light bulb and the other sounds. She would rather face the knife than go in there.

She stumbled into her bedroom, almost falling. Quick, quick, use the last of her strength to move the bed, to block the door! But she was barely able to grasp the footboard. Before the bed had even shifted, he shouldered his way into the room.

As he saw what she was trying to do, he smiled; at least, his face split to reveal his glistening teeth. For a grotesque moment it seemed he meant to help her. Still gripping the knife, he dragged the bed against the door, trapping her.

She ran to the curtains and wrenched them apart. They entangled her like blankets during a fever. Struggling free, she fumbled open the louvers at the top of the frame. "Help! Help!" she screamed. The opening was meager, and filled by the clamor of rain. She had no chance at all of being heard.

He knew it, and was taking his time as he closed in, waiting for her to back herself into a corner. They both knew that the point of the knife would drive her back. If only she had a weapon—but perhaps she had. She stooped and managed to pull off one of her shoes.

The effort threw her against the window. She felt the pane bend under her weight, threatening to hurl her into the night. She shoved herself away, heart clenching. Then at once she knew what to do.

She clubbed the pane with the heel of her shoe. The glass vibrated, once, twice. For a substance which had felt so fragile when she'd leaned against it, it now seemed impossibly strong. She struck the glass again with all the power she could command, which was very little. Glass splintered, and a handful of shards flew out, leaving a gap hardly larger than her heel.

She began to scream for help as she smashed at the edge of the hole. Outside was nothing but the hedge, threshing and glittering beneath the streetlamp. No, there was a car in the drive, painted black by the night. If anyone across the road could hear her screams and the breaking of glass, they were probably deploring another boisterous party. Nobody would help her, even if they could hear her above the downpour.

But he seemed to think that they might, for he was using the kinfe to prod her away from the window, toward the corner opposite the door. Each time the point darted toward her, her nipple twinged. Was he indifferent to her panic, or secretly pleased? His face was as bland as his baldness.

As he forced her toward the dressing table she began to seize objects—empty perfume bottles, an old hairbrush—and fling them at him. He knocked them aside, looking amused by the feebleness of her defense.

She threw a comb. It clawed him just above one eye, and visibly maddened him. The game was over. It was time to finish her off. She was still crying for help, but the downpour outshouted her. As he stepped forward, raising the blade, he seemed silent as a dream.

There seemed to be so much noise that neither of

them heard the movement of the bed. In any case they couldn't look away from each other, not even when the door was flung open.

"I think you'd better give me that," Colin said, "and quickly."

It was like awakening. Everything seemed apart from her, occurring on a different plane, not quite comprehensible. She saw the bald man's face turn viciously petulant, like a child robbed of an insect he was torturing. He hurled the knife at Colin. It rebounded from Colin's shoulder, and drew a shriek of fear or rage from Gladys, who was behind him.

Colin stepped forward, glancing solicitously at Rose, warily but confidently at her attacker. The bald man turned back toward Rose; he was coming at her again. "Leave her alone!" Gladys cried, and ran forward, ready to claw him.

Colin glanced back at her, startled. The man dodged past both of them and raced for the stairs. Before he reached them Gladys was above him on the landing, grabbing at him. Rose saw him lose his balance and fall like a giant toy; bump, bump, bump. Then she was falling too, for there was nothing to hold her.

XLIV

As Colin caught Rose and lowered her onto the bed, Gladys flustered into the room. "I don't know if he's dead," she said nervously.

"I shouldn't think so. We'll see." He stooped to examine Rose, gazing deep into her eyes. His hands and his calm bronze face meant to be reassuring. His time in England had tarnished his color, Rose observed. "You'll be all right now, Rose. He's dealt with. Gladys will stay here with you while I call the police."

She was struggling to tell him that she was by no means all right. He peered into her eyes. "What is it, Rose? What do you want to say?"

She wasn't sure. She couldn't tell him about the parasite which might still be within her; he could only probe her mind for it, and that would make it worse. She just didn't want him to leave her. She didn't want to be left alone. Whenever she tried to speak, the swollen hole in her face twitched uncontrollably. At last it managed to pronounce, "Take me home."

"But you are home, Rose."

"No, home." At least the voice was her own. That was heartening, insofar as anything was. "Ormskirk."

"If that's what you want we'll drive you there. Just let me deal with this fellow and make sure of the police. Do you know who he is?"

Her head lolled back and forth, meaning no. As her cheeks touched the pillow they felt like gelatin meeting ice. She succeeded in grabbing his wrist with her hand, a stuffed glove of skin. "Can't talk to police," she mumbled.

"Don't worry, I'll take care of them."

She heard his murmuring downstairs. The replaced phone rang. Now he was outside, leaving the front door open, for the sizzle of rain had increased. Presumably the bald man must be safely unconscious, but Gladys was glancing nervously toward the bedroom door. To think she of all people was guarding Rose! The irony was nerve-racking.

Here was Colin, hurrying upstairs. "No, he's just out for the count," he told Gladys. "They'll be here shortly. Now I want you to take all of these," he said to Rose, lifting her head gently and feeding her a sip of water from a glass.

She swallowed capsules: one, two, three. Their effect felt like a flood of indifference. At least it made her helplessness more bearable. Her body was a bath, congealed and rubbery, in which she was floating.

When a car drew up outside the house, it sounded as though the gravel was a gritty marsh. The doorbell rang. Colin went down, and she heard a long incomprehensible discussion. He must be persuading them to leave her alone. She didn't care now whether or not they came upstairs, so long as they didn't mind her lying here mutely.

Car doors slammed. Wheels rolled away. How could gravel squelch? Perhaps the gray was taking over. Colin reappeared. "Well, that's taken care of. Shall we go?"

They supported Rose to the car. She was a disinterested observer which her body was carrying about. As she stood in the drive, the drenching rain seemed not to reach her. She was armored by indifference.

Colin drove. Gladys sat in the back with Rose. As the headlights groped into the road, raindrops flew up like shards of glass. The pavements appeared to be seething. They looked unstable, as everything was.

As the Fiat moved into the road, she glanced back. Her house was crawling with rain. Beyond the broken bedroom window the curtain was waving, a mockery of a farewell. Gladys reached timidly over and squeezed her arm.

The reassurance meant nothing to Rose. Her mind felt packed in wadding. It was safely shelved inside the box of her head. Impressions reached her, none more important than the rest. The car smelled faintly of petrol. Raindrops hopped ahead of it toward Aigburth Road. The pipes of villas dripped and splashed incontinently. Colin resembled a bust propped before the wheel. Gladys was fussing with her capacious bag. The tic of the windshield wipers was constant, monotonous. If Rose had been less drugged she might have screamed.

At the junction with Aigburth Road a van flashed its lights and gave way to them. Colin headed into Sefton Park, toward Queens Drive. The park was a mass of hectic glimmering. Leaves and grass and stone appeared to be swarming or melting. Everything hissed shrilly. The arch of a railway bridge above Queens Drive looked like an underwater grotto. As she glanced back, a speeding van resembled a fish slipping out of a cavern.

Queens Drive went on for miles. Colin drove leisurely, in case there were still any patches of ice. He spoke only once, to ask Gladys to open her window a little. The smell of petrol must be bothering him; it made Rose feel slightly sick. Beneath the sodium lamps the trees were sweating orange paint, with which the drains had to gargle, because they were unable to close their throats.

Blocks of houses sailed by, halted by traffic lights. It was like an electronic race, where the lights sent the car back to the start of the simulated course. Now the car was turning, toward Walton Hospital. Was Colin taking her there? No, he had slowed while a man with an injured foot went skipping across the road. She was incurable. Beyond the hospital was Walton Prison. Perhaps she ought to be locked up.

The car was hastening onward, through a few streets of pubs and small shops—crowded takeouts, a confectioner's called Le Petit Gourmet—and out into the first patch of countryside. Aintree Racecourse drifted by. It looked dead now that it was denied the Grand National. Darkness occupied it, and interrupted the streetlamps, making a van behind the car look intermittently black.

Maghull went by, a bunch of lighted streets which the dark quickly dealt with. Now there was nothing but miles of dual carriageway. The last of the rain dangled trembling from sodium lights. Occasional ranks of houses looked built of cardboard bathed in lurid oil.

Patches of orange which appeared disturbingly irregular lay beneath the lamps and kept staining the van behind the car.

Near Ormskirk the dual carriageway merged into a single road, and grew dimmer. The road was strewn with animals and birds which had been too slow for the traffic. The surrounding dark spilled between the infrequent streetlamps, like earth through a flimsy subterranean wall. Headlights flailed vainly at it, the car's and the van's. But the van had turned away toward Altcar, leaving Colin's lights to fend off the dark as best they could. Once Rose had heard a hare at Altcar, screaming like a kitten as it was pulled apart by two dogs at the Waterloo Cup, the annual hare coursing. She hadn't been able to sleep for days.

She mustn't think of such things now. She was going home. How could that make a difference? There must have been a time when she had been whole, herself alone, but how could she reach back to that? Surely it no longer mattered where she went. For a moment her sense of perspective went awry in the night, and part of the dark seemed to stand over her, or over the world, on thin stilts of limbs.

Ormskirk was twinkling below. As the car descended Holborn Hill, the fire station was bright as a beacon. She felt unexpectedly eager. Dimly she made out the tower and adjacent steeple of the parish church, the view which had met her whenever she cycled down on the tandem. She was going home.

The center of town was almost deserted, except for shoals of cars outside the pubs. A few of the uprights of market stalls had been left poking up from the streets, like breathing-tubes. Outside the Ribble bus station, ranked passengers sat inside a gloomy long-distance coach. They looked inert and grimy, models trapped inside a worn-out toy. They made her glad that she hadn't much farther to go.

But as soon as the car crossed the lights it halted, at

the start of the Wigan Road. A lorry was manuevering while several cars fumed. Now that the car was standing, the smell of petrol was stronger. Perhaps because of the delay, Gladys had begun to rummage in her bag. Rose felt sick and edgy, but for none of these reasons. The car had halted in sight of the butcher's shop, whose upper window was curtained and lit.

All at once her homesickness was frightening. Was she anxious to return to her parents' house, or to this one? She fought her eagerness, suppressed it, tried to ignore it, to obscure it. She seemed to be dodging about her mind, near to panic. But she couldn't dodge very long, for the drugs lulled her. She struggled to think only of her parents' house. Something must be threatening her mind, for the petrol didn't smell quite like petrol.

The lorry roared away. The first of the cars jerked forward. The next grumbled away, and the next. Colin's way was clear. What was he waiting for? "We aren't there yet," Rose told him. Nervousness sharpened her voice.

"Yes, I'm afraid we are." He turned in his seat as Gladys's hands emerged from the bag. "You're home at last," he said, and then he was holding Rose while Gladys pressed over her nose and mouth the wad soaked in ether, which no longer smelled like petrol at all.

XLV

At first, when she regained consciousness, she didn't know where she was.

Apart from the chair on which she was propped, the room was bare of furniture. Ancient wallpaper, which resembled bark on a dead tree, patched the walls. The floorboards looked scrubbed, but they were dull with age and disuse; dust had lodged in their whorls, like grime in fingertips. A lamp with a grubby tasseled shade loomed above her head. Beyond the curtains of the window, light shifted dimly. It was hardly a place to wake alone—but as she gained some control over the giddy movements of her head, she saw that she was surrounded by people.

Their presence seemed welcome. She knew many of them, and felt daunted by none. All were gazing at her as if they had no concern in the world except her well-being. There was Colin, absolutely calm, and Gladys, who looked determined to be brave. There was the magistrate from their party, the newspaper editor, Frank Sherratt the cinema owner, the young explorers, and people whom she'd seen in Ormskirk: a stout red-faced man, a youth whose hair made it seem that his head was bubbling rustily. All were soberly dressed—out of respect, she thought vaguely. Some, including the magistrate, wore small Union Jacks in their lapels.

She wished someone would step forward and help her. She was unable to stand up, and felt in danger of toppling from the chair. Her face was slack, incapable of expressing her thoughts, let alone of speaking. Why were they standing back against the walls? What were they waiting for? It was not until she recognized the red-faced man that she knew where she was.

At once she remembered the sound of his cleaver, whose chopping seemed in retrospect to have resounded throughout Ormskirk. At once the stench of blood was overpowering, and the dead and corrupt creature was advancing eagerly—but she could no longer pretend to herself that the creature was hidden in the shop. It was rising from within her. She knew instinctively, though the instinct might not be her own, that the smell of blood and the eagerness were only hints of Grace's dream.

She was beyond horror. Besides, her dizziness preoccupied her. Perhaps they had fed her more drugs, or perhaps the ether was to blame. Was it her dizziness that made the floor beneath the chair feel like a crust, ready to split, to let corruption well up? She would be content to sit on the chair, not touching the floor, to sit absolutely still until she ceased to be.

But she couldn't, not until she knew who was behind her. She turned her head, though the room staggered drunkenly. She heard Colin whisper, "No, it's all right." Here were more people she recognized, though it took her a moment to know why: a small woman whose brightest detail was the Band-Aid which held her spectacles together, a burly young man who was dribbling. The woman was gripping his hand as though she wanted him to make the best impression possible.

As Rose glanced at her, the woman fumbled in her pocket and dragged out an object which she clapped clumsily over her face. It was a black mask. "You don't need that now," Colin said.

Rose should have known—not that these people had been hunting her, not that some of them had called her out of her body that night, but that everything would betray her; nothing was trustworthy. When her head wobbled in the opposite direction, and she recognized another face, she was beyond reacting. Between two large dour young men who looked like policemen there stood, bruised but conscious, the bald man.

Her surge of hatred was not hers. As their eyes met, he started forward. The two men seized him at once, but not before the circle of watchers grew tense and Gladys darted forward, crying, "Don't you touch her!"

In her haste she dropped her bag. There was a smash, and pieces of china flew out. As she grabbed the bag and began to sweep the fragments into it, she looked at the moment near to hysteria. She glanced hopefully at Rose, but Rose had already seen that one of the fragments was a tiny perfect hand which belonged to the Chinese figurine.

She'd had enough. She withdrew into herself, where nothing could touch her, not even the luxurious squirming in her head. Let them all do whatever they wanted. It was as though they were performing a play, trying vainly to impress her, Gladys crying at the bald man, "Just you stay away from her. Don't you dare spoil things now. We haven't suffered so much for it all to come to nothing."

"I shouldn't let him bother you, Gladys. He can't harm us now." Colin seemed to be reveling in his own calm. "I doubt that he ever could. Those who followed him must have been as mad as he is. My only regret is that they aren't here to see how little his efforts were worth. What do your readers call themselves?" he asked the bald man slyly. "Not Alcoholics Anoymous, no—Astral Armament."

Smiling faintly, he turned to Rose. "Of course, you didn't know who he was. That must have been bewildering. Allow me to introduce Hugh Willis, author of the popular *Astral Rape*."

Munich. The English Garden. The bald man by the waterfall. He'd said she had been infested when young, Willis had. No wonder Grace had erased the incident from her conscious mind. She was able to remember now, because neither Willis nor anyone else could prevent what was going to happen.

But he was still trying. He was staring at her. "I tried to save you until it was too late. I knew it was no use trying to reason with these people." He glanced away aghast, as though he'd realized suddenly that he was addressing a corpse. "None of you has any idea what you're trying to set free," he cried.

"Just you shut your evil mouth," Gladys hissed. "Colin spent half his life working for this, and your sole ambition is to prevent him, you pitiful worm. You're scared of anything you don't understand. You can't bear anyone who's better than yourself. You and your kind are what's wrong with the world."

"You mustn't overrate him," Colin said. "He's only a failed writer, after all. At least he made such a fuss that we always knew where he was and what he was doing."

Rose watched. It was a play performed by madmen, a parody of a struggle between good and evil. The Hays and their followers appeared more reasonable, hence no doubt were more dangerous.

"I won't be hushed, Colin. It's time some people knew how much you've done. The way I suffered when I lost my parents was nothing compared to how you suffered in searching for the truth. And with only me to look after you—not your father, good riddance to him! Yet you," she spat at Willis, "you have to surround yourself with protectors, yet all you can do is destroy. Shut him up, Colin. I can't stand him."

"What, and let him think he could have swayed us? I for one would be fascinated to learn what he planned to achieve with that carving knife."

"To destroy your evil at the source." Fanaticism blanked his eyes. "I wouldn't have been killing her. She must be destroyed by now, eaten away from within."

Rose agreed mutely, indifferently, but Colin shook his head. "You have no sense of what she is. She was chosen to be his vessel. Since then she has been more than human."

"You must all be possessed, not only her," Willis cried, staring. "She was somewhere he could grow. Her personality was a mask for him. He used her as ruthlessly as he's going to use all of you."

"Don't you say that about her." Gladys seemed maternally furious. "She was more than that. I was never sure who she was or if she knew what we were thinking. I used to be afraid of her, I'm not ashamed to admit it, but I took care of her."

"He transfigured her from within," Colin said. "He gave her the strength to carry him. She became far more than the child she was would have grown up to be. You could see none of this, Willis, because you have no vision."

Rose was bored. Her flesh and her innards felt restless. Perhaps the circle was bored too, for Frank Sherratt said, "How long are you going to waste arguing?"

"His time is not like ours. He'll make it clear when he is ready." Colin glanced deferentially at Rose. "No need to be impatient," he said more sharply to the others. "We should have learned that by now."

Before anyone else could interrupt, he went on. Something about Willis had troubled his calm. "Perhaps you never knew what my vision was. Do you know why I felt compelled to search? Because I felt partly responsible for the state of the world. All psychiatry is. It exploits the weak and diminishes the strong. It makes weakness and laxity acceptable, even fashionable. No wonder Hitler called it the Jewish science."

"So why do you still pretend to be a psychiatrist?" Willis demanded. "It isn't only a cover. You treat some of these people for the effects of what you're doing. You contradict yourself all the way."

"It has its uses." Colin didn't bother glancing at the others, none of whom looked convinced by Willis. "But you're trying to prevent me from telling you my vision. It's quite simple. The civilized world is growing soft because there is no continuity of strength. Each generation is softer than the last. The only solution to this is to preserve strength undying. I came to see that the answer lies in the occult. All over the world there are signs of an occult revival. Many of us here realized independently that these are signs of a new order, if only the occult can be wielded. It was I who saw where the answer lay. Perhaps you can appreciate the irony, though in fact it shows that we are in the right. I saw the answer as soon as I read your book."

Willis looked betrayed. His glistening forehead jerked as though snagged by pain. "Do your followers know how you had your visions? Do they know why you left South Africa in such a hurry?" He seemed to expect to be silenced before he could say, "He had his visions while he was using drugs."

"Of course," Colin said. "I had to find a way to free my mind. Someone had to see farther."

For the first time the circle seemed uneasy, Sherratt and the magistrate especially. Colin's nonchalance had troubled them. A few glanced restlessly toward a sound of passing footsteps on the street below.

"You make him sound like an addict, a wastrel," Gladys said hotly. "He risked himself on behalf of others. If any of you had seen him as I did you would know."

After an awkward silence the magistrate said, "The vision's the important thing, not how it was achieved."

"But that was only the start of it." Willis had seen his advantage. "Don't you know he's still involved in drugs? What do you think he sells to nearly all his so-called patients? How do you think he managed to afford a house in Fulwood Park?"

"Oh, why do we have to listen to him? Won't someone shut him up?" Gladys was glaring about, perhaps for a weapon. The footsteps on the street had halted and were coming back.

"It isn't worth upsetting yourself, Gladys. He knows that we know he's lying." Colin's tarnished head shook once, precisely and sadly. "Our house was subsidized by others who share our beliefs. It's a pity that more of our overseas friends can't be with us tonight."

He gazed clinically at Willis. "Look how frightened he is. You can tell that from his arguments. He knows he's in the presence of someone far greater than himself. Even you can't deny that, Willis. His survival proves his greatness."

"God Almighty, you'd believe anything rather than admit you were wrong." Willis's hands appeared to be trying to choke each other's wrists. "Grace is using you. He's completely mad. He isn't even human. All he wants is to destroy."

Rose knew this was so, as did the parasite, which began writhing impatiently in her skull. Perhaps it would deal with Willis, but it seemed there was no need: the circle was closing in on him, having had enough of him. Suddenly they were still, and listening. The footsteps had halted outside the house.

Colin hurried to the window and sneaked aside an edge of the curtain. His shoulders moved brusquely, impatiently. "It's her husband, Bill," he muttered. "He's seen our car."

At first Rose didn't know who he meant. Gladys, however, cried out at once. "Oh, good God, we left her bag on the seat!"

Bill. It was Bill. Abruptly Rose knew why she'd failed to recognize him in bed: a consciousness other than her own had got in the way. Instinctively, without thinking, she called his name. Perhaps because it had been mute for so long, her voice was shockingly loud.

Several people—the magistrate, Sherratt, Gladys— ran at her, but she had already been silenced from within. The men who looked like policemen had seized Willis; one held their prisoner's mouth shut with a grip that looked close to breaking his jaw. In the silence, the knocker thudded against the front door.

"He heard her," Colin said irritably. Indeed, after several bouts of knocking, the footsteps retreated a few paces and Bill called, "Rose?" The voice meant nothing to her; it took all her strength to preserve some faint sense of herself.

The footsteps were advancing. They seemed to pass beneath the house, to turn into a spinster's, prim and shrill. Echoing stone had transformed them. "He's going through to the back," Colin said. "Can he get in?"

"He won't like it if he does," the butcher said. "I'll give him a welcome." He hurried downstairs amid a chorus of creaking. There were creaks elsewhere, more muffled and tentative, and then a click of metal. That was the door into the yard, which Bill had opened somehow. Rose found it difficult to concentrate, to follow the action. The footsteps which were padding across the ground floor of the house, toward the back—ah, they were the butcher's. That was the sound of the back door. Now it was open, and silence was gaping. Was that a scuffle? She'd forgotten who was involved.

Chunk. There was silence for a moment, then the sound of a heavy fall. She knew the previous sound, if she could only recall. The smell of blood thickened. Of course, it had been the sound of a meat cleaver.

Her mouth opened. "Now we shall begin," said her lifeless voice.

XLVI

And now the last act was about to begin, as the audience stood back respectfully from the bare stage of the room. Her body staggered upright on the chair; her head jerked erect, nodding and swaying. Its movements had nothing to do with her, but she was distantly aware of all her joints, arranging themselves obediently but awkwardly as a puppet's. She felt hemmed in by eyes.

Still, she was not quite the center of attention. The circle was listening to sounds below, the back door opening, footsteps in the yard. The footsteps were slow and uneven, as though the man was burdened. "What in God's name is he doing?" Gladys demanded.

"What do you think?" Colin said impatiently.

Rose had no idea what he meant, but her voice apparently did. It felt like an insubstantial crawling in her mouth. "Well," it said with a kind of vicious petulance, "will you spend all night listening to his performance?"

Colin looked taken aback, almost vulnerable. "We were waiting until he comes back."

"You are enough without him." The voice sounded secretly amused. "Close the door."

When someone did so, the door did not entirely shut out the world. Along the road, a woman was calling a dog. A bus was leaving the Ribble station. A plane rumbled along the horizon like a dull wooden ball. All of this was meaningless to Rose, who knew only that the eyes watching her were too numerous. Within the room, an audience was gathering.

She couldn't see them yet, but she sensed their eagerness. It felt like fever, but was far more oppressive. They were eager for tonight's experiment to succeed, though it seemed impossible that it could fail. Had that drawn them, or had they been attracted to the bloodshed down below, like flies? She could smell them. They had been dead for a long time.

Neither Colin nor his followers appeared to notice the intrusion. Only Willis's eyes were twitching from side to side; his skull looked oily and plastic. Colin was trying to seem both respectful and dignified as he faced Rose, but it was clear that the soft, absolutely lifeless voice had perturbed him deeply. "How may we help you?" he said.

"How indeed. I think you have done quite enough."
The voice had the wary tonelessness of paranoia. "You
have almost drawn attention to me several times. Well,
at least you have brought me a vessel. Bring him to
me."

At once the small woman stepped timidly forward,
dabbing at her eyes. She was leading her retarded
son, who looked dazed. Rose's body began to jerk
wildly, flapping its hands in a kind of senile rage. Her
body must be hampered by the drugs, but the voice in
her mouth was viciously controlled. "Take that thing
away."

Rose heard the watchers grow uneasy, but the
mother seemed aware only of the rebuff. She looked as
though she had been denied a last chance. "But he's
strong, and his mind is weak," she protested tearfully.
"We thought it would be easy for you—"

"You expect me to go into an idiot?" A note of cruel
humor crept into the voice. "Well, my opinion of the
mass of humanity was never high. I shall be generous
tonight and assume you have as little sense as he has."

Now the mother understood what he was threatening, and grew as fearful as the rest of them. Even Colin
was glancing about in the hope that he wouldn't be
chosen. All of them were too anxious for themselves to
notice that in the shadowy corners of the room, vague
pale shapes were stirring. Rose could only loll on the
chair like a ventriloquist's dummy as her mouth said,
"Bring me the writer who would not be warned."

A ripple of intense relief went through the circle. As
they dragged Willis in front of her, the two men who
might be policemen were actually smiling. Perhaps
Willis would put up a fight, futile though it might
be—but as soon as the gaze of her eyes fastened on his,
he wilted. Even his look of fear collapsed. Only his
forehead was still active, streaming.

"Now put out the light and encircle us," the voice
said softly, eagerly.

When someone put out the light, not everything

grew vaguer. In the dimness she could see the shapes beyond the closing circle more plainly. They were pale blotches that bulged from the walls like fungus. They were no longer confined to the corners, but crowded all the darkest areas of the room.

Light crawled over the curtains, which appeared to shift. That was a mockery of anticipation, for nothing was about to intervene. She could read that in Willis's face: a dreadful resignation. She could see him although the parasite was gazing at him through her eyes. Framed in the doorway, and frozen by her gaze, he looked unreal as a painting—but nobody would have wanted to paint the look on his face.

Around her everyone was absolutely still. Colin and Gladys were smiling faintly, nervously, with what looked grotesquely like parental pride in her. She felt suffocated, by more than the dim room. The fascination of the circle hemmed her in. Their eyes held her, as did the eyes of the blotches on the walls.

Her paralysis was a hint of her imminent fate in the gray church. Though nothing moved, she felt as though the circle was tightening about her, like a noose. That must be the force of their will—theirs, and the will of the swellings on the walls, which were exhorting Grace to succeed on their behalf.

Something was moving: something besides the sweat which trickled unchecked into Willis's eyes. She could feel it, gathering inside her, preparing to emerge. Her mouth gaped as though to vomit it forth. But it rushed into her eyes, and bloated them poisonously. For a moment she was blind, trapped behind cataracts.

Then, as though she had been puffed up by the poison, she seemed to deflate. She fell from the chair like discarded clothes. When she struck the floor, it felt thin, undermined by decay. She was drained, incapable of movement. She watched Willis only because he was in front of her.

His face writhed and crumpled with unutterable horror. His hands were jerking by his sides. She knew they were trying to reach his head, to claw out the intruder. She couldn't pretend she felt very sympathetic, for she was too relieved that it had left her.

His eyes were changing. It was as though poison was seeping into them. He had looked mad, but at least he'd seemed human, sometimes pitifully so. Now his eyes were a corpse's eyes, which were nevertheless moving slowly, luxuriously, gleefully. Their dead light was intensifying, until it seemed they might almost burst into flame.

Colin stepped forward tentatively. It was clear that he didn't know whether to stretch out his hands in greeting. Some of his followers broke the circle, but seemed unsure whether or not to stay back. None of them appeared to notice the half-formed faces in the shadows, faces growing pallidly on the walls. Presumably, since Rose could see them, she must still be capable of psychic glimpses—not that it could do her any good.

She was watching the timid overtures of Colin and his followers, as the dead eyes bulged gleefully in the bald head—she was watching because she could do nothing else—when the door burst open and the figure with the bloody cleaver came in.

He was wearing a blue windbreaker, whose hood flapped emptily behind his head. His hair was tousled, his face was flushed; his left cheekbone was dark with a bruise; one arm of his glasses hung broken, like an animal's limb. He looked dismayed and furious, unable to believe what was happening but determined not to let his incredulity hinder him. His clothes made him resemble a vengeful blue monk. He was Bill.

He saw Rose lying at the bald man's feet. His eyes filled with rage. He rushed forward, lifting the cleaver, but a twinge of revulsion seemed to obstruct him. He turned the cleaver and brought the blunt edge down with all his force.

The blow sounded excruciatingly sharp. Perhaps the bald head had cracked. Yet Willis took a long time to fall, and the dead eyes were struggling not to be doused. Bill looked distressed by his own action, but defiantly willing to repeat it if necessary. He had clearly resolved to ignore his bewilderment until he had saved Rose.

All at once, with an intensity of emotion which she'd thought lost to her, she loved him. Whatever he had done in London, he hadn't abandoned her. He hadn't changed beyond redemption, after all. Nobody else would have come here to rescue her. He had given her back some sense of herself.

Willis, or the thing within him, was collapsing at last. The dead eyes went out, grew simply blank. But he was only the first of Bill's adversaries, if perhaps the worst. How could Bill fight off Colin and the others? Were the watchers on the dark walls capable of intervening? Rose was unable to help him or even to stir: had he any chance of carrying her away?

None at all, it seemed—at least, not in any hopeful sense. The cleaver fell from his hand and stuck trembling in the floor. The dead eyes were still in the room. They were lurid with triumph. It took her a moment to see that they were in Bill's face.

XLVII

Oh, please let her be mistaken, please let it be a trick of the dimness! Surely her emotions hadn't been reawakened for this. But Bill was smiling a corpse's smile that might have been produced by the withering of skin. It had nothing to do with life. It said that Grace was in complete control.

She was helpless. Her body was slack as rags; her mouth jerked like the mouth of a drowning fish. If she cried out, vocally or inwardly, she would never stop; but what would that achieve? If she let herself feel at all, that would destroy her. Perhaps that would be welcome—but her emotions had retreated deep into her, unable to bear further injury. She could only lie there and wish that everything was over.

"At last," Bill's mouth said softly. He might have been greeting a predestined end. He began to pace around the circle, peering at each face. He no longer walked like Bill, but like someone taller, boasting of his straightness. His back was stiff as rigor mortis.

At least he was ignoring her. She prayed not to see what his face had become; one glimpse had been enough. Some of the members of the circle managed not to shrink back as he approached them, one or two succeeded in meeting his gaze, but all of them were terrified. It seemed especially dreadful that anyone should react thus to Bill.

But it was not Bill. It was the essence of the corrupt house. The room had given birth at last. Muffled lights sank beyond the curtains, swollen shadows groped over the ceiling, pale bulges nodded impatiently forward from the walls, and at the center of all this Bill was saying, "So you want to learn my secrets? First I must be sure of you."

His voice had grown cruel. It sounded revengeful, righteous as paranoia. "You will have to prove yourselves to me," he said.

It wasn't Bill, though his windbreaker rustled and the arm of his glasses dangled by his ear. It was as though someone had stolen his corpse and was using it as a puppet, making it stalk about, imitating Grace. Bill could never behave like that. He wasn't in control. He was—

Perhaps this was a worse horror. Her mind flinched away, tried not to think. If it was true, there was nothing she could do—but the insight which had seemed pitifully reassuring had grown treacherous. Now that Grace had occupied Bill's body, where was Bill? Was he in the fungoid church?

He could never survive; he would go mad. Perhaps that would be merciful—but he might have to suffer an immeasurable time before his mind gave way. She remembered how the gray had held her fast. It might hold him so fast that he could not even break, only suffer.

Her cry of horror was growing. If she was unable to voice it, it would explode in her mind. It wouldn't stop until it had seared her mind raw, and then she could only slump within herself until the next useless cry. Nobody would hear her, nobody would come to her aid. She was alone.

Or was she?

Yes, she thought she was, except for Bill's stalking body, and the nervous circle, and the pale intent swellings on the walls. But those swellings, appalling though they were, meant something else to her now. Since she could still perceive them, some of her powers must remain. Could she use her powers to summon the presence which had saved her once before?

She could just move her eyes, though they felt half-deflated, rolling awkwardly. She sneaked a glance at the thing that was Bill. He was scrutinizing Gladys's face. Gladys appeared to be trying to free her hands, which squirmed together before her like beaten dogs; her face was shivering, unable to retain any expression. He seemed to find her antics amusing, and might linger for a while. Warily, terrified that he might sense what she was doing, Rose sent a plea into the dark.

He didn't turn. Either he was too preoccupied with his new life, or he felt her cry wasn't worth acknowledging. Yes, he must know he was safe. As her plea reached into the night, into the spaces between the stars, it found only a wider night, an infinite void without warmth or life. Whatever she had glimpsed

before was there no longer. It was far beyond her
range. Her plea dwindled in the darkness and went out.

He was still parading Bill's body around the circle,
and had reached Colin, who gazed steadily at him.
Colin's face was calm—or was it expressionless only
because he was holding back his fear? For a moment
Rose almost wished he would be able to outstare the
thing in front of him; Colin at least was human. But
before long his gaze wavered, dodged aside.

Rose looked away in despair. How much longer must
she lie here awaiting her fate? If she were able to move
she would crawl to the top of the stairs, throw herself
down. Or would that be the beginning of her torments
rather than the end? Perhaps at least she would be with
Bill. She musn't think of him, he was beyond help. Her
eyes roved loosely in their sockets, seeking rest, and
caught sight of the darkest corner of the room.

If she could have shuddered, she would have been
unable to stop. She felt trapped in her slumped flesh.
She glanced aside wildly, anywhere rather than into
that corner. Two eyes like ovals of bright scum had
been glaring from a pale bulge on the wall. As she'd
met them she had glimpsed their thoughts.

A moment more and she would have been unable to
look away. She could still feel their gaze, plucking at
her like hooks, and their thoughts: cripples hanging by
their feet in a dead place that looked like the moon,
their throats cut, their bodies writhing feebly as they
drained; an old Jew castrated, feeding leeches; a youth
like a living sculpture, training a flamethrower on a
hospital ward full of mothers and children, most of
them black. These were joyful dreams, which had fed
on themselves outside time. She didn't need to make
out the face that had begun to form in the corner, on
the pale swelling.

If there were powers that could prevent its rebirth,
how could they have allowed such yearnings to survive
at all? No, there was nothing to oppose the forces

gathered in the room. She knew that from the failure of her plea for help.

That wasn't true. There were powers, for she'd experienced them. Not only her memory of being rescued proved that. Grace's voice had admitted as much, for it had accused Colin of nearly drawing attention to him. Could that attention still be drawn?

The gaze from the corner was trying to fasten on her, to force her to look, perhaps so that it could feed on her terror. She sent another plea into the night. Perhaps her panic lent her strength, for her cry seemed to reach farther before failing. That only made her more aware of the endless dark that surrounded her. She recoiled, back to her sense of the dim room.

Bill stood above her, his dead eyes gazing down at her.

Had he sensed her call? There was no apprehension in his eyes, nor even anger: only contempt that bordered on revulsion. "Did I have to rely on you for so long?" he said, so softly as to be scarcely audible. "That was the lowest of their treacheries—to make me have to need something like you."

He stepped back as though from treading in filth. Now she felt she was nothing. The way Bill was looking at her had destroyed her. He was sneering, though the way his lips moved was not absolutely lifelike, more like the stirring of corruption. "Crawl to me," he said.

She could not, even if she would have. She could defy him because of the state in which he had left her; she supposed that was a kind of triumph. She lay inert, trying not to see the grublike movements of Bill's lips.

She sensed his mounting hatred and frustration. The members of the circle must have sensed his feelings too, for they began to prod her with their feet. Some were kicking her. Were they making a scapegoat of her to show their allegiance to him, or were they afraid that her disobedience was going to lose them his secrets? It scarcely mattered, for she could not move.

Without warning he stepped forward and snatched up the cleaver. He loomed over her, raising the blade. The circle grew still, as though out of respect for a ritual. Only the retarded youth was mumbling uneasily, and sounded afraid for Rose.

Did Bill mean to kill her, or to torture her until she gave him satisfaction? The smell of blood was overpowering. She could feel that he hated her more than anything else in the world. As the cleaver soared up, she could only flinch within herself.

The cleaver faltered. "No," he whispered in delight, almost to himself. He paced away from Rose, glancing back to make sure that she could see what he was doing, and seized the mumbling youth by the elbow. Though the youth began to mutter and struggle uneasily, Bill urged him backwards. Gripping one of the young man's wrists, he flattened his hand against the wall.

The youth's mother started forward. Colin restrained her, hissing, "It's all right." Did he think Bill would do nothing, or didn't it matter to him? He seemed to have soothed or cowed her, for she gestured her son to be still. Perhaps she could feel that the rest of the circle was impatient to finish this interlude.

Bill was raising the cleaver. "Now will you crawl?" He must think that even if Rose refused to move in order to save herself, she would make the effort to save someone else. She made the only effort that remained to her: she cried a last desperate plea into the dark.

He must have sensed it, for at once he smiled viciously. The cleaver trembled at the height of its arc. His eyes glared, bright with a challenge or with triumph. Rose lay helpless. The cleaver came down.

She heard it bite into the wall, and a small object dropped to the floor. The mother began screaming. The two policemen had to hold her back and silence her. The youth was moaning in a loud clogged voice and staring dully at the stump of his finger.

Though he was struggling, Bill held his arm against the wall and smiled at Rose. "Shall I continue?" he said.

Oh, why couldn't she lose consciousness? Then at least he would know he had nothing to gain by torturing the youth—but that mightn't stop him, he was enjoying it so much. The bulges on the walls were nodding gleefully, as though trying to peel themselves free. There was nothing beyond them except the empty dark. Rose's pleas had failed, not because the great impersonal presence was unaware—surely it was never that—but because it was indifferent. The forces in this room were too trivial to be acknowledged.

All at once her mind tried to close into itself. Whether it was drawn by her pleas or by the evil that filled the house, something was approaching.

Her pleas had widened her awareness far too much. She sensed the immense darkness, broken by stars like infrequent flaws. The light of each star seemed trapped within its rim, unable to touch the dark. Part of the deepest darkness was moving.

Was it composed of the darkness? Perhaps, for the filaments with which it was reaching out between the stars seemed as infinite. Perhaps it would draw itself along the filaments once they had seized its prey, or perhaps it had no need. In a moment she might sense its thoughts, at the moment when it touched her, and then at last she would go mad.

Bill seemed to have sensed it, for his dead eyes flickered back and forth. Did he welcome it, or was he uneasy? Now Colin and the others were glancing about vaguely but warily, except for the mutilated youth and his mother, who was still trying to tear herself free. Rose was struggling within herself with a fury she'd thought she no longer possessed. Her body was an immobile suffocating burden which trapped her in the room. Even if she remembered how to voyage, would she have time to do so?

In fact nobody had achieved anything when the presence came into the room.

It was as though the void of outer space had swallowed the house. Everything and everyone within it were all at once infinitesimal, almost insubstantial, for that was how they appeared to the presence. It was enormous and cold and pitiless, and unbounded by space or time. It seemed hardly to resemble life.

Rose's spirit was paralyzed, held fast by the alien view of her. She might even have preferred to be hated. It was regarding all of them with a disinterested regret, as though they were flaws too trivial to be distinguished. It made no exceptions. Now it was reaching out purposefully, and Rose could not flinch back.

Not until the half-formed faces began to retreat into the walls did she realize this was the presence she had called.

It hadn't come in response to her pleas. Perhaps it was here to frustrate the dark predator she'd sensed approaching. Before, when it had saved her, its remoteness had made it far less terrible. Now she realized how impossible it was to glimpse it or its motives. It was too profoundly alien.

But the faces were sinking into the walls, like stains, and Bill had begun to snarl or to snigger out of vicious bravado. Though he was clearly unable to move, his skin appeared to be writhing. Would the struggle which was taking place within him crack him open?

Something dark squeezed between his lips, as if through the tip of a chrysalis, but it was only his tongue. His face was darkening; perhaps it would be the pressure of blood that burst his shell. His eyes were guttering luridly. The presence of Grace was flickering within them, but there was no sign of Bill.

Abruptly he collapsed, as though the scaffolding of muscle had been pulled away. At once the great impersonal presence had gone. Rose was too stunned to think, but she wished instinctively that she had been able to comprehend its intervention. Though the faces had vanished, she wished she could be sure that they had been driven back far enough, if not destroyed.

She lay. Now that the presence had gone, the room and everyone within it seemed unreal, shrunken fragile shells of themselves. Colin and the others stood looking dazed and shaken; it was impossible to tell how much they'd sensed. They began to move gingerly, like accident victims testing their limbs. Suddenly a common terror seemed to possess them. They crowded toward the door, though Colin made an ineffectual plea for order, and down the stairs.

The mother stumbled over to the retarded youth, who was still moaning piteously, and who had wrapped his mutilated hand in the folds of his overcoat. She seemed ashamed to look at him. As though performing a grotesque parody of tidiness, she picked up a small object from beside his feet, then hurried him away, saying "Come on" in a tone which sounded actually accusing. When Colin offered to help her, she snatched up the fallen cleaver and drove him back. With a last glance at the room—a glance which combined frustration, fear, and resignation—he followed her downstairs.

Rose lay, her body and her emotions inert. It seemed the play was over. Bill and Willis lay on the bare boards. Perhaps they were dead. She heard activity downstairs and in the yard, as though props were being dragged into the wings. Footsteps hurried through the house and through the stone passage between houses. Car doors slammed, a series which seemed interminable, like trapped echoes. The theater crowd was leaving. Cars roared away, quick as panic. Soon the night seemed empty and neutral, like the room and the entire house.

She couldn't tell how much time passed before Bill moved: hours, it seemed. His lips began shifting in a way that she had never seen before. A low dull sound escaped them, again and again. Perhaps they were almost uncontrollable, for he was having difficulty in opening his slumped eyelids. She was afraid to hear what he was saying, afraid to see his eyes.

His eyes opened. The muttering continued, toneless, unchanging. Was there any awareness within his blank eyes? Yes, there was a glimpse, though it looked stunned and feeble. Now she could hear what he was muttering. "Police," he was repeating, over and over, like a charm.

It was Bill, or what was left of him. She would have to go to him when she was able. Around him the room was bare and innocent, as though nothing had happened. But what he had done to her and to the retarded youth was still happening, again and again, in her mind.

Epilogue

When Rose looked out of the bedroom window there wasn't much left of Fulwood Park. Fifty yards on either side of her, the roadway was wiped out by fog. The field beside the Mersey paled into nothingness like a photograph invaded by a glare of light. Boats lowed on the river, wet birds perched in the tattered trees. Gazing out, she felt cozy and safe. The new window made the house feel warmer still.

She blinked the last of her nap from her eyes, then she went carefully downstairs. The fire was painting the living room orange; in the kitchen, Bill's casserole was simmering. At the end of the garden, the greenhouse looked carved out of fog. "Bill?" she called, but there was no reply.

He ought to be home by now. He had only gone down the road to the shops in Aigburth Vale. She made coffee for both of them, then she sat for a while and gazed at the steaming mugs. Eventually she fetched her key from her handbag and went to the end of the drive to look for him.

The late October fog receded from her, and the trees and the hedge of the field grew clear, like a television image that was being tuned from black and white to color. As far as she could see along the road, it was deserted. The railway bridge looked plugged with dust, even when a train came hurtling out with a muffled shriek. Everything was muffled by the gray—the restless murmur of the city, the mournful cries of ships, the blurred houses of Fulwood Park, the car headlights of the lawyer who lived next door, even his greeting to Rose as he opened his front door. When she turned to answer him, she saw that the gray was creeping up on her house.

But here was Bill, striding out of the screen of fog. As soon as he saw Rose he hurried to her. "What's wrong? Is it the baby?"

"No, I just wondered where you were."

"I'm sorry if I was a long time. I ran into Dr. Thursaston in the chemist's, and we were talking."

"What did he have to say?"

"Oh, nothing new. He still thinks it's a miracle."

Of course he would think so, but Rose was sure that it had been the lurking presence in her body which had made her sterile. Once she was exorcised, there had been nothing to inhibit her fertility. She could hardly tell Dr. Thursaston that, even though he was her gynecologist.

"Come in out of the cold," Bill said. "We don't want you catching a chill, not now."

When they reached the kitchen he became gently reproving. "Look, I would have made the coffee. I thought you were going to rest. Why don't you have a lie-down until dinner's ready? You can call me if you need anything."

They seemed closer than ever. He had never been so attentive to her; he was reluctant to let her out of his sight now that her labor was imminent—he came home whenever he wasn't lecturing, he scarcely left her alone at weekends. She could thank the baby, and possibly his lapse with Hilarly as well, for her newfound peace. She never mentioned Hilary: overlooking the incident seemed a small price to pay. It was extraordinary how safe Bill and the baby made her feel, hardly a year after that last night in Ormskirk.

She lay down on the couch, which was soft as a bed. Within the great invulnerable pouch of her belly the baby swam, kicking. On the shelves the books were multiplying—translations and increasingly popular American editions. Bill had managed to complete the introductions to *Rediscoveries in Film,* and it was already their most successful book. They didn't need to write any more for a while, any more than Rose had needed to go back to work. The books could be trusted to multiply by themselves, which was all to the good, for there was a cot in the workroom now, and rabbits on the wallpaper. Everything was knitting together at last.

She lay and felt her body feeding the life within her. She felt perfectly at ease with herself. An airliner rumbled above the fog, a double slam of car doors announced that the lawyer and his wife were going out to dinner, and eventually Bill came to call her to hers. As they ate she could see the fog, a luminous wall of lard beyond the kitchen window. It didn't bother her at all.

Afterward they sat, arms around each other, on the couch before the fire. The house was theirs again, steeped in memories of their life. Her memories of terror had been driven out as though they had never been. The dancing firelight kept the shadows at bay. Bill stroked her hair, and she felt an almost sexual eagerness to bear their child.

They watched television for a while. In a pilot film, a cut-price exorcist was praying for a television series for himself. "Maybe we should think of doing a book about television," Rose said, feeling comfortable enough even to consider writing. Bill didn't answer; of course the baby would give her no time to write for years.

Still she felt happy to plan the future. "When I've had the baby I want to stay with my parents for a while."

Bill glanced at her. "I'm glad you feel able to go back to Ormskirk."

Did that mean he remembered what had happened? During the first months she hadn't dared to ask, those months when, every so often, his eyes would go momentarily blank. That blankness had vanished for good as soon as she was pregnant—her pregnancy had helped both of them recover—and then she'd been glad to forget. But she felt safe enough to talk about it now; talking about it should make her feel even safer. "What do you remember about that night?" she said.

"Well, nothing really," he said, as she'd hoped he would. "No doubt I called your parents when I found you weren't here, but you remember they said afterward that their phone was out of order. I suppose I would have gone to Ormskirk to look for you, but presumably I thought I'd better check first that you weren't at Colin's. But as I say, I really don't remember, not after Colin gave me that stuff."

She'd told the police that she and Bill had been drugged, an explanation which they readily believed once they found the cache of LSD and other drugs at Colin's. She'd said that Colin had been experimenting on her with drugs while purporting to treat her nervous trouble—that when she'd confronted him with this he had drugged her. When Bill appeared, Colin had tricked him with a drugged drink, then had driven them to Ormskirk, apparently planning to leave them there, dead of overdoses. "Thank heaven that was all that was wrong with you all the time," Bill said now, stroking her cheek. "Just drugs."

Rose suppressed a wry smile. He was using her elaborate lie to explain away what had happened to her, but no doubt it was best for him to believe it was true; he might not be able to bear remembering what had really happened. No doubt he had needed to forget in order to recover. It felt odd to have her own lie quoted back at her as reassurance, but it didn't matter: the baby was moving. When she guided Bill's hand to the secret movement, she had never seen his eyes so bright.

After a while he said, "It was a good thing that bald fellow turned up when he did."

He was right, though not in the way he meant: Willis had saved them. In the hospital he'd proved to have been stunned into sanity, at least for a while. He had been strolling through Ormskirk when he'd glimpsed a struggle in a car on the Wigan Road, he'd told the police. Someone from the nearby butcher's had come out to intervene, but had been driven back with his own meat cleaver; then the man and woman from the car had dragged their victims, Bill and Rose, into the house. The victims had looked drugged, Willis had said, giving Rose the basis for her lie. When he'd gone into the house to intervene, the woman had stunned him with the cleaver.

For a moment Rose felt uneasy: having to maintain the lie was bringing her uncomfortably close to the memory of what it disguised. The baby was kicking within her, almost as if she were making it restless. Bill must have sensed her unease, for he held her more tightly. "Never mind," he said. "They're all dead now. Dead and cremated."

Colin and the others must have been driving recklessly in panic, for they had scarcely left Ormskirk when they had been involved in a multiple car crash on an unlit country road. Most of the bodies had been unrecognizable. Willis had died in a fire too, months later—certainly he must have been the bald man who'd been noticed loitering near the house on the Wigan Road shortly before it burned down, even if the police assumed the body to be that of a tramp. All the people she might fear were dead, and the only thing that was making her nervous was her body, which had begun to act in an unfamiliar way. "I think the contractions are beginning," she said.

Bill held her gently while muscles clenched and relaxed in her belly. The baby was still now, as if waiting. When she was certain she said, "I think I'd like Dr. Thursaston to be here if he can."

The gynecologist was especially interested in her case, and he lived nearby. "You lie down," Bill said. "I'll call him."

It took him a while to get a reply, long enough for her to grow tense while trying not to. But he said "Bill Tierney" urgently at last, and she relaxed. "She seems to be going into labor. Ten minutes? Fine."

Ten minutes passed, fifteen, and there was no sign of the doctor. He mustn't have realized that the fog was worse. Bill peered through the velvet curtains at the towering slab of gray. Rose breathed from her diaphragm while her belly clenched again. She knew what to do, she certainly didn't need the gynecologist yet, but the presence of someone experienced would be reassuring. "I ought to let my mother know I've started," she said.

"All right, you stay there while I see if she's at home." He seemed more nervous than she was, and glad to have something to do—the classic expectant father, she thought wryly. He dialled, then listened for a minute or so. "They must be out. There's no reply."

It was like a reenactment of that night a year ago, except that then he must have been far more nervous. All at once the similarity made her realize what he'd said a few minutes ago, and it was so unexpected that she spoke without thinking. "Why, Bill, it never occurred to me—you do remember something about that night. You remember that all those people were involved, not just Colin and his mother."

At once she wished she hadn't spoken, for he looked uneasy—the look of a schoolboy caught red-handed, which she hadn't seen for a year. Of course he must have been trying to protect her by pretending to remember as little as possible, in an attempt to help her forget—but he must have been trying to forget as well: suppose she'd forced him to recall things he had almost succeeded in suppressing? The sound of the doorbell came as a relief to both of them. "He's here now," Bill said.

As he went to let in the doctor, Rose felt a little guilty: it was rather early to call him, now that she thought about it—she might not be fully in labor for hours, it might even be a false alarm. Still, she had to admit that she already felt more at ease now that he was here. She heard the front door open; a hint of chill seeped into the house. The door slammed, the two men came marching down the hall, and the first to enter the room was Colin.

Her whole body convulsed as if meant to destroy the baby, or Rose herself, or even what she was seeing. Of course it was no use. Colin was still there, more tanned and more self-confident than ever. He was smiling broadly, though certainly not at her.

Worse yet, Bill had come into the room and was trying to look as though he weren't involved. "I'm sorry," he mumbled, though he seemed relieved to be able to speak freely at last. "Not everyone was killed in the crash."

The hatred she'd felt in the hotel room in London was nothing compared to the detestation she felt now. When Colin saw how she was looking at Bill he tried, grotesquely, to reconcile them, a family friend doing his best to patch 'up a marriage. "Don't blame your husband. Nobody Grace ever touches is ever free of him." After a pause he added, "You least of all."

The baby moved within her, a slow secretive movement that she hadn't felt before, and all at once she knew what he meant. She was beyond horror, for it was as if nothing had changed: the trap had taken one more year to close, that was all. She *had* felt that movement before, but it had been lurking in her skull, not in her womb.

If she'd had any doubts, Colin left her none. He was watching her keenly as a snake, watching to see if she realized what he meant. At once she knew what she must do, and it must have shown in her eyes, for he stepped forward to prevent her. He was opening his bag and taking out a hypodermic. She still had time, there was no other course of action she could follow—but then a new contraction seized her belly, and she could do nothing at all.

She still had a chance. She had only to lie there while the contraction passed. She was trying to breathe from her diaphragm and praying for the spasm to be over—for everything to be over—while Colin screwed the needle into the barrel of the hypodermic. At least Bill was hanging back, looking too abashed to hold her down. "Let him do it, Ro," he said soothingly. "He only wants to make it easier for you."

She had to be calm so that the contraction didn't exhaust her. She had to appear calm so that the men would think she had resigned herself. Her breath was trembling, but she managed to breathe from her diaphragm while Colin punctured the ampule and drew the fluid into the syringe. Bill continued to loiter, obviously hoping that he wouldn't have to restrain her. He stepped forward reluctantly as Colin approached her with the needle.

Everything was all at once hallucinatory, oppressively precise: Colin's glistening eyes that meant to look reassuring, Bill's eyes that had turned aside from her, the razor-sharp flash of light from the needle, the gleaming drop of fluid at its tip. But her chance was even clearer, and the contraction was over. As Colin reached her, she knocked the syringe out of his hand.

"No point in doing that," he said harshly, and stooped to retrieve the syringe, which the thick carpet had prevented from breaking. Bill made to grab the hypodermic as he did, and they tangled irritably for a few moments—long enough for her to scramble to her feet and reach the door.

"Don't make things more difficult," Bill pleaded as he saw what she was doing. "Once you've given birth to him you need never see him again."

She didn't trust herself to speak to him, and in any case she had no time. She stumbled down the hall, though her belly threatened to overbalance her, especially now that the creature within it had begun to struggle. She slammed the front door behind her and floundered into the fog.

It was even closer, a dim gray tent which surrounded her and glided with her as she hurried as best she could to the end of the drive. When she reached the gateposts she couldn't see the house. Vague whitish blotches of light denoted streetlamps. The road was reduced to a dark filmy patch less than twenty yards long, a strip of pavement dripping with grass-blades, a few clumps of hedge poking through the fog. She hung onto the gatepost for a few minutes, her fingers gritting on wet stone, and shivered as the chill seeped through her dress.

When she heard the front door crash open she jerked forward, into the road. She could try to reach the nearest lit house, but what would be the use? It would be even more pointless to head for the main road, and besides, she could never outrun her pursuers. No, she knew what she had to do. She could do something definite at last. As she heard the footsteps on the gravel drive she made for the residents' garden, as quickly and quietly as she could.

She was leaving the light behind. She noticed the chain barely in time to save herself from falling over it; the bollards were indistinguishable from the fog, a few glistening links seemed to float unsupported in midair. She had crossed the squelching garden and was at the concrete fence before she was sure that the men were following. "Come back, Ro," Bill pleaded, and she heard the links rattling. "It's no use."

She was through the gap in the concrete at once, and slithering down the grassy slope. He mustn't have called the gynecologist at all, nor her parents. It didn't matter now, they couldn't help. She found that she no longer hated him; no doubt Grace could make him do anything. Nobody Grace had touched could defy him—nobody except her.

She crossed the dirt road and found the gap in the

wire netting, from which she clambered up the path to the plateau. At the top there was nothing but fog, a thickening of the darkness which looked even closer. Nevertheless she wasn't about to lose her way, for she could hear the foghorns ahead.

She was some way across the plateau when she had another contraction. She sat down on the grass, and her dress was soaked at once. The contraction passed, but the baby was still moving, struggling now. She heard the jangle of wire netting as the men reached the path. Perhaps Bill had realized which way she would go, or perhaps Grace was guiding the men to her.

She stumbled across the plateau, though the fog made her feel blindfolded, and all at once she was skidding down the slope to the promenade. A concrete pole held a dish of white light above a clearing in the fog. She could make out a lone bench beside a patch of grass verge like sodden blackened carpet, an arc of lit promenade, a stubby tangent of promenade rail. Nearby a lamp had gone out; she could hear the creaking of the dish as it cooled. Otherwise there was nothing but the slopping of the river. It sounded thick as oil.

As she ventured onto the promenade she made out the red light of a buoy on the river, an open wound in the fog, pumping red every couple of seconds. She crossed the promenade and held the rail, which felt like ice. Her soaked dress clung to her; she was shivering uncontrollably. She held onto the rail as though it were a lifebelt, and stared back at the plateau.

She couldn't hear the men. They must be creeping toward her through the fog, closing in. She stared at the bushes beyond the grass verge, which were no color at all. Was she waiting until she saw the bushes move? No, she was terrified to do what she had to do. The fog reminded her too much of the gray church.

Suddenly her eyes widened. If Grace had been able to send her there now, he would already have done so.

His struggles within her were growing desperate, and that showed how helpless he was. The tiny body must have trapped him. He was trapped within Rose. She smiled bitterly, triumphantly, and turned to the rail—and realized fully at last what she planned to do.

At once her hands were clinging to the rail to prevent her from acting. Her body was paralyzed, a dead weight that wouldn't climb. How could she have thought she would be able to do it? Everything she could see, and everything that was left of her life, seemed to be weighing her down, holding her back. Nobody in her right mind could do what she'd planned to do. Surely it was the ultimate admission of despair.

Then the baby jerked within her—perhaps it was calling to the men—and she remembered her glimpse of its dream, the revenge on the living, the eternal psychotic revenge. She heaved herself up at once, refusing herself more time to think.

It was far more difficult than she had anticipated: the rail bruised her belly, the wire mesh for the protection of children ripped her tights and scratched her legs. Her arms were trembling with effort before she managed to lift one foot over the rail. Absurdly, she was afraid of losing her balance.

She had just levered one leg over the rail when Colin and Bill appeared at the edge of the fog. "Come back!" Colin screamed, but she didn't think he was talking to her. "Come back, Ro," Bill cried, and she heard grief in his voice. He sounded free of Grace's influence. She would be saving him. She dragged her other leg over the rail, and let herself drop.

The stone incline thumped the breath out of her, and scraped the skin from the back of her legs. The shock of the icy water was so great she would have cried out if she had been able to do so. The current seized her at once, rushing her and Grace out to sea, beyond anyone's reach. The gray closed in, and she remembered the polluted depths of the water. But it would soon be over for her, and she would be bound wherever she was going. For Grace, who was struggling more and more desperately within her, she thought it would never end.

THE EVIL BORN IN THE BROWNSTONE LIVES ON...

Chandal Knight survived a fiery tragedy that has left a cloud upon her mind. Now she must come face to face with a supernatural horror that has laid claim to her sanity, her life, her very soul...

THE BLOODSTONE
KEN EULO

COMING IN OCTOBER from POCKET BOOKS

Wherever paperbacks are sold!

THE OCCULT:

events sometimes real, sometimes
imagined. Always haunting.
Psychological thrillers guaranteed to
keep readers in the grip of fear.
Chilling books—

available now from
POCKET BOOKS

_____	42240	JULIA, Peter Straub $2.95
_____	82215	DEVIL'S GAMBLE, Frank G. Slaughter $2.50
_____	82222	SEA CLIFF, Michael T. Hinkemeyer $1.95
_____	43381	EDUCATION OF OVERSOUL #7, Jane Roberts $2.75
_____	81948	DEMON SUMMER, Elaine Booth Selig $1.95
_____	82803	DARK SUMMER, Mark Upton $2.25
_____	81769	THE HELL CANDIDATE, Thomas Luke $2.75
_____	42377	GHOST STORY, Peter Straub $3.50

POCKET BOOKS Department OCA
1230 Avenue of the Americas, New York, N.Y. 10020
Please send me the books I have checked above. I am enclosing
$_____ (please add 50¢ to cover postage and handling, N.Y.S.
and N.Y.C. residents please add appropriate sales tax). Send check
or money order—no cash or C.O.D.s please. Allow six weeks for
delivery.

NAME_____

ADDRESS_____

CITY_____ STATE/ZIP_____

118